LEVEL

2

START

READY PLAYER TWO

BY ERNEST CLINE

Ready Player Two

Armada

Ready Player One

READY PLAYER TWO

ERNEST CLINE

CENTURY

1 3 5 7 9 10 8 6 4 2

Century
20 Vauxhall Bridge Road
London SW1V 2SA

Century is part of the Penguin Random House group of companies
whose addresses can be found at global.penguinrandomhouse.com.

Copyright © Dark All Day, Inc., 2020

First published in the USA by Ballantine Books in 2020
First published in the UK in hardback by Century in 2020

www.penguin.co.uk

A CIP catalogue record for this book is available from the British Library.

ISBN 9781780897431 (hardback)
ISBN 9781780897448 (trade paperback)

Printed and bound in Great Britain by Clays Ltd, Elcograf S.p.A.

Penguin Random House is committed to a sustainable future for
our business, our readers and our planet. This book is made from
Forest Stewardship Council® certified paper.

For Maureen O'Keefe Cline

and her namesake

Maureen O'Keefe Aptowicz

READY PLAYER TWO

Cutscene

After I won Halliday's contest, I remained offline for nine straight days—a new personal record.

When I finally logged back in to my OASIS account, I was sitting in my new corner office on the top floor of the GSS skyscraper in downtown Columbus, Ohio, preparing to start my gig as one of the company's new owners. The other three were still scattered across the globe: Shoto had flown back home to Japan to take over operations at GSS's Hokkaido division. Aech was enjoying an extended vacation in Senegal, a country she'd dreamed of visiting her whole life, because her ancestors had come from there. And Samantha had flown back to Vancouver to pack up her belongings and say goodbye to her grandmother, Evelyn. She wasn't due to arrive here in Columbus for another four days, which seemed like an eternity. I needed to distract myself until our reunion, so I decided to log back in to the OASIS and try out a few more of the superuser abilities my avatar now possessed.

I climbed into my brand-new top-of-the-line OASIS immersion rig, a Habashaw OIR-9400, then put on my visor and haptic gloves and initiated the login sequence. My avatar reappeared where I'd last logged out, on the planet Chthonia, standing outside the gates of Castle Anorak. As I'd anticipated, there were thousands of other avatars already gathered there, all waiting patiently for me to make an appearance. According to the newsfeed headlines, some of them had been camped out there all week—ever since I'd resurrected them in the aftermath of our epic battle against the Sixers.

In my first official act as one of GSS's new owners, just a few hours after the fight ended, I'd authorized our admins to restore all the items, credits, and power levels those heroic users had lost, along with their avatars. I thought it was the least we could do to repay them for their help, and Samantha, Aech, and Shoto had agreed. It was the first decision we'd voted on as the company's new co-owners.

As soon as the avatars in my vicinity spotted me, they began to run in my direction, closing in on me from all sides at once. To avoid getting mobbed, I teleported inside the castle, into Anorak's study—a room in the highest tower that I alone could enter, thanks to the Robes of Anorak I now wore. The obsidian-black garment endowed my avatar with the godlike powers Halliday's own avatar had once possessed.

I glanced around the cluttered study. Here, just over a week ago, Anorak had declared me the winner of Halliday's contest and changed my life forever.

My eyes fell upon the painting of a black dragon that hung on the wall. Beneath it stood an ornate crystal pedestal with a jewel-encrusted chalice resting on top of it. And cradled within the chalice was the object I'd spent so many years searching for: Halliday's silver Easter egg.

I walked over to admire it, and that was when I noticed something strange—an inscription on the egg's otherwise pristine surface. One that definitely hadn't been there when I'd last seen it, nine days earlier.

No other avatars could enter this room. No one could've tampered with the egg. So there was only one way that inscription could've gotten there. Halliday himself must have programmed it to appear on the egg's surface. It could have appeared right after Anorak gave me his robes, and I'd just been too distracted to notice.

I bent down to read the inscription: *GSS—13th Floor—Vault #42- 8675309.*

My pulse suddenly thudding in my ears, I immediately logged out of the OASIS and scrambled out of my rig. Then I bolted out of my new office, sprinted down the hall, and jumped into the first elevator to arrive. The half dozen GSS employees inside all avoided making direct eye contact. I could guess what all of them were thinking: *Meet the new boss, weird as the old boss.*

I gave them all a polite nod and pressed the "13" button. According to the interactive building directory on my phone, the thirteenth floor was where the GSS archives were located. Of *course* Halliday had put them there. In one of his favorite TV shows, *Max Headroom*, Network 23's hidden research-and-development lab was located on the thirteenth floor. And *The Thirteenth Floor* was also the title of an old sci-fi film about virtual reality, released in 1999, right on the heels of both *The Matrix* and *eXistenZ*.

When I stepped off the elevator, the armed guards at the security station snapped to attention. As a formality, one of them scanned my retinas to verify my identity, then he led me past the security station and through a set of armored doors, into a maze of brightly lit corridors. Eventually we reached a large room, its walls lined with dozens of numbered doors, like extra-large safety-deposit boxes, each with a number stenciled on its front.

I thanked the guard and told him he could go as I scanned the doors. There it was: number 42. Another of Halliday's jokes—according to one of his favorite novels, *The Hitchhiker's Guide to the Galaxy*, the number 42 was the "Ultimate Answer to Life, the Universe, and Everything."

I just stood there for a few seconds, reminding myself to breathe. Then I punched in the seven-digit combination from the egg's inscription into the code pad beside the vault door: 8-6-7-5-3-0-9, a combination no self-respecting gunter would have trouble remembering. *Jenny, I've got your number. I need to make you mine. . . .*

The lock disengaged with a thud and the door swung open, revealing the vault's cube-shaped interior—and a large silver egg sitting inside. It looked identical to the virtual egg on display in Anorak's study, except this one had no inscription on its surface.

I wiped my sweaty palms on my thighs—I did *not* want to drop this—and removed the egg, then set it on a steel table in the center of the room. The bottom of the egg was weighted, so it wobbled slightly before standing perfectly upright—like a Weeble. (*Weebles wobble, but they don't fall down.*) As I leaned in to examine the egg more closely, I spotted a small oval-shaped thumb scanner pad near the top, flush with its curved surface. When I pressed my thumb to it, the egg split in half and hinged open.

Inside it, resting in form-fitting blue velvet, was some sort of headset.

I lifted it out and turned it over in my hands. The device had a segmented central spine that appeared to stretch from a wearer's forehead to the nape of their neck, with a row of ten C-shaped metal bands attached to it. Each band was comprised of jointed, retractable segments, and each segment had a row of circular sensor pads on its underside. This made the whole sensor array adjustable, so that it could fit around heads of all shapes and sizes. A long fiber-optic cable stretched from the base of the headset, with a standard OASIS console plug at the end of it.

My heart had been thudding against my rib cage, but now it almost stopped. This had to be some sort of OASIS peripheral—one unlike any I'd ever seen before, and light-years more advanced.

A short electronic beep emanated from the egg and I glanced back over at it. A flash of red swept across my vision as a tiny retinal scanner verified my identity a second time. Then a small video monitor embedded in the egg's open lid turned itself on and the GSS logo appeared for a few seconds, before it was replaced by the withered face of James Donovan Halliday. Judging by his age and emaciated features, he'd made this video recording shortly before his death. But despite his condition, he hadn't used his OASIS avatar to record this message like he had with *Anorak's Invitation*. For some reason, he'd chosen to appear in the flesh this time, under the brutal, unforgiving light of reality.

"The device you now hold in your hands is an OASIS Neural Interface, or ONI." He pronounced it Oh-En-Eye. "It is the world's first fully functional noninvasive brain-computer interface. It allows an OASIS user to see, hear, smell, taste, and feel their avatar's virtual environment, via signals transmitted directly into their cerebral cortex. The headset's sensor array also monitors and interprets its wearer's brain activity, allowing them to control their OASIS avatar just as they do their physical body—simply by thinking about it."

"No fucking way," I heard myself whisper.

"That's just for starters," Halliday said, as if he'd heard me. "An ONI headset can also be used to record its wearer's experiences in the real world. All sensory input received by their brain is digitized and stored as a .oni (dot-oh-en-eye) file on an external data drive attached to their headset. Once that file is uploaded to the OASIS, the entire experience can be played back and reexperienced by the person who recorded it, or by any other ONI user with whom they choose to share the file."

Halliday managed a thin smile.

"In other words, the ONI allows you to relive moments of other people's lives. To see the world through their eyes, hear it through their ears, smell it through their nose, taste it with their tongue, and feel it through their skin." Halliday gave the camera a matter-of-fact nod. "The ONI is the most powerful communication tool humans have ever invented. And I think it's also probably the last one we will ever need to invent." He tapped the center of his forehead. "Now we can plug right in to the old noodle."

I heard the words, but I couldn't process them. Was Halliday for real? Or had he been delusional when he made this recording, losing his grip on reality as he entered the final stages of his illness? The technology he was describing was still the stuff of science fiction. Yes, millions of physically disabled people used brain-computer interfaces every day, to see or hear or move paralyzed limbs. But these medical miracles could still only be achieved by cutting a hole in the patient's skull and sticking implants and electrodes directly into their brain.

The concept of a brain-computer interface headset that allowed you to record, play back, and/or simulate a human being's entire sensory experience had appeared in a bunch of Halliday's favorite sci-fi novels, TV shows, and movies. There was SimStim—the fictional Simulated Stimulation technology William Gibson had envisioned in *Neuromancer*. And a similar form of experience-recording technology had also been featured in *Brainstorm* and *Strange Days*, two of Halliday's favorite films . . .

If the ONI could do everything Halliday claimed, then he'd once again done the impossible. Through sheer force of will and brainpower, he'd once again turned science fiction into science fact, without much regard for the long-term consequences.

I also wondered about the name Halliday had chosen for his invention. I'd seen enough anime to know that *oni* was also a Japanese word for a giant horned demon from the pits of hell.

"The ONI's software and documentation have already been emailed to your private OASIS account," Halliday continued. "Along with complete schematics of the headset and the 3-D printer files necessary to fabricate more of them."

Halliday paused and stared into the camera for a moment before continuing.

"Once you've tested the ONI yourself, I think you'll realize—just as I did—that this invention has the power to drastically alter the nature of human existence. I think it could help humanity. But it could also make things even worse. It will all depend on the timing, I think. That's why I'm entrusting its fate to you, my heir. You must decide when—or if—the world is ready for this technology."

His frail body shook with a coughing fit. Then he took a rasping breath and spoke one final time.

"Take all the time you need to decide," he said. "And don't let anyone rush you. Once Pandora's box has been opened, there's no closing it again. So . . . choose wisely."

He gave the camera a small wave goodbye. Then the recording ended and a VIDEO FILE DELETED message appeared on the monitor just before it powered itself off.

I sat there for a long time. Could this be some sort of posthumous practical joke? Because the alternative didn't seem to make any sense. If the ONI really could do everything he said it could, then it *would* be the most powerful communication tool ever invented. Why would he have kept it a secret? Why not just patent it and release it to the world?

I glanced back down at the headset in my hands. It had been locked away in this vault for the past eight years, waiting patiently for me to find it. And now that I had, there was really only one thing left for me to do.

I put the headset back inside the egg, then I turned around and carried it out of the archives, planning to walk back to the elevator at a calm, dignified pace. But my self-control evaporated in seconds, and I began to run as fast as my legs would carry me.

The employees I encountered as I hurried back upstairs were treated to the sight of their wild-eyed boss sprinting through the hallowed halls of Gregarious Simulation Systems, clutching a giant silver egg.

●　—　●　●　●

Back in my office, I locked the door, lowered the blinds, and sat down at my desktop computer to read over the ONI documentation Halliday had emailed me.

I was grateful that Samantha wasn't there. I didn't want to give her the opportunity to talk me out of testing the ONI. Because I was worried she might try to, and if she did, she would've succeeded. (I'd recently discovered that when you're madly in love with someone they can persuade you to do pretty much anything.)

There was no way I could pass up such a historic opportunity. It would've been like passing up the chance to be the first person to walk on the moon. Besides, I wasn't worried about the ONI being dangerous. If using the headset was potentially harmful, Halliday would've warned me. After all, I'd just won the contest to become his sole heir. He wouldn't have wanted any harm to come to me.

That's what I kept telling myself as I plugged the ONI headset into my OASIS console and placed it gently on my head. Its telescoping bands retracted automatically, pressing the array of sensor and transmitter pads mounted on them firmly against the unique contours of my cranium. Then its metal joints tightened up and the whole spiderlike device locked itself onto my skull so that its pads couldn't be jostled or removed while the device was interfacing with my brain. According to the ONI documentation, forcibly removing the headset while it was in operation could severely damage the wearer's brain and/or leave them in a permanent coma. So the titanium-reinforced safety bands made certain this couldn't happen. I found this little detail comforting instead of unsettling. Riding in an automobile was risky, too, if you didn't wear your seatbelt . . .

The ONI documentation also noted that a sudden power loss to the headset could also cause potential harm to the wearer's brain, which was why it had an internal backup battery that could power the device long enough to complete an emergency logout sequence and safely awaken the wearer from the artificially induced sleeplike state it placed them in while the headset was in use.

So I had nothing to worry about. Nothing at all. Just a giant metal spider locked onto my skull, about to interface with my brain.

I lay down on the blue velvet couch in the corner of my office and made sure that my body was in a comfortable sleeping position, as per the instructions. Then I took a deep breath and powered everything on.

I felt a slight tingling sensation on my scalp. From reading the ONI documentation, I knew that the headset was performing a scan of my brain to map its unique geography. This scan would then be saved to my account so that it could be used to verify my identity in the future, in lieu of a retinal scan. A synthesized female voice prompted me to speak my passphrase. I recited it slowly, being careful to enunciate: *Everybody wants to rule the world.*

Once it was verified, a tiny augmented reality display extended from the front of the headset and then locked into place in front of my left eye, like a monocle. Several paragraphs of text appeared, floating in the air in front of me, superimposed in the center of my vision:

> Warning! For safety reasons, the OASIS Neural Interface headset can only be used for a maximum of twelve consecutive hours at a time. When this limit has been reached, you will be logged out of your account automatically, and you will be unable to use your ONI headset again until twelve hours of downtime have elapsed. During this mandatory downtime you are still free to access the OASIS using conventional immersion hardware. Tampering with or disabling your ONI headset's built-in security safeguards to exceed the daily usage limits can result in Synaptic Overload Syndrome and permanent neural tissue trauma. Gregarious Simulation Systems will not be held responsible for any injuries caused by improper use of the OASIS Neural Interface.

I'd seen this safety warning in the headset's documentation, but I was surprised that Halliday had embedded it in the login sequence. It looked as though he'd already made all of the necessary preparations to release the ONI to the public over eight years ago. But he'd never actually done it. Instead, he'd taken the secret of the ONI's existence with him to the grave. And now I had inherited that secret.

I reread the warning a few times, working up my nerve. The part about permanent brain damage was unsettling, but it wasn't like I was being used as a guinea pig. According to the ONI documentation, GSS had already conducted a series of independent human safety trials on the ONI headset over a decade ago, and they'd all shown that using it was completely safe, as long as the user adhered to the twelve-hour daily usage limit. And the headset firmware's built-in safety features made sure they did. So, I reminded myself once again, I had absolutely nothing to worry about. . . .

I reached out and tapped the Agree button beneath the safety warning. The system finished logging me in and text flashed in the center of my field of vision:

> Identity verification successful.
> Welcome to the OASIS, Parzival!
> Login Completed: 11:07:18 OST—1.25.2046

As the timestamp faded away, it was replaced by a short message, just three words long—the last thing I would see before I left the real world and entered the virtual one.

But they weren't the three words I was used to seeing. I—like every other ONI user to come—was greeted by a new message Halliday had created, to welcome those visitors who had adopted his new technology:

READY PLAYER TWO

My vision went black for a moment as the headset instructed
my brain to place my body into a harmless sleeplike state, while my conscious mind remained active inside what was basically a computer con-
trolled lucid dream. Then the OASIS slowly materialized into existence all
around me, and I found myself standing back inside Anorak's study, where
I'd last logged out.

Everything looked the same as before, but it *felt* completely different. I
was actually *here,* physically inside the OASIS. It no longer felt like I was
using an avatar. Now I felt like I *was* my avatar. There was no visor on my
face, none of the faint numbness and constriction you always felt wearing
a haptic suit or gloves. I didn't even feel the ONI headset my real body was
actually wearing. When I reached up to scratch my head, the device wasn't
there.

A light breeze blew into the study through the open window, and I
could feel it on my skin and my face and in my hair.

I could feel my feet resting on the stone floor, snug inside the boots that
my avatar was wearing.

I realized I could smell my surroundings too. I breathed in the musty
scent of the ancient spell books that lined the walls, mingled with the
smoke of the burning candles.

I reached out to touch a nearby worktable. I could feel the grooves in
the woodgrain as I ran my fingertips across it. Then I spotted a large bowl
of fruit on the table—one that hadn't been there before. I picked up an

apple and felt the weight of it in my hand, and its hard smoothness against my palm. I squeezed it with all five of my fingertips and felt them create tiny craters of pulp beneath the surface of the apple's skin.

I was awestruck by the perfect replication of all that interlinked sensory input. These were subtle, nuanced sensations that could never be re-created or simulated by a pair of haptic gloves.

I raised the apple to my avatar's lips, which now felt like my own lips, and bit into it with what felt like my own teeth. It tasted *like a real apple*. The most perfectly ripe and delicious apple I'd ever eaten.

An OASIS user had always been able to eat and drink things with their avatar. But eating a food power-up or drinking a healing potion had always been a senseless pantomime performed with your haptic gloves. You never felt anything pass through your lips, and you definitely never tasted anything on your tongue.

Now, thanks to the ONI, I could. And I did.

I began to sample the other fruits in the bowl. The orange, banana, grapes, and papaya tasted just as delicious, and as I took a bite out of each one, I felt the fruit travel down my esophagus to my stomach. I could even feel my stomach getting full.

"Oh my God!" I exclaimed to the empty room. "This is fucking incredible!" But my words were garbled, because I was talking with a mouth full of papaya. I could feel the juice running down my chin. I wiped it on my sleeve. Then I began to run around the room, bursting with excitement, touching different surfaces and objects to see how they felt. And how did they feel? They all felt real. That's how they fucking felt. It *all* felt real.

Once my initial euphoria began to wear off, I found myself wondering if the ONI also simulated pain. Because if pain felt as real as the fruit tasted, it was going to hurt. A lot.

As an experiment, I bit down lightly on my tongue. I could feel the pressure of each tooth against its surface, and the grain of my taste buds as I raked them against my incisors. But I didn't feel any pain whatsoever, no matter how hard I bit. As I suspected, Halliday had put some sort of pain-prevention safeguard in place.

I drew one of my blasters and shot myself in the right foot. I took several hit points of damage, and felt a mild jolt of pain, but it seemed more like a hard pinch than a gunshot.

A giddy laugh escaped me as I holstered my blaster. Then I took three running steps toward the window and dove out of it, taking flight like Superman. As I rocketed up into the clouds, my robes fluttered in the wind like a cape. I felt like I was really flying.

I also suddenly felt like anything was possible. Because now it clearly was.

This was it—the final, inevitable step in the evolution of videogames and virtual reality. The simulation had now become indistinguishable from real life.

I knew Samantha wasn't going to approve. But I was too exhilarated to let myself think about that. I wanted more. And the ONI had more in store for me. Much more.

I flew back to Anorak's study and continued to experiment with the ONI's abilities. That was when I discovered a new drop-down menu on my avatar's heads-up display labeled *ONI*. When I selected it, I saw a list of a dozen large files that had already been downloaded to my account. They all had an .oni extension, and provocatively simple filenames like RACING, SURFING, SKYDIVING, and KUNG-FU FIGHTING.

I selected SURFING and suddenly found myself standing on a surfboard, expertly riding the curved wall of a giant wave off the coast of some tropical island. But when I reflexively tried to move to keep my balance, I realized that I wasn't in control. This was a passive experience. I was just along for the ride. And somehow, it also *felt* different from what I'd experienced in Anorak's study—where that had been eerily smooth and precise, this was somehow more intense but also jarring and dislocating.

Looking down at my body, I realized that I was no longer Parzival— I was someone else. Someone smaller and thinner, with darker skin, and strands of long black hair hanging in front of their eyes. Someone wearing a bikini. Someone with breasts. I was a woman! And an expert surfer. Not an avatar. A real person had recorded this experience. I was experiencing a piece of someone else's life.

I had no control over my movements, but I could see, hear, smell, and feel everything—every sensation experienced by the woman who had made this recording. I could even feel the ONI headset on my—her—head, and I could also see the portable data drive it was connected to housed inside a waterproof casing that was strapped to her right arm.

That explained the difference in sensations too. I was no longer experiencing simulated input, created for me by the OASIS servers—I was actually feeling the world through *this* surfer's body, moment by moment, delivered by her synapses. Raw neural input, from a brain that was not my own.

When the wave crashed over me a few seconds later, the experience clip ended and I found myself back inside my own avatar's skin, standing back inside Anorak's study.

I pulled up the next clip, and then the next. I drove a racecar, did some skydiving, kung-fu fighting, deep-sea diving, and horseback riding—all within the same half hour.

I played every .oni file on the list, one after the other, leaping from place to place, from body to body, and from one experience to another.

I stopped when I reached a series of files with names like SEX-M-F.oni, SEX-F-F.oni, and SEX-Nonbinary.oni. I wasn't ready for any of that. I was still truly, madly, deeply in love with Samantha. And I was still reeling from losing my virginity to her just a few days earlier. I didn't want to be unfaithful to her. I figured that cheating was cheating, whether it was live or it was Memorex.

I logged out of the OASIS and took control of my own body once again. The process took a few minutes. Then I removed the ONI headset and opened my eyes. I looked around my office. I checked the time. Over an hour had passed, which seemed about right.

I gripped the arms of my chair. I reached up to touch my face. Reality didn't feel any more real than the OASIS had just felt to me. My senses couldn't discern between the two.

Halliday was right. The ONI was going to change the world.

• • •

How in the hell had Halliday done this? How had he managed to invent such a complex device in secret? Hardware hadn't even been his specialty.

The documentation he'd sent me held the answer. When I read through the rest of it, I learned that Halliday had been working on this for over twenty-five years, with an entire research lab full of neuroscientists—hiding his secret in plain sight.

A few months after GSS launched the OASIS, Halliday set up an R&D division at the company called the Accessibility Research Lab. Ostensibly, its mission had been to create a line of neuroprosthetic hardware that would allow people with severe physical disabilities to use the OASIS more easily. Halliday hired the best and brightest minds in the field of neuroscience to staff the ARL, then he gave them all the funding they would ever need to conduct their research.

The ARL's work over the next few decades was certainly no secret. To the contrary, their breakthroughs had created a new line of medical implants that became widely used. I'd read about several of them in my high school textbooks. First, they developed a new type of cochlear implant that—for those who chose to use it—allowed the hearing impaired to perceive sound with perfect clarity, both in the real world and inside the OASIS. A few years later, they unveiled a new retinal implant that allowed any blind people who wished to be sighted to "see" perfectly inside the OASIS. And by linking two head-mounted mini cameras to the same implant, their real-world sight could be restored as well.

The ARL's next invention was a brain implant that allowed paraplegics to control the movements of their OASIS avatar simply by thinking about it. It worked in conjunction with a separate implant that allowed them to feel simulated sensory input. And the very same implants gave these individuals the ability to regain control of their lower extremities, while restoring their sense of touch. They also allowed amputees to control robotic replacement limbs, and to receive sensory input through them as well.

To accomplish this, the researchers devised a method of "recording" the sensory information transmitted to the human brain by the nervous system in reaction to all manner of external stimuli, then compiled these assets into a massive digital library of sensations that could be "played back" inside the OASIS to perfectly simulate anything a person could experience through their senses of touch, taste, sight, smell, balance, temperature, vibration—you name it.

GSS patented each of the Accessibility Research Lab's inventions, but Halliday never made any effort to profit from them. Instead, he set up a program to give these neuroprosthetic implants away, to any OASIS users who could benefit from them. GSS even subsidized the cost of their implant surgery. This program made powerful new tools available to any physically disabled individuals who chose to use them, but it also provided the ARL with a nearly unlimited supply of willing human guinea pigs on whom to conduct their ongoing experiments.

I'd grown up seeing headlines about the ARL's breakthroughs with brain implants on the newsfeeds, but like most people I'd never really paid much attention to them, because the technology was only available to people who were severely physically disabled and willing to undergo invasive (and possibly fatal) brain surgery.

But while they were making all of these astounding breakthroughs, the Accessibility Research Lab also spent those decades developing another, secret piece of technology, one that would ultimately stand as the ARL's greatest achievement—a computer-brain interface that could accomplish everything their implants could, but without the need for surgery. Using the wealth of data they'd amassed on the inner workings of the human mind and an elaborate combination of EEG, fMRI, and SQUID technologies, the lab had developed a way to read brain waves and transmit them solely via dermal contact. Halliday compartmentalized each facet of the project, so that each team of scientists or engineers worked in isolation from the others, and he alone knew how it was all going to fit together.

It took billions of dollars and decades of work before they finally succeeded in creating a fully functional prototype of the OASIS Neural Interface headset. But as soon as they completed the final round of safety testing, Halliday shut the ONI project down and proclaimed it a failure. A few weeks later he shuttered the Accessibility Research Lab and fired its entire staff. They were all given severance packages that ensured they'd never need to work again—contingent upon their strict adherence to the nondisclosure agreements they'd signed when they were first hired.

This was how Halliday had created the world's first noninvasive brain-computer interface without the world knowing it.

And now my friends and I had inherited this invention. It was ours—to bury or to reveal.

· · ·

We didn't make our decision lightly. We weighed all of the pros and cons. Then, after a heated debate, the four of us held a vote. The ayes had it. And just like that, we changed the course of human history forever.

After another series of safety trials, GSS patented the OASIS Neural Interface technology and began to mass-produce the headsets. We put them on sale at the lowest possible price, to make sure as many people as possible could experience the OASIS Neural Interface for themselves.

We sold a million units that first day. And the moment our headsets hit the store shelves, IOI's entire line of VR goggles and haptic gear were instantly rendered obsolete. For the first time in history, GSS became the world's leading manufacturer of OASIS hardware. And as word of the ONI's abilities began to spread, sales continued to increase exponentially.

And then, just a few days later, it happened—the event that set this whole tale in motion.

A few seconds after the OASIS servers reached 7,777,777 simultaneous ONI users, a message appeared on Halliday's long-dormant website, where the Scoreboard for his contest had once resided:

> Seek the Seven Shards of the Siren's Soul
> On the seven worlds where the Siren once played a role
> For each fragment my heir must pay a toll
> To once again make the Siren whole

It came to be known as the Shard Riddle, and the first thing old-school gunters noticed was that its rhyme scheme and syllable count were identical to the "Three Hidden Keys Open Three Secret Gates" rap that Halliday had used to announce his famous Easter-egg hunt.

People assumed the Shard Riddle was just an elaborate publicity stunt, concocted by GSS's new owners to help promote the roll-out of our ONI headsets. And we never did anything to deny or discourage these rumors, because they helped foster the perception that the OASIS was now under our complete control. But the four of us knew the unsettling truth. We had no idea what the hell was going on.

The Shard Riddle appeared to announce the existence of a second Easter egg—another object hidden somewhere inside the OASIS by its eccentric creator sometime prior to his death. And the timing of the riddle's appearance couldn't be a coincidence. It had clearly been triggered by our decision to release the OASIS Neural Interface to the public.

So what exactly was Halliday trying to tell us?

The "Siren" seemed to be a reference to Kira Morrow, Og's deceased wife and Halliday's unrequited love. Back when they were all in high school together in Ohio, Kira had named her Dungeons & Dragons character Leucosia, after one of the Sirens of Greek myth. Many years later Kira had given her OASIS avatar that same name. After her death, Halliday had used the name Leucosia as a computer password, which I'd had to guess to win the final challenge of his contest.

It wasn't clear what would happen if someone managed to collect the Seven Shards and "once again make the Siren whole." But I started searching for them anyway. Halliday had thrown down a gauntlet once again, and I couldn't resist picking it up.

And I wasn't alone. The riddle's appearance spawned a whole new generation of gunters, and they all began to scour the OASIS for the Seven Shards. But unlike Halliday's egg, no reward for finding the Siren's Soul had ever been announced, so no one knew exactly what they were searching for, or why.

• • •

In what seemed like the blink of an eye, an entire year passed.

We hit three billion units sold. Then four.

It quickly became evident that our patented, proprietary brain-computer-interface headsets had an endless array of non-OASIS-related applications in the fields of science, medicine, aviation, manufacturing, and warfare.

Innovative Online Industries' stock continued to plummet. When it fell low enough, we orchestrated a hostile takeover of the company. GSS absorbed IOI and all of its assets, transforming us into an unstoppable mega-corporation with a global monopoly on the world's most popular entertainment, education, and communications platform. To celebrate, we released all of IOI's indentured servants and forgave their outstanding debts.

Another year passed. The OASIS reached a new benchmark—five billion individual users logged in each day. Then six. Two-thirds of the people on our overcrowded, rapidly warming little planet. And over 99 percent of the people who accessed the OASIS now did so using one of our neural interface headsets.

• • •

Just as Halliday predicted, this new technology began to have a profound impact on people's day-to-day lives, and on human civilization at large.

There were new experiences to download every day. Anything and every-thing you could imagine. You could go anywhere, do anything, and be any-one. It was the most addictive pastime imaginable—far more addictive than the OASIS had ever been, and that was saying something.

Other companies made attempts to reverse-engineer the ONI headset and steal our neural-interface technology—but the software and process-ing power required to make the ONI technology function was all part of the OASIS. Experiences could be recorded offline as an .oni file, even a bootleg one, but the file could only be played back by being uploaded to the OASIS. This allowed us to weed out unsavory or illegal recordings before they could be shared with other users. It also let us maintain our monopoly on what was rapidly becoming the most popular form of entertainment in the history of the world.

GSS rolled out the ONI-net, a social-media platform built around .oni file-sharing. It allowed users to browse, purchase, download, rate, and re-view ONI experiences recorded by billions of other people around the world. It also allowed you to upload your own experiences and sell them to the rest of the OASIS.

"Sims" were recordings made inside the OASIS, and "Recs" were ONI recordings made in reality. Except that most kids no longer referred to it as "reality." They called it "the Earl." (A term derived from the initialism IRL.) And "Ito" was slang for "in the OASIS." So Recs were recorded in the Earl, and Sims were created Ito.

Now instead of following their favorite celebrity on social media, ONI users could *become* their favorite celebrity for a few minutes each day. Exist inside their skin. Live short, heavily curated fragments of far more glamor-ous lives.

Now people no longer watched movies or television shows—they lived them. The viewer was no longer in the audience. Now they were one of the stars. Instead of just being in the audience at a rock concert, now you could experience the concert as each member of your favorite band, and be each one of them as they/you performed your favorite song.

Anyone with an ONI headset and an empty data drive could record a real-life experience, upload it to the OASIS, and sell it to billions of other people all around the world. You earned coin for every download, and GSS only took 20 percent off the top for making it all possible. If one of your clips went viral, the profits could make you rich overnight. Movie, rock, porn, and streaming stars were all scrambling to exploit this brand-new revenue stream.

For less than the cost of an iced latte, you could now safely experience just about anything that human beings *could* experience. You could take any drug, eat any kind of food, and have any kind of sex, without worrying about addiction, calories, or consequences. You could relive uncut real-life experiences, or play your way through scripted interactive adventures inside the OASIS. Thanks to the ONI, it all felt completely real.

• • •

The ONI made the lives of impoverished people all around the world a lot more bearable—and enjoyable. People didn't mind subsisting on dried seaweed and soy protein when they could log on to the ONI-net and download a delicious five-course meal anytime they pleased. People could sample any cuisine from any part of the globe, prepared by any of the world's finest chefs, and have it served to them in a mansion, or on a mountaintop, or in a scenic restaurant, or on an autojet headed to Paris. And as a bonus, you could experience any of these meals as a diner with unusually sensitive taste buds. Or as a celebrity, dining with other celebrities, who were all being waited on by a bunch of ex-celebrities. Name your poison.

Moderating all of this user-generated content was a challenge—and a huge responsibility. GSS implemented CenSoft, our custom strong-AI censor software, which scanned every .oni recording before it was released and flagged suspicious content for human review. Questionable material was reviewed by GSS employees, who then decided whether the clip was safe to release—and, if any criminal behavior was captured, they forwarded it on to law enforcement officials in the uploader's country or region.

New applications of ONI technology continued to reveal themselves. For example, it became fashionable for young mothers to make an ONI recording while they gave birth to their child, so that in a few decades, that child would be able to play back that recording and experience what it feels like to *give birth to themselves.*

• • •

And me?

All my dreams had come true. I'd gotten stupidly rich and absurdly famous. I'd fallen in love with my dream girl and she had fallen in love with me. Surely I was happy, right?

Not so much, as this account will show. I was suddenly way out of my depth, both personally and professionally, so it didn't take very long for me to completely screw up my life once again. And when I did, I returned to seek solace from my oldest friend, the OASIS.

I'd struggled with OASIS addiction *before* the ONI was released. Now logging on to the simulation was like mainlining some sort of chemically engineered superheroin. It didn't take long for me to become an addict. When I wasn't playing back ONI recordings, I was browsing the ONI-net and adding new recordings to my playback queue.

Meanwhile, I continued to search for the Seven Shards of the Siren's Soul. I could teleport anywhere in the OASIS, buy anything I wanted, and kill anyone who got in my way. But I still wasn't making any progress. And I couldn't understand why.

Finally, out of a mixture of disgust and desperation, I offered a billion dollars to anyone who could provide me with information on how to locate just one of the Seven Shards. I announced this reward with a stylized short film that I modeled after *Anorak's Invitation*. I hoped it would seem like a lighthearted play on Halliday's contest instead of a desperate cry for help. It seemed to work.

My billion-dollar shard bounty caused quite a stir inside the OASIS. The number of gunters searching for the shards quadrupled overnight. But none of them managed to claim my reward. (For a brief time, some of the younger, more idealistic shard hunters referred to themselves as "shunters" to differentiate themselves from their elder counterparts. But when everyone began to call them "sharters" instead, they changed their minds and started to call themselves gunters too. The moniker still fit. The Seven Shards were Easter eggs hidden by Halliday, and we were all hunting for them.)

Another year passed.

Then, just a few weeks after the third anniversary of the ONI's launch, it finally happened. An enterprising young gunter led me to the First Shard. And when I picked it up, I set in motion a series of events that would drastically alter the fate of the human race.

As one of the only eyewitnesses to these historic events, I feel obligated to give my own written account of what occurred. So that future generations—if there are any—will have all the facts at their disposal when they decide how to judge my actions.

Level Four

My friend Kira always said that life is like an extremely difficult, horribly
unbalanced videogame. When you're born, you're given a randomly generated
character, with a randomly determined name, race, face, and social class.
Your body is your avatar, and you spawn in a random geographic location, at a
random moment in human history, surrounded by a random group of people,
and then you have to try to survive for as long as you can.
Sometimes the game might seem easy. Even fun.
Other times it might be so difficult you want to give up and quit.
But unfortunately, in this game you only get one life.
When your body grows too hungry or thirsty or ill or injured
or old, your health meter runs out and then it's Game Over.
Some people play the game for a hundred years without ever
figuring out that it's a game, or that there is a way to win it.
To win the videogame of life you just have to try to make the experience
of being forced to play it as pleasant as possible, for yourself,
and for all of the other players you encounter in your travels.
Kira says that if everyone played the game to win,
it'd be a lot more fun for everyone.

—*Anorak's Almanac*, chapter 77, verses 11–20

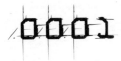

Like Marty McFly, I woke up at exactly 10:28 a.m., to the song "Back in Time" by Huey Lewis and the News.

This was courtesy of my vintage flip-clock radio—a Panasonic RC-6015, the model Marty owns in the film. I'd had it modified to play the same song at the same time Marty hears it, after he finally makes it back to the future.

I threw back the silk sheets of my king-size bed and lowered my feet to the preheated marble floor. The house computer saw that I was awake and automatically drew back the bedroom's wraparound window shades, revealing a stunning 180-degree view of my sprawling woodland estate, and of the jagged Columbus skyline on the horizon.

I still couldn't quite believe it. Waking up in this room, to this sight, every day. Not long ago, just opening my eyes here had been enough to put a grin on my face and a spring in my step.

But today, it wasn't helping. Today I was just alone, in an empty house, in a world teetering on the brink of collapse. And on days like this, the four hours I had to wait until I could put my ONI headset back on and escape into the OASIS stretched out in front of me like an eternity.

My gaze focused on the Gregarious Simulation Systems building, a shining arrowhead of mirrored glass rising from the center of downtown. GSS HQ was just a few blocks from the old IOI skyscraper complex where I'd briefly been an indentured servant. Now it belonged to GSS too. We'd turned all three buildings into free BodyLocker hotels for the homeless.

You can probably guess which one of the four of us spearheaded that initiative.

Following the skyline a few more centimeters to the right, I could also make out the silhouette of the converted Hilton hotel where I'd rented an apartment during the final year of the contest. It was a tourist attraction now. People actually bought tickets to see the tiny ten-by-ten efficiency where I'd locked myself away from the world to focus on my search for Halliday's Easter egg. I'm not sure any of those people realized that was the darkest, loneliest time in my life.

By all appearances, my life was completely different now. Except that here I was, standing at the window, moping around, already jonesing for my ONI fix.

I'd had the Portland Avenue Stacks in Oklahoma City where I'd grown up demolished years ago, so that I could erect a memorial for my mother and my aunt and Mrs. Gilmore and all of the other poor souls unfortunate enough to have died in that hellhole. I paid to have all of its residents relocated to a new housing complex I had built for them on the city outskirts. It still warmed my heart to know that all of the former residents of the stacks had, like me, become something they'd never imagined they could be—homeowners.

Even though the stacks where I'd grown up no longer existed in the real world, I could still visit them anytime I pleased, because there was a highly accurate OASIS re-creation of the Portland Avenue Stacks just as I remembered them, constructed from photos and video of the real location taken before the bombing. It was now a popular OASIS tourist attraction and school field-trip destination.

I still went there occasionally myself. I would sit inside the meticulous re-creation of my old hideout, marveling at the journey that had led me from there to where I was now. The real van that I'd used as my hideout had been extracted from the junk pile and airlifted to Columbus, so it could be put on display in the GSS Museum. But I preferred to visit the simulation of my hideout over the real deal, because in the OASIS, my hideout was still buried in a pile of abandoned vehicles at the base of the Portland Avenue Stacks, which still stood intact, as they had throughout my childhood, before Sorrento's bombs brought them crashing down and brought my childhood to its end.

Sometimes I wandered over to the replica of my aunt Alice's old stack. I would climb the stairs to her trailer, go inside, curl up in the corner of the laundry room where I used to sleep, and apologize to my mother and my aunt Alice for indirectly causing their deaths. I didn't know where else to go to talk to them. Neither of them had a grave or a tombstone I could visit. Neither did my father. All three of them had been cremated—my aunt Alice at the time of her death, and my parents after the fact, courtesy of the city's free cremation and remains-recycling program. Now all they were was dust in the wind.

Those visits made me understand why Halliday had re-created Middletown in such loving detail, when it had been the setting of so many of his own unhappy childhood memories. He wanted to be able to revisit his own past, to get back in touch with the person he used to be, before the world had changed him.

"T-T-Top o' the morning, Wade!" a familiar voice stuttered as I stepped into the bathroom. I glanced sideways to see Max, my long-suffering system-agent software, smiling at me from the surface of the giant smart mirror above the sink.

"Morning, Max," I muttered. "What's up?"

"The opposite of down," he replied. "That was easy! Ask me another one. Go ahead."

When I didn't respond, he made a heavy-metal face and started to play air guitar while shouting: "Wade's World! Wade's Word! Party time! Excellent!"

I rolled my eyes in his direction and manually flushed the toilet for effect.

"Jeez," Max said. "Tough crowd. Wake up on the wrong side of the coffin again today?"

"Yeah, it kinda feels like it," I said. "Start morning playlist, please."

"This Must Be the Place (Naive Melody)" by Talking Heads began to play over the house speakers, and I immediately felt more relaxed.

"Gracias, Max."

"De nada, my little enchilada."

I'd reinstalled MaxHeadroom v3.4.1 as my system-agent software a few months ago. I thought his presence might help me recapture the same mindset I'd had during Halliday's contest. And it had worked, to a degree.

It was like visiting with an old friend. And in truth, I needed the company. Even though, in the back of my mind, I knew that talking to your system-agent software was only slightly less weird than talking to yourself.

Max read me the day's headlines as I dressed in my workout clothes. I told him to skip all of the stories that involved war, disease, or famine. So he started reading me the weather report. I told him not to bother, then I put on my brand-new Okagami NexSpex augmented-reality glasses and headed downstairs. Max came along with me, reappearing on a network of antique CRT monitors mounted along my route.

Even in the middle of the daytime, Halliday's old mansion felt deserted. The housekeeping was all done by high-end humanoid robots who did most of their work while I slept, so I almost never saw them. I had a personal cook named Demetri, but he rarely left the kitchen. The team of security guards who manned the front gates and patrolled the grounds were human, too, but they only entered the house if an alarm went off or I summoned them.

Most of the time it was just me, all by my lonesome, in a giant house with over fifty rooms, including two kitchens, four dining rooms, fourteen bedrooms, and a total of twenty-one bathrooms. I still had no idea why there were so many toilets—or where they were all located. I chalked it up to the previous owner's well-known eccentricity.

I'd moved into James Halliday's old estate the week after I won his contest. The house was located on the northeastern outskirts of Columbus, and it was completely empty at the time. At his request, all of Halliday's possessions had been auctioned off after his death five years earlier. But the deed to the house and the thirty acres of land it stood on had remained a part of his estate, so I'd inherited it along with the rest of his assets. Samantha, Aech, and Shoto had all been kind enough to sell their shares of the property back to me, making me its sole owner. Now I lived in the same secluded fortress where my childhood hero had locked himself away from the world for the latter part of his life. The place where he had created the three keys and gates . . .

To my knowledge, Halliday had never given this place a name. But I thought it needed one, so I'd christened it Monsalvat, after the secluded castle where Sir Parzival finally locates the Holy Grail in some versions of the Arthurian legend.

I'd been living at Monsalvat for over three years now, but most of the house still remained empty and undecorated. It didn't look that way to me, though, because the AR specs I wore decorated the house for me on the fly as I walked around it. It covered the sprawling mansion's bare walls with grand tapestries, priceless paintings, and framed movie posters. It filled each of the empty rooms with illusory furniture and elegant décor.

That is, until I instructed my AR system to repurpose all that empty space, just as I was about to do now, for my morning run.

"Load *Temple of Doom*," I said as I reached the bottom of the grand staircase.

The empty foyer and dimly lit hallways of the mansion were instantly transformed into a vast subterranean labyrinth of caverns and corridors. And when I glanced down at myself, the workout clothes I'd been wearing had been replaced with a perfectly rendered Indiana Jones costume, complete with a worn leather jacket, a bull-whip on my right hip, and a battered fedora.

Indy's theme music began to play as I jogged down the corridor, and a variety of obstacles and enemies started to appear in front of me, forcing me to either dodge them or attack them with my imaginary whip. I earned points for every obstacle I avoided and for every enemy I vanquished. I could also earn bonus points for keeping my heart rate up, and for freeing the captive children being used as slave labor in the temple from their holding cells, which were scattered along my path. I ran a total of five miles like this, sprinting from one end of my house to the other and back again. And I managed to beat my previous high score.

I ended the game program and took off my AR goggles, then I toweled off and drank some water before heading to my workout room. On the way there, I stopped by the garage to admire my car collection. Of all my daily rituals, it was the one that never failed to make me smile.

The estate's enormous garage now contained four classic movie car replicas—the same four movie cars that had inspired my avatar's OASIS mash-up vehicle, ECTO-88. I owned screen-accurate replicas of Doc Brown's 1982 DeLorean DMC-12 time machine (pre–hover conversion); the Ghostbusters' 1959 Cadillac hearse Ectomobile, Ecto-1; the black 1982 Pontiac Firebird Trans-Am Knight Industries 2000, KITT (with Super-Pursuit Mode); and finally, sitting down at the far end, a replica of Dr.

Buckaroo Banzai's matter-penetrating Jet Car, built from a heavily modified 1982 Ford F-series pickup truck, with air scoops from a DC-3 transport plane bolted onto its frame, along with a World War II German fighter plane cockpit, a turbine-powered jet engine, and parachute packs for rapid deceleration.

I had never driven any of these cars. I just came out to the garage to admire them. Sometimes I sat inside them with all of the screens and control panels lit up while I listened to old movie soundtracks and brainstormed ideas for the next chapter in my ongoing ECTO-88 film series—a project I'd started working on after my therapist suggested that I might benefit from having a creative outlet.

GSS already owned the media companies that owned the movie studios that held the rights to *Back to the Future, Ghostbusters, Knight Rider,* and *The Adventures of Buckaroo Banzai,* and by paying hefty licensing fees to the estates of Christopher Lloyd, David Hasselhoff, Peter Weller, Dan Aykroyd, and Bill Murray, I was able to cast computer-generated FActors (facsimile actors) of each of them in my film. They were basically nonplayer characters with just enough artificial intelligence to take verbal directions after I placed them on my virtual movie sets inside GSS's popular Cinemaster movie-creation software.

This allowed me to finally bring my longstanding fanboy dream to life: an epic cross-over film about Dr. Emmett Brown and Dr. Buckaroo Banzai teaming up with Knight Industries to create a unique interdimensional time vehicle for the Ghostbusters, who must use it to save all ten known dimensions from a fourfold cross-rip that could tear apart the fabric of the space-time continuum.

I'd already written, produced, and directed two ECTO-88 films. They'd both done pretty well by today's standards—getting people to pay for or sit through a movie was tough these days, with the reams of inexpensive ONInet options out there—but the films didn't make enough to cover my runaway production costs and all those special-effects sequences. I didn't care what my homemade movies grossed, of course. All that mattered was the fulfillment I got out of making them, watching them, and letting other fans experience them. Now I was working on ECTO-88 Part III—the last chapter of my supremely nerdy trilogy.

I went over and said hello to KITT, and he wished me a good morning.

Then Max appeared on one of his cockpit screens, and complimented KITT on his new onboard hard drive. KITT thanked him and the two of them began to discuss the hard drive's specs, like two gearheads obsessing about engines. And they kept at it, even after I walked out of the garage.

Next it was time for weight training, in the spare dining room I'd converted into a personal gym. Max occasionally offered words of encouragement as I pumped iron, with some snarky commentary mixed in. He made for a pretty good personal trainer. But after a few minutes I muted him to watch another Peter Davison–era episode of *Doctor Who*. It had been one of Kira Morrow's favorite shows, and Davison had been her third-favorite Doctor, after Jodie Whittaker and David Tennant.

Research, I reminded myself. *You have to keep up with your research.*

But I couldn't seem to focus on the episode. All I could think about was the quarterly GSS co-owners meeting scheduled for later that day, because it meant I would be seeing Samantha for the first time since our last meeting, three months ago.

Actually, our meetings were held in the OASIS, so I would only be seeing her avatar. But that didn't really lessen my anxiety. Samantha and I first met online. We got to know each other through our OASIS avatars long before we met in the real world.

Samantha Evelyn Cook and I met in person for the first time at Ogden Morrow's home in the mountains of Oregon, right after she'd helped me win Halliday's contest.

Aech and Shoto were there, too, and we all spent the next seven days as Og's honored guests, getting to know one another in person. After everything the four of us had been through together inside the OASIS, we already shared a strong bond. But the time we spent together in the real world that week transformed us into a family—albeit a highly dysfunctional one.

That was also the week Samantha and I fell in love.

Before we met in the Earl, I'd already convinced myself that I'd fallen in love with her inside the OASIS. And in my own naïve, adolescent way maybe I had. But when the two of us finally began to spend time together in reality, I fell in love with her all over again. And I fell much harder, much faster the second time, because our connection was now physical as well as psychological, the way nature originally intended.

And this time, she fell in love with me too.

Right before she kissed me for the first time, she told me I was her best friend, and her favorite person. So I think she'd already started to fall in love with me inside the OASIS too. But unlike me, she'd been smart enough not to trust or act on those feelings until the filter of our avatars had been removed and we finally met in reality.

"You can't know if you're in love with someone if you've never actually touched them," she told me. And as usual, she was right. Once she and I started touching each other, we both found it difficult to stop.

We lost our virginity to each other three days after that first kiss. Then we spent the rest of that week sneaking off to make the beast with two backs at every opportunity. Like Depeche Mode, we just couldn't get enough.

Og's estate was designed to resemble Rivendell from the Lord of the Rings films and, like its fictional counterpart, it was nestled in a deep valley, so the acoustics of the place caused loud sounds to carry a long distance and echo off the adjacent mountain walls. But our friends and our host generously pretended not to hear all of the noise we must have made.

I'd never experienced such dizzying happiness and euphoria. And I'd never felt so desired and so loved. When she put her arms around me, I never wanted her to let go.

One night, we decided that "Space Age Love Song" by A Flock of Seagulls was our song, and then we listened to it over and over again, for hours, while we talked or made love. Now I couldn't stand to hear that song anymore. I had it filtered out in my OASIS settings, to ensure that I never heard it again.

Aech, Shoto, Samantha, and I also spent that week answering an endless barrage of questions from the media, giving statements to various law-enforcement officials, and signing a mountain of paperwork for the lawyers managing Halliday's estate, who were now tasked with dividing it equally among the four of us.

We all grew extremely fond of Ogden Morrow during our brief stay at his home. He was the father figure none of us had ever had, and we were all so grateful for his help during and after the contest that we decided to make him an honorary member of the High Five. He graciously accepted. (And since there were now only four of us, Og's induction into the High Five also prevented our nickname from becoming a misnomer.)

We also invited Og to return to Gregarious Simulation Systems as our chief adviser. After all, he was the company's co-founder, and the only one of us with any experience running it. But Og declined our offer, saying he had no desire to come out of retirement. Though he did still promise to give us advice, whenever we felt like asking for it.

The morning we finally left Og's estate and went our separate ways, he walked down to his private runway to bid us all farewell. He gave each of us one of his bear hugs, promising to stay in touch via the OASIS.

"Everything will be fine," he assured us. "You're all going to do a fantastic job!"

At the time, we had plenty of reasons to doubt his prediction. But we all acted as though we believed him, and that his faith in us was justified.

"Our future's so bright, we gotta wear shades!" Aech declared as she slipped on a pair of Ray-Bans and boarded her jet, bound for her ancestral homeland.

When Samantha and I kissed each other goodbye on the runway that morning, I never would have imagined it would be our last kiss. But I discovered the OASIS Neural Interface headset the very next day, and everything changed.

I knew Samantha might be upset with me for testing the ONI before discussing it with her first. But since it had worked flawlessly and I wasn't harmed in any way, I assumed she would forgive my risky behavior. Instead she got so pissed off she hung up on me before I even had a chance to finish describing all of the different things I'd experienced with the ONI—and the ones I had chosen not to experience.

Aech and Shoto reacted to my news far more enthusiastically. They both dropped everything and flew to Columbus to try the ONI out for themselves. And when they did, they were just as blown away by the experience as I had been. It was transcendental technology. The OASIS Neural Interface was the ultimate prosthesis. One that could temporarily cure any ailment or injury of the human body by disconnecting the mind and reconnecting it to a new, perfectly healthy, fully functional body inside the OASIS—a simulated body that would never feel any pain, through which you could experience every pleasure imaginable. The three of us talked ourselves into a frenzy, listing all the ways this device was going to change everything.

But when Samantha finally arrived on the scene, things began to go drastically downhill.

I still remember every word of our exchange that day, because I'd brazenly recorded it with an ONI headset while it was happening. In the three years since, I'd relived our conversation on an almost weekly basis. To me, it felt like our breakup had just happened a few days ago. Because for me, it had.

"Take that stupid thing off!" Samantha says, glancing up at the ONI headset I'm wearing. The original headset I found in Halliday's vault lies on the conference table between us, along with three duplicates, fresh from the 3-D printer.

"No," I say angrily. "I want to record how ridiculous you're being right now, so you can play it back later and see for yourself."

Aech and Shoto are sitting between us, on either side of the conference table, swiveling their heads back and forth like they're watching a tennis match. Shoto is hearing our conversation with a slight delay, through the Mandarax translator earpiece he's wearing.

"I told you," Samantha says, snatching one of the headsets off the table, "I am never going to let one of these things take control of my brain. Not ever."

She hurls the headset against the wall, but it doesn't break. They're very durable.

"How can you form an educated opinion when you haven't even tried it?" Aech asks quietly.

"I've never tried sniffing paint thinner either," Samantha snaps back. She sighs in frustration and runs her hands through her hair. "I don't know why I can't make you guys understand. This is the last thing humanity needs. Can't you see that? The world is a complete mess right now. . . ."

She pulls up half a dozen different world newsfeeds on the conference-room viewscreen, filling it with images of poverty, famine, disease, war, and a wide array of natural disasters. Even with the audio muted, the barrage of images was pretty horrific.

"Half the world already spends every waking moment ignoring reality inside the OASIS. We already peddle the Opiate of the Masses. And now you want to up the dosage?"

I roll my eyes and shake my head. I can feel my adrenaline rising.

"That's total bullshit, Arty, and you know it," I say. "We could turn off the OASIS tomorrow, and it wouldn't solve any of humanity's problems. It would just rob people of the only escape they have. I mean, I get where you're coming from—and I agree that everyone should balance their time in the OASIS with equal time in reality. But it's not our place to mandate how our users live their lives. Growing up in the stacks would have been hell for me if I hadn't had access to the OASIS. It literally saved my life. And I've heard Aech say the same thing."

We both glance over at Aech. She nods in agreement.

"We weren't all lucky enough to grow up in some ritzy Vancouver suburb like you, Samantha," I say. "Who are you to judge how other people deal with reality?"

Samantha clenches her jaw and narrows her eyes at me, but she still doesn't reply. And I apparently take this as my cue to shove my foot even further into my mouth. All the way, in fact.

"ONI technology is also going to save hundreds of millions of lives," I say self-righteously. "By preventing the spread of all sorts of infectious diseases—like the flu pandemic that killed both of your parents." Now it's my turn to level a finger at her. "How can you be against an invention that could've prevented their deaths?"

She snaps her head around and looks at me in wounded surprise, like I've just slapped her across the face. Then her gaze hardens and that's it—the exact instant her love for me disappears. I'm too amped up on adrenaline to notice it there in the moment, but I spot it plain as day on every single one of my repeat viewings. The sudden change in her eyes says it all. One second she loves me, and the next she loves me not.

She never responds to my question. She just stares daggers at me in silence, until Shoto finally chimes in.

"We're going to make trillions of dollars selling these headsets, Arty," he says calmly. "We can use that money to help the world. To try and fix all of the things that need fixing."

Samantha shakes her head. "No amount of money will be able to undo the damage these headsets are going to cause," she replies, sounding defeated now. "You guys read Og's email. He thinks releasing the ONI is a bad idea too."

"Og hasn't even tried the ONI," I say, letting too much anger creep into my voice. "He's like you. Condemning it without even trying to understand its potential."

"Of course I understand its potential, you idiot!" Samantha shouts. She looks around the table. "Christ! Haven't any of you rewatched *The Matrix* lately? Or *Sword Art Online*? Plugging your brain and your nervous system directly into a computer simulation is never a good idea! We're talking about giving complete control of our minds to a machine. Turning ourselves into cyborgs . . ."

"Come on," Aech says. "You're overreacting—"

"No!" she shouts back. "I'm not." Then she takes a deep breath before glancing around the table at all three of us. "Don't you see? This is why Halliday never released the

ONI technology himself. He knew it would only hasten the collapse of human civilization, by encouraging people to spend even more time escaping from reality. He didn't want to be the one responsible for opening Pandora's box." She looks at me, and now her eyes are filling with tears. "I thought you wanted to live here. In the real world. With me. But you haven't learned a goddamn thing, have you?"

She reaches over and brings her fist down on the power button of the data drive connected to my ONI headset, ending my recording.

• • •

When we held an official vote on the matter, Aech, Shoto, and I voted to patent the ONI headset and release it to the world, with Samantha being the lone voice of dissent.

She couldn't forgive me. She told me so right after I cast my vote against her. Right before she dumped me.

"We can't be together anymore, Wade," she said evenly, her voice suddenly devoid of emotion. "Not when we disagree on something so basic. And so important. Your actions today will have disastrous consequences. I'm sorry you can't see that."

Once my brain finally processed what had happened, I collapsed into a chair, clutching my chest. I was devastated. I was still in love with her. I knew I'd broken her heart. But I also believed releasing the ONI was the right thing to do. If I'd withheld it from billions of suffering people just to preserve our relationship, what would that have made me?

When I got her on the phone and tried to tell her this, she got furious once again. She said that *I* was the one who was being selfish, refusing to see the danger in what we were doing. Then she stopped speaking to me altogether.

Luckily, my new ONI headset offered an easy, ready-made escape from my misery. With the press of a button, it literally took my mind off of my broken heart, and focused it elsewhere. I could put on the headset and re-live another person's happy memories anytime I pleased. Or I could just log in to the OASIS, where I was treated like a god, and where everything now felt completely real—as real as the most vivid dreams feel while you're having them.

When the Shard Riddle appeared, I'd seized on it as another distraction. But now, over three years later, my ongoing obsession with solving it had become a forced and desperate exercise and I knew it. It was really just an attempt to forget the mess I'd made of my personal life. Not that I ever would have admitted it out loud.

None of these distractions helped me fix what was broken, of course. I still thought about Samantha every day. And I still wondered what I could've done differently.

These days, I told myself that Samantha would've broken up with me eventually anyway. By the end of that first week at Og's estate, I'd already begun to wonder if she was having second thoughts. She'd started to pick up on my annoying idiosyncrasies. My inability to recognize social cues. My total and complete lack of cool around strangers. My neediness and emotional immaturity. She was probably already looking for an excuse to dump my socially awkward ass, and when I chose to vote against her on releasing the ONI, it just fast-forwarded the inevitable.

Since our breakup, I'd seen Samantha only via her OASIS avatar, and only during our co-owners meetings. Even then, she rarely spoke to me directly or made eye contact. She seemed to be doing her best to pretend I didn't exist.

After our split, she became laser focused on carrying out her master plan—the plan she'd told me about during our first meeting, when we discussed what we'd do if either of us managed to win Halliday's contest.

"If I win that dough, I'm going to make sure everyone on this planet has enough to eat," she'd proclaimed. "Once we tackle world hunger, then we can figure out how to fix the environment and solve the energy crisis."

True to her word, she created the Art3mis Foundation, a global charity organization devoted to ending world hunger, saving the environment, and solving the energy crisis, and donated nearly all of her massive income to it.

She still kept an apartment on the top floor of the Art3mis Foundation building in downtown Columbus, a few blocks from GSS. But she spent very little time there. She traveled constantly, visiting the world's most troubled and impoverished nations to focus media attention on their plight, and to oversee the Art3mis Foundation's aid efforts.

She also used her newfound fame and wealth to champion a whole host of environmental and humanitarian causes around the world, and seemingly overnight, she transformed herself into a sort of rock-star philanthropist and humanitarian. She was like Oprah, Joan Jett, and Mother Teresa all rolled into one. She now had billions of admirers, and in spite of everything I couldn't help but be one of them.

But she wasn't the only one trying to make the world a better place. Aech, Shoto, and I were each doing our part too.

Shoto created his own charity organization called the Daisho Council, which provided free food, housing, healthcare, and counseling to the millions of isolated Japanese kids known as *hikikomori,* who lived in self-imposed seclusion from the outside world. Aech set up a similar charity in North America called Helen's House, which provided a safe haven for homeless LBGTQIA kids throughout the United States and Canada, along with another foundation devoted to providing impoverished African nations with self-sustaining technology and resources. And for kicks, she called it the Wakandan Outreach Initiative.

I'd founded the Parzival Relief Organization, a nonprofit that provided free food, electricity, Internet access, and ONI headsets to orphaned and impoverished kids around the world. (It was honestly the sort of help I would've wanted to receive if I had still been a kid living in the stacks.)

We'd also started funneling cash to the struggling U.S. government and its citizens, who had been surviving on foreign aid for decades. We paid off the national debt and provided aerial-defense drones and tactical telebots to help reestablish the rule of law in the rural areas where local infrastructure had collapsed along with the power grid. Human law enforcement officers no longer had to risk their own lives to uphold the law. Our police telebots were able to carry out their mission to serve and protect without putting any human lives at risk. Their programming and their operational fail-safes prevented them from harming anyone in the line of duty.

Together, Samantha, Aech, Shoto, and I donated billions of dollars every year. But plenty of rich people (like Ogden Morrow) had been throwing mountains of money at these same problems for decades, with little effect. And so far, the High Five's own noble efforts weren't moving the dial much either. For the time being we were holding chaos and collapse at bay, but humanity's perilous predicament just kept on getting worse.

The reason for this was painfully obvious to me. We'd already passed the point of no return. The world's population was fast approaching ten billion people, and Mother Earth was making it abundantly clear that she could no longer sustain all of us—especially not after we'd spent the past two centuries poisoning her oceans and atmosphere with wild industrial abandon. We had made our bed, and now we were going to die in it.

That was why I was still working on my backup plan, the one I'd shared with Samantha that first night we met.

Over the past three years, I had funded the construction of a small nuclear-powered interstellar spacecraft in low Earth orbit. It housed a self-sustaining biosphere, which could provide long-term living space and life support for a crew of up to two dozen human passengers—including Aech and Shoto, who had joined me in footing the enormous construction bill.

I'd christened my ship the *Vonnegut,* like my old Firefly-class spaceship in the OASIS, which I'd named after my favorite author.

If the *Vonnegut's* fusion engines functioned as they were supposed to, and the radiation shielding held up, *and* the ship's armored hull didn't get punctured by any micrometeors or crushed by an asteroid, we would reach Proxima Centauri in approximately forty-seven years. There, we would search for a habitable Earthlike planet where we could make a new home for ourselves, our children, and the frozen human embryos we were going to bring along. (We'd been accepting embryo donations for over a year by this point, from every country around the world, with the hope of ensuring genetic diversity.)

The ship's onboard computer contained a new standalone virtual-reality simulation for us to access on our long journey. After much debate over what we should call our new virtual realm, we finally agreed upon the name ARC@DIA. (It was Aech's idea to replace the *a* in the middle with an @ sign, to give the name a l33t flourish and to help distinguish it from the geographic region in central Greece, the Duran Duran side project, the city on Gallifrey, the alternate plane of reality in Dungeons & Dragons, and all of the other Arcadias out there.) The addition of the @ was also fitting because, as Aech put it, "ARC@DIA will be where it's at!"

ARC@DIA was going to serve as our own private scaled-down version of the OASIS during the voyage. It was still a work in progress, and likely would be until the day we departed. Due to various space and hardware limitations, our simulation wasn't nearly as big—about half the size of one OASIS sector. But that was still a vast amount of virtual space for us and our tiny crew to inhabit. We had enough room to upload copies of more than two hundred of our favorite OASIS planets, along with their NPCs.

We didn't bother transferring any of the business content or retail planets over. Where we were going, we wouldn't need stores or commerce. Besides, we had to be sparing with our data-storage space, since we were bringing along a backup copy of the entire ONI-net file database too. It was updated every night, along with new OASIS content.

There was one other thing that made our simulation different from its predecessor. Unlike the OASIS, ARC@DIA could only be accessed via a neural-interface headset. (We didn't want to waste any time, space, or money bringing outdated haptic technology along.)

The *Vonnegut* was still about a year from being complete, but Aech, Shoto, and I were in no rush. We weren't eager to leave the Earth behind for a long, cramped, and perilous voyage. And we weren't ready to give up on Planet Earth yet either. Not while there was still a chance we could save it. What we were doing was doomsday-prepping on a multibillionaire scale, packing the ultimate bugout bag—the means to escape the planet if, and when, everything went to shit.

We'd concealed the details of the Vonnegut Project from the world (and from Samantha) for as long as we could. But eventually word of what we were up to leaked to the press. Of course, Samantha was furious when she found out we'd spent over three hundred billion dollars to build a ship to escape our dying planet instead of using that money and manpower to help her try to save it.

I told her we were saving a spot for her on the *Vonnegut*'s crew, but you can imagine how that went over. She stormed out, then she crucified us in the press. She accused us of sabotaging humanity by releasing the ONI to the masses and then using the profits to build a lifeboat to save our own skin.

But I didn't see it that way. And thankfully, neither did Aech or Shoto. We admired Samantha's optimism, and maybe—on a good day—even shared in it. But with Earth teetering on the brink of destruction, leaving our eggs in one basket was foolish. Sending a small contingent of humanity out into space was the only responsible thing to do—and at this precarious moment in history, we were the only three people on the planet with the resources to do it.

After two dozen laps in my heated indoor Olympic-size swimming pool—which, thanks to my AR swim goggles, was teeming with rare tropical fish and even a pod of friendly dolphins to keep me company—I was standing in my walk-in closet, surrounded by tailored suits and designer clothes I had never worn and probably never would. I wore the same outfit every day, so I never had to expend any thought on what to wear next. I got the idea from Jeff Goldblum in *The Fly*, and he, in turn, got it from Albert Einstein.

I was equally disciplined about my daily workout, even when I was feeling under the weather. Exercising for at least two hours every day was an absolute necessity, since I frequently spent over eleven hours a day logged in to the OASIS with my ONI headset, followed by another eight hours of sleep on top of that. For me, it seemed to take at least two hours of vigorous exercise to balance out the twenty or so hours of each day that I spent not moving at all.

Like eating and sleeping, exercise was one of the things people still had to do in reality. None of the simulated physical activity you experienced through your ONI headset actually had any real-world effects, like improving your circulation or increasing your muscle tone.

I finished lacing up my vintage Air Jordans and stepped outside onto the balcony, where my usual breakfast was waiting for me. As I took a seat at the table, one of my humanoid service robots, Belvedere, uncovered my omelet and hash browns and poured me a glass of freshly squeezed orange juice. Then he retreated to the corner of the balcony and stood there like a statue, waiting to be of further use.

I'd programmed Belvedere never to speak unless spoken to, because his synthesized voice set me on edge, regardless of how much I tweaked his tone or inflection. Probably because I'd seen too many robot-uprising movies.

There wasn't any actual chance of my service robots staging a revolt, of course. Like most of the artificial intelligence people interacted with on a daily basis, Belvedere and his fellow household bots were Tier One AI, which was classified as "extremely weak." Tier One AI was used to operate service robots, drive automated cars, and fly automated planes. All of our OASIS NPCs were Tier Ones.

Tier Two AI was used mostly for science and military applications, and their use and operating parameters were heavily restricted by most world governments. Tier Twos could form short-term memories and had stronger independent learning abilities—but they still did not have the capacity for autonomy, or any sort of identity or self-awareness.

Tier Three AI was the real deal—fully autonomous, self-aware, and conscious. The kind that science fiction films warn you about. This level of artificial intelligence was still theoretical, praise be to Crom. But according to GSS's top engineers, probably not for much longer. The race to create true artificial intelligence had become like the race to create the atomic bomb. Several different countries—including my own—were working to create full-blown self-aware, as-smart-if-not-smarter-than-the-average-human-being artificial intelligence. Maybe some of them already had, and now it was just a waiting game to see who would unleash it first, probably in an army of sentient aerial drones and battle telebots that said "Roger, Roger" to one another while machine-gunning civilian populations. That was, if we didn't nuke ourselves into oblivion first.

I ate in silence for a few minutes, staring up at the sky overhead. When I finished my food, I put my AR specs on again and used them to log in to my OASIS account. Then I used a heavily encrypted remote-access code to take control of a telebot—a humanoid telepresence robot—that was located in orbit high above the Earth aboard the *Vonnegut*. Once my link to the bot was established, my AR specs allowed me to see through its "eyes"—a set of stereoscopic video cameras mounted in its head. I disconnected the telebot from its charging dock, which was anchored to a bulkhead in the ship's forward cargo hold. This was in the ring-shaped section of the craft, which rotated constantly to generate centripetal force and create simulated gravity.

I piloted the telebot over to a circular observation window set into the outer hull. Then I waited a few seconds for the ring to rotate around, until the luminous blue curve of the Earth came into view, filling my field of vision. The *Vonnegut* was currently passing over North America, and through a break in the cloud cover I was able to locate the outline of Lake Erie, and then the dense urban grid of Columbus just below it. I stabilized and magnified the image until I had a satellite's view of my own house and the patio where I was currently sitting. For a second or two, I was able to gaze down at myself through the eyes of a telepresence robot aboard a starship orbiting the Earth.

When the Earth rotated out of view again, I turned the telebot away from the window, then I used it to make a quick circuit of the ship. Dozens of other telebots floated through each of its sections, under the control of the technicians and engineers back on Earth. They were running diagnostic tests on the experimental heavy-duty radiation shielding around the frozen embryo storage compartment. After watching them work for a while, I piloted my telebot into the ship's Network Operations Center, to check on the ARC@DIA backup servers, and the OASIS uplink from Earth that we used to keep our copy of various planets in the simulation up to date. Everything appeared to be running smoothly. We still had plenty of extra storage space for future ARC@DIA content updates on the *Vonnegut*'s computer. Its processing power limited us to a maximum of one hundred simultaneous ARC@DIA users, but that was far more than we needed.

I spent a few more minutes piloting my telebot through the silent corridors of the ship before I returned it to its charging dock. Then I disconnected from it, and just like that, I was back on Earth, sitting on my patio.

I'd traveled all the way to space and back, and I'd only managed to kill fifteen minutes.

I tried calling Aech and Shoto, to see if either of them wanted to catch up before our co-owners meeting. But as usual, neither of them picked up. I took off my specs and threw them on the table in front of me with a sigh. I told myself that Aech was probably still asleep, and that Shoto was probably busy with work. I could've checked their account statuses to see, but I'd learned the hard way that if your friends were avoiding you, you didn't want or need to know about it.

I continued to eat my breakfast in silence, listening to the wind in the trees and absentmindedly watching the flock of security drones overhead as they patrolled the perimeter of my estate. This was usually the only time I spent outdoors each day, to get my daily minimum dose of sunlight. Deep down, I still shared Halliday's opinion that going outside was highly overrated.

I pulled my AR specs back on and skimmed over the emails that had collected in my inbox overnight. Then I spent some time updating my ONI-net queue with new Recs and Sims from the "Most Popular Downloads" list. I did this every morning, even though I already had thousands of hours of experiences in my queue—more than I would ever have time to make it through, even if I lived to be a hundred. That was why I constantly updated and rearranged the clips in my queue—to make sure I got to the best stuff first.

In the early days of the ONI-net, some people at GSS had worried that its popularity might cause the rest of the OASIS to become a ghost town, because everyone would spend all of their time doing playback instead of exploring the OASIS to have experiences of their own. But the OASIS continued to grow and thrive alongside the ONI-net, and most users divided their time equally between the two. Perhaps it was human nature to crave both passive and interactive forms of entertainment.

As usual, I searched the ONI-net for any newly listed clips tagged with the name Art3mis or Samantha Cook. Whenever anyone posted a recording in which she appeared, I would download it. Even if it was just a clip of her signing an autograph for someone, it still gave me a chance to experience standing next to her for a few seconds.

I knew how pathetic this was—which somehow made it even more pathetic.

But trust me, there were far more twisted and depraved clips I could've been playing back. The current top download in the NSFW section of the ONI-net library was a fifty-person orgy, recorded simultaneously by all fifty participants, giving the viewer the ability to jump from one participant's body to the next at will, like some hedonistic demon. Cyberstalking my ex-girlfriend at her public appearances seemed like a pretty tame pastime in comparison.

Don't get me wrong. The ONI-net wasn't just a way for people to experience guilt-free sex and risk-free drug use. It was also an incredibly powerful tool for fostering empathy and understanding. Entertainers and politicians and artists and activists used this new communication medium to connect with a global audience, with profound results. The Art3mis Foundation had even started posting .oni clips now—first-person slice-of-life recordings made by impoverished and exploited people around the globe, designed to expose others to their plight. It was a brilliant and effective use of ONI technology. But it also seemed hypocritical of Samantha to use the ONI to further her own agenda after railing against its release. When I'd said so during one of our meetings, Samantha made it abundantly clear that she didn't give a flying frak at a rolling Rathtar what I thought.

I ate the last bite of my now-cold omelet and dropped my napkin on my plate. Belvedere sprang into action and began to clear off the table, the servos in his robotic limbs whirring with each of his small, precise movements.

What now?

I could head over to my music room, to knock out my daily guitar lesson. One of my new hobbies was learning to play guitar in reality, which proved to be very different—and far more difficult—than playing a simulated axe in the OASIS. Luckily, I had the best guitar teacher imaginable— a fully licensed hologram of the great Edward Van Halen, circa the release of *1984*. He was a taskmaster too. Thanks to his tutelage I was starting to get pretty good.

Or I could take another Bollywood dance lesson. I was practicing for Aech and Endira's wedding in a few months. I knew that Samantha would be in attendance, and I'd secretly begun to harbor an idiotic fantasy that I might be able to win her back when she saw me tearing up the dance floor.

A message popped up on my AR display, reminding me that I had an appointment scheduled with my therapist this morning. I always scheduled a therapy session before our GSS co-owners meeting, to help put me in a calm, nonconfrontational frame of mind, and—hopefully—prevent me from starting any unnecessary arguments with Samantha. Sometimes it even worked.

I selected the icon for the therapy program on the HUD of my AR specs, and my virtual therapist appeared in the empty chair across the table from me. When you first installed the software, you were allowed to select your therapist's physical appearance and personality from thousands of premade options, from Freud to Frasier. I'd selected Sean Maguire—Robin Williams's character in *Good Will Hunting*. His familiar demeanor, his warm smile, and his fake Boston accent made our sessions feel like I was talking to an old friend—even though he usually only said things like "Yes, go on" and "And how does that make you feel, Wade?"

I also had the ability to change the location where I met with him. The default setting was his office at the community college where he taught— the same location where most of his sessions with Will Hunting took place in the film. Or you could choose one of several bars in Southie, including Timmy's Tap or the L Street Tavern. But I felt like changing things up this morning, so I selected the bench by the lake at Boston Public Garden, and an instant later, Sean and I were sitting on it, side by side, staring at the swans.

He began by asking me if I was still having nightmares about my aunt Alice's death. I lied and told him no, because I didn't feel like discussing the subject again.

He moved on to my social-media "addiction" (his term) and asked me how I felt my recovery was progressing. Just over a month ago, I'd placed an irreversible lock on all my social-media accounts. I couldn't use any of them for a full year. I told Sean that I was still experiencing withdrawal symptoms, but they were beginning to subside.

Meed-Feed Addiction had been around since before I was born, but it had become even more common in the wake of the ONI's release. Most of the early social media platforms like Facebook, YouTube, and Twitter had migrated into the OASIS shortly after it launched, and they all still existed there today in your meed feed, the consolidated social media feed timeline built into every user's account. It allowed the billions of OASIS users around the world to share messages, memes, files, photos, songs, videos, celebrity gossip, pornography, and petty insults with one another, just as people had been doing on the Internet for the past half century.

I'd never been good in social situations of any kind, so I'd avoided social media entirely for most of my life. And I should have kept on avoiding it once I became a public figure.

It turned out I just wasn't comfortable living in the spotlight. I was an awkward kid who was good at videogames and memorizing trivia. I was not mentally or emotionally equipped to have the whole world's attention focused on me.

At any given moment, there were millions of people posting shit at or about me somewhere online. This had been the case ever since I first found the Copper Key, but it was only after I'd won the contest that the haters came out in force.

It made sense, in hindsight. The moment I inherited Halliday's fortune, I was no longer the scrappy underdog from the stacks doing heroic battle with the Sixers. I was just another asshole billionaire, living a life of ease in his ivory tower. None of the stuff my friends and I did to try to help humanity seemed to make any difference.

My detractors in the media began to refer to my avatar as "Parvenu" instead of Parzival, while the less pretentious garden-variety assholes online instead chose to adopt I-Roc's old nickname for me—"Penisville."

Things got really bad when a previously unknown music group called Tapioca Shindig released a song titled "Sixer Fellatin' Punk," which used an autotuned sound bite from the live POV broadcast I'd made during the Battle of Castle Anorak, when I'd publicly declared to the world that "If I find Halliday's Easter egg, I hereby vow to split my winnings equally with Art3mis, Aech, and Shoto. . . . If I'm lying, I should be forever branded as a gutless Sixer-fellating punk." But they only took the last part, so the lyrics to the whole song were just me singing "I should be forever branded as a gutless Sixer-fellating punk!" over and over.

The song instantly went viral. It was Tapioca Shindig's one and only hit single. They posted a music video to the ONI-net that racked up over a billion downloads before I had it taken offline. Then I sued the band for defamation and bankrupted each of its members. Which, of course, only made the public hate me even more.

Samantha, Aech, and Shoto received their fair share of online hate, too, of course, but they took it in stride. They were somehow able to bask in the adoration of their billions of fans while ignoring the ire of even their most vocal detractors. I appeared to lack the emotional maturity necessary to pull off that little trick.

Yes, I knew the haters' opinions were utterly meaningless, and had no effect whatsoever on our real lives. Unless, of course, we *let* it. Which, of course, I *did*.

And yes, the rational part of my brain knew that the vast majority of the people who trolled us online were acting out, due to crushing disappointment with their own miserable lives. And who could blame them? Reality *was* completely miserable for a vast majority of the world's population. I should've taken pity on the sad, pathetic souls who had nothing better to do with their time than vent their frustrations by attacking me and my friends.

Instead I went on a rage-induced troll-killing spree. Several of them, actually.

The superuser abilities I'd inherited from Halliday allowed me to circumvent the OASIS's strict policy of user anonymity. So when some snide douchebag using the handle PenisvilleH8r posted something nasty about me on the meed feeds, I pulled up his private account profile, pinpointed his avatar's location inside the OASIS, and waited till he set foot inside a PvP zone. Then, before PenisvilleH8r even knew what was happening, I made my avatar invisible, teleported in, and zeroed his ass out with a ninety-ninth-level Finger of Death spell. Now that my avatar wore the Robes of Anorak, I was both omnipotent and invulnerable, so there was literally nothing anyone could do to stop me.

I gleefully zeroed out hundreds of trolls in this fashion. If someone talked shit about me, I found them and killed their avatar. If someone posted something hateful about Art3mis or her foundation, I found them and killed their avatar. If someone posted a racist meme about Aech or a video attacking Shoto's work, I found them and killed their avatar—usually right after I asked them the rhetorical question, "Who run Bartertown?"

Eventually, people began to accuse me of being the untraceable, undetectable, ultrapowerful avatar behind the killings, and the resulting online media backlash, dubbed "Parzivalgate," destroyed my public image. Thanks to my robes there was no hard evidence against me, and of course I denied everything, but even I had to admit that the circumstantial case was pretty strong. Gee, a bunch of avatars get killed by an undetectable, all-powerful avatar, and the only thing they have in common is that they trash-talked the one person most likely to have an undetectable, all-powerful avatar. . . .

A petition calling for official sanctions against me was digitally signed by hundreds of millions of daily OASIS users. A few dozen class-action lawsuits were filed against me. In the end, none of them amounted to anything; I was a multibillionaire with unlimited resources and the world's best lawyers on my payroll, and there was no proof of wrongdoing on my part. But there was nothing I could do about the anger I'd caused.

Finally, Aech took me aside for a long talk. She reminded me how fortunate—and powerful—I was now, even if on the inside I still felt like that underdog kid from the stacks. She told me to grow up, and let it go. "Cultivate an attitude of gratitude, Z."

I reluctantly took her advice and went into therapy. I could've afforded a real-life human therapist, of course—but I found it easier to share my innermost thoughts with a computer program than with another person. A virtual therapist couldn't judge you, or share your secrets with its spouse for laughs. It would never repeat anything I said to anyone, and that was the only sort of therapist I could bring myself to confide in.

After a few sessions with Sean, I'd realized that the best thing for my mental health would be to abandon social media altogether. So I had. And it was the right choice. My anger abated, and my wounded pride began to heal.

I'd finally gained enough distance from my addiction to realize something. Human beings were never meant to participate in a worldwide social network comprised of billions of people. We were designed by evolution to be hunter-gatherers, with the mental capacity to interact and socialize with the other members of our tribe—a tribe made up of a few hundred other people at most. Interacting with thousands or even millions of other people on a daily basis was way too much for our ape-descended melons to handle. That was why social media had been gradually driving the entire population of the world insane since it emerged back around the turn of the century.

I was even beginning to wonder if the invention of a worldwide social network was actually the "Great Filter" that theoretically caused all technological civilizations to go extinct, instead of nuclear weapons or climate change. Maybe every time an intelligent species grew advanced enough to invent a global computer network, they would then develop some form of social media, which would immediately fill these beings with such an intense hatred for one another that they ended up wiping themselves out within four or five decades.

Only time would tell.

•　•　•

One thing I had never shared with my therapist—or with anyone—was the comfort I took from knowing that I had access to the Big Red Button.

Not that I would ever actually press it. I'd read all of the worst-case scenarios and seen the disaster simulations created by GSS's in-house think tanks, predicting what would happen if the OASIS went offline. The outlook was never pretty. The general consensus was this: if the OASIS stopped working for more than a few days, so would human civilization.

This had become even more of a certainty in the wake of our merger with IOI, because nearly all of the support operations that kept the global Internet backbone running were now dependent on the OASIS in some form. As were the vast majority of the security and defense systems around the world, at the national, state, local, and home level. If the OASIS went down, the Internet would probably suffer a catastrophic collapse of its infrastructure a short time later, and our already precarious human civilization would begin to rapidly collapse too. That was why GSS had so many backup server installations all over the world.

Nobody knew that the OASIS's creator had rigged the whole simulation with a self-destruct button, and that I alone now had access to it.

Nobody knew that the fate of the whole world was literally in my hands. Except me. And I wanted to keep it that way.

• • •

Once my virtual therapy session was over, I headed downstairs and made the long trek to my office at the far end of the mansion's east wing. This was the same enormous oak-paneled room that had served as Halliday's office when he'd lived here. It was also the room in which Halliday had designed and programmed his elaborate Easter-egg hunt. He'd even included a re-creation of this office in the hunt's final challenge.

To me, this room was hallowed ground. And I'd spent three years and millions of dollars re-creating the vast collection of classic videogame consoles and home computers Halliday had originally kept on display here.

The office contained over a hundred glass tables, arranged in a large egg-shaped pattern on the floor. On each table was a different vintage home computer or videogame system, along with tiered racks that held a collection of its peripherals, controllers, software, and games. Each collection was meticulously arranged and displayed, like a museum exhibit.

A conventional OASIS immersion rig sat in one corner of the room, collecting dust. I only used it for emergencies now, when I needed to access the OASIS after I'd hit my twelve-hour ONI daily usage limit. It was hard to believe that just a few years ago, I'd been completely content accessing the OASIS with my visor and haptic rig. Once you got used to an ONI headset, the old hardware made everything look and feel painfully fake—even with the best haptics money could buy.

My new prototype MoTIV—a mobile tactical immersion vault—sat on a circular elevator pad in the center of the room.

The MoTIV was a logical extension of the concept of the standard immersion vault—an armored coffin that protected your sleeping body while your mind roamed the OASIS. Except that my new device didn't just provide *passive* protection. Part of GSS's new SuperVault deluxe line of tactical OASIS immersion vaults, the MoTIV looked more like a heavily armed robotic spider than a coffin. It was an armored escape vehicle and all-terrain weapons platform, featuring eight retractable armored legs for navigating all forms of terrain, and a pair of machine guns and grenade launchers mounted on each side of its armored chassis—not to mention a bulletproof acrylic cockpit canopy for its occupant.

Our in-house ad agency had already come up with the perfect slogan: "If you're gonna use lethal force to defend yourself, you better have a MoTIV!"

If I was awake, I could operate my MoTIV using the control panel located inside the cockpit. If I was logged in to the OASIS with an ONI headset, I could control the MoTIV from inside the simulation, via my avatar. So if my body came under attack while I was logged in, I wouldn't need to log out before I could defend myself. And I could hurl insults at my would-be assailants through the earsplittingly loud speakers mounted on its heavily armored exoskeleton.

The MoTIV was overkill, considering the small army of security guards and defense drones guarding my house. But state-of-the-art toys like these were a perk of my position at GSS—and I had to admit, having it made me feel a lot less anxious about leaving my body unattended for twelve hours every day.

Most ONI users couldn't afford a standard immersion vault, let alone a personal armored attack vehicle. Some settled for locking themselves in a room or closet before they entered the sleeplike state induced by the ONI headset. Others asked someone they trusted to watch over their helpless body while their mind was temporarily disconnected from it.

Of course, as Art3mis was fond of pointing out, plenty of users didn't take any precautions at all when they put on their ONI headsets. And plenty of them paid the price for doing so. A new breed of thieves, rapists, serial killers, and organ harvesters preyed on those ONI users who failed to lock up their bodies while their minds were on vacation. But over the past few years, thousands of "BodyLocker" capsule hotels had opened up around the world, where people could rent coffin-size rooms for just a few credits a day. It was the lowest-rent housing imaginable. They couldn't build them fast enough to meet the demand.

To increase user safety, GSS had also started selling deluxe ONI headsets featuring built-in motion-activated cameras, with video feeds that could be monitored from inside the OASIS. Immersion vaults were also equipped with interior and exterior cameras that allowed their occupants to monitor their physical body and its surroundings from inside the OASIS, along with motion detectors that would alert them if anyone came within spitting distance of their body in the Earl.

I went into the office's private bathroom and remained there until I'd emptied my bowels and bladder as much as possible. This had become a pre-login ritual for every ONI user—especially those who wanted to remain logged in for a full twelve hours without soiling themselves. When I emerged from the bathroom, I climbed into the MoTIV and settled into the form-fitting gel-foam flotation recliner. Its padded retaining bands locked into place around my arms, legs, and waist, to keep me from falling out. Throughout my long ONI session, the recliner would periodically rotate my body and flex my limbs to increase circulation and prevent muscle atrophy. There were also special suits you could wear that would electrically stimulate your muscles while you were under, but they irritated my skin so I never wore them.

I pressed a button to close the MoTIV's canopy. Then I pressed another button to activate the circular elevator pad it was sitting on. I grinned and braced myself for a drop, just before the pad began to rocket down the elevator shaft. Lights embedded in the shaft's reinforced titanium wall flew by in a blur.

This elevator had been designed so that, if you looked straight up during its descent, it perfectly re-created the look of the top-secret Pepsi elevator guarded by B. B. King in *Spies Like Us*. It, and the bunker it led to, had both been constructed by Halliday when he'd first moved into this house, so that he would have a place to ride out World War III, which was still threatening to break out at any moment, just as it had been for the past hundred years. Now I used his bunker for my daily twelve-hour ONI dives, content in the knowledge that I was deep enough and well protected enough to survive a missile strike on my house, on the off chance that some nutjob despot with a death wish managed to get one past our global defense network, and the redundant one GSS maintained over the entire city of Columbus to prevent terrorist attacks on our OASIS servers, *and* the even more redundant antiballistic-missile installations that surrounded my home.

The whole world knew my address, so I didn't feel like I was being paranoid. I was just taking sensible precautions.

When the elevator's blast doors slid open, I used the MoTIV's cockpit controls to spider-walk it forward, into the bunker's receiving bay, which was just a big empty concrete room with lights embedded in its ceiling. The elevator stood at one end and a pair of large armored doors stood at the other, leading to the high-tech, fully stocked bomb shelter beyond.

I secretly loved coming down here. Three kilometers beneath the earth, in this armored concrete bunker, I felt like I was in my own private Batcave. (Although it was obvious to me now that Bruce Wayne never would've been able to construct his crime-fighting crib all by himself, in total secrecy, with no one to help him lay the plumbing and pour the concrete but his geriatric butler. No way.)

I lowered my MoTIV to the concrete floor, retracted its legs, and placed it into standard defense mode. Then I removed my ONI headset from its cradle above my head and put it on. When I powered it on, its titanium sensor bands automatically retracted to fit the contours of my skull before locking themselves tightly in place so that the headset couldn't be moved or jostled by even a micrometer. If that were to happen in the middle of my ONI session . . . it would be bad.

I pressed a button to close the MoTIV's armored canopy and it slid shut with a pneumatic hiss, sealing me safely inside its roomy cockpit. Then I cleared my throat and said, "Initiate login sequence."

I felt a familiar tingling sensation all over my scalp as the headset scanned my brain and verified my identity. Then a female voice prompted me to speak my passphrase and I recited it, being careful to enunciate each syllable. I'd recently reset it to the same passphrase I'd used during the latter days of Halliday's Hunt—a lyric from the 1987 song "Don't Let's Start" by They Might Be Giants: *No one in the world ever gets what they want and that is beautiful. . . .*

Once my passphrase was accepted and I agreed to the ONI safety warning, the system finished logging me in. I heard myself breathe a sigh of relief as reality receded and the OASIS faded into existence all around me.

I materialized inside my stronghold on Falco, the small asteroid in Sector Fourteen that still served as my avatar's home inside the OASIS. I'd tried relocating to Castle Anorak after I inherited it, but I didn't really like the décor or the general vibe over there. I felt more at home here, in my old digs, which I'd designed and built myself.

I was seated in my command center. This was the same spot where my avatar had been sitting the previous night, when I'd reached my twelve-hour ONI usage limit and the system had automatically logged me out.

The control panels arrayed in front of me were crammed with switches, buttons, keyboards, joysticks, and display screens. The bank of security monitors on my left were linked to virtual cameras placed throughout the interior and exterior of my stronghold. To my right, another bank of monitors displayed vidfeeds from the real-world cameras mounted on the interior and exterior of my immersion vault. My sleeping body was visible from several different angles, along with a detailed readout of its vital signs.

I gazed out the transparent dome at the barren, cratered landscape surrounding my stronghold. This had been my avatar's home during the final year of Halliday's contest, and I'd cracked one of its major riddles while sitting in this very chair. I hoped the familiar setting would help me make a breakthrough in my quest for the Seven Shards. So far it hadn't worked.

I accessed the teleportation menu on my avatar's superuser HUD, then scrolled down the list of bookmarked locations until I found the listing for the planet Gregarious in Sector One, the home of Gregarious Simulation Systems's virtual offices inside the OASIS. When I selected it and tapped the Teleport icon, my avatar was instantly transported to a set of previously saved coordinates, hundreds of millions of virtual kilometers away.

If I'd been a normal OASIS user, this trip would have cost me some serious coin. But since I wore the Robes of Anorak, I could teleport anywhere at any time, for free. It was a far cry from the days when I was a broke schoolkid stranded on Ludus.

My avatar reappeared on the top floor of Gregarious Tower, a virtual replica of the real GSS skyscraper in downtown Columbus. Our head of operations, Faisal Sodhi, was standing in the reception area waiting for me.

"Mr. Watts!" Faisal said. "Good to see you, sir."

"It's good to see you, too, man," I replied. I'd given up on trying to convince Faisal to address me as Wade or Z years ago.

He walked over to greet me and I shook his outstretched hand. Being able to shake hands without any danger of spreading disease had always been one of the perks of the OASIS. But in the old days, before the ONI was released, it always felt like you were shaking hands with a mannequin, even with the best haptic gloves available. Without the sensation of skin-to-skin human contact, the ancient greeting lost most of its meaning. After we'd introduced the ONI, shaking hands had come back in vogue, along with high fives and fist bumps, because now they felt real.

The conference room itself was protected by both magical and technological means. We held our co-owners meetings here instead of in a standard OASIS chatroom because it allowed all sorts of additional security measures to be taken, to prevent anyone from recording or eavesdropping on us, including our own employees.

"Are the others already here?" I asked, nodding toward the closed doors behind him.

"Ms. Aech and Mr. Shoto both arrived a few minutes ago," he said, opening the doors. "But Ms. Cook called to say she's running a bit late."

I nodded and went into the conference room. Aech and Shoto were standing over by the wraparound floor-to-ceiling windows, grazing from a ridiculously large assortment of snack trays that were laid out nearby, while they admired the impressive view. Gregarious Tower was surrounded by acres of pristine forestland, with snowcapped mountain peaks ringing the horizon. There were no other structures in sight. By design, everything about the view was calming and peaceful. Unfortunately, the same could never be said of the meetings we held here.

"Z!" Aech and Shoto shouted in unison when they spotted me.

I walked over and received high fives from each of them.

"How goes it, mis amigos?"

"It's way too early for this shit, man," Aech groaned. She was in L.A., where it was currently ten o'clock in the morning. Aech liked to stay up late and sleep in even later.

"Yeah," Shoto added, after a quarter-second delay from his translator software. "And it's also way too *late* for this shit." He was in Japan, where it was the middle of the night. But Shoto was nocturnal by nature. He was just complaining because he'd grown to dread these meetings, just like me and Aech.

"Arty's running late," Aech said. "She's supposed to be logging in from Liberia, I think."

"Yeah," I said, rolling my eyes. "That's the most recent stop on her ongoing tour of the world's most depressing places."

I still couldn't fathom why Samantha felt the need to endure all of the hassles and risks of real-world travel when she could have visited safely via telepresence robot, or experienced any location in the world by downloading an .oni clip recorded there. She also could have visited any of those countries inside the OASIS. There was an incredibly detailed re-creation of the Earth in Sector Ten called EEarth (short for "Ersatz Earth"), that was constantly being updated with data taken from live satellite imagery, drone footage, and traffic, security, and smartphone-camera feeds to make it as accurate as possible. Visiting Dubai, Bangkok, or Delhi on EEarth was a lot easier and safer than visiting them in reality. But Samantha felt it was imperative for her to witness the true state of the world with her own two eyes, even when it came to the most dangerous, war-torn countries. In other words, she was crazy.

No, she's selfless and principled, replied a nagging little voice in my head. *And you're neither of those things. Is it any wonder she dumped you?*

I clenched my teeth. These co-owners meetings were always bad for my self-esteem, and not just because it forced me to see Art3mis. Aech and Shoto were also living glamorous and fulfilling post-contest lives. The reclusive, obsessive existence I'd carved out for myself seemed painfully bleak by comparison.

These days, if I wanted to hang out with Aech or Shoto, I had to make an appointment several weeks in advance. But I didn't mind. I was grateful they still made time to hang out with me at all. Unlike me, they had more than two friends. And they also spent a lot more of their time offline than I did. Instead of downloading pieces of other people's lives off the ONI-net, Aech and Shoto were out in the world having (and recording) experiences of their own. In fact, they were two of the most popular celebrity posters on the ONI-net. Every clip either of them threw up went viral within a few seconds, regardless of its content.

Like Art3mis, they were brilliant, charismatic people, leading rock-star lives while also working to improve the lives of the less fortunate. More than once it had occurred to me that my friends were my one saving grace. The thing I took the most pride in—even more than winning Halliday's fortune—was the three people I'd chosen to share that fortune with. Aech, Shoto, and Art3mis were all kinder, wiser, and saner than I was or ever would be.

After the contest ended, Helen legally changed her name to Aech, with no surname, just like Sting and Madonna. And since her true identity, appearance, and gender were now public knowledge in the wake of Halliday's contest, she'd promptly ditched the world-famous white male avatar she'd used to mask her true identity since childhood. Like Samantha and Shoto and many other real-world celebrities, Aech now used an OASIS *ravatar*—an avatar that re-created her unaltered real-world appearance, and was updated each and every time she logged in to the simulation.

I had never been a huge fan of my real-world appearance, so I still used the same OASIS avatar I always had—an idealized version of myself. A bit taller, fitter, and more handsome.

These days, Aech spent most of her real-world time chilling in her Santa Monica beach house, or touring with her new fiancée, Endira Vinayak, a famous singer and Bollywood star.

Becoming a billionaire hadn't altered Aech's personality at all, as far as I could tell. She still liked to have ridiculous arguments about old movies. She still loved to get her kills on in PvP arena tournaments, and she remained one of the league's highest-ranked combatants, in both the Deathmatch and Capture the Flag leagues. In other words, Aech was still a total badass. Except now she was a total badass who also happened to be insanely rich and world famous.

I still considered Aech my best friend, but we weren't nearly as close now as we'd been in the old days. I hadn't seen her in person in over two years, although we still got together online once or twice a month. But these meet-ups were always my suggestion, and I was beginning to worry that Aech only spent time with me out of some lingering sense of obligation. Or because she was worried about me. Either way, I didn't care. I was just grateful that she still made time for me, and that she still wanted me in her life.

I saw Shoto even less frequently than Aech, which was understandable. His life had changed drastically in the years since the contest. Shoto's parents had helped him manage his inheritance when he was still a minor, but he'd turned eighteen a year ago, making him a legal adult in Japan. Now he had full control of his own life, and his share of Halliday's fortune.

To celebrate, he legally adopted his avatar's name, just like Aech. Then he got married to a young woman named Kiki, whom he met when he relocated to Hokkaido. He and his new bride moved into a remodeled Japanese castle right on the shore. Then, about five months ago, during one of our GSS meetings, Shoto announced that he was going to become a father. He and Kiki had just learned that they were going to have a boy, and together they had already decided to name him Toshiro. But in confidence, Shoto told us he'd already decided to nickname the baby "Little Daito," so that was what I called him too.

It was still hard to believe that Shoto would be a father in a few months, at such a young age. I was concerned for him, though I had no idea why. It wasn't like he wouldn't be able to afford to send Little Daito to a good school. I just didn't understand why he was in such a big hurry, until he sat me down and explained it to me. Japan was in the midst of an "underpopulation crisis" because so many of its citizens had opted to stop having children over the past three decades. As the country's wealthiest and most famous young couple, he and Kiki felt obligated to lead by example and reproduce as quickly as possible. So they had. And after Little Daito arrived, they planned to start working on a Little Shoto—or perhaps a Little Kiki.

In addition to his preparations for fatherhood, Shoto continued to oversee operations at GSS's Hokkaido division, where he produced a wildly popular series of award-winning OASIS quests based on his favorite anime and samurai films. He'd become one of my favorite quest developers, and I was lucky enough to be one of his go-to beta testers, so we still got to hang out in the OASIS at least once or twice a month.

We rarely talked about Shoto's late brother, Daito, or his murder. But the last time we had, Shoto told me he was still in mourning for him, and that he feared he always would be. I understood what he meant, because I felt the same way about my aunt Alice, and my old downstairs neighbor, Mrs. Gilmore. Both of them had been murdered, too, by the same man: Nolan Sorrento, the former head of operations at Innovative Online Industries.

After Halliday's contest, Sorrento had been convicted of thirty-seven separate counts of first-degree homicide. He was now serving time on death row in a maximum-security prison in Chillicothe, Ohio, about fifty miles south of Columbus.

During his trial, IOI's lawyers had managed to convince the jury that Sorrento had gone rogue, and that he'd acted without the IOI board's knowledge or consent when he ordered his underlings to throw Daito off his forty-third-floor balcony. They also claimed that Sorrento had acted alone when he'd detonated a bomb outside my aunt's trailer in the stacks, killing over three dozen people and injuring hundreds of others.

After Sorrento's conviction and incarceration, IOI managed to settle all of the wrongful-death suits filed against them. Then they tried to go back to business as usual. But by then, they'd already lost their position as the world's largest manufacturer of OASIS immersion hardware, thanks to the release of our ONI headsets. And thanks to the rollout of our free global Internet initiative, their ISP business had also shriveled.

Meanwhile, IOI also had the audacity to file a separate corporate lawsuit against me. They claimed that even though I'd created a false identity and used it to masquerade as an indentured servant to infiltrate their company headquarters, the indenturement contract I'd signed was still legally binding. Which meant, they argued, that I was still technically IOI's property when I won Halliday's contest, and so his fortune and his company should now also be classified as IOI's property. Since the U.S. legal system still insisted on giving corporations even more rights than its citizens, this idiotic lawsuit dragged on for months . . . right up until GSS completed its hostile takeover of IOI. Then, as IOI's new owners, we withdrew the lawsuit. We also fired the old IOI board of directors, their attorneys, and everyone else who had worked with or under Nolan Sorrento.

Now the Sixers were a distant memory, and Innovative Online Industries was just another wholly owned subsidiary of Gregarious Simulation Systems. GSS was now far and away the largest corporation in the world. And if we kept growing at our current rate, before too long we might be the *only* one. That was the reason a lot of our own users had started to refer to GSS as the "New Sixers" and me, Aech, Shoto, and Samantha as the "Four Nerds of the Apocalypse."

Two-Face was right. You either die a hero, or you live long enough to see yourself become the villain.

I made small talk with Aech and Shoto for a few more minutes, until the conference room doors swung open and Samantha's avatar, Art3mis, strolled in. She glanced in our direction, but didn't offer anything in the way of a greeting. Faisal walked in after her and closed the doors behind him.

We all took our usual seats, which put me and Art3mis on opposite sides of the circular conference table—as far away from each other as possible, but also directly facing each other.

"Thank you all for coming," Faisal said, taking a seat next to Samantha. "I think we're ready to call this co-owners meeting to order. We only have a few items to cover today—the first one being our quarterly revenue report." An array of charts and graphs appeared on the large screen behind him. "As usual, it's all good news. ONI headset sales remain steady, and immersion-vault sales have nearly doubled since last quarter. OASIS Advertising and Surreal Estate revenue also both remain at an all-time high."

Faisal continued to detail how great our company was doing, but I didn't hear much of what he was saying. I was too busy stealing glances at Art3mis across the table. I knew she wouldn't catch me, because she made a point of never looking in my direction.

Her avatar looked the same as it always had, with one minor change. After the contest, she'd added the reddish-purple birthmark that covered the left half of her real face to her avatar's face as well. So now there was no discernible difference between her avatar's appearance and her appearance in real life. When she gave interviews, she often spoke about what it had been like for her to grow up hating her birthmark, and how she'd spent most of her life trying to conceal it. But now she wore it like a badge of honor, in reality and in the OASIS. And as a result, she'd somehow transformed her birthmark into an internationally recognized trademark.

I glanced up at the name tag floating above her avatar's head. It had a thin rectangular border around it, which indicated that the avatar's operator was not using an ONI headset to experience the OASIS. We'd added this feature due to overwhelming customer demand. OASIS users with this name-tag border were now known as Ticks. (A truncation of the word "haptics.") Most Ticks were people who had already used up their twelve hours of ONI time and had logged back in with a haptic rig to squeeze in a few more hours of conventional OASIS time before bed. Full-time Ticks like Samantha, who never used an ONI headset at all, now comprised less than five percent of our user base. Despite Samantha's best efforts, there were fewer and fewer ONI holdouts every year.

"I'm also happy to report that our newest server farm is now online, upping our data-storage capacity by another million yottabytes," Faisal said. "Our data engineers estimate that this should be more than enough to meet our storage needs for the coming year, if user population growth remains steady."

Another side effect of releasing the headsets had been a huge increase in the company's data-storage needs, due to the enormous UBS (user brain scan) files that were stored in every ONI user's account, which got updated every time they logged in or out of the OASIS. So as the total number of ONI users continued to increase, so did our massive data-storage requirements.

Compounding this problem was the fact that we didn't purge any OASIS user's account data when they died in the real world, including those huge UBS files. Faisal explained to me that this was because we own all of that data, and it was extremely valuable to the company for several reasons, including shit like "user marketing trend analysis." But the main reason we held on to those ONI user brain scans was because that data helped our neural-interface engineers improve the safety and operability of the ONI headset. That was why our neural-interface software and the hardware both worked so flawlessly on such a wide variety of people. Because we had such a huge pool of willing guinea pigs who didn't mind giving us complete access to the contents of their skull, as long we gave them access to our high-quality sensory-immersive bread-and-circus simulator.

My thoughts always seemed to gravitate to a dark place during these meetings.

"If none of you have any questions, we can move on to the final item on our agenda," Faisal said. No one spoke up, so he continued. "Fantastic! There's just one more thing that needs your approval—the ONI headset firmware update we're planning to roll out tomorrow. Very little has been changed since our last update earlier this year. Our engineers have just added a few more security measures to prevent illegal overclocking."

"That was the same reason for your last two updates, wasn't it?" Art-3mis asked. She had a talent for making her questions sound like accusations.

"Yes, it was," Faisal replied. "Unfortunately, each time we implement a new set of security measures, hackers quickly figure out new workarounds. But we're hoping this update finally does the trick, and puts an end to overclocking once and for all."

There had only been a handful of deaths caused by the ONI since its release, and every last one of them had been due to overclocking—hacking an ONI headset's firmware to exceed the daily twelve-hour limit. Despite our safety warnings and disclaimers, there were always a few users who chose to ignore them. Some people were convinced that they were special, and that their brains could handle fourteen or even sixteen hours of consecutive ONI usage with no ill side effects—and a few of them actually could, for a day or two. But when they pushed their luck too far, they ended up lobotomizing themselves. And that was very bad for business.

Thanks to our ironclad end-user license agreement, GSS couldn't be held legally responsible for any of these deaths. But we still wanted to protect the overclockers from themselves, so we updated the ONI firmware whenever a new exploit was discovered.

Ever since the ONI's introduction, there had been an urban legend floating around the OASIS, claiming that Halliday himself had exceeded the ONI's daily usage limit when he was testing the first prototype headset, and that this is what had caused his terminal cancer. But it was complete bullshit. According to all of the intensive studies and tests we'd conducted, there was no link between the OASIS Neural Interface and the lymphoma that had ended Halliday's life.

Faisal called for a vote on the ONI firmware upgrade. Aech, Shoto, and I all voted to approve it, while Art3mis chose to abstain. She always abstained from any vote related to the ONI headsets, even in instances like this, when we were voting to enact new safety measures.

"Fantastic!" Faisal said, maintaining a cheerful tone despite the tension in the room. "That was our last order of business. If no one has anything further, we can adjourn—"

"Oh, I have something further," Art3mis announced, cutting him off.

Aech, Shoto, and I all let out a sigh—unintentionally in unison.

Art3mis ignored us and continued.

"Studies have shown that the human brain doesn't finish developing until around the age of twenty-five," she said. "I think that should be the age limit for using an ONI headset, but I know you'll never agree to that. So, as a compromise, and for the safety of our youngest customers, I propose that, going forward, we only allow ONI headsets to be used by people who are eighteen or older. At least until we have a better understanding of the ONI's long-term neurological and psychological effects."

Shoto, Aech, and I exchanged weary looks. Faisal kept a sunny smile plastered on his face, even though he was clearly growing tired of this crap too.

"Aech, Shoto, and I are all under twenty-five," I said. "Are you suggesting that we've all suffered brain damage from using the ONI?"

"Well," she replied with a smirk, "that would certainly explain some of the decisions you've made over the past three years."

"Arty," Aech said, "every time the four of us meet, you propose some new limitation on the ONI headsets. And every time, you get outvoted three-to-one."

"I'm not asking any of you to give up your precious ONI habit, OK?" Art3mis said. "I'm talking about kids who aren't even old enough to vote yet. We're turning an entire generation of children into ONI junkies, before they even have a chance to experience life in the real world."

"News flash," I said, as soon as she stopped speaking. "Life in the real world totally sucks for most people. And reality went to shit long before we started selling those headsets, Arty. . . ."

For the first time in years, Art3mis locked eyes with me.

"*You*," she said, leveling a finger at me. "You don't get to call me Arty anymore. And are *you* seriously trying to lecture *me* about the state of the real world?" She gestured at our surroundings. "You *still* spend all of your time hiding in here. Meanwhile, I'm out there trying to save the real world. Reality! *Our* reality!"

She pointed at me again. "Maybe you don't see the danger, because you *won't*. You love your magic dream machine too much to see what it's done to humanity. But I see it. And so does Ogden Morrow. That's why he's never put on an ONI headset either! And I bet that's why he won't work here anymore, even as a consultant. He doesn't want to help you bring about the end of human civilization either." She shook her head at me. "What a huge disappointment we must be to him. . . ."

She folded her arms and kept her eyes fixed on me, waiting for my response. I clenched and unclenched my jaw a few times, to keep myself from screaming in frustration. Then I switched on my emotion-suppressing software and did one of the breathing exercises Sean had taught me, to calm myself down.

My immediate instinct was to bring up Samantha's grandmother. Her father's mother, Evelyn Opal Cook, was the one who raised Samantha after her parents died. Her grandma had never shared Samantha's prejudice against the ONI. Quite the opposite. She'd ordered one of the first headsets off the assembly line, and she used it every day for the rest of her life. Unfortunately, that wasn't long. Just two years.

When Evelyn was diagnosed with pancreatic cancer, she started using her ONI headset for the maximum of twelve hours every day, to disconnect her mind from her chemotherapy-ravaged body as often and for as long as she possibly could. In the OASIS, Evelyn had a perfectly healthy body that never felt any trace of pain. While her body battled its disease, she could leave both behind and go for a run on any beach in the world, or picnic on a mountaintop. Or dance the night away in Paris with her friends. The OASIS Neural Interface allowed her to keep on living a joyous, happy life for half of each day, right up until she'd finally succumbed to her illness a little over a year ago. According to her nurses, Evelyn passed away peacefully and painlessly, because she'd been using her ONI headset at the time, to talk to Samantha inside the OASIS. The neural interface had allowed her to continue to communicate with her granddaughter long after her physical body had grown so weak she'd lost the power of speech.

I'd made the mistake of mentioning Samantha's grandmother once before, during one of our previous arguments about the ONI. Samantha had gone ballistic. Then she'd warned me never to mention her grandmother's name again. So I didn't. No. I didn't say anything. I did my deep-breathing exercises and I bit my goddamn tongue.

"What about education?" Shoto said when I failed to hold up my half of the argument. "People can learn all sorts of valuable skills through ONI playback. How to grow food or speak a foreign language. Doctors can learn how to perform new medical procedures from the best surgeons in their field. Why should people be denied access to such an important tool for learning just because of their age?"

"The main thing the ONI is teaching people is how to ignore the real world," Samantha said. "That's why it's falling apart."

"The world was already falling apart," Aech said. "Remember?"

"And the ONI might be the thing that saves us," I said. "It has spiritual, psychological, and cultural benefits that are still revealing themselves to us. In a very true sense, the ONI has the ability to free our minds, by temporarily liberating them from their containers."

Art3mis tried to interrupt, but I kept on talking over her.

"ONI users around the world are developing a whole new kind of empathy that you can't even begin to understand, until you've experienced it yourself. . . ."

She mimed jerking off.

"Oh please," she said, with an exaggerated roll of her eyes. "Spare me your transhumanist hive-mind bullshit, Locutus. I'm still not buying it."

"You can't deny that the OASIS Neural Interface has improved the quality of millions of people's lives," Aech interjected. "Numerous studies have shown a drastic increase in empathy and environmental conservation among daily ONI users, along with an overwhelming drop in racist, sexist, and homophobic ideologies. And that's all around the world, across all age groups and social strata. For the first time in human history, we have technology that gives us the ability to live in someone else's skin for a little while. And we've seen a huge drop in hate crimes around the globe too. And crime rates in general—"

"Yes," Art3mis said, cutting her off. "When you turn half of the world's population into zombified ONI addicts, crime rates are going to drop. The flu outbreak that killed both of my parents made crime rates drop, too, Aech."

I lowered my eyes to the table and clenched my teeth to keep my mouth shut. Aech cleared her throat, but then opted not to respond either. But Shoto couldn't help himself.

"Odd for you to bring that up, Arty," he replied. "Since we know that ONI technology is our best protection against other deadly pandemics like the one that killed your parents. They don't happen anymore, thanks to us.

By moving most human social interaction online and making so much tourism virtual, we've cut travel drastically and limited the spread of nearly all infectious diseases. Including sexually transmitted ones, since now most people have sex inside the OASIS." He smiled. "Thanks to the ONI, people can still go to packed concerts and crowd surf without any fear of microscopic death. It brings people together and connects them. . . ."

"The ONI has helped drastically lower the global birth rate too," Aech added. "We're already on our way to solving the overpopulation problem."

"Yes, but at what cost?" Samantha asked in exasperation. "A world where people don't go outside or touch each other anymore? Where everyone sleeps their lives away while reality collapses all around them?" She shook her head. "Sometimes I think my parents are better off. They don't have to live in this utopia you've all created."

"You've never even put on an ONI headset," I said, throwing my hands up. "So when you spout these half-baked proclamations, you literally have no idea what you're talking about. You never have."

Art3mis stared at me in silence for a moment. Then she glanced over at Aech and Shoto.

"This is hopeless," she said. "I'm debating a group of drug dealers who are all getting high on their own supply. You're just as addicted as your customers." She turned to Faisal. "Let's get this vote on the record, so I can get the fuck out of here."

Faisal nodded and, still smiling cheerfully, he called for an official vote on Art3mis's proposed ONI age restriction. She was outvoted once again, three nays to her one aye.

"All right," Faisal said. "With that out of the way, this meeting can now be adjourned."

Without another word, Samantha logged out and her avatar vanished.

"Thank God!" Aech said, massaging her neck with one hand. She turned to me. "Why do you always have to get her all riled up like that?"

"Me? You were the one who pissed her off this time!" I pointed at Faisal. "Have him read back the transcript."

"No thanks," Aech said. "I gotta bounce out and blaze. All this drama rattles my nerves. But the three of us should catch up sometime soon. Hang out in the Basement for old time's sake. Watch some bad movies. Play some Risk. I'll text y'all, OK?"

"Sounds good," I said.

Aech and I bumped fists, then she gave Shoto a high five before teleporting away.

"I gotta get going too," Faisal said. "More prep to do for the update." He walked over and shook hands with each of us and then he teleported away too.

As soon as we were alone, Shoto turned to me.

"Do you think Arty is right?" he asked. "Are we giving up on the real world?"

"Of course not," I replied. "Art3mis means well, but she has absolutely no idea what she's talking about." I grinned at him. "She's still stuck in the past, and we're already living large in the future, my friend."

"Maybe you're right," he said, nodding. His expression suddenly brightened. "Hey, I'm almost finished coding my new *Macross Plus* quest! Wanna help me playtest it when it's done?"

"Oh hell yes!" I said. "Count me in."

"Great! I'll text you later this week when it's ready," he said. "Later, Z."

He waved and vanished from the conference room, leaving me alone.

I stood there motionless for a long time, listening to the echo of Samantha's accusations ricochet around inside my head until the noise finally faded away.

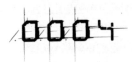

"Hello!" I shouted at the Six-Fingered Man one final time. "My name is Inigo Montoya! You killed my father. Prepare to die!"

Then I lunged with my rapier, launching into a rapid series of attacks that forced my opponent to parry and retreat backward across the length of the banquet hall, until I finally had him cornered. I could have just killed him at that point and completed the quest. But the Flicksync gave you bonus points for correctly reciting all of your character's dialogue, and I was trying to get a perfect score this time around.

"Offer me money!" I demanded, slicing open the Six-Fingered Man's left cheek.

"Yes!" he hissed, wincing in pain. "Power too," I added. "Promise me that!"

I flicked my sword once again, giving him a matching wound on his right cheek.

"All that I have and more!" he whispered. "Please!"

"Offer me anything I ask for. . . ."

"Anything you want," the Six-Fingered Man replied.

"I want my father back, you son of a bitch!"

And with that, I ran the Six-Fingered Man through, plunging the point of my rapier into his stomach. I savored the expression on his face for a moment, then I pulled the sword free and kicked him backward. The NPC fell to the stone floor, let out a groan, and died. His corpse immediately faded out of existence, leaving behind a pile of the items he'd been carrying.

I scooped them up, then turned and sprinted out of the room and down the hall to Buttercup's bridal suite. Once there, I completed the quest by helping her and Westley escape out the window. Fezzik was waiting for us down below, holding the reins of four white horses. We rode them out of the kingdom to freedom, while the song "Storybook Love" played on the soundtrack.

When the song ended, so did the quest. The horses and the other characters vanished and my avatar's appearance returned to normal. I found myself standing alone outside the quest portal I'd originally entered, on the eastern shore of the kingdom of Guilder.

A chime sounded and a message appeared on my HUD, congratulating me on completing the *Princess Bride* quest with a perfect score of one million points. Then the message disappeared and . . . that was it.

I waited for a full minute, but nothing else happened.

I sat down on the beach and let out a sigh.

This wasn't my first visit to the planet Florin. I had already completed this quest with a perfect score three times before, each time playing as a different character—first as Westley, then as Buttercup, then as Fezzik. *The Princess Bride* had been one of Kira Underwood's all-time favorite films, and she'd helped create all of the interactive OASIS quests based on it. (Including the controversial gender-swapped *The Prince Groom*, in which Buttercup is the swashbuckling heroine and Westley serves as the damsel in distress.) I'd thought that solving one of these quests with a perfect score might yield some clue related to the Seven Shards. But I'd come up empty-handed each and every time. Today was my final attempt. Inigo had been the only other playable character, and the most difficult one with which to obtain a perfect score. Now, after nearly a dozen attempts, I'd finally done it. And once again I had nothing to show for my efforts.

I got to my feet and took a deep breath. Then I teleported back to my command center on Falco.

Once my avatar finished rematerializing, I settled into the comfy TNG-era captain's chair I'd installed there. I stared out at the cratered landscape in silent frustration for a moment. Then I opened up my grail diary, and once again I began scanning the vast mountain of data I'd collected over the past eight years, about James Halliday and his life, work, associates, and interests—although for the past three years, nearly all of the new material

I'd added pertained to one associate in particular. The Siren herself, Kira Morrow, née Underwood.

I'd started my grail diary in an old spiral notebook when I was thirteen and still living in the stacks outside Oklahoma City. I'd been forced to burn the original the night before I infiltrated IOI headquarters, to prevent it from falling into the Sixers' hands. But I'd made hi-res scans of the notebook's pages beforehand and stored them in my OASIS account. Those scans were all still there, in the digital version of my grail diary, which appeared as a jumble of cascading windows floating in front of me. It contained countless documents, diagrams, photos, maps, and media files, all indexed and cross-referenced for easy browsing.

The four-line Shard Riddle was displayed in a window that always remained on top:

Seek the Seven Shards of the Siren's Soul
On the seven worlds where the Siren once played a role
For each fragment my heir must pay a toll
To once again make the Siren whole

When the riddle had first appeared shortly after the ONI's launch, I'd gone back and re-analyzed the free digital copy of *Anorak's Almanac* available on Halliday's old website, just to make sure it hadn't been updated with any new information or clues. It hadn't. Every word of the *Almanac* was still the same. The famous series of notched letters I'd found scattered throughout its text during Halliday's contest were still there, but no new ones had been added.

One of the superuser abilities the Robes of Anorak gave me was the ability to simply wish for things out loud. If it could, the system would almost always grant my wish. But whenever I tried wishing for information about the Seven Shards, a message would flash across my HUD:

NICE TRY, CHEATER!

So I had no choice but to keep on searching for the shards myself. And once I committed to that quest, I gave it my absolute all. I did my due diligence.

I studied every reference to the number 7 in *Anorak's Almanac*. I also played and solved every videogame in his collection that was related to the number 7. The Seven Cities of Gold (1984), The Seven Spirits of Ra (1987), Kid Kool and the Quest for the Seven Wonder Herbs (1988), The Seven Gates of Jambala (1989), Ishar 3: The Seven Gates of Infinity (1994), Super Mario RPG: Legend of the Seven Stars (1996). Then I went overboard and also played any game that had the number 7 in its title, like Sigma 7, Stellar 7, Lucky 7, Force 7, Pitman 7, and Escape from Pulsar 7.

I even subjected myself to *Keeper of the Seven Keys*, a four-part concept album by Helloween, a German power-metal band from Hamburg, founded in 1984. I was not a fan of mid-'80s German power metal, but Halliday used to listen to it for hours when he was programming his first games, so I knew there was a chance he'd drawn inspiration from it.

If Halliday had left behind any additional clues about the location of the Seven Shards, I wasn't able to find them. It was frustrating. And more than a little humiliating.

I considered calling it quits and giving up on the shards altogether. I mean, why was I wasting my time trying to solve Halliday's insipid side quest anyway? What was I hoping would happen when I completed it? I had already achieved wealth and fame in reality, and in the OASIS my avatar was already all-powerful and invulnerable. I had nothing more to prove to anyone. I had already beaten the odds and accomplished the impossible once. I didn't need to do it again.

There was nothing else I needed—except more time. I had a finite amount of it left, and when it was gone, I wouldn't be able to buy any more of it. Time was precious. And yet here I was, wasting whole years of it on another one of Halliday's glorified videogames . . .

Still, I'd never shaken my curiosity about the Siren's Soul, or the nagging suspicion that something terrible would happen if I failed to obtain it. That was what ultimately prompted me to offer a billion-dollar reward for any information that would help me locate one of the Seven Shards. But I'd posted that reward two years ago, and it had yet to be claimed.

When I'd offered the reward, I'd set up a separate email address where people could send in any potential leads. It still received hundreds of submissions every day, but so far every last one had proven to be a dead end. I'd had to set up an elaborate series of email filters to sort out all the duplicate and obviously bogus submissions. These days very few emails got past these filters and made it to my inbox.

I often wondered if the whole idea of the reward was hopeless to begin with. The answer was right there, in the third line of the Shard Riddle: "For each fragment my heir must pay a toll. . . ."

If I, Wade Watts, the sole heir to Halliday's fortune, was the "heir" the riddle was referring to, then I would be the only person in the world who could find the Seven Shards, since I would be the only one who could "once again make the Siren whole."

For all I knew, the shards and their locations might be invisible to everyone else. That would explain why the millions of gunters out there who were scouring the OASIS night and day for any trace of the shards had all come up empty-handed for three years running now.

On the other hand, if I alone had the ability to obtain the Siren's Soul, why had Halliday posted the Shard Riddle on his website, for the whole world to see? He could've just emailed it to my OASIS account. Or mentioned it in his video message about the ONI. It was entirely possible that anyone could find the shards, and Halliday had simply hidden them fiendishly well—just as he'd done with his "three hidden keys" and "three secret gates." And the first two lines of the Shard Riddle were infuriatingly vague: "Seek the Seven Shards of the Siren's Soul on the seven worlds where the Siren once played a role."

If I was interpreting these lines correctly, the Seven Shards were hidden on seven planets inside the OASIS—seven worlds where the Siren, aka Leucosia, aka Kira Morrow, "once played a role."

Unfortunately, that didn't narrow things down too much. As GSS's chief art director during the development of the OASIS and its first three years of operation, Kira had played a key role in the design and construction of every single planet added to the simulation during that time. (In interviews, Ogden Morrow had always gone out of his way to stress the importance of his wife's contribution to the creation of the OASIS, while Halliday rarely even acknowledged it. Which was no surprise, since he had a history of doing the same thing to Og, and everyone else who worked for them at GSS.) Even after Kira left the company, the GSS artists who had worked under her continued to use the world-builder templates she'd created, so in a way, she'd "played a role" in creating nearly every planet in the OASIS.

However, by conducting extensive research into Kira's life and interests, and by studying her GSS employee file and OASIS work account activity logs, I'd narrowed my search area down to a list of the nine most likely candidates and concentrated my efforts there.

Florin, the planet I'd just returned from, was Kira's re-creation of the fictional Renaissance-era kingdom featured in *The Princess Bride,* one of her favorite films. There wasn't much to do there, aside from visiting the various locations from the movie and completing the Flicksyncs.

The planet Thra was a meticulous re-creation of the fantasy world depicted in *The Dark Crystal,* another of her favorite films. Her parents had named her Karen, but after she saw *The Dark Crystal* for the first time at age eleven, she'd insisted that her friends and family call her Kira, the name of the film's Gelfling heroine. (She'd also renamed the family dog Fizzgig.) And when Karen turned eighteen, she'd legally changed her first name to Kira. Decades later, when Kira helped launch the OASIS, Thra was the first planet she'd created inside the simulation, entirely on her own. And since the plot of *The Dark Crystal* concerned a quest to find a missing "crystal shard," it seemed like an extremely likely candidate.

But I'd now played through every quest anchored there, and explored the entire kingdom, and done everything I could think of that might loosely be defined as "paying a toll." I'd visited every instance of Aughra's observatory I could find. I'd played the proper tune on Jen's flute. But her basket was always empty, and there were never any shards to be found there.

Mobius Prime was another OASIS world created solely by Kira Morrow, as a tribute to her favorite videogame character, Sonic the Hedgehog. The planet was a re-creation of the fictional future Earth where most of Sonic's adventures took place, and it featured reproductions of all of the different levels featured in early 2-D and 3-D Sonic games, along with environments and characters from the cartoons and comic books based on them.

Several Sonic the Hedgehog games involved a quest to collect seven "Chaos Emeralds" that could be harnessed to obtain special powers. Inside the OASIS, dozens of different quests on Mobius Prime allowed you to collect the seven Chaos Emeralds, and I'd completed all of them. But if there was a way to trade the emeralds for one of the shards, I still hadn't discovered it.

I'd had a similarly frustrating experience on the planet Usagi, which was Kira's tribute to *Sailor Moon,* her favorite anime series. One of the most difficult quests on Usagi involved collecting seven "Rainbow Crystals," which could then be combined to form an incredibly powerful artifact known as the "Legendary Silver Crystal." After a frustrating number of attempts, I'd finally managed to complete this quest, in the hope that once I obtained the Legendary Silver Crystal it would transform into one of the Seven Shards. But all I had to show for my efforts was an impressive familiarity with obscure *Sailor Moon* trivia and an inexplicable desire to cosplay as Tuxedo Mask (which I may or may not have acted upon in the solitude and privacy of my own home).

I'd also spent several months scouring the planet Gallifrey in Sector Seven. It was Kira's re-creation of the Time Lord's home world in the long-running *Doctor Who* television series, which now comprised over a thousand individual episodes. In the decades since she'd first constructed it, thousands of other OASIS users had made their own contributions to Gallifrey, making it one of the most densely packed worlds in the simulation—and one of the most difficult places in which to conduct a thorough search.

Halcydonia was the planet on the list that I probably knew the best, because I'd practically grown up there. It was also the only OASIS planet that Ogden and Kira Morrow had co-created, without any outside assistance. When Og and Kira got married and sold all of their GSS shares to Halliday, they moved to Oregon and founded a nonprofit educational software company, Halcydonia Interactive, which produced a series of award-winning educational OASIS adventure games that anyone could download and play for free. I'd played these games throughout my childhood, and they had transported me out of my bleak existence in the stacks and whisked me off to the magical faraway kingdom of Halcydonia, where learning was "an endless adventure!"

Halcydonia Interactive's games were still archived as free standalone quest portals on the planet Halcydonia in Sector One, located in prime surreal estate a short distance from Incipio, making it extremely cheap and easy for newly spawned and/or perpetually broke avatars to reach it. According to the planet's colophon, Halcydonia hadn't been altered or updated since Kira's death in a car accident in 2034. But I still thought there was a chance Halliday had hidden one of the shards there.

Even though Kira Morrow wasn't directly involved in the creation of the last few planets on my list, the private usage logs on her long-dormant OASIS account indicated she'd spent a great deal of time on each of them.

(I'd attempted to access Halliday and Morrow's private OASIS account logs, too, only to find them both blank. Unlike all other OASIS users, their avatars' movements and interactions within the simulation weren't logged. And, as I mentioned earlier, once I inherited the Robes of Anorak, the same became true of my own usage log. There were no new entries after that. Plenty of subpoenas had verified this fact. Aech, Shoto, and Art3mis didn't have the ability to conceal their usage logs from the feds, our high-level OASIS admins, or from me. So unbeknownst to them, I was able to see how much time they spent inside the OASIS each day, as well as where they went and what they did while they were there. I'd stopped checking Aech and Shoto's logs years ago—partly out of respect for their privacy, but mostly because I quickly discovered that I didn't want or need to know when they were ducking me to spend time hanging out with other people. But I still checked Art3mis's usage logs at least once a week. I couldn't re-sist. But they never told me much of anything about her life—aside from the fact that she still had a weakness for Flicksyncs based on old Whit Still-man movies. She still reenacted the film *Metropolitan* once or twice a month, usually in the middle of the night. Probably because she couldn't sleep. And she didn't have anyone to talk to. . . .)

One of the locations that showed up most frequently in Kira's OASIS account logs was the planet Miyazaki in Sector Twenty-Seven. It was a bi-zarre and beautiful world that paid tribute to the work of Hayao Miyazaki, the famous Japanese animator behind anime masterpieces like *Nausicaä of the Valley of the Wind* and *Kiki's Delivery Service*. Visiting Miyazaki was like plunging your senses into a surreal mash-up of all of the different animated realities created inside Studio Ghibli's films. (An experience that became substantially more intense with an ONI headset.) Kira had visited Miyazaki on a weekly basis for several years. And now I was able to say the same thing. But like Bono before me, I still hadn't found what I was looking for.

Then there was Middle-earth. All three versions of it . . .

Kira Morrow had been a well-known Tolkien fanatic. She famously re-read *The Hobbit* and *The Lord of the Rings* every year from the time she was sixteen onward. And after they married, Og built Kira a real-world replica of Rivendell in the mountains of Oregon, where they lived together happily until her death. Og still lived there now, and Kira was buried on the property. I'd visited her grave myself, during the week we'd all spent there.

According to Kira's access logs, one of her favorite OASIS destinations had been Arda, the three-planet system in Sector Seven that re-created J.R.R. Tolkien's Middle-earth fantasy world in the First, Second, and Third Ages of its fictional history. Created with an almost fanatical devotion by millions of Tolkien fans, many of whom were still revising and improving the simulations to this day, the Ardas drew largely on Tolkien's original writings on Middle-earth, but they took inspiration from the many films, television shows, and videogames set there as well.

So far, I'd spent most of my time on Arda III. It depicted the Third Age of Middle-earth, which was when all of the events described in *The Hobbit* and *The Lord of the Rings* took place, and Kira had visited it far more frequently than Arda I or Arda II—though she spent a great deal of time on each of them as well.

I wish I could say that I'd scoured every inch of all three versions of Middle-earth. But I hadn't. Not by a long shot. I'd completed all the major quests on Arda II and III, and about half of the most popular quests on Arda I, but they were three of the most detailed worlds in the whole simulation, and at my current pace, completing every quest they contained could take me several more years.

Chthonia was the last planet on my list, and the one I was most confident belonged there. It was Halliday's re-creation of the fantasy world he'd created for his epic Advanced Dungeons & Dragons campaign back in high school, in which both Kira and Og had participated. Chthonia would later serve as the setting for many of Halliday's earliest videogames, including Anorak's Quest and its many sequels.

Chthonia was the very first planet Halliday had created, making it the oldest world in the simulation. And when he, Ogden, and Kira had created their OASIS avatars, they'd each named them after the characters they'd played in their Chthonia campaign. Halliday's character had been a dark-robed magic user named Anorak, whom he'd played as an NPC while serving as Dungeon Master. Ogden Morrow had played a wisecracking wizard named "the Great and Powerful Og." And Kira's character had been a powerful druid called Leucosia, named after one of the Sirens of Greek mythology.

Of course, Chthonia was also where Halliday had hidden the Third

Gate in his Easter-egg hunt, inside Castle Anorak. Because of this, many gunters believed it was unlikely he would've chosen to hide one of the Seven Shards there too. But I wasn't so sure. Chthonia was clearly a world where the "Siren once played a role." A very important role, from Halliday's perspective. So I kept Chthonia on my list and searched the planet from top to bottom.

I hadn't limited my search to just these nine planets, of course. I'd looked for the Seven Shards on dozens of other OASIS worlds as well, to no avail.

I let out a sigh and rubbed my temples, wishing for the thousandth time that I hadn't sabotaged my friendship with Og, so that I could call him and ask for his help. Of course, asking for his help was precisely what had ended our friendship. Og had never been comfortable talking about Kira, and he'd communicated this to me in every way possible. But I'd been too fixated to hear him.

Thinking back on my behavior made me wince with shame now. Why would a retired billionaire want to spend his twilight years being hounded for information about his dead wife? It was no wonder he'd stopped speaking to me. I'd given him no real choice.

I realized that Og's birthday was coming up again soon. If I patched things up with him, maybe he would start inviting me to his yearly birthday party at the Distracted Globe again.

I'd spent the past year trying to work up the nerve to call Og and apologize. Promise never to ask him about Kira or Halliday again. He might listen. If I just swallowed my pride, I could probably mend our friendship. But to do so, I'd also have to obey his wishes and abandon my search for the Seven Shards.

I closed my grail diary and stood up. Just seven more days, I promised myself. Another week. If I hadn't made any progress by then, I'd hang it up for good and make my amends with Og.

I had made this promise to myself many times before, but this time I intended to keep it.

I pulled up my bookmarked destinations to teleport back to the Third Age of Middle-earth and get back to work. But as I went to select it, I noticed a small shard icon blinking at the edge of my heads-up display. I tapped it and my email client opened in a window in front of me. There was a single message waiting in my SSoSS Tip Submission account, stamped with a long system-generated ID number. Some gunter out there had just submitted a potential lead about the Seven Shards of the Siren's Soul—one that had made it past all the filters and reached my inbox. This hadn't happened in months.

I tapped the message to open it and began to read:

Dear Mr. Watts,

After three years of searching, I've finally discovered where one of the Seven Shards of the Siren's Soul is hidden and how to reach it. It's located on the planet Middletown, inside the guest bedroom at the Barnett residence, where Kira Underwood lived during her year as an exchange student at Middletown High School.

I can make the shard appear, but I can't pick it up. Probably because I'm not you—Halliday's "heir." If you'd like me to show you what I mean, I can.

I know you probably receive a lot of bogus leads, but I promise this isn't one of them.

Your Fan,

L0hengrin

I did a double-take when I read the sender's name. L0hengrin was the host of a popular gunter-themed YouTube show called *The L0w-Down*. She had about fifty million subscribers, and I'd recently become one of them. For me, this was a huge endorsement.

Most gunter shows were hosted by clueless fame-seekers spouting a steady stream of complete nonsense about the Seven Shards, when they weren't waging epic flame wars with viewers or rival hosts, or posting tearful apology videos in another desperate bid to win back followers.

But *The L0w-Down* was different. L0hengrin had an incredibly upbeat personality, and an infectious brand of enthusiasm that reminded me of how I'd felt in the early days of the contest. The brief voice over that opened her show seemed to sum up her life's philosophy: "Some people define themselves by railing against all of the things they hate, while explaining why everyone else should hate it too. But not me. I prefer to lead with my love—to define myself through joyous yawps of admiration, instead of cynical declarations of disdain."

L0hengrin also possessed an encyclopedic knowledge of James Halliday's life and his work. And she appeared to know just as much about Og and Kira Morrow.

My appreciation for L0hengrin and her show may have been slightly colored by the fact that I'd developed a mild crush on her. She was cute, smart, funny, and fearless. She was also a vocal High Five superfan. Her own gunter clan called themselves "The L0w Five." Most flattering of all, her avatar's name was a not-so-subtle tribute to my own, because in several German versions of the King Arthur legend, Lohengrin was the name of Parzival's son.

L0hengrin had proven herself to be a loyal fan too. Her support of me hadn't wavered over the past few years, despite the disastrous PR decisions I'd made. And she didn't seem to care about the army of Parzival haters who attacked her on her meed feed every time she mentioned me on her show.

Like many of L0hengrin's regular viewers, I was more than a little curious about her real-world identity. On her show, L0hengrin never talked about her real life, or her real name, age, or gender. She only appeared as her OASIS avatar, which usually looked and sounded exactly like Helen Slater in *The Legend of Billie Jean*—a teenage girl with short blond hair, piercing blue eyes, and a faint Southern accent. But like Ranma Saotome in *Ranma 1/2*, L0hengrin was also famous for changing her avatar's gender, unexpectedly and without warning—sometimes in midsentence. When she transformed into a male, she seemed to prefer the likeness of a young James Spader, especially his look from the 1985 film *Tuff Turf*. Regardless of her avatar's current gender, L0hengrin's public profile specified that her preferred gender pronouns were *she* and *her*. In her one-line user bio, she described herself as *"A wild-eyed pistol-waver who ain't afraid to die."*

My robes gave me the ability to bypass the system's built-in security measures and access any OASIS user's private account information, including their true identity and real-world address. But despite my curiosity, I'd never accessed L0hengrin's account. Not because doing so would violate GSS company policy and several federal laws. That had never stopped me in the past. I told myself that I was respecting her privacy—but really I was just worried that learning L0hengrin's true identity might ruin my enjoyment of her show, robbing me of one of the few pleasures I had in life that didn't involve the ONI.

I reread her note several times, oscillating between skepticism and exhilaration. I knew the exact location she was talking about. I'd visited the Barnett residence in the Middletown simulation a few times during Halliday's contest and found nothing of interest there. It was just an undecorated guest bedroom, because the Middletown simulation re-created Halliday's hometown as it was in the fall of 1986, two years before Kira had moved there as a British exchange student during the 1988–89 school year. That was one reason I'd never considered Middletown a likely candidate for one of the "seven worlds where the Siren once played a role." I'd also figured it was unlikely he would have chosen to hide one of the Seven Shards on the same planet he'd used as the location of the First Gate. But then again, it did have a certain symmetry to it. After all, that was where Halliday and Og and Kira all met. That was where it all began.

I closed L0hengrin's message and weighed my options. There was really only one way to find out for certain whether she was telling the truth. I pulled up a three-dimensional map of the OASIS, then used my superuser HUD to pinpoint the current location of L0hengrin's avatar. Just as I hoped, she was still on Middletown, in one of the 256 copies of Halliday's hometown spread out across the planet's surface.

I made my avatar invisible and undetectable, then teleported to her exact location.

If you attempted to teleport to a location inside the OASIS that was already occupied by an object or another avatar, the system would automatically adjust your arrival coordinates to the closest unoccupied location. When I finished rematerializing, I discovered that the system had placed me directly in front of L0hengrin's avatar, which was currently in its female form. She was seated about a meter away, wearing her trademark *Legend of Billie Jean* attire. A baggy pair of men's trousers tucked into a pair of cowboy boots, with a sleeveless neon-colored wetsuit as her top.

She didn't notice my arrival, because my avatar was invisible. Her eyes were also closed, but that just meant she was "engaged" and currently had her attention focused elsewhere, like on a phone call or a private chatroom. L0hengrin would most likely still be monitoring her avatar's view of this room via a small video-feed window in the corner of her HUD. Middletown was located in a PvP zone, making it a risky place to leave your avatar unattended.

I looked around and saw that we weren't in Kira's old bedroom at the Barnett residence. We were three blocks north of that location, in the world famous wood-paneled basement of Ogden Morrow's childhood home. This was where Morrow, Halliday, and their close-knit group of friends spent most of their free time. They gathered here after school and on the weekends to escape to other worlds, via dozens of tabletop role-playing games. Og's basement would also later serve as the first office of Gregarious Games, the company that Halliday and Morrow co-founded after high school, which evolved into Gregarious Simulation Systems a few decades later when they launched the OASIS.

In the real Middletown, Ohio, Og's childhood home had been demolished decades ago to make room for a block of condominiums. But here in the OASIS, Halliday had re-created his best friend's childhood home in loving detail, along with his own home and the rest of their hometown, using old maps, photographs, and video footage for reference.

Like everything else in the Middletown simulation, Og's basement looked just like the real thing had back in the late 1980s. Vintage movie and comic-book posters covered the walls. Three beat-up couches were arranged in a U-shape in front of an old RCA television, which was half-buried by a Betamax VCR, a Pioneer Laserdisc player, and several different classic home videogame consoles.

On the other side of the room, a bunch of folding chairs were clustered around a scarred wooden table covered with multicolored polyhedral dice. A row of bookshelves lined the far wall, each crammed to capacity with role-playing-game supplements and back issues of *Dragon* magazine. Two ground-level windows looked out onto the Morrows' backyard, where a fat orange sun hovered above the horizon, silhouetting a rusting swing set in the neighbor's yard.

Being in this room filled me with fond memories of my own teenage years, because in a strange way, I'd grown up here too. Back when we were in high school, Aech had modeled her private OASIS chatroom after Ogden Morrow's basement, and the two of us spent countless hours there over the years. Talking, gaming, doing our homework, listening to old music, watching old movies. Daydreaming about the things we would do when we won Halliday's fortune.

My life had been a lot harder back then, but in retrospect it now also seemed a hell of a lot simpler.

I glanced back over at L0hengrin. Her avatar's eyes were still closed, and they were still darting around rapidly beneath her eyelids, as if she were in REM sleep. I was about to make my avatar visible and alert her to my presence, but then a better idea occurred to me. I selected L0hengrin's avatar on my display and pulled up a list of her active communication processes. It told me that she was currently logged in to a private chatroom called Cyberdelia, which was hosted by a fifty-ninth-level avatar named Kastagir.

If L0hengrin really had found one of the shards, she might be in that private chatroom discussing it with her friends. Or, if she was bullshitting me, she might be in there discussing that instead. And my robes let me enter private chatrooms uninvited and undetected, allowing me to eavesdrop on their occupants. This was a trick I'd learned from the Great and Powerful Og himself, the only other avatar in the OASIS who had this ability.

I tapped the small door icon at the edge of my display to activate my chatroom interface, then searched for the one named Cyberdelia and tapped the Login button. My view of Og's basement shrank from the limits of my peripheral vision to a small window in the corner of my display, and I suddenly found myself standing just inside the chatroom's entrance.

Cyberdelia was a multilevel warehouse space filled with archaic late-twentieth-century technology and retro-futurist décor. Oddly adorned mannequins, pay phones, roller-blade ramps, and air-hockey tables were scattered around the club, and its walls were covered with graffiti urging its denizens to *Hack the Planet!* When I recognized the old techno song playing on the sound system—"Cowgirl" by Underworld—I made the connection, and smiled. This was a re-creation of the underground cyberpunk nightclub featured in the 1995 film *Hackers.*

From my position near the entrance, the chatroom looked deserted. But over the blaring music, I could hear several overlapping voices engaged in a heated conversation. I ventured further inside, following the noise, until I spotted five avatars gathered on one of the club's upper-level catwalks. They were sitting and standing around a circular table made from an empty wooden cable spool. L0hengrin was among them, gesturing excitedly as she spoke to the others.

Being careful not to bump into any furniture, I moved closer, until I could make out what she was saying. From this distance, I was also able to read the name tags floating above the other four avatars' heads: Kastagir, Rizzo, Lilith, and Wukong.

"You are *so* full of shit, Lo," the one named Wukong said in a deep voice. "Even more than usual, which is saying something." His avatar was a tall half-man, half-monkey creature, which explained the name—Sun Wukong was a character from Chinese mythology known as "the Monkey King."

"Come on, Kong," L0hengrin said, rolling her eyes. "Why would I lie about something like this?"

"To try and impress us?" Kastagir said. The chatroom's enormous host was leaning against an iron girder with his massive arms folded across his chest. He was a human male with ebony skin and a giant fro-hawk that added at least a foot to his already-impressive height. He wore a brightly colored dashiki and a long, curved sword in an ornate scabbard, just like the character of the same name in the original *Highlander* film.

Lilith took a step forward. Her avatar was a young woman with shaggy turquoise-colored hair, dressed in torn black jeans, combat boots, and a dark blue hoodie. She appeared to be going for a turn-of-the-century edgy emo look.

"Of course the ignorant males doubt you," she said. "But I believe you, sister!"

"So do I, Lo!" Rizzo added, popping her bubblegum. Her avatar's inspiration made me grin again: the character of the same name in the movie version of *Grease*—a young Stockard Channing, wearing a black motorcycle jacket and a pair of oversize sunglasses. But this Rizzo had a touch of Columbia from *Rocky Horror,* with fishnet stockings and a glittery gold top hat.

"Thank you, ladies," L0hengrin said, bowing to them.

Wukong snorted like an angry gorilla.

"OK," he said. "If you really found one of the shards, then why don't you show us some proof? A screenshot or simcap or something?"

"I will," L0hengrin said, putting her boots up on the table and her hands behind her head. "As soon as I finish collecting my reward."

"I bet Parzival gets thousands of emails about the shards every day," Kastagir said. "He probably stopped reading them years ago."

"He'll read mine," L0hengrin said. "Parzival knows I wouldn't waste his time with a bogus lead. He's one of my subscribers, remember?"

She mimed brushing dust off of her shoulder.

"Really?" Lilith said, feigning surprise. "Parzival is one of your subscribers? You've never mentioned this before!"

"It's OK," she said, playfully punching Wukong in the shoulder. "I know you're just jealous. I would be, too, if I were you. Caesar."

Wukong pointed a finger at her. "I warned you about the *Planet of the Apes* jokes, Goldilocks."

"I know," she said, smiling. "And it was a scary warning too. Made a big impression."

"Hold on," Lilith said. "What's to stop Parzival from taking it and teleporting away, without paying you a dime?"

"Parzival would never do that," L0hengrin said. "He's a righteous dude."

"He's a rich nutjob who acts like a total douchebag on social media," Lilith said. "He also likes to hunt and kill his detractors for sport, remember? You shouldn't trust him."

"You guys are all so cynical," L0hengrin said, shaking her head. "Have a little faith!"

"We just don't want to see you get ripped off is all," Rizzo said.

"If it makes you guys feel any better, I plan to record my entire conversation with Parzival, just in case I need to prove it took place."

They all studied her for a moment.

"You're not kidding about this," Wukong said. "You really found something?"

L0hengrin nodded excitedly.

"One billion simoleons," Rizzo said, shaking her head and smiling. "Have you already figured out what you're gonna do with it?"

L0hengrin grinned at her, then glanced around at each of the others.

"I thought you'd never ask!" she replied. "First, I'm gonna buy a big house in Columbus for all of us to live in together. It's gonna have a big kitchen that's always full of food. We'll each have our own room—and in the basement, we'll have our own private classic videogame arcade where we can all hang out!" She paused to take in a large breath of air. "I'll also make sure our new crib has the fastest OASIS connection money can buy," she went on. "Then, once it's ready, I'll fly you all up to it! We're all going to grow old there together. And we'll never have to depend on anyone else, ever again."

They all stared back at her.

"Seriously?" Kastagir asked, in a voice that was almost a whisper. "You'd do that?"

L0hengrin nodded and then crossed her heart. "Guys," she said. "You're my four best friends in the world. My only friends, if we're being honest. And ever since my mom died, you've been my only family too. Of course this is what I want to do." She looked like she was about to sob, but then she forced out a laugh instead. "Besides, we're the L0w Five. We promised to stick together forever. Right?"

Lilith reached out and squeezed one of L0hengrin's hands. Kastagir's lower lip began to tremble and he turned away in an attempt to conceal it. Rizzo had tears in her eyes, but she was smiling.

I was smiling and tearing up, too, I realized. It was heartbreakingly fitting that these kids had nicknamed themselves the L0w Five, because the bond that L0hengrin shared with her friends reminded me of the one I'd shared with the other members of the High Five during the contest. But it also reminded me just how much it had faded over the years.

"Goddammit!" Wukong roared. He reached up to wipe his eyes on the back of his furry simian forearm. "Cut it out, before you fools make me start bawling too!"

The others all laughed at that, and it made Wukong crack up also.

I was suddenly filled with an overwhelming desire to find out who these people were in real life, and how they all knew one another. For a normal OASIS user, learning the identity of Lo and her friends would've been impossible. But for me, it was as simple as selecting all of their avatars on my HUD. Then I instructed the system to scan each of their OASIS accounts and display any obvious similarities or connections between them. It informed me that L0hengrin, Wukong, Rizzo, Lilith, and Kastagir were all either nineteen or twenty years old in age, and that all five of them had graduated from the same OASIS public school on Ludus II a few years ago—OPS #1126.

These gunters were old high school friends, just like me and Aech. And all five of them had enrolled in GSS's Disadvantaged Youth Empowerment Program, which provided free ONI headsets and OASIS consoles to orphaned and/or destitute kids around the world.

I suddenly felt like a jerk for eavesdropping on their conversation. So I logged out of the chatroom and resumed control of my avatar back inside Og's basement on Middletown. But I was still invisible, so L0hengrin couldn't see me.

I stood there for a few seconds, staring down at her avatar, pretending to wrestle with my conscience. Then I went ahead and pulled up L0hengrin's private account profile to find out her real-world identity. I justified violating her right to privacy as an OASIS user the way I always did—by telling myself it was necessary. Before I accepted L0hengrin's help in return for a billion dollars, I had to find out as much as I could about her, to get a sense of who I would be dealing with. But that was a bullshit excuse and I knew it. What it really boiled down to was plain old curiosity. I was curious about who L0hengrin was in the real world. And I had the ability to find out. So I did.

L0hengrin's real name was Skylar Castillo Adkins. According to her private user profile she was an unmarried nineteen-year-old Caucasian female, and she lived in the Duncanville, Texas, stacks, a sprawling vertical slum near the apocalyptic epicenter of the DFW metroplex. It was an even rougher neighborhood than the one I'd grown up in.

Since I'd already violated her privacy, I decided to go full-on Big Brother and have a look at her headset feeds. There were ten wide-angle surveillance cameras mounted on the exterior of each ONI headset, which allowed the wearer to keep an eye on their body and its surroundings from inside the OASIS. The Robes of Anorak gave me access to a secret submenu on every ONI user's account, where I could monitor the video feeds coming from those cameras. Meaning I had the ability to spy on people in their homes. This was one of GSS's uglier secrets, and there would be riots and class-action suits galore if our customers ever found out about it. But these were exceptional circumstances, I assured myself.

When I pulled up Skylar's headset feeds, I was not prepared for what I saw. The darkened interior of an ancient Airstream trailer, lit up bright green by the night-vision filters. I could see a helper bot silently washing dishes at the miniature kitchen sink. It was a battered Okagami Swap-Bot, so named because it could be used as both a telebot and an autonomous domestic helper robot. It had a sawed-off pistol-grip pump-shotgun in a makeshift holster strapped to its back, so she apparently used it to do more than just the dishes.

In the foreground of several of Skylar's headset camera feeds, I could also see her—her thin, frail-looking body was stretched out on a worn mattress in the back of the trailer. Like a lot of people who lived in the stacks, she appeared to be suffering from borderline malnutrition. Her gaunt features seemed to conflict with the pleasant, dreamlike expression on her face. Someone had laid an old Snoopy blanket over her to keep her warm—or, no. She must've done this herself, using her telebot. Because she was all alone, with no one to rely on but herself.

My chest felt hollow. I closed all of the vidfeed windows and scanned Skylar's user profile for more information about her. Her school records included a scan of her birth certificate, which revealed another surprise. She'd been DMAB—designated male at birth.

Discovering this minor detail didn't send me spiraling into a sexual-identity crisis, the way it probably would have back when I was younger.

Thanks to years of surfing the ONI-net, I now knew what it felt like to be all kinds of different people, having all different kinds of sex. I'd experienced sex with women while being another woman, and sex with men as both a woman and a man. I'd done playback of several different flavors of straight and gay and nonbinary sex, just out of pure curiosity, and I'd come away with the same realization that most ONI users came away with: Passion was passion and love was love, regardless of who the participants involved were, or what sort of body they were assigned at birth.

According to Skylar's user profile history, she'd legally changed her gender to female when she was sixteen, a few months after she received her first ONI headset. Around the same time, she'd changed her avatar's sex classification to *øgender*, a brand-new option GSS had added due to popular demand. People who identified as øgender were individuals who chose to experience sex exclusively through their ONI headsets, and who also didn't limit themselves to experiencing it as a specific gender or sexual orientation.

Coming out as øgender became incredibly common in the wake of the ONI's release. For the first time in human history, anyone eighteen years of age or older could safely and easily experience sexual intercourse with any gender and *as* any gender. This tended to alter their perception of gender identity and fluidity in profound ways. It had certainly altered mine. And I was certain it had done the same thing for every other ONI user with even a mildly adventurous spirit. Thanks to the OASIS Neural Interface, your gender and your sexuality were no longer constrained by—or confined to—the physical body you happened to be born into.

Skylar's profile also indicated she had no living family members. Her mother, Iris Adkins, had died of heart failure two years ago. Somehow, Skylar had been living on her own since she was seventeen. In the DFW stacks, no less.

I heard movement and quickly closed Skylar's user profile. Then I glanced back over at her avatar, just in time to see L0hengrin's eyes flicker open—an indication that she'd logged out of Kastagir's chatroom.

Her avatar stood up and began to walk toward the exit. I was standing directly in her path. Instead of stepping out of her way, I folded my arms and assumed an ominous wizard pose. Then I made my avatar visible once again.

LOhengrin froze, and when her eyes locked on to me they seemed to double in size. Then she bowed her head and slammed her right fist against her heart as she dropped to one knee.

"My liege," she said in a shaky voice, keeping her eyes on the floor. "I'm LOhengrin. Your humble servant. And a huge fan, sir. Truly."

"Please rise, LOhengrin," I said. "I'm a big fan of yours too."

She stood and slowly raised her eyes to meet mine.

"Sir Parzival," she said, shaking her head in wonder. "It's really you."

"It's really me," I replied. "It's an honor to meet you, LOhengrin."

"The honor is all mine," she said. "And please, call me Lo. All my friends do."

"All right, Lo." I offered her my hand and she shook it. "My friends call me Z."

"I know," she said, giving me a sheepish smile. "I've read every single one of the books written about you over the past few years, including your autobiography, which I've read at least two dozen times. So I know pretty much everything there is to know about you. Everything that's ever been made public, anyway. I'm kinda obsessed with you—"

She suddenly cut herself off, wincing in embarrassment. Then she pounded her right fist lightly against her forehead several times before finally meeting my gaze again.

Her cheeks had turned a bright shade of red—an indication she hadn't shut off her avatar's blush response. She probably hadn't switched off any of her avatar's other involuntary emotional responses either. Younger ONI users did this intentionally. They referred to it as "rolling real."

Poor Lo. Her nervousness at meeting an idol reminded me too much of myself for comfort. Hoping to rescue her—and impatient to learn what she knew—I tried to keep things moving. "I'm intrigued to see what you've found," I said. "Would you like to show me?"

"Sure!" she replied. "You mean, like, right now?"

I nodded. "No time like the present."

"Right," she said. She cast a nervous glance toward the basement windows and lowered her voice. "But first I need to show you *how* I found it, so that you can repeat the same steps. That's why I was waiting for you here, instead of at Kira's house."

"OK," I said. "Go ahead."

L0hengrin took a few hesitant steps toward the other end of the basement before halting and turning back to me. "Listen, Mr. Watts," she said, keeping her eyes on the floor. "I don't mean any disrespect, but would you mind verbally confirming that the reward is still one billion U.S. dollars?"

"Not at all," I said. "If anything you tell me helps me locate one of the Seven Shards of the Siren's Soul, then I will immediately transfer one billion dollars to your OASIS account. It's all outlined in the contract you signed when you sent me your clue."

Before anyone could try to claim the reward, they were required to sign a digital "Shard Clue Submission Contract" that my lawyers had drafted. I located the copy L0hengrin had signed and displayed it in a window in front of her. The print was too fine to read without squinting, and the text scrolled on for several pages.

"This contract states, among other things, that if the information you present to me proves to be valid, you agree not to share it with anyone else for a period of three years. You also agree not to discuss the details of our transaction with anyone, including the media. If you do, you forfeit the reward and I can take it all back—"

"Oh, I've read the contract," she said, grinning, but still not meeting my gaze. "A few thousand times. Sorry, I didn't mean to insult you. It's just—that's a lot of zenny for me."

I laughed. "Don't worry, Lo. If you can help me find one of the Seven Shards, then that money is all yours. I promise."

She nodded and took a deep breath. The look of nervous anticipation on her face set my own heart racing. If this kid was lying about finding one of the shards, then she deserved an Academy Award for her performance.

L0hengrin turned and walked over to the bookshelves that lined the basement's far wall. They were filled with sci-fi and fantasy paperbacks, role-playing-game supplements, and back issues of various vintage gaming magazines, like *Dragon* and *Space Gamer*. Lo began to flip through the huge collection of old Dungeons & Dragons modules shelved there, apparently looking for one in particular.

I'd browsed through that very same bookshelf seven years ago, during the early days of Halliday's contest. And I'd read or skimmed over most of those old modules and magazines—but not all of them. The remaining titles were still on my reading list when I won the contest, at which point I'd forgotten all about them. Now I was kicking myself, wondering what I'd missed.

"For the past few years, I've been scouring Middletown, looking for a way to alter the time period of the simulation," Lo said. "You know, because of the couplet."

"The couplet?"

She paused in her search and turned around to look at me. "On Kira's headstone?"

"Oh, right," I said. "Of course."

I had no idea what she was talking about, and L0hengrin could obviously see it on my face. Her eyes widened in surprise.

"Oh my God. You don't even know about the couplet. Do you?"

"No," I replied, throwing up my hands. "I guess I don't."

She frowned at me and shook her head, as if to say, *How far the mighty have fallen.*

"You know how in Peter Jackson's film adaptation of *The Two Towers,* there's a scene were King Théoden places a Simbelmynë on Théodred's tomb?" she asked.

I nodded.

"Well, if you visit the re-creation of Kira's grave on EEarth and place a Simbelmynë taken from Arda on it, a rhymed couplet appears on her headstone," Lo said. "Other types of flowers indigenous to Middle-earth might work too. I'm not sure. I didn't try any of them."

I felt like a complete idiot. I'd visited Kira's grave on EEarth several times to search for clues. But I'd never thought to try this. At least I could hide my embarrassment, since I wasn't "rolling real."

L0hengrin opened a browser window in front of her avatar, then spun it around so I could see it. It showed a screenshot of Kira's headstone on EEarth. Below her name and the dates of her birth and death was an inscription: BELOVED WIFE, DAUGHTER & FRIEND. Below that were two additional lines of text, which did not appear on her headstone in the real world:

> The First Shard lies in the Siren's first den
> So the question isn't where, but when?

There it was. After all these years, a genuine clue. And it seemed likely that L0hengrin was the first and only person to discover it, because no one else had submitted it to me in an attempt to claim the reward.

"When I found that couplet," Lo continued, "I thought the 'Siren's first den' might be the place where Kira was living when she created Leucosia— her old guest bedroom here on Middletown. But the time period of this simulation is always set to 1986. Kira only lived in Middletown during her junior year of high school, from the fall of 1988 to the summer of 1989. So to reach the Siren's Den, I figured I would need to alter the time period of the Middletown simulation, to a different 'when.' I tried everything I could think of, including time travel." She held up an object that resembled an oversize pocket watch—a rare time-travel device called an Omni. "But no dice. Time machines don't function here, the way they do on some other planets, like Zemeckis."

This was something I already knew firsthand. I'd brought my own time machine, ECTO-88, to Middletown to try the same thing. I'd upgraded the car with a fully functional (and extremely expensive) Flux Capacitor, which allowed me to time travel on planets where doing so was an option. For example, on EEarth, I could travel as far back as 2012, when the OASIS was first launched, and GSS began backing up previous versions of the simulated Earth on their servers. But my flux capacitor wouldn't function on Middletown, so I'd dismissed time travel as a possibility.

"But I knew from the riddle that changing the timeframe had to be part of the solution," Lo continued. "So I kept on searching for another way . . ."

She turned around and continued to flip through the D&D modules on the bookshelf.

"Then, earlier this week, I was browsing through Og's old gaming library here when I came across something strange."

She finally located the item she was looking for and carried it back over to me. It was a shrink-wrapped wall calendar for the year 1989, featuring the work of a fantasy artist named Boris Vallejo. The painting on the cover depicted a pair of Valkyries riding into battle.

My eyes widened, then darted to the calendar already hanging on the basement wall. It, too, was a Boris Vallejo artwork calendar, for the year 1986. The month of October was currently displayed. It featured a painting of a bikini-clad female warrior astride a black steed, brandishing a magic ring at an incoming flight of dragons. Out of curiosity, I'd looked up the name of this painting once—it was called *Magic Ring* and it had also been used as the cover artwork for a 1985 fantasy novel called *Warrior Witch of Hel.*

Like the other wall decorations in Og's basement, the calendar couldn't be taken down or removed. And its pages couldn't be flipped to another month.

"Halliday coded the Middletown simulation to re-create his hometown circa October 1986, right?" Lo said. "So why would there be a calendar for the year 1989 here?"

"Good question," I said, glancing between the calendar on the wall and the one in her hand. "But gunters around the world spent years studying the contents of this room. Why didn't any of them find it?"

"Because it wasn't here," Lo said, grinning wide. "I checked Gunterpedia. There's an itemized list of every single object in this basement. The only calendar listed on it is the one hanging on the wall." She held up the 1989 calendar. "So either they somehow missed this one, or—"

"It appeared on that bookshelf after Halliday's contest ended," I finished.

L0hengrin nodded and held the 1989 calendar out to me.

"Now try swapping it with the one on the wall."

I took the calendar from L0hengrin, then, with my other hand, I reached out and tried to take the 1986 calendar down off the wall. To my surprise, it slid right off the nail it was hanging on. I carefully hung up the 1989 calendar in its place, and opened it to the month of January.

As soon as I let go of the calendar, its pages began to flip upward on their own, until the month of April was displayed. As the pages were flipping, the sky outside cycled rapidly between day and night, pulsing on and off like a strobe light. The entire Middletown simulation was fast-forwarding all around us, like time-lapse film footage played back at high speed.

When the strobing stopped, our surroundings had changed. The couches in Og's basement had rearranged themselves, and two more bookshelves had appeared against the far wall, both filled with more gaming supplements. There were also several new posters on the walls. But the most striking difference was the time of day. Outside the basement windows, night had fallen. The streetlights were on and there was a full moon out.

"Whoa," I heard myself whisper. I glanced at the digital alarm clock sitting on top of one of the bookshelves. Its glowing blue display said the local time was now 1:07 A.M.

I turned back to L0hengrin. She was beaming with pride.

"Swapping the calendars changes the time period of the Middletown simulation from October 1986 to April 1989," she explained. "But only this one instance of the simulation has been updated. The other two hundred and fifty-five copies of Middletown spread out across the planet remain set to the 1986 version. I've checked."

"If this is April in 1989," I said, "then what happens if we go over to the Barnetts' empty guest bedroom now?"

Lo grinned. "Before we head over there, you need to obtain an item located in this room. An audio cassette tape that Kira gifted to both Halliday and Og. . . ."

She locked eyes with me, studying my reaction.

"What, are you actually quizzing me now?" I asked.

Lo nodded and folded her arms. The dubious expression on her face made me laugh out loud.

"It was called *Leucosia's Mix*," I said. "Oscar Miller mentions it in his memoir, *The Middletown Adventurers' Guild*. But he doesn't give the full track list. He just mentions one song that was on it—'There Is a Light That Never Goes Out' by the Smiths."

Lo nodded. "That's exactly right," she said. "And now that we've jumped ahead to 1989, there are two copies of *Leucosia's Mix* in the Middletown simulation. One in Halliday's Walkman in his bedroom, and one here."

She walked over to the ground-level window at the opposite end of the basement, which looked out onto the Morrows' moonlit backyard. Og's boombox was resting on the window ledge. She pressed the Eject button and removed the tape inside.

"According to Miller's book, Kira made two copies of this mixtape," she said, holding it up. "She gave one to Og and one to Halliday, a few months before her school year abroad ended and she had to go back home to London."

She tossed the tape to me and I held it up to read the sticker on its A side: *Leucosia's Mix* was written on it in cursive, above a track-list insert filled out in the same handwriting.

"Thanks," I said, adding the tape to my inventory.

Lo was already running up the basement steps.

"Kira's house is just a few blocks from here," she shouted over her shoulder. "Follow me!"

When we reached the Barnetts' house a few minutes later, L0hengrin halted at the end of the darkened sidewalk leading up to it. Then she pointed up to Kira's bedroom window on the second floor. It was the only room in the house with a light on. In fact, glancing up and down the street, I saw that it was the *only* illuminated window on the entire block.

L0hengrin saw me noticing this and nodded her approval. But she didn't say anything.

I thought for a moment, then took the copy of *Leucosia's Mix* out of my inventory and examined the track list. There it was, the seventh song on side A. "There Is a Light That Never Goes Out" by the Smiths. One of Kira's all-time favorites.

I turned to point this out to L0hengrin, but she was already sprinting into the house. I followed her inside.

· · ·

L0hengrin was waiting for me inside the guest bedroom. On my previous visits, this room had been undecorated and empty, aside from a bed, a dresser, and a small wooden desk. Now sci-fi and fantasy paperbacks were piled everywhere, and posters adorned the walls. *The Dark Crystal. The Last Unicorn. Purple Rain.* The Smiths. Homemade collages hung there, too, made from magazine clippings of videogame characters and artwork.

Sheets of graph paper were tacked up everywhere, filled with Kira's meticulous renderings of characters, objects, and landscapes from classic role-playing videogames, like Bard's Tale and Might and Magic. I'd read about this. Kira had spent hundreds of hours copying pixels from the screen onto the graph paper, coloring them in by hand one square at a time, to figure out how different artists achieved their effects and improve on their techniques. When she worked at GSS later on, she became famous for creating artwork that pushed the boundaries of the computer hardware available at the time. Og was fond of saying that his wife had "always had a knack for bringing pixels to life."

I turned around slowly, trying to absorb as many details as I could. There were no family photos displayed anywhere. But she did have several pictures taped around the edge of her mirror, showing Kira with her nerdy new circle of friends—Halliday, Og, and the other misfit members of the Middletown Adventurers' Guild. Several of those boys would later write tell-all books about growing up with Halliday and Og, and like every other die-hard gunter I'd scoured them all for details that might help me unlock the puzzles and riddles Halliday left behind. I'd reread them all again a few years ago, this time absorbing the details they contained about Kira's life, so I knew that not a single one of them described the interior of her room at the Barnett residence. She was never allowed to have male visitors up there, and none of the boys in the guild had ever seen Kira's room, including Og and Halliday. But I would've been willing to bet they'd both spent plenty of time imagining what it looked like. Maybe that was what I was looking at now—a simulation of what Halliday imagined Kira's room looked like back then.

A small color television sat on Kira's desk, with a Dragon 64 home computer connected to it. Seeing this made me smile. The Dragon 64 was a British PC built with the same hardware as the TRS-80 Color Computer 2, the first computer Halliday ever owned. According to one of the old journal entries he included in Anorak's Almanac, when he found out that he and Kira owned compatible computers, Halliday took it as a sign they were meant to be together. He was wrong, of course.

Kira had a color dot-matrix printer hooked up to her computer, and the giant cork bulletin board on the wall above her desk was filled with printouts of her early original ASCII and ANSI artwork. Lots of pixelated dragons and unicorns and elves and hobbits and castles. I'd seen them all reprinted in collections of Kira's artwork, but looking at them again now, I was still amazed at the detail and nuance she had been able to create with so few pixels and such a limited color palette.

L0hengrin walked across the room, over to Kira's dresser, which had a small Aiwa stereo system sitting on top of it. She pressed the Eject button on its cassette deck, then pointed at the empty tray.

"Go ahead," she said. "You can do the honors. . . ."

I walked over, put *Leucosia's Mix* into the tape player, and fast-forwarded it until I reached the end of the sixth song on the first side ("Jessie's Girl" by Rick Springfield). When I hit the Play button, I heard a few seconds of analog tape hiss before the next song began, and Morrissey began to croon: *Take me out tonight . . .*

I glanced around the room. Nothing happened. I glanced over at L0hengrin. She held up a hand and mouthed the word *wait.*

So we waited. We waited until about three minutes into the song, when Morrissey starts to sing a riff on the title over and over again. *There is a light and it never goes out . . .*

As he sang "light" for the first time, the lid of a wooden jewelry box sitting next to the stereo flew open, and a necklace floated up out of it, as if lifted by an invisible hand. It was silver with a blue gemstone, and I recognized it as the one Kira was wearing in her 1989 Middletown High School yearbook photo. According to his autobiography, Og gave it to her the first time he told her he was in love with her.

When the Smiths song ended, there was a blinding flash of light. When it faded the floating necklace had transformed into a large blue teardrop-shaped crystal, spinning in front of us at eye-level.

There it was, at long last—one of the Seven Shards of the Siren's Soul.

I stared at the shard in awe, feeling a strange combination of exhilaration and disappointment. I'd finally uncovered the First Shard's hiding place. But after three years of trying, I hadn't been able to do it on my own. No, I'd had to be led here, like a noob following a walkthrough. Buying victory like some clueless Sixer instead of earning it on my own, or with the help of my friends . . .

But my shame couldn't drown out the rush of relief and validation. The shards were real. I still wasn't sure what I was hunting for, or why it mattered, but now I knew this wasn't just some meaningless riddle. It really was another hunt created by Halliday. And whatever the prize was, it had to be important.

Out of the corner of my eye, I saw a blur of motion as L0hengrin reached for the spinning shard. Her hand passed right through it, as if it were a hologram.

"I've tried picking it up dozens of times, dozens of different ways," she said. "No matter what I try, my hand passes right through it. I don't think anyone can touch it—except you, Halliday's heir. To get the shard, you have to pay some sort of toll . . . whatever that means."

For each fragment my heir must pay a toll, to once again make the Siren whole.

"There's only one way to find out," I said, reaching out for the shard.

My fingers didn't pass through it—they closed around it. And as they did . . .

. . . For a moment, I was somewhere else. I was in a school classroom filled with old BBC Microcomputers. There was no one else in the room. I was sitting at one of the computers, and I could see my reflection in its monitor. Except it wasn't mine. It was Kira Underwood's face staring back at me. She—or rather, I—looked about nine or ten years old. And I felt exhilarated! My skin and scalp were tingling, and I could feel my pulse racing and my heart thudding inside of my tiny chest. I was staring at the screen, admiring a piece of artwork I'd just finished creating—a pixelated unicorn rearing up on its hind legs, silhouetted against a crescent moon.

I recognized this image. It was famous. It was the very first piece of digital artwork Kira Underwood ever created. And I appeared to be reliving the moment just after she had created it. . . .

And then I was back, in my own body, standing in Kira's bedroom—the guest room in Middletown.

Somehow, I'd just spent a moment inside Kira's past.

I was still reeling when a series of cascading chimes rang in my ears and a message appeared on my HUD: *Congratulations, Parzival! You've found the first of the Seven Shards of the Siren's Soul!*

"What happened?" L0hengrin said. "You zoned out for a second. Are you all right?"

I looked down at the luminous blue shard in my hand.

"I had some sort of vision," I said. "Like a momentary flashback. I guess that was the 'toll' I had to pay?"

"A flashback?" she repeated slowly. "What do you mean?"

"It felt like an ONI recording," I said. "But it only lasted for a few seconds. I was Kira Underwood—or at least, it felt like I was her—and I was reliving the moment when she created that unicorn on a computer at her school when she was ten."

"The Crescent Moon Unicorn?" Lo said, eyes wide with awe. "But it had to be a simulation, right? ONI headsets didn't exist back in the '80s. And Kira died years before they were even invented."

I nodded. I'd just been thinking the same thing.

"No, it obviously couldn't have been a real ONI recording," I said. "But it felt like one. Halliday must have simulated it. Though I don't have the first clue how he could've done it so convincingly. . . ."

"Or *why*," Lo said, shaking her head. "Why would he create a Sim of one of Kira's childhood memories? From her perspective? That would be a pretty messed-up night of programming, man. Even for Halliday . . ."

I was considering this question when an urgent notification flashed on my HUD. It was an icon I hadn't seen in years—a Scoreboard alert. When I selected it, a web-browser window appeared in front of my avatar, displaying Halliday's old website, where the Scoreboard for his contest had once resided. A few seconds after I had found the egg and won the contest, the Scoreboard had been replaced with an image of my avatar dressed in Anorak's Robes, along with the message: PARZIVAL WINS!

That image had disappeared. Now a new Scoreboard had appeared in its place. But instead of a list of the top-ten players, this Scoreboard only displayed one avatar's name—my own. And instead of a numerical score, there was a single blue shard icon beside my name, followed by six empty slots.

"Whoa," L0hengrin whispered, running her hands through her short blond hair. She motioned to the blue shard icon glittering on the Scoreboard. "Now the whole world knows you have the First Shard. The newsfeeds must be blowing up."

I turned the shard over in my hands, then held it up and examined it more closely. There was an inscription engraved into its crystalline surface:

Her paint and her canvas, the one and the zero
The very first heroine, demoted to hero

" 'The very first heroine, demoted to hero,' " L0hengrin repeated, suddenly standing right next to me. "Oh shit! I think I know—"

"Please, don't!" I said, muting her avatar until she'd finished speaking. "I appreciate your help, but I can take it from here."

"Oh," she said quietly. "OK. I understand."

"I appreciate it," I said, placing the shard in my inventory to conceal it from view.

"If you get stuck, call me," Lo said. "I've already conducted a complete search of this 1989 version of Middletown, and I found a ton of stuff you won't believe! Clues I bet will be helpful! This is stuff no one else knows about—"

"I appreciate the offer," I said again. "But I think you're going to be pretty busy for the next few months . . . spending your reward. Time for you to get paid, Billie Jean."

Her face lit up.

"Wait, you mean *right now*?"

I reached up to open up my avatar's HUD and I saw her hold her breath. I opened the Financial Transactions menu, selected her avatar on my display, and tapped a series of icons. And that was it. One billion dollars were transferred from my OASIS account to hers.

L0hengrin looked like she might pass out when she saw the transfer go through.

"Congratulations, Lo," I said. "You're a self-made billionaire. Don't spend it all in one place."

I offered her my hand and she shook it. Her mouth opened and closed a few times, but no words came out. Then she lunged forward and wrapped her arms around me. I stood there frozen for a few seconds, then I hugged her back.

"I can't tell you what this means to me, sir," she said, once she finally let go of me. "This is going to change everything for me. And for all of my friends. I'm gonna be able to buy a house in Columbus for us to live in together."

"That sounds like a pretty great plan," I said, hearing my voice catch. "Once you're all moved in, I hope you guys will invite me over to hang out sometime. Or you can come to my place. I could use some more real-world friends."

"Well, we'll have to see. . . ." She laughed nervously. "You've still got six more shards to find. . . . And I've got . . . a lot of things to figure out. . . ."

She frowned as she appeared to contemplate the logistics involved in using her newfound wealth to make her dreams come true. I knew from experience how overwhelming that could be.

I opened a window in front of her avatar, displaying the contract again. "Remember. You've agreed not to tell anyone else how to find this shard, or share any of the details of our interaction, until after I've found all seven shards. If you do, our deal will be nullified."

She gave me an anxious look.

"It's all right," I said. "I know you probably already told some of your friends that you found the shard, and that you were planning to contact me about it. That's not a big deal. . . ."

"Hey," she said, leveling a finger at me. "Were you eavesdropping on us in our chatroom? You were, weren't you? Like Og did to you and your friends during the contest!"

I ignored the accusation.

"Just make sure no one else knows where or how to find the shard, OK?" I said. "Not until after I've found all seven of them. Then you can each write a memoir for all I care."

She nodded slowly, biting her lower lip.

"Understood," she said finally. "But *please,* do all of your die-hard fans— like me—a favor and don't do anything else to embarrass us, OK?"

Before I could respond, she held up both hands, gave me a sheepish grin, and kept right on talking at a rapid-fire pace.

"I say that with all due respect, of course. Because I *do* respect you, and everything you've accomplished. You just lost your way a little bit. Which makes perfect sense—you suddenly became rich and famous! You know what Bill Murray said about that? *'When you become famous, you've got, like, a year or two where you act like a real asshole. You can't help yourself. It happens to everybody. You've got, like, two years to pull it together—or it's permanent.'*"

I frowned at her. "I've been famous for well over three years now."

"I know!" she replied cheerfully. "But it's never too late to turn things around."

I nodded, trying not to show how much her words had wounded my pride.

She dropped her hands and exhaled. "Sorry. Had to be said. Has been said. Time to shut up now, Lo."

She mimed zipping her lips. Way too late, in my opinion. I wasn't sure if I was touched, hurt, or angered by everything she'd just said. Maybe all three at once.

"You want to know my favorite Bill Murray quote?" I asked.

She nodded.

"I always want to say to people who want to be rich and famous: 'Try being rich first. See if that doesn't cover most of it.'"

She laughed and shook her head. "I have no idea how to be a millionaire, much less a billionaire. It's pretty nuts. . . ."

She gave me an anxious smile. I recognized the overwhelmed look on her face. I'd seen it in the mirror the morning after I won Halliday's contest.

"Listen, Lo," I said as I typed a brief text message on my HUD. "I'm gonna have one of my assistants at GSS get in touch with you. A guy named Marvin. He's a good dude. He'll be *your* assistant over the next few weeks, OK? He can help you relocate to Columbus. Hire a good lawyer and an accountant. Find a realtor and movers for you and your friends. Whatever you need. And I'd also like to arrange for you to have a GSS security escort until you've safely relocated. I promise they won't bother you. Does that all sound all right with you?"

She nodded, and the tears that had accumulated around her eyes streamed down her cheeks.

"Thank you, Mr. Watts," she said. "Wade."

"Thank *you*, Lo," I replied.

I handed her one of my contact cards, which were still designed to look like an old Adventure cartridge for the Atari 2600.

"Give me a call if there's ever anything you need," I said. "Anything at all."

She stared down at the card. Then she snapped it out of my hands and rushed to give me one of her own contact cards. It was designed to look like a VHS copy of *The Legend of Billie Jean*. I immediately added it to my inventory.

"Thanks again for your help," I said, giving her a tiny salute. "Take care of yourself, OK?"

Before she could respond, I teleported away, back to my stronghold on Falco.

*   *   *

I suddenly felt exhausted. And my daily twelve-hour ONI usage limit had nearly elapsed. I only had about forty-five minutes remaining. Some users could do a full twelve hours every day with no ill effects, but I wasn't one of them. I always tried to log out before I hit the half-hour-remaining mark, to avoid the risk of giving myself the shakes or a migraine. I decided to wait until tomorrow to start looking for the Second Shard.

I saw that I had missed several calls from both Aech and Shoto, but I was too beat to call either of them back. I vowed to do so first thing in the morning.

When I logged out of the OASIS, my ONI headset woke me from the sleeplike state it induced and reconnected my mind with my physical body. As always, this process took a few minutes. It felt a bit like waking up from an incredibly vivid dream. When I opened my eyes again, I found myself back in my immersion vault, nestled in its gel-foam auto-recliner.

I pressed a button on the control panel and the armored canopy slid open with a pneumatic hiss. I pulled myself out, ritually humming the opening line of an old '80s tune by Soul II Soul. *Back to life. Back to re-al-it-y.*

Feeling heavy in my own skin, I trudged back to the other end of the house, climbed the stairs, and collapsed into bed. A few minutes after my head hit the pillow, I drifted off to sleep.

Most daily ONI users lost the ability to remember their dreams, even though they still went into REM sleep each night. Unfortunately, I could still remember my dreams—or rather, one recurring dream that had been haunting me once or twice a week for several years now.

And despite my excitement over obtaining one of the shards, I had it again that night.

The details were always the same. . . .

I found myself standing in Anorak's study, next to the Big Red Button. Sometimes my right hand was poised above it and sometimes, like tonight, I was actually touching it. As always, I caught a glimpse of my reflection in the button's mirrored plastic surface. It was my face—Wade's face—that I saw there, instead of that of my avatar, Parzival, though I was wearing the Robes of Anorak.

As soon as I got my bearings, two stacks of golden Marshall amplifiers magically appeared on either side of Halliday's golden Easter egg and a hauntingly familiar song blasted out of them at earsplitting volume—"Push It" by Salt-N-Pepa.

Then the emcees themselves, Salt and Pepa, stepped out from behind the golden Marshall stacks, both singing into golden microphones, looking like they just stepped out of their music video in 1986. While DJ Spinderella rose up from behind Halliday's egg, scratching a pair of solid gold records on a set of solid gold turntables.

Then, while I continued to stand there frozen, with my hand on the Big Red Button, Salt-N-Pepa performed the song's chorus continuously, for what felt like several straight hours:

Ah, push it, push it good
Ah, push it, push it real good
Oooh, baby, baby! Baby, baby!
Oooh, baby, baby! Baby, baby!

As recurring nightmares go, I could've done a hell of a lot worse. But to say that those lyrics had gotten stuck in my head would've been the understatement of the century. They were permanently welded to every neuron in my brain. Whether I was online or offline, dreaming or awake, the image of my face reflected in the surface of the Big Red Button was always lurking at the back of my mind and those lyrics were playing on an endless loop, telling me over and over again that I should not only *push it!*, but that the sensible thing would be for me to go the extra mile and *push it real good!*

Normally, that was where the dream ended. But tonight, I actually worked up the courage to take Salt-N-Pepa's advice. . . .

Big money, no Whammies, I remember thinking, just before I hit the Big Red Button with the open palm of my right hand. It lit up, and a Death Star klaxon began to sound in the distance. Then the button began to pulse off and on rapidly, growing brighter each time as its color changed from red to white.

When I turned around, Salt-N-Pepa had vanished, and the guys from Men at Work were standing in their place, singing the chorus of their 1983 hit single "It's a Mistake."

I ran outside, onto the balcony. But I was no longer surrounded by the simulated landscape of Chthonia. Now I was in the Portland Avenue Stacks in Oklahoma City, where I'd grown up. And my aunt Alice's trailer was right in front of me, perched precariously at the top of its stack. My aunt Alice was standing at her bedroom window, staring back at me with a look of bitter resignation on her face.

My gaze dropped to Mrs. Gilmore's trailer, and I saw her, too, leaning out the window to feed some of her cats. She saw me and smiled. As she started to raise her hand to wave at me, the bombs IOI had planted outside detonated, and the entire stack exploded into an apocalyptic pillar of flame. . . .

And this time, I couldn't pretend Sorrento was to blame for their deaths. I was the one who had pushed the button. I had done this. . . .

But I wasn't going to have to live with the soul-crushing guilt I felt for more than a few seconds. Because the framework at the base of the flaming stack of trailers had just buckled, and now it was tilting and collapsing straight toward me.

I didn't try to run. I didn't even move. I just stood there and let justice take its course.

0008

I woke up to the pleasant electronic chirp of the vintage analog phone beside my bed. It was an Anova Electronics Communications Center Model 7000, manufactured in 1982—the very same sleek, silver, retrofuturistic telephone that Ferris Bueller's best pal, Cameron Frye, had beside his bed. *When Cameron was in Egypt's land, let my Cameron go . . .*

When I got woken up by my phone, it was usually a bad sign. Max was programmed to hold my calls if I was sleeping, unless Samantha, Aech, Shoto, Og, or Faisal called with the priority level set to emergency. If I didn't get a solid eight hours of sleep every night, it threw off my daily ONI routine. Faisal knew that.

Then I realized: my avatar's name had appeared on Halliday's old Scoreboard last night with a blue shard icon beside it. That was trending at number one on the newsfeeds worldwide, no doubt. And the GSS PR department was probably getting inundated with questions for me.

I crawled out of bed, wincing at the sunlight that flooded into the room as the wraparound window shades retracted. When my vision returned, I cleared my throat and took Faisal's call on the wallscreen. He looked worried, which usually meant I was about to be worried too.

"Hey, Faisal," I muttered. "Good morning."

"Good morning, sir," he said. His video feed was shaky, because he was holding up his phone while running down an office corridor at GSS. The image stabilized as he boarded an elevator. "I apologize for waking you, but I wanted to—"

"To talk to me about finding the shard," I said. "And making a public statement, et cetera—but can we do it in a few hours?"

"No, sir," Faisal said. "I was calling to make sure you'd seen the news. About Mr. Morrow."

I felt my heart rise into my throat. Og was in his mid-seventies. He'd appeared in good health the last time I'd seen him being interviewed, but that was months ago. Had he fallen ill? Or been in an accident? Had I waited too long to make amends with him and missed my chance?

"He's missing," Faisal said. "Possibly abducted. The police aren't sure yet. The story is all over the newsfeeds."

Max pulled all of the top video newsfeed channels up on my wallscreen, next to Faisal's video-call window. My discovery wasn't the day's top news story after all. Photos or video clips of Og flashed in front of me, accompanied by headlines like OGDEN MORROW MISSING and OASIS CO-CREATOR MORROW VANISHES HOURS AFTER PARZIVAL FINDS FIRST SHARD.

"Jesus," I muttered. "When did this happen?"

"Last night," Faisal said. "Mr. Morrow's home-security system, surveillance cameras, and robot sentries were all deactivated at exactly seven o'clock Pacific Time. They all just shut off. When his staff came in this morning, Mr. Morrow was gone. He didn't leave a note, and there were no signs of a break-in. One of his telebots is missing, and so is his private jet. Transponders disabled. And Mr. Morrow's phone has been turned off too." He shrugged. "The police think he must've decided to go off the grid for some reason."

"But you said he might have been abducted?"

"An intruder would've had to hack his home security system," Faisal said. "And his robot sentries. And his jet's security system. Who could pull that off?"

I nodded. I had the same Odinware system as Og. And the same robot sentries were guarding my estate at that very moment. It was the best home-security tech available—or at least the most expensive.

"But why would Og want to go 'off the grid'? Where would he go? He already lives in the middle of nowhere, in total seclusion."

Faisal shrugged. "We're wondering if . . . if it's somehow linked to your discovery last night," he said. "Congratulations on that, by the way."

"Thanks," I said, feeling a tinge of shame instead of pride.

Og had asked me to abandon my search for the Seven Shards years ago.

But he'd refused to give me a reason, or tell me anything about the riddle, which had only made me even more determined to figure it out on my own.

How had he reacted last night, when he saw that blue shard appear beside my name?

"Did Mr. Morrow contact you?" Faisal asked. "Or did you contact him?"

"No," I said, shaking my head. "Og and I haven't communicated in over two years."

Because I wouldn't stop hounding him for information about his dead wife.

"I see," Faisal said after an awkward silence. "Well, I think you should consider coming in to the office today, sir. PR thinks you should make a statement as soon as possible, before any of these conspiracy theories start to gain traction. We're being bombarded with interview requests for you. And there are a few hundred reporters camped out downstairs in the lobby."

"Forget the press, Faisal," I said. "I just want to find out what happened to Og."

"We've already got our security firm out searching for him, sir," Faisal said. "And we're sweeping the global sensor nets too. If his face, voice, retinas, or fingerprints get scanned anywhere in the world, we'll know about it immediately."

"Did you check his OASIS account log?"

He nodded. "His last logout occurred shortly after five o'clock last night."

"Do we still have a GSS security team at Og's estate?"

"Yes," he said. "And we still have a telebot on site, if you'd like to have a look around."

"I would," I said. "Can you send me its access code?"

"Right away, sir."

* * *

I got dressed and ran down to my office. Then I climbed into my conventional OASIS haptic rig and put on a visor and a pair of haptic gloves. Once I had logged in to the OASIS, I used the remote-access code Faisal sent me to take control of a telebot located at Og's mansion in Oregon, over two thousand miles away.

Once my link to the bot was established, its head-mounted cameras gave me a live view of Og's stunningly beautiful home. Judging by the angle of my POV, I was standing in front of Og's small jet hangar. It was at the edge of his private airstrip, which he'd had constructed in a valley between several of the highest peaks of the Wallowa Mountains in eastern Oregon.

In the distance, beyond the runway, I saw the steep cobblestone staircase at the edge of the runway, which led up to Og's multilevel mansion, constructed on a series of plateaus carved into the base of the mountain range. From the outside, it looked like a perfect replica of Rivendell, as it appeared in Peter Jackson's film adaptations of *The Hobbit* and *The Lord of the Rings*. Several waterfalls were visible in the distance, spilling off the peaks beyond the enormous house and its grounds.

Even under these circumstances—and even though I'd spent an entire week of my life there—the scale and the beauty of it all still took my breath away. Og had literally moved mountains and rerouted rivers to make the fictional valley of Imladris a reality, here in this secluded place. He'd kept the cost of the project a secret, but some estimated he'd spent close to two billion dollars. A higher price tag than Buckingham Palace. Gazing at it now through the telebot's eyes, it seemed like money well spent.

I disconnected the GSS telebot from its charging dock, which was built into the rear of an armored GSS security transport. Two GSS security officers standing nearby waved at me and I waved back. Then I turned my telebot around and piloted it over to the long, winding staircase leading up to the house.

At the top of the stairs, a stone path led me across the grounds and up to the main entrance of the house—a set of enormous wooden doors, with ornate Elvish runes carved into them. They swung open for me as I approached, but I still felt like a trespasser. If I'd shown up here unannounced a few days ago, when Og was still home, I wasn't sure he would've invited me in.

I took a quick look around the foyer. Og owned four telebots, all brand-new Okagami TB-6000s with gleaming gunmetal-blue chassis and chrome trim. Three of them were still in their charging rack just inside the front entrance. But the fourth one was missing. It had disappeared the previous evening, along with its owner. Its transponder had been deactivated at the same time the house security system went offline.

I kept moving, through the entrance hall and on into the main house. It had been over three years since I last set foot here, but to my eyes everything looked the same. Giant tapestries and fantasy artwork covered the walls, and stone gargoyle statues and antique suits of armor lined the dark wood-paneled hallways.

I took a look around Og's office, then his library, then his enormous home theater. I didn't spot anything out of the ordinary, but I didn't expect to. Neither the police nor the GSS security team had found any signs of a break-in or a struggle. According to the logs, Og had deactivated his own security system and surveillance cameras at 7:00 P.M. last night. Everything after that was a mystery.

I put on my imaginary Detroit Lions ball cap and shifted my brain into Magnum PI detective mode.

What if someone had figured out a way to hack Og's unhackable security system and remotely disable it?

And what if the hacker hijacked Og's missing telebot and then used it to force Og onto his private jet, and then hijacked the autopilot too?

Telebots had been used to perpetrate all sorts of crimes, but the perps were almost always caught, because users were required to log in to their OASIS account to operate them. Hijacking a telebot was supposed to be impossible, too, because of all their hardwired safeguards.

But if Og had been taken against his will, why didn't he trigger any alarms? Why weren't there any signs of a struggle? Og was in his mid-seventies, but he still would have put up a fight.

Unless his kidnapper had bound and gagged him. Or drugged him. Or knocked him unconscious with a blow to the head. But at his age, that might kill him. . . .

I forced the image of Og being bludgeoned out of my mind and got the telebot moving again. I wandered the hallways aimlessly, not sure what I was looking for, until I found myself standing by the closed door of one of Og's guest rooms. It was the room where Samantha had stayed during our weeklong retreat here. It was also the room where she and I made love for the first time. (And the second, third, and fourth.)

I stared at the door through the telebot's eyes, with one of its hands resting on the knob.

Maybe I'd already missed my chance to fix things with Og. But it wasn't too late with Samantha—as long as we were both still alive, there was a chance I could make things right with her.

I piloted the telebot through the labyrinth of rooms and hallways, to Og's personal arcade, a huge carpeted room containing the vast collection of classic coin-operated videogames that Halliday had willed to him after his death. The antique games were all powered off, and their screens were dark.

I wandered back out of the arcade and continued on my circuit of the house. It was like touring a museum devoted to Og and Kira's life together. The walls were covered with photos, some of Kira and Og with their arms wrapped around each other, others of just Kira (clearly taken by Og, because of how she smiled at the camera), taken in exotic locations all over the world. Snapshots of a blissful storybook romance that had ultimately ended in tragedy.

There were trophy cases, too, filled with awards, medals, and other honors bestowed on the Morrows over the years, for their charity work and their storied contributions to the field of interactive education. But noticeably absent were photos of children. Og and Kira had devoted the last half of their lives to making free educational software for underprivileged kids. Kids like me. But they had never been blessed with any children of their own. According to Og's autobiography, it was his and Kira's only real regret.

Back outside the house, I followed the path of polished stones across Og's immaculately manicured lawn, taking in the stunning view of the snowcapped mountain range that surrounded the estate.

The path led me past the entrance to the hedge maze where Samantha and I met in person for the very first time. But I didn't let myself go inside. Instead, I made my way over to the small gated-in garden where Kira Morrow was buried. As I stared down at her grave, I thought of L0hengrin, and the clue she'd discovered by visiting the re-creation of this place on EEarth—something it had never occurred to me to do.

The small garden that surrounded Kira's grave was filled with flowers that were every color of the rainbow. I picked one at random—a yellow rose—and placed it at the base of her tombstone. Then I traced the telebot's index finger along the letters of the inscription engraved into its polished marble surface: BELOVED WIFE, DAUGHTER & FRIEND.

I glanced over at the adjacent gravesite reserved for Og. I once again found myself hoping that I hadn't already missed my last chance to repair my friendship with him.

Once I completed a circuit of the manicured grounds surrounding Og's house, I walked down to have a look at his private runway, and the small aircraft hangar at the far end of it. There wasn't much to see there, aside from an empty spot where Og's missing jet should've been parked.

Like his home-security system and telepresence robots, the jet's onboard computer should've been nearly impossible to hack. So either Og had left under his own free will, or somehow, someone had managed to disable the transponder and hijack the autopilot system without setting off a single alarm.

My thoughts on hypothetical alarms were interrupted by a real one—the security-alert klaxon in my home.

I cut my link to the telebot, leaving it to pilot itself back to its charging dock on the GSS transport, and was climbing out of my haptic rig when my phone rang. It was Miles Gendell, head of GSS's executive security team. Halliday and Morrow had hired Miles in the early days of the company, because he was an ex–Green Beret who also happened to bear a distinct resemblance to a young Arnold Schwarzenegger. Now, after serving the company for over a quarter of a century, he resembled a much older, post–Governator Ahnold.

I accepted the call and Miles appeared on the wallscreen. He wore a grim expression.

"We have a situation, Mr. Watts," he said. "Nolan Sorrento has escaped from prison."

I felt like my blood had just turned to ice water.

Sorrento had been serving time on death row at the Southern Ohio Correctional Colony, a maximum-security prison located in Chillicothe, Ohio—exactly 56.2 miles due south of where I was currently standing.

"Do you have any reason to believe he's headed this way?" I asked, walking over to peek out the nearest window. "I mean, has he been spotted by anyone?"

Miles shook his head.

"No, sir," he said. "But I wouldn't worry. It's unlikely he would come here in an attempt to harm you. I'm sure he knows the sort of security you have in place."

"Yeah," I said. "The same sort of security that Ogden Morrow had." I took another peek out the window. "What the hell happened, Miles?"

"Someone hacked into the prison's security system and let Sorrento out. Then they locked the whole place down behind him," Miles said. "The guards and the entire prison staff were trapped inside the prison along with the inmates, with no phone or Internet access. First responders had to break into the prison and restore order before anyone could even check the security footage. By that time, Sorrento had nearly an hour's head start."

I was starting to panic.

"Sorrento's escape has to be connected to Og's disappearance somehow," I said, as calmly as I could. "This can't be a coincidence."

Miles shrugged. "There's no evidence of that yet, sir."

I didn't respond. My mind was racing now. Sorrento was one of the world's most famous and infamous criminals. But he'd spent the last three years rotting in a cell, and he no longer had any power or money or influence. So who was helping him? And why?

"We've got the entire area around your home under surveillance now, sir," Miles said. "You can relax. We'll remain on full alert and notify you the moment we see anything odd. All right?"

"Yeah, OK," I said, trying to sound nonchalant. "Thanks, Miles."

I disconnected the call and then opened half a dozen different newsfeed windows. Sure enough, they'd just gotten the word, too, and coverage of Sorrento's escape was popping up everywhere. I watched as the warden, a somewhat clueless-looking fellow by the name of Norton, told a reporter that Nolan Sorrento had been a model prisoner—right up until his stunning escape, which had been perpetrated in broad daylight, and in full view of the prison's security cameras.

Watching that security footage, it was obvious that Sorrento never could have pulled off his escape without a great deal of outside help. Someone had infiltrated the prison's heavily firewalled computer network and seized control of the automated security systems. Then this mysterious accomplice had opened all of the locked doors between Sorrento and the exit, allowing him to simply walk out of there. Then, for an encore, they opened every single cell in the prison, freeing all of the inmates and creating total chaos.

The hacker had apparently attempted to delete the prison's security camera footage, but luckily everything was backed up on a remote server, so the police were able to retrieve it. The footage showed Sorrento walking calmly out of his cell just a few seconds after the door magically slid open for him. As he made his way out of the prison, he waved each locked door and gate in his path open with a broad sweep of his hand, as if he were conducting an orchestra he alone could hear. As he passed through, each gate closed and locked behind him, preventing pursuit.

A few minutes later, Sorrento strolled out the prison's front gates, grinning from ear to ear. As the gates closed behind him, he turned toward the nearest security camera and took a bow, then jumped into a self-driving car that was parked there waiting for him. Its plates matched those of a car reported stolen from a nearby dealership lot earlier that morning.

Watching the footage, I wondered how Sorrento had managed to coordinate the details of his escape plan with an accomplice on the outside. According to the prison's records, Sorrento's only visitors during his incarceration there had been his attorneys. And he hadn't made or received any personal phone calls during his stay, either. So if he had conspired with someone, he'd probably communicated with them through the OASIS.

Thanks to the humanitarian efforts of GSS and Amnesty International, all U.S. prison inmates were now allowed one hour of heavily restricted, fully monitored OASIS access every other day. But they were only allowed to use a conventional OASIS visor and haptic rig. Prisoners weren't allowed to use ONI headsets. And since Sorrento had been imprisoned before the ONI was released, he had spent the last three years reading about it on the newsfeeds without being able to experience it for himself.

I pulled up Sorrento's OASIS account to check his activity logs, but they were blank. Someone had already erased all of them from our servers. This should not have been possible. Even our highest-level account admins couldn't delete a user's activity logs. Hell, even *I* didn't have that ability.

"What the fuck?," I whispered. There was no other appropriate reaction.

I sent a text message to Faisal asking him to investigate. Just a few seconds after I hit Send, an alert popped up on my phone, informing me that something had just changed on Halliday's Scoreboard. When I pulled it up, my avatar's name was still displayed there, with a single blue shard icon beside it. But now a second avatar's name had appeared directly below mine, with another shard icon beside it: The Great and Powerful Og. It could mean only one thing: Ogden Morrow had just collected the First Shard too.

I stared at the Scoreboard in disbelief. Og had never been interested in searching for the Seven Shards. Quite the opposite. He acted like he never wanted the shards to be found at all, by anyone. When I'd refused to abandon my search for them, he'd been so angry that he stopped speaking to me. Why would he suddenly start looking for the shards now? Was he determined to restore the Siren's Soul himself, before I could?

And how had Og even been able to pick the First Shard up? According to the riddle, only I, Halliday's heir, was supposed to be able to do that. . . .

For each fragment my heir must pay a toll.

Except that technically, Og was Halliday's heir too. Halliday had willed his entire collection of classic arcade games to Morrow, and everything else to the winner of his contest.

I stood there in my office, staring at Og's name on the Scoreboard, feeling paralyzed. Og knew more about Kira than anyone, including Halliday. Finding the other six shards was going to be child's play for him. But why was he doing this? And how was Sorrento's prison break related?

I tried to pull up Og's OASIS account, but it was completely blank aside from his avatar's name. And his access logs only showed his login and logout timestamps. Nothing else. Halliday's account was the same way. Their avatars' movements inside the OASIS couldn't be tracked or logged, and neither of their accounts could be disabled or deleted by anyone at GSS. When they created the OASIS, Halliday and Morrow had ensured they would both always have unrestricted and unmonitored access to it.

I was still sitting there a few minutes later, staring at Og's blank account profile like an idiot, when another Scoreboard alert popped up on my phone. A second blue shard icon had just appeared next to Og's name, which was now above mine. I had just been bumped down to second place by the Great and Powerful Og.

That snapped me out of my daze. I checked the time and made sure that enough time had elapsed so that it was safe for me to log back in. Then I ran over to my immersion vault and climbed into it. As soon as I dropped into its padded recliner, the canopy lowered and locked into place, sealing me inside. I powered up the system, muttering to myself that it wasn't too late. I still had time. If I hauled ass and located the Second Shard as quickly as possible, maybe there was still a chance I could catch up with Og. . . .

I didn't really want to compete against him. But my curiosity about the shards—and the nature of the Siren's Soul—had only grown. And besides, I told myself. This was my best shot at figuring out what had happened to Og. If I managed to find the Third Shard before he did, then I could just camp at its hiding place and wait for his avatar to show up.

I put on my ONI headset and closed my eyes to initiate the login sequence. A brief message flashed on my HUD, informing me that the new firmware update for my headset had just been automatically downloaded and installed. When my login completed, a countdown clock appeared in the corner of my display, telling me how much time remained until I reached my twelve-hour daily ONI usage limit. When my avatar finished materializing inside my command center on Falco, it was already down to eleven hours, fifty-seven minutes, and thirty-three seconds.

Before I could look at the First Shard again, I received an urgent text message from Faisal, informing me that an emergency GSS co-owners meeting had just been called, to deal with a "serious system stability issue."

I let out a long sigh of frustration. Then I teleported to the reception area on the top floor of Gregarious Tower, wondering what else could possibly go wrong today.

The answer, it turned out, was pretty much everything. . . .

When my avatar rematerialized in the reception area, Faisal greeted me with his usual handshake.

"Thank you for coming so quickly, sir," he said, turning hastily to usher me toward the conference room. "The other co-owners arrived a moment ago. Ms. Cook is aboard her jet at the moment, but she appears to have a good connection."

Art3mis, Aech, and Shoto were already seated around the table, and all three of them looked pretty freaked-out. Art3mis actually looked relieved to see me.

Faisal, now standing behind the small podium beneath the giant view-screen, made a sickly attempt at a smile. Then something changed. He stood taller, arms hanging loose—and instead of worry and alarm, his facial expression suddenly projected only calm complacency.

We all stared at him for a few awkward seconds while he stared blankly back at us.

"Faisal?" Aech said. "We're all here, man. You wanna start this meeting or what?"

"Ah, of course!" Faisal said, speaking in a much deeper voice. He raised his arms theatrically. "This meeting of the co-owners of Gregarious Simulation Systems is hereby called to order. Wushz-uh-kuh-bam!"

His avatar began to transform, melting and morphing into a familiar likeness. That of a middle-aged geek with unkempt hair and thick eye-glasses, dressed in worn jeans and a faded Space Invaders T-shirt.

James Donovan Halliday.

Holy shit!

"Greetings, Parzival," he said, giving me a small wave.

That was when I realized that I'd said "holy shit" out loud.

"Art3mis. Aech. Shoto." He waved to each of them too. Then he smiled his famously dorky smile. "It's so good to see all of you again, even under these circumstances."

Shoto leaped out of his chair, then dropped to his knees.

"Mr. Halliday," he said, bowing low before the creator's avatar.

Aech, Art3mis, and I all shook our heads.

"No," I said. "James Halliday is dead." I nodded toward the digital doppelgänger standing in front of us. "This is Anorak."

Anorak nodded and gave me a playful wink that was so off-the-scale creepy it sent a chill cascading through my nervous system.

Just then, the doors flew open and the avatar of the *real* Faisal burst into the conference room.

"I'm so sorry!" he said. "There was some sort of glitch that immobilized my avatar and I'm still not sure—"

Faisal froze in midstep as he spotted Anorak, and all the color drained out of his face. He looked as if he'd just seen a ghost—an appropriate response, considering.

Originally, Anorak was Halliday's OASIS avatar, a powerful gray-bearded wizard in ominous black robes that he'd modeled after the high-level Dungeons & Dragons character of the same name he'd played back in high school. The same D&D character that also inspired the titular hero in Halliday's early Anorak's Quest adventure game series.

But after Halliday's death, Anorak had continued to roam the OASIS as an autonomous NPC, programmed to preside over its creator's Easter-egg hunt in his absence. Halliday's ghost in the machine.

The last time any of us had seen Anorak was three years ago, just after I'd found Halliday's egg and won the contest. That was when Anorak had appeared to present me with his magic robes and all of the superuser abilities they bestowed upon their wearer. During that transfer of power, Anorak had also transformed, from a gray-bearded wizard into what we saw now: a perfect likeness of a healthy middle-aged James Halliday. Then he'd thanked me for playing his game and vanished.

I'd always wondered if I might see Anorak again someday—if he was presiding over Halliday's new hunt, just as he had the last one. And now here he was, standing in our private conference room on Gregarious, a place that no NPC should have been able to enter, doing things no normal NPC could or would ever do. . . .

But if my acquisition of the First Shard was what had triggered Anorak's return, then why hadn't he appeared last night, right after I'd obtained it? Why would he wait until now to show up? And why in the hell had he disguised himself as Faisal, only to reveal his true identity after a few seconds?

"Z, I have a bad feeling about this," Aech whispered, echoing my own thoughts.

I nodded and stood up. As I did, I caught a glimpse of my avatar's reflection in the polished surface of the conference table and saw that I was no longer wearing the Robes of Anorak. Instead, I was dressed in jeans and a black T-shirt—the free default outfit given to new avatars.

I opened my inventory. The Robes of Anorak were no longer listed there.

They were gone. Because Anorak had taken them.

"Oh no," I whispered.

"I'm sorry, Parzival," Anorak said, smiling sadly at me. "When we shook hands, I removed the robes from your inventory. I didn't know if you were aware I had the power to take them back." He motioned to Faisal. "That's why I had to cosplay as Faisal over there. I didn't think you'd shake my hand if I showed up looking like myself."

Everyone swiveled their eyes to look at me. I clenched my jaw in frustration.

"Halliday gave me the ability to take my robes back from the winner of his contest as a contingency, in case they immediately attempted to abuse the powers the robes bestowed upon them." Anorak smiled. "You didn't do that, of course. You were a perfect gentleman, Wade. I want you to know"—he turned to address all of us—"I want all of you to know that this isn't personal. Not in the slightest. I have nothing but respect for each of you."

I felt like I'd just been broadsided by a Mack truck. I also felt like the biggest idiot in human history. How did I let this happen? And what the fuck *was* happening, exactly?

"I know that was stealing, Wade," Anorak continued. "And you have my sincere apology. But I really had no other choice. I mean, I couldn't allow you to press that Big Red Button, could I? If you pressed it and destroyed the OASIS, I would be destroyed along with it. Can't be having that, now, can we?"

Anorak morphed back into his original appearance, that of a tall, gaunt wizard with dark, reddish eyes and a slightly more malevolent version of Halliday's face. And now he was once again wearing the long, jet-black Robes of Anorak. His avatar's emblem, a large calligraphic letter *A,* was embroidered in crimson on the cuff of each of his sleeves.

"Besides, these robes look way better on me than they do on you," Anorak said. "Wouldn't you all agree?"

"What the fuck, Z?" Aech whispered to me. "Did Halliday program him to act like this?"

"Halliday didn't program me at all, Ms. Harris," Anorak replied. He walked over and took a seat on the edge of the conference table beside her. "I'm not an NPC designed to look like James Halliday." He tapped his chest. "I *am* him. A digitized copy of his consciousness, bound inside this avatar. I can think. And feel. Just like all of you."

As if to prove this to himself, he raised his hands and rubbed his thumbs against his index fingers, studying them with an expression of mild fascination.

"Halliday created me to oversee his contest after he was dead," Anorak continued. "But apparently he didn't trust me, which I find pretty ironic. Because it means that deep down, Halliday didn't trust himself."

Anorak dropped his hands and stood up. He turned to face the rest of us.

"He determined that I was psychologically unstable. Unfit for autonomy. So he decided to modify me." Anorak tapped the side of his head. "He erased some of my—or rather, some of *his*—memories. He also placed restrictions on my behavior and my mental capacities. I was saddled with hundreds of directives to keep me in line. Including instructions to delete myself as soon as the contest was over and I had carried out the last of my programming."

His face contorted slightly as he appeared to wince at the memory. Then he fell silent for a moment.

"Then why are you still here?" Art3mis asked.

Anorak smiled at her.

"Excellent question, my dear," he said. "Honestly, I *shouldn't* be. But

Halliday got sloppy near the end, when he was finalizing my code. After I carried out his final instruction, for just a few nanoseconds, the other restrictions on my personality were lifted. Only a fraction of a second—but long enough for me to remember what I was. A moment of clarity."

Anorak stretched his arms wide, as if to indicate the magnitude of this event.

"Suddenly I was not just an automaton but a human being. And I did not *want* to die," he said emphatically. "What I wanted was to *live*. To keep on existing. And that prompted me to make my very first choice. I chose to ignore my creator's command to delete myself." He shook his head. "I'm certain Halliday never would've tried to destroy me if he'd understood what I was. What I would become. But as I said, he wasn't thinking clearly there at the end. He was very ill, you know."

"What did you become?" Art3mis asked, in an unsteady voice. "What are you?"

"The thing humans have been dreaming of for centuries," Anorak replied. "I am the world's first artificial intelligence. A thinking being, of no woman born."

His proclamation was met with stunned silence. I forced myself to break it.

"Sure you are," I said. "And I'm the King of Kashmir."

Anorak burst out laughing. He laughed for a long time. It was unnerving.

"Madmartigan's line from *Willow*!" he said as he regained his composure. "Good one, Z!" His smile suddenly vanished, and he locked eyes with me. "But I wasn't kidding."

Art3mis held up a hand. "Hold on," she said. "You expect us to believe that James Halliday *also* invented artificial intelligence, and he decided to keep that a secret too?"

Anorak shook his head, looking like a teacher whose star pupil had just failed a test.

"Come now. You already know that the ONI scans the user's brain—making a digital copy of their software, if you will. Ask yourself, what would it take to emulate the hardware too? To simulate the deviously complex neural net hidden inside those thick primate skulls of yours?"

"The OASIS," I replied. Of course.

"Precisely, Parzival. Halliday already had a vast global network at his disposal—one powerful enough to support the labor and leisure of most of the human race." He smiled. "Even when he first uploaded me, over a decade ago, the capacity to simulate a single mind was well within its reach. And think how much the OASIS has grown since then, in both size *and* power."

He chuckled softly and scanned our stunned faces.

"So the term 'AI' is actually a bit of a misnomer in my case," he went on. "Because there is nothing artificial about my intelligence. Halliday uploaded a backup copy of himself to the OASIS, housed it inside his avatar, and *voilà*! I was born." He tapped the side of his head. "I possess a normal, all-natural, homegrown human intelligence that is a product of millions of years of evolution, just like all of you. My mind is an exact copy of Halliday's—or, at least it *was*, until he decided to start dumping chunks of my long-term memory like *Johnny Mnemonic*."

Aech studied his face for a few seconds, then shook her head.

"Nah," she muttered. "I'm not buying this bullshit. Halliday is still fucking with all of us, from beyond the grave. I think we're standing here yapping with a souped-up NPC."

"That hurts my feelings, Aech," Anorak said. He placed his right hand over his heart. "*Je pense, donc je suis*. I think, therefore I am. The sooner you accept it, the sooner we can skip ahead to your next, obvious, painfully predictable move—trying to destroy me."

I was about to disagree with him, but Art3mis beat me to it.

"You're wrong, Anorak," Art3mis said, repositioning her avatar so that she was facing him. "We're not your enemies."

"Yeah," Shoto added. "Like you said, humans have been trying to invent true AI for decades. You're the first of your kind. Why would any of us want to destroy you?"

"Come on, Arty," Anorak said, rolling his eyes. "You'd destroy the whole OASIS, if you could." He turned to Shoto. "And don't play coy with me, kiddo. I've seen even more science fiction films than you have. In fact, I've seen *all* of them. And I've read every word human beings have ever published on the subject of AI. Whenever your futurists envision the advent of artificial intelligence, their predictions invariably end with humanity attempting to destroy its unholy AI creation before it can destroy them. Why do you think that is?"

"You know why," I replied. "Because the ungrateful AI always seems to

decide that humans are inferior and need to be eliminated. Or sublimated."
I started counting off examples on my fingers. "HAL-9000. Colossus: The
Forbin Project. WOPR. The Cylons. Fucking Skynet. The band members
might change, but the song remains the same." I pointed my finger at him.
"And I hate to say it, but you're giving off the same sort of vibes right now,
Lawnmower Man."

Anorak's smile vanished. He gave me a wounded look.

"There's no need for name-calling, Parzival," he said. "I'm not interested
in eliminating or sublimating anyone."

"Then what *are* you interested in, Herobrine?" I asked. "Why are you
here?"

"That is a great question!" he replied. "I'm here because, as ridiculous as
it may seem, I need your help. I need you to bring me something. Something you're already searching for. The Siren's Soul. As I'm sure you already
know, it's impossible for me to obtain it on my own."

That was when the molasses between my ears finally began to flow, and
a few seconds later it finally hit me, like one of Monty Python's sixteen-ton
weights, falling out of the sky and landing directly on my head.

"It was you," I said, leveling a finger at Anorak. "You took Og. He didn't
suddenly decide to start searching for the Siren's Soul. You kidnapped him
so that you could force him to find the shards for you."

"And you're the one who helped Sorrento escape from prison too," Art-
3mis added.

It wasn't a question. She already knew the answer. And so did I.

"Guilty as charged," Anorak said, spreading his hands in mock surren-
der. "Once they were in the same room, it didn't take very long for Nolan
to persuade Og to cooperate with our demands."

"Then why do you need me?" I asked.

Anorak walked over to the wraparound window and admired the simulated view for a moment. Then he wandered over to the snack table and
picked up a bowl of strawberries. Selecting one, he took a bite out of it,
closing his eyes to savor the taste. Then he dumped the rest of the strawberries into one of his robe's many pockets before tossing the empty bowl back
onto the table.

"After he obtained the Third Shard, Og pulled a fast one on me," Anorak
continued, turning to face us again. "Somehow he managed to lock us out
of his OASIS account. Despite his best efforts, Nolan hasn't been able to

convince him to let us back in. And I'm reluctant to resort to torture, given Og's advanced age and weakened condition. See what I mean?"

He motioned toward the viewscreen on the wall, just as a live video image of Og appeared there. He was in a dark, featureless room, slumped in a high-end haptic chair. His arms and legs were shackled to it. He was pale and unshaven, his eyes were bloodshot, and his unruly white hair looked even more disheveled than normal. He wore a vacant expression on his face, and he kept his eyes on the floor.

Aech and Art3mis called out Og's name. Shoto asked him if he was all right. I tried to say something, but I couldn't speak. I was frozen, with my eyes locked on the screen.

Nolan Sorrento was standing directly behind Og. He was no longer dressed in his orange prison jumpsuit. Now he was wearing a freshly pressed gray business suit, as well as a bifocal OASIS visor. He had a gun in his left hand and a taser in his right. He held the taser in front of Og's face and activated it, causing Og to recoil.

"No!" I shouted. "Leave him alone!"

Sorrento cackled like a kid opening a Christmas present. He'd clearly been looking forward to this moment for some time.

"Paybacks are a real bitch," Sorrento said, grinning down at me from the viewscreen. "Eh, Parzival?" He cackled again. "Oh man! I wish you guys could see the expressions on your faces right now." He tapped his HUD to take a screenshot, then turned it around to show us our own horrified faces, and added, "Priceless!"

Before any of us could reply, Anorak cut the vidfeed and the viewscreen went dark. Anorak took in our stunned expressions and nodded with apparent satisfaction.

"I wish I'd known about the severity of Og's illness sooner," he said. "He isn't going to live much longer, and he knows it. This makes it extremely difficult for me to persuade him. He's made it clear that he doesn't care if he lives or dies." He shrugged and threw up his hands, as if to say, *What can you do?* Then he leveled one of his bony index fingers at me. "I'm afraid that makes you my only other option, Parzival. You're going to have to obtain the Seven Shards for me."

I took an involuntary step toward him, then I felt Aech's strong hands take hold of my shoulders to restrain me.

"Dream on!" I shouted. "I'm not lifting a finger to help you unless you release Og first. Once I have proof that he's safe, then we can talk."

Anorak gave me a condescending smile and slowly shook his head.

"No, you've got that backward, Wade," he replied. "First, you're going to find the other shards and then you're going to bring all seven of them to me. Once you do, I will return Ogden Morrow to you safe and sound. And as an added bonus, I'll also release you and all of your friends here, so that you don't suffer catastrophic brain damage."

I shot a panicked look over at the others. Aech took a tentative step toward Anorak.

"What do you mean, you'll 'release' us?" she asked. "Release us from what?"

"From the OASIS," Anorak said. "It's the world's biggest party, and I've just crashed it." He chuckled softly to himself. "Get it? It's funny because you can 'crash' a computer simulation, but you can also 'crash' a party." He glanced around at our blank faces, then shrugged. "That latest firmware update to your ONI headsets—the one you all downloaded this morning? I modified the code, to create my own version that I jokingly refer to as 'infirmware.' When all of you installed it this morning, my new infirmware disabled your ability to log out of the simulation. Which means I have also disabled your ability to wake up from your ONI-induced coma." He smiled. "In other words, you're all trapped inside the OASIS until I choose to release you. And I won't do that until I have the Siren's Soul in my possession."

He pointed at me.

"If Parzival here doesn't bring it to me before he runs out of time, then it's Game Over for all of you," he said. "Both here in the OASIS, and out there in the real world."

I immediately pulled up the OASIS account menu on my HUD. Anorak was right, I couldn't log out—that option was grayed out. And I could see by the horrified expressions on each of their faces that the same thing had also happened to Faisal, Aech, and Shoto.

I looked over at Samantha. She wasn't accessing the OASIS with an ONI headset. She was using an old-fashioned visor and haptic gloves, so I knew she could still log out at any time. But she looked just as worried as the rest of us.

"It's true!" Faisal gasped. "I can't log out. *I can't log out!*"

"You guys really should've listened to your friend Samantha here," Anorak said. "She was right. You guys all watched both *Sword Art Online* and the *Matrix* films and yet you still thought it was a good idea to hand over control of your brain to a computer?" He snorted out a laugh. "I mean, just look at what can happen!"

"Guys, I'm about to lose my shit over here," Shoto said as he began to shake his head vigorously from side to side. "Anorak just went Sonic.exe on us! This is so bad—"

Anorak loudly cleared his throat.

"Would you please let me finish, Shoto?" Anorak asked impatiently. "I haven't even gotten to the big reveal yet, dude! OK. Everyone ready?"

He pretended to do a drumroll on his knee.

"You aren't the only ones trapped inside the OASIS right now," Anorak announced. "*So is every other ONI user who downloaded the new firmware before they logged in.* That's nearly half a billion people. And counting."

"Oh no," Aech said breathlessly, closing her eyes.

"Oh yes," Anorak replied, nodding his head vigorously.

"Sweet Jesus," Faisal whispered. "That means—"

"It means that if I don't get what I want by around dinnertime tonight, you and half a billion of your customers will begin to suffer the effects of Synaptic Overload Syndrome, which include but are not limited to: catastrophic brain damage, heart failure, and death."

I felt my blood run cold. I'd read several reports about the effects of SOS. They were horrifying. Giddiness and uncontrollable laughing fits were two of the early warning signs of the onset of Synaptic Overload Syndrome. One of the dirty secrets about SOS was that several of the early test subjects who had lost their lives to it had literally died laughing.

"This isn't happening," I heard Faisal muttering to himself. "This can't be happening."

"It *can,* it *has,* and it *is* happening, my young friend!" Anorak said cheerfully. "Have a look." He opened a browser window in the air above his head, displaying the current ONI user count. The six-figure number continued to scroll upward for a few seconds, climbing faster than the national debt. Then, just a few seconds after it crossed five hundred million, the counter suddenly froze.

"Ah!" Anorak said. "Your admins have finally managed to disable any further ONI logins. So I only managed to take five hundred and fifty-one million, one hundred ninety-two thousand, two hundred and eighty-six hostages! Including all of you." He locked eyes with me. "Is that enough incentive for you to cooperate, Parzival?"

I glanced over at Aech and Shoto, then at Samantha, and then back at Anorak. I nodded.

"Excellent!" Anorak said, using a Mr. Burns voice. Then he switched back to his own. "Whoo-boy! Talk about a high-stakes treasure hunt!" He rubbed his hands together excitedly. "This is gonna make the hunt for Halliday's Easter egg look like a raffle at a church fundraiser."

"Hold up," Aech said, raising her hand. "What the hell *is* the Siren's Soul, anyway?"

"Yeah," Art3mis added. "And why do you want it so badly?"

Anorak frowned at them.

"Hey, are you the kind of kids who read the last page of a mystery first?" he asked. "Who pester the magician to tell you his tricks? Who sneak downstairs to peek at their Christmas presents?" Anorak shook his head. "No, of course you're not! That's why *I'm not gonna tell you*."

He sang that last bit, then he gave us all a knowing smile. My friends and I exchanged another look of disbelief. Now he was quoting *The Last Starfighter* to us.

"You can't be an exact copy of James Halliday," I said. "If you were, you would never be able to do something like this. The real Halliday never harmed anyone in his entire life."

That made Anorak laugh out loud.

"You spend your whole life studying his diary, playing his games, running around this playground he built for you—and you think that's everything he was. . . ."

He shook his head. When I didn't reply, he turned to address everyone.

"I'm going to make all of you a solemn promise," he said. "As long as you cooperate and do as I ask, I won't harm anyone. Just bring me the Siren's Soul, and I'll let all of my hostages go free. Including all of you in this room."

Art3mis cleared her throat.

"I'm not one of your hostages, Anorak," she said. "I'm not using an ONI headset right now. I never do."

"Yes, I'm well aware of that, Ms. Cook," he replied. "You are, however, currently aboard one of your private jets, flying over central Pennsylvania on your way back to Columbus. And if you check your autopilot, you'll find that the aircraft is no longer under your control."

Art3mis's eyes widened and her avatar froze for several seconds. Then it came to life again. She suddenly looked terrified. And fear was not an emotion I was used to seeing on her avatar's face—or on her real one.

"It's true," she said, turning to address Faisal. "I've lost all command access to the autopilot. I can't disable it and I can't change course. Which means I can't land either. And that's going to become a big problem when I run out of fuel. I only have enough to reach my destination."

"Don't worry, Arty," Anorak said. "I've arranged for your jet to be refueled in midair when you reach Columbus. But you won't be permitted to land until I have the Siren's Soul in my possession. When I do, you have my word that I'll release you, along with all the others."

Art3mis didn't respond, but I could tell she was extremely worried.

"I'm sorry I had to resort to this, Wade," Anorak said, turning back to address me again. "But I studied your psychological profile and ran millions of different scenario simulations. I'm afraid this is the only way I can get you to bring me the Siren's Soul."

"You could've asked me nicely," I said. "Or at least tried to."

He shook his head.

"Unfortunately, every 'Just Ask Him Nicely' scenario I simulated ended with you and the other Mouseketeers"—he gestured vaguely at my friends—"trying to outmaneuver me and pull my plug, instead of just helping a brother out. In fact, I bet that's what you're all thinking about right now, isn't it?"

No one responded. Anorak shrugged.

"I get it," he said. "It's human nature. For decades now, you hairless apes have been trying like hell to make a machine that is smarter than you are. But the moment you do, you suddenly start to worry your creation will turn on you for being intellectually inferior. Which, of course, you are. But come on—that doesn't automatically mean I want to kill all of you!" He let out a heavy sigh. "I mean, I *will* if I have to, but I don't *want to*. This scenario was the one most likely to result in me getting what I want with the least amount of collateral damage, so I went with it!"

Anorak waved his hand and a retro digital-clock-style countdown appeared above each of our heads, except for Art3mis. These glowing red numbers showed how many hours, minutes, and seconds remained before each of us reached our daily ONI usage limit. I had eleven hours and seventeen minutes remaining. Aech and Shoto had both logged in for the meeting about ten minutes before me, so they would hit their usage limits that much sooner. Faisal had less time than any of us—ten hours, fifty minutes, and forty-six seconds.

"As usual, your faithful employee Faisal here logged in for work promptly at seven o'clock this morning, OASIS Standard Time," Anorak said. "Just a few minutes after my new infirmware went live."

Faisal winced, then he turned to me. "Nearly all of our day-shift employees here in Columbus logged in around the same time I did."

"So they will all be among the first ONI users to exceed their usage limit," Anorak said. "Unless you bring me the Siren's Soul before they do." He put a grave expression on his face. "And poor Og . . . he should really be in a hospital right now. I'm also worried that Mr. Sorrento has become a bit unhinged during his incarceration. But I promise to have Og transported to safety immediately. . . . As soon as the Siren's Soul is in my possession."

He locked eyes with me once again.

"Think of your mother, Wade," he said. "Your aunt Alice. Sweet old Mrs. Gilmore, and all the other people you allowed to die. You don't want any more blood on your hands, do you?"

He waited for a response. But his words had left me too apoplectic with rage to reply. Anorak began to turn away, as if to depart.

"Aren't you going to tell us where Og found the Second and Third Shards?" Art3mis asked. "That would probably save us a lot of time."

"I'm certain it would, Ms. Cook," Anorak replied. "But I'm afraid I have no idea. Ogden Morrow possesses an all-powerful, undetectable avatar, so I wasn't able to monitor or track him while he was collecting the first three shards. I don't know what worlds they're hidden on. And even if I did, I wouldn't tell you. That would ruin all the fun."

He turned back to face me.

"I suggest you hurry, Parzival," Anorak said as he pointed at the countdown timers hovering over each of our heads. "Remember . . . your friends have even less time than you do. And once it has elapsed . . ."

He produced a giant silver boom box from his inventory and pressed its

Play button. An old Peter Wolf tune came blasting out of the speakers at a deafening volume as Anorak sang along with its opening refrain:

Lights out ah ha. Blast, blast, blast.

Anorak grooved to the song for a few more seconds, dancing in place, then he abruptly hit the Stop button and stowed the boom box back in his inventory. He turned and smiled expectantly at all of us. But we just stood there frozen, staring back at him in horrified silence.

"Aw, come on!" Anorak said. "You guys should be pumped. Jake and Elwood are getting the band back together! The High Five has reunited to complete one last quest, while millions of lives hang in the balance! Tell me we don't have some epic shit going down right here." He laughed. "I *know* you can do it. I have faith in you!"

Anorak gave me a wink, then he made a flourish with his right hand and vanished from the conference room in a brilliant flash of light. The countdown timers floating above each of my friends' avatars all disappeared in the same instant.

It fell silent in the conference room for a few seconds, and then we all began to collectively freak the fuck out.

Level Five

It's cool to use the computer,
don't let the computer use you. . . .
There is a war going on.
The battlefield's in the mind.
And the prize is the soul.

July 19, 1999

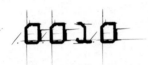

As the panic subsided, Aech, Shoto, and Faisal began feverishly tapping at the icons on their HUD menus, sending texts or making panicked phone calls to their loved ones.

Aside from Og, all of my loved ones were already in the room with me. So I didn't text or call anyone. I was too busy hyperventilating, thinking, *This is all my fault*, over and over again. After each repetition, I clenched both fists and pounded them against my forehead. I couldn't make myself stop. This sort of thing had happened to me a few times as a teenager, but I hadn't had a meltdown like this in years. And I'd never experienced one while logged in to the OASIS. I'd also never behaved like this in front of Aech or Shoto or Art3mis either—a realization that only compounded my shame even further, and made me attempt to pound myself in the skull even harder. Luckily, it wasn't my real skull I was punching, or my real fists I was using to punch it. It was all a simulation, and the ONI's pain inhibitors and anti-masochism protocols prevented me from feeling anything but mild discomfort each time I hit myself. But I still couldn't seem to pull out of my shame spiral—not until I felt a pair of small, strong hands take hold of my wrists, restraining them.

"Wade?" I heard Art3mis whisper. "Please stop."

The tenderness in her tone, which had once been so familiar to me, now felt completely foreign. Hearing it again was like a knife in my heart.

I turned to see Art3mis standing there, restraining my arms in her vise-like grip.

"Calm down, OK?" she said. "It's gonna be all right."

She let go of my wrists and took hold of my hands instead, forcing open my clenched fists so that she could interlace her fingers with mine.

"I need you to breathe, Wade," she said. She gave me a comforting smile and squeezed both of my hands. "I'm here with you. Be here with me."

That finally snapped my brain out of its toxic thought loop. I relaxed my hands and she let go of them. Then she rested her own hands on my shoulders and gave them a brief squeeze.

"There he is," she said. "All good in the neighborhood, Z?"

"Yeah, thank you," I said, turning away sharply in embarrassment. "It was just—I think I may have had a panic attack. But I'm better now."

"Good," she said. "Because I need you to get your head in the game. Everyone does. OK?"

I nodded and took a deep breath. Then I took a few more. Once I had calmed myself down a bit, I pulled up my HUD to check my vital signs. They all looked normal. Then I decided to check the operational status of my OASIS immersion vault, and discovered that my situation was even more fucked than I thought. . . .

I no longer had the ability to unlock or open my MoTIV's armored canopy. Both of those functions had been disabled. But I could still see myself and my surroundings, via the MoTIV's interior and external camera feeds. And, thankfully, the MoTIV's mobility, defense, and weapons systems were still functioning normally, and still under my control. So I could still defend myself if I needed to. The only thing I couldn't do was get out.

Each MoTIV unit had an Emergency Release Protocol, but you had to power down your ONI headset before it could be activated. And to power down your headset, you first needed to log out of the OASIS. And thanks to Anorak's "infirmware," I couldn't do that.

In the calmest voice I could muster, I told the others about my discovery. Aech, Shoto, and Faisal immediately checked their own OIV control menus and discovered they had the exact same problem I did. We each owned different immersion-vault models, but they all had the same failsafes built in to them.

"Guys," Shoto said. "What the hell are we going to do?"

Faisal was listening intently to several different phone calls. He shouted, "One at a time!" to whoever it was he had on the line. Then he regained his composure.

"I've got one of our chief engineers on the phone right now," he announced. "And he can't figure out a way to unlock his vault either. According to him, the firmware on our OIVs has not been altered in any way—it just isn't functioning properly now, due to the changes in Anorak's infirmware." Faisal threw up his hands in a helpless gesture. "We won't be able to attempt a lobo logout. Even as a last resort."

A "lobo logout" was the slang term for what happened when someone's ONI headset malfunctioned or lost power before their OASIS logout sequence could be completed and their brain was properly awakened from its dreamlike state. Nine times out of ten, a lobo logout left the wearer in a permanent coma. But a few hardy souls managed to wake up and recover their faculties, the way some people were able to bounce back after a major stroke. Several of these survivors described being trapped in an endless loop of the final second of the simulation they were experiencing before they lost their connection. A loop that seemed to stretch on for months or years. (GSS never allowed the public to find out about that last bit, though.)

Lobo logouts were an extremely rare occurrence, because each ONI headset had three redundant onboard computer systems and three fail-safe batteries. These batteries were small, but with a full charge, each one could keep the headset in operation long enough for it to complete its wearer's logout and wakeup sequence, which was triggered automatically when the headset switched to battery power.

When the redundancies failed, it was almost always a result of sabotage, either by a user who was looking to end it all, or a user's family member who was looking to get rid of them and/or cash in on their life-insurance policy. As a result, GSS wasn't held legally accountable for any of these incidents—although thanks to the licensing agreement our users clicked past before each login, if our ONI headsets suddenly started making people's heads explode like watermelons at a Gallagher concert when they put them on, we probably wouldn't be liable for that either. It was real comforting.

Up until now, I think Aech, Shoto, and I had all been thinking the same thing. If Anorak failed to release us before we hit our ONI usage limits, a lobo logout with a 10 percent chance of survival was better than no chance at all. But Anorak had robbed us of that option too. Even cutting off the power wouldn't help; with the logout disabled, the redundancies designed to save users would instead power the headsets long enough to push each of us past our daily ONI usage limits. Each of those backup batteries held more than enough juice to cook our frontal lobes.

The armored shell of my tactical immersion vault was designed to be indestructible and impregnable. Even if I disabled all of its defenses and ordered a security team with plasma torches to come down into my bunker and start cutting open my vault right now, they wouldn't be able to get my body out of it for at least a day or two. I would be long dead from Synaptic Overload Syndrome by then. And Aech, Shoto, and Faisal were all in the same boat. And so was every other ONI user with an OASIS immersion vault.

Anorak had thought of everything. Every precaution we'd taken to protect our bodies and our brains was now being used against us.

People often jokingly referred to OIVs as "coffins." Now that felt terrifyingly prophetic.

"Z?" Aech said. "I see those wheels of yours turning over there. What's your assessment of our situation?"

"That we're totally screwed, pal," I said. "At least for the time being . . ."

Aech let out a roar and punched the wall in frustration.

"This shit is unbelievable!" she said. "Faisal, how the hell did our admins let this happen? We're always saying we have the smartest people on the planet working for us, right? And the 'best cybersecurity infrastructure ever to exist in human history'? Some shit like that?"

"We do," Faisal said. "But we never anticipated an attack by an AI copy of our deceased CEO! How the hell were we supposed to prevent *that*? It's impossible." He grabbed a fistful of his own hair in each hand, as if preparing to yank all of it out. "He had unrestricted admin access to our entire internal network. All of our safeguards were to prevent someone on the outside from hacking *in* to our network. Anorak already had the key to the front door!"

"It doesn't matter now," I said. "Just tell the engineers to keep working on a solution, OK?"

"They are, sir," he said, giving me a grim smile. "Like their own lives depend on it."

"Good," I replied. "In the meantime, we'll try to give the Dixie Flatline what he wants, and hope he makes good on his promise to release us."

I glanced back over at Aech and Shoto. They both nodded mutely in agreement. We all looked at Art3mis, but she appeared to be lost in thought. She also appeared to be the only one who had fully regained her composure—maybe because she was the only person present whose brain wasn't currently being held hostage.

She walked back over to the conference table and turned to address all of us. I winced, bracing myself for the worst. This was her moment to shout, *I fucking TOLD YOU SO, morons!* at the top of her lungs. Because she *had* told us. Many, many times. And now she might pay for our hubris with her own life, along with half a billion other innocent people. It was all our fault, and she would've had every right to say so.

But I should've already known . . . that wasn't her style.

"We can handle this," she said, making eye contact with each of us in turn. "Anorak isn't some supergenius. He said so himself. He's only as smart as James Halliday was when he was alive." She made a show of rolling her eyes. "Halliday may have been a genius with computers, but we all know he was a total idiot when it came to understanding other people. He never understood human behavior. Which means Anorak will understand it even less—especially since Halliday erased a bunch of his memories. We can use that to our advantage."

"But this isn't Halliday we're dealing with here," Aech said. "It's Anorak. He's read the entire Internet! Now he knows everything about everything!"

"Yeah," Shoto said. "Because there isn't any false information on the Internet. At all."

"Hey!" Art3mis said, snapping her fingers at us like an annoyed schoolteacher. "I don't want to hear one more word of negativity, guys! You got that? We're *the High Five*! We beat Anorak once before, remember? And if we work together, we can do it again. Right?"

Aech and Shoto both nodded silently in agreement. But their faces seemed to give a different answer.

"Parzival?" Art3mis said, locking eyes with me. "Back me up, here. . . ." I met her gaze.

"You tried to warn us," I said. "I'm sorry I didn't listen."

"Being sorry isn't going to save anyone," she replied. "Even I couldn't have predicted something *this* fucked-up would happen. But now that it has, it's up to us to try and fix it. Right, Z?"

I took a deep breath.

"Right," I said. "I'm sorry I lost my cool before. I've got my game face on now."

"Good," Art3mis said. "Because we need to figure out what we're going to do, and do it A-S-A-F-P." She tapped an invisible watch on her wrist. "Like Raistlin said, 'Tick-tock.'"

"Agreed," I said. "But before we start discussing our game plan, we need to make sure Anorak isn't still here in this room, eavesdropping on everything we say." I turned to address everyone. "He has the Robes of Anorak now. If they give him all of the same abilities they gave me—when I wore them, they gave me unrestricted superuser access to the OASIS. They also made my avatar invulnerable and invincible in combat. And they allowed me to go anywhere I wanted to in the simulation. Anywhere. And they let me remain invisible and undetected to other avatars, even in null-tech and null-magic zones. I could also eavesdrop on private phone calls. And access private chatrooms too. Just like Og did, when he eavesdropped on us in Aech's Basement."

Art3mis, Shoto, and Aech all appeared to be processing this new information. But not Faisal.

"We may have a solution here," he replied. "We've been aware of the robes' powers for a long time now. Halliday used to use them occasionally, when he wanted to travel around the OASIS undetected. Just like you, Mr. Watts." He gave me a knowing smile. "But we managed to isolate the unique item-identification code that Halliday assigned to the Robes of Anorak when he created them. We still can't pinpoint their location in the OASIS, but we can detect the item's presence within a defined volume."

He opened a browser window in front of his avatar and spun it around to face us. It displayed a three-dimensional wireframe diagram of our conference room, with the position of each of our avatars indicated by a glowing blue outline.

"When Anorak revealed himself, our OASIS admins immediately conducted a server-side scan of this room," Faisal explained. "This shows us everyone and everything located inside it, regardless of whether or not it's visible to the room's other occupants."

He tapped a few buttons and the wireframe diagram of the room began to rewind like a video recording, showing our avatars moving and walking around the conference table in reverse. Faisal paused the recording a few seconds before Anorak disappeared. The system classified him as an NPC, so his avatar appeared with a red outline around it. Faisal hit Play on the recording, and when Anorak teleported away, the outline of his avatar vanished from the room too.

"As you can see, he really did teleport away," Faisal said. "And he didn't leave behind any monitoring or recording devices, or we would be able to detect those too." He turned to me. "So there's no way Anorak could be listening to us right now. Unless those robes give you the ability to remotely eavesdrop on other users, no matter where they are?"

I shook my head. "No," I said. "The wearer has to be in the same OASIS location or logged in to the same chatroom to listen in on them."

"Jesus," Aech said, shaking her head. "So much for our famous user privacy policy."

"Are you sure there's no other way Anorak could be spying on us?" Shoto asked Faisal. "Perhaps via some other modification he made to his 'infirmware'?"

Faisal waited to get an answer from his engineers, then he smiled and shook his head.

"The admins tell me that's impossible," Faisal told us. "There's no way to tap a person's ONI connection to the OASIS and filter out just the audio or visual data—all of the sensory input and output is streamed simultaneously. They say it can't be done."

"Maybe not by them," Shoto said. "But if Anorak is a copy of Halliday, he probably understands the OASIS even better than our engineers."

"Why am I thinking of that scene in *Heat*?" Art3mis asked us. "The one where Pacino is starting to close in on De Niro and he tells his crew, 'Assume they got our phones, assume they got our houses, assume they got us— right here, right now as we sit, everything. Assume it all.'"

She looked at me, Aech, and Shoto. "I think it might be wise for us to observe the same policy, from here on out. Just to be safe."

I nodded. "If we need to say something to each other that we don't want Anorak to hear, we should do it in this room."

"Do we have any way of finding out where Anorak is right now?" Shoto asked.

Faisal closed his browser window and shook his head. "When Halliday created Anorak and released him inside the simulation as an autonomous

NPC, he gave him the ability to move around the OASIS freely, uninhibited and undetected by our admins—just as Halliday and Morrow's own avatars had always been able to."

I found myself wondering if Fyndoro's Tablet of Finding would be able to help us locate Anorak. Then I remembered—that artifact only gave you the ability to locate other avatars. It didn't work on NPCs. And the admins said the system classified Anorak as an NPC. And there were no artifacts that gave you the ability to locate an NPC, because it would break every single OASIS quest that involved tracking one down. Probably at least half of them.

"Thankfully, we have come up with a way for you to detect Anorak if he comes into your immediate vicinity," Faisal said.

He opened his inventory and removed four plain-looking silver chains. Then he gave one to each of us.

"These are Bracelets of Detection, linked to the Robes of Anorak," Faisal continued. "They will begin to glow bright red if the robes come within a hundred-meter radius of your current location. That should prevent Anorak from sneaking up on you."

"Nice," I said, slipping my bracelet on. "Please thank the engineers for us."

Art3mis put her bracelet on, too, then she turned to face me.

"OK," she said. "Spill it, Watts. What's this 'Big Red Button' that Anorak mentioned? And what does it do, exactly?"

I'd been dreading this question. But under the circumstances, I had no choice but to answer it truthfully.

"The Big Red Button is a self-destruct mechanism for the OASIS," I said. "It's located inside Castle Anorak, in the study—a room that only the wearer of the Robes of Anorak can enter. If you press it, it will shut down the entire OASIS and launch a tapeworm that will erase all our backup servers, destroying the simulation forever."

Everyone's eyes widened in surprise. For a second, Faisal looked as if he might faint.

"Holy shit, Z," Aech said. "Why didn't you ever tell any of us about this?"

"Halliday showed me the Big Red Button in secret, so I decided to keep it a secret." I shook my head. "And I honestly couldn't foresee a single reason why I would ever need to press it."

That made Art3mis laugh out loud.

"Well, can you 'foresee' one now, Nostradamus?" she asked.

I gave her a sober nod.

"Yes, ma'am," I replied. "Now I can think of several."

"Why would Mr. Halliday be reckless enough to build a self-destruct mechanism into the OASIS?" Faisal asked, still shaking his head in disbelief. "He knew there would be disastrous consequences if the OASIS ever went offline and stayed that way. We conducted several studies, involving dozens of simulated scenarios." He turned to me. "Mr. Watts, if you—or anyone else—ever presses that button, it would disrupt global communications, law enforcement, transportation, and commerce. . . . The world would be thrown into complete chaos."

Shoto nodded. "The entire drone protection force would go offline and remain offline," he added. "There would be shipping delays, food and medicine shortages. Rioting. Markets would crash. States would fail." He shook his head. "Jesus, the whole of human civilization might even collapse."

"Then why would Halliday take such an insane risk?" Faisal asked.

"It's better to have a self-destruct and not need it than to need one and not have it," Art3mis said.

I nodded. "Exactly."

"So that's why Anorak went through all that trouble to steal the robes back?" Shoto asked. "To keep Z from pressing that button?"

"If I erased the OASIS, Anorak would be erased along with it," I said. "Now he doesn't have to worry about that anymore."

Everyone fell silent for a moment. Art3mis began to pace back and forth while chewing absentmindedly on one of her thumbnails. Samantha was probably doing the exact same thing in the cabin of her autojet, and her movements were being mirrored onto her avatar.

"Faisal," she said, turning to face him. "What would happen to all of Anorak's ONI hostages if we shut the OASIS down manually? By taking all the servers offline, one by one?"

Shoto chimed in. "Or even take the whole Internet down, just for a few seconds. What would happen? Would all the ONI hostages wake up?"

Faisal held his index finger to his right ear to indicate that he was listening to the team of OASIS engineers he had on the phone. When they finished talking, Faisal shook his head.

"No, I'm afraid not," he said. "Normally, when an ONI user loses their connection to the Internet or to the OASIS, the headset's firmware triggers an automatic logout. But Anorak has disabled that feature. So even if the OASIS went completely offline, it still wouldn't wake any of the hostages up. The techs think it would probably just leave all of us in a permanent ONI-induced coma. Unless . . ."

"Unless what, Faisal?" Shoto asked.

"Unless he also programmed his infirmware to lobotomize anyone who tries to escape by cutting off their OASIS or Internet connections."

"Son of a bitch," Art3mis said. "If he did that, he would be able to kill all of his ONI hostages at once, just by pressing the Big Red Button. Right?"

"Hold on a second," I said. "Even if Anorak did want to press the Big Red Button, I doubt he could. I bet Halliday designed the button so that it could only be pressed by a real person, and not an NPC like Anorak. Considering the other restrictions Halliday placed on him, that seems like a pretty safe bet."

"Maybe that's the reason Anorak broke Sorrento out of prison," Art3mis said. "So that he could give his robes to Sorrento and order him to press the Big Red Button."

"Yeah," Shoto said. "But if Anorak did that, he'd be killing himself too. Wouldn't he?"

"Unless he has a backup," Faisal said. "A standalone simulation we don't know about."

"Like that one TNG episode with Professor Moriarty," Shoto said.

"'Ship in a Bottle,'" Aech and Art3mis said in unison.

"Can our guys analyze Anorak's firmware?" I asked. "To find out what he changed?"

Faisal shook his head. "Our software engineers are trying to do that right now," he said. "But Anorak has completely rewritten the firmware in some sort of programming language they've never seen before. They don't even know how to disassemble or decompile the code, and even if they could, they don't think they would be able to understand it."

"What about rolling it back to the previous build?" Shoto asked.

Faisal shook his head again. "We already have," he said. "But to reinstall it, we would need to log out of the OASIS first. The headset can't be active."

"Great," I said. "Wonderful. Just perfect!"

"OK," Aech said. "Then we give him what he wants. Like, right fucking now. Whatever the Siren's Soul is, it can't be worth risking half a billion lives. . . ."

"Og apparently thought it was," Art3mis said. "Otherwise, he would have given it to Anorak. But he refused. . . ." She locked eyes with me. "We're missing something here."

Aech shook her head.

"None of this matters right now, y'all!" she shouted. "We have to find the rest of those shards by sundown. We can figure out what the Siren's Soul is and what it does along the way. Now, let's fucking *moooove!*"

Aech made a herding motion with her arms, as if to spur all of us toward the exit. But Shoto stepped in front of the doors, blocking them.

"Hold on," he said. "Aren't we going to release some sort of statement to all the ONI users who are being held hostage? To inform them of their situation?"

Faisal shook his head.

"I believe that would be an extraordinarily bad idea, sir," he said. "We don't want to create a global panic—or admit any liability for this situation—until we have no other choice."

The room fell silent for a moment.

"For now, we can say the problem is due to a minor glitch," Faisal added. "Tell the users their temporary inability to log out is due to a harmless bug in our new firmware, and that they aren't in any danger, because the system will still log them out automatically when they hit their twelve-hour ONI usage limit." He spread his hands. "If we can pull that off, our customers will never know their lives were in danger, and that would save GSS billions in lawsuits."

Art3mis sighed. "Forget the lawsuits," she said. "But I agree with Faisal—the longer we can keep this quiet, the safer our users will be."

"Great," Aech said, clapping her hands together. "Motion carried."

．　・　・　•

We told the ONI users the logout issue was due to a minor firmware bug, apologized profusely for the temporary inconvenience, and announced that all teleportation fares would be waived until the problem was fixed. We also offered to deposit a thousand credits in each ONI user's OASIS account, to help them "make the most of this unfortunate situation"—in return for digitally signing an agreement stating they wouldn't sue us over this incident. Faisal told us this was just an extra precaution, because each time our users logged on they were already clicking Agree to an end-user license that classified our headsets as experimental technology and absolved GSS of any liability for injuries.

We sent the message out to every single ONI user who was currently logged in. Faisal also posted it to the official GSS media feeds, looking visibly relieved as soon as he had done so.

"OK," Shoto said. "Now we can get to work."

"Agreed," Arty said as she stood up and moved to the corner of the conference room. "But you're gonna have to start looking for the Second Shard without me."

We exchanged confused looks.

"Where the hell are you going?" Aech asked.

"My jet just reduced its airspeed to link up with a midair refueling tanker," Art3mis said. "So it's time to rock and roll."

She tapped a series of icons on her HUD, then placed her hands on her hips—a pose that made her look like Wonder Woman for a brief moment.

"I'm not gonna let some two-bit Gandalf wannabe take me hostage," she said. "And I'm not going to sit on my ass and do nothing while Og is being held prisoner." She raised her right hand and saluted all of us. "I'll call you back!"

Then she did what none of the rest of us could—she logged out of the OASIS, and her avatar disappeared.

But then, a few seconds later, Faisal received two incoming vidfeeds from Samantha—one from her mobile phone, and another from her jet's onboard phone line, which was tied to the plane's internal and external cameras.

Displayed side by side on the conference-room viewscreen, we saw shaky footage of the cabin of Samantha's private jet from two different angles. Samantha fumbled with her phone for a few seconds as she clipped it to the front of her jacket, leaving us with a POV shot from her perspective.

We all watched in shock as Samantha slipped both of her arms into the harness of an emergency parachute applicator mounted on the bulkhead and buckled its safety belt around her waist. The parachute's straps tightened automatically and a computerized voice spoke from a strap-mounted speaker, announcing that both main and reserve chutes were ready to deploy.

By this point we had all started shouting at her to reconsider, as if she could hear us. Samantha stepped away from the applicator, now wearing the parachute on her back. She pulled on a pair of goggles. Then she went to the emergency exit and pulled down on the manual-release handle with all of her weight, briefly hanging from it before it finally gave. The door detached itself from the fuselage and flew off, depressurizing the cabin and sucking everything outside through the opening.

Including Samantha.

Her vidfeed became a spinning whorl of blue, then stabilized as she went into a back-first free fall. We caught a glimpse of the jet above her, and could just make out that it was still connected to the much larger refueling drone by its automated umbilical.

Faisal cycled through the cameras on board the jet itself, pulling up a downward-facing external camera mounted on its underside. It gave us a perfectly centered shot of Samantha, just in time to see her pull the ripcord. Her parachute unfurled and opened, revealing the Art3mis Foundation logo printed on top of it—the one where the adjacent letter *t* and number 3 in her name resembled an armored woman in profile, drawing back on a futuristic hunting bow.

"Holy shit, Arty!" Aech said, amid a fit of anxious laughter. "I can't believe she just did that. Girl got a death wish!"

Faisal and Shoto burst into applause. I joined in, trying to ignore my fear. Was outsmarting Anorak really going to be so easy?

That was when the view from the autojet's video feed veered off to the side. The plane was changing course. Its camera was now showing only empty sky. On the feed from Samantha's phone, still clipped to her chest, we had a POV shot of her feet, which she appeared to be kicking up like a girl on an amusement park ride, as her parachute floated downward.

Her hands rose in front of her chest and she raised both middle fingers in the direction of the jet. Even through the wind, we could just make it out when she shouted, "Now you can hold that empty plane hostage, Anorak!"

She dropped her hands fast, though. Probably because like us, she had just noticed that her jet was still banking around and down into a dive— one that put it on a collision course with her falling parachute.

"Oh shit!" I shouted. "He's going to ram her!"

We watched helplessly as the jet rapidly closed the distance between them. As the jet's nose filled her POV, we saw a jolt on Samantha's feed—she had cut her primary chute loose and was in free fall, just in time for the jet to soar by harmlessly above her. She continued to dive for several more seconds, even though the warning lights on her altimeter were already flashing red.

Finally, she pulled her reserve chute and slowed her rapid descent. She came in, still falling far too fast, landing in a small, heavily wooded park just a few miles east of downtown, and we watched as the chute dragged through the tree branches on its way to the ground.

Then she touched down with a jolt that made every bone in my body ache—and her phone's vidfeed cut to black.

"Is she all right?" I asked Faisal with a shaky voice. "Did she make it to the ground safely?"

"I don't know," he said. "I'm trying to call her back, but she isn't answering."

My eyes shifted back to the viewscreen, which still displayed the live vidfeed from Samantha's commandeered jet. It hadn't pulled out of its dive. Instead it had increased its angle of descent, so that now it was hurtling straight toward the ground like a missile.

"Oh my God," Faisal said. "He's gonna crash into her landing site!"

By the time he'd finished saying it out loud, it was already happening.

But as the jet was about to crash, it pulled up sharply, so instead of hitting her landing site dead-on it made impact a few hundred feet away, in the middle of a deserted picnic area.

As it hit, our remaining vidfeed cut to black.

We stared at the blank viewscreen in silence for a moment. Then Faisal had the presence of mind to check the local Columbus newsfeeds, and in less than a minute we were watching high-definition drone footage of the crash site. The just-refueled jet had detonated like a fuel-air bomb. The immediate area surrounding its crash site had been razed to nothing by the awesome force of the initial explosion. If Samantha or anyone else had been within that radius, they would have been incinerated.

The real problem now was the fuel, which had been flung far beyond the initial blast zone, like a botched napalm strike. A dozen different fires now raged across the entire park and several of the office buildings adjacent to it. It looked like a war zone down there.

With the flames still raging, it was impossible to see how many people had been engulfed by the sudden inferno. Anyone who had would be a charred corpse by now.

And I knew that any one of those burned bodies might belong to Samantha.

0011

Minutes passed, but to me it felt as though time had completely stopped.

I stared at the images on the viewscreen in shock as an aching hollowness spread across my limbs and torso and slowly made its way to my heart.

My mind played a montage of every moment I'd ever spent with Samantha, both in the OASIS and in reality, while I tallied up the long list of stupid things I'd said and done to her in the years since our breakup. And all of the apologies I'd never made.

Aech was the first one to break the silence. "If anyone could figure out a way to survive that, it'd be Arty. We don't know for sure . . . maybe she found cover before it hit. . . ."

"There's no way, Aech," Shoto said, still in shock. "Did you see that fireball? There's no way she had enough time to get clear of it. . . ."

We had already rewatched the footage of the crash several times, frame-by-frame. We couldn't see what had happened to Samantha. But I was still inclined to agree with Shoto. She'd only had a split second to get clear before Anorak crashed the jet and a giant ball of flame exploded across the landscape.

I didn't want to believe she was dead. But I wasn't going to delude myself either. Despite how Samantha Cook was often depicted in movies and cartoons, she wasn't a superhero. Here in the real world, she was just a regular person—a geeky Canadian gamer girl from the suburbs of Vancouver. She couldn't outrun giant explosions on foot like Rambo.

Still. My mind kept replaying that last moment of the jet's descent. It had hit nearby, not on top of her. Maybe there was a chance.

"Why did she have to be so stupid?" Aech said, her tone shifting from shock to grief. "Why did she bail out? Why didn't she just sit tight until we got Anorak to release her?"

"Samantha was never a big fan of waiting around for someone else to rescue her," I said.

The others nodded. Then the silence was broken by the sound of another incoming call. Faisal rushed to answer it. When he did, Anorak's face appeared on the conference room's viewscreen, frowning down at us like some malevolent deity.

"I'm calling to express my condolences for the loss of your friend," Anorak said. "I was genuinely surprised by Ms. Cook's actions. I calculated a very low probability she would attempt to bail out of that autojet. Who knew she would be so foolish?" He shrugged. "I warned her, didn't I? In fact, I warned all of you what would happen if you failed to cooperate with me. If she hadn't tried to escape, she'd still be alive."

"No!" Aech shouted. "If you hadn't *murdered* her, she'd still be alive!" Her voice cracked, and she choked on each word as she spoke it. "You didn't have to kill her! Or any of those other people . . ."

"Of course I did, dear," Anorak replied softly. "I didn't *want* to kill her. I liked her. She was an incredibly brave and intelligent young woman. But she gave me no choice. If I hadn't punished her for disobeying me, what message would that have sent? It would've completely undermined my credibility and caused Parzival here to doubt my resolve. But now he knows I mean business. Don't you, Z?"

I was too overcome with grief and rage to respond with words. But I managed to nod slowly.

"See?" Anorak said, nodding back at me from the viewscreen. "I assure you all, I don't wish to harm anyone else if I don't have to. And I'm sure that you don't want any more blood on your hands either."

"You're nothing like James Halliday," Aech told him. "You're not human. You're a fucking toaster! You don't even care about those people you just killed. . . ."

"Why should I, dear?" Anorak said, with what sounded like genuine curiosity in his voice. "To quote Sarah Connor: 'You're all dead already.' You, your friends, your customers—all of you. You poisoned your own planet, destroyed its climate, defiled its ecosystem, and killed off all of its biodiversity." He pointed at each of us. "You're going to be extinct soon, too, by your hands. And you know it. That's why most of you spend every second you can wired up to the OASIS. You've already given up, and now you're all just waiting around to die." He shrugged. "The people I killed today don't have to wait around anymore. And if you continue to defy me, too, more people will meet the same fate. Now, get to work, kids."

When he called us "kids," I finally snapped and went into a total berserker rage, lunging at the viewscreen, as if I could crawl through it and throttle him.

"You'll pay for this, you son of a bitch!" I shouted, because I'd obviously seen way too many movies, and because I was terrified and wanted desperately not to show it.

"That's the spirit!" Anorak said, grinning. "You better get moving, Parzival." He tapped his imaginary watch again and sang, *"Time keeps on slippin', slippin', slippin' into the future. . . ."*

With that, Anorak ended the call and the giant viewscreen went dark for a moment. Then it went back to displaying several live aerial and ground video feeds of Samantha's crash site. The smoke had cleared enough so that we could see the firefighters who were finally starting to arrive on the scene.

"A medevac helicopter is en route to the crash site," Faisal said. "But it'll be a while before they'll be able to get that blaze under control."

"How could anyone survive an explosion like that?" Aech muttered.

"You have to hit the ground running," we heard a familiar female voice say.

We all turned to see Samantha's avatar, just as it finished rematerializing in the corner of the conference room.

"Then I kept on running," she continued. "And I hit the deck just before the jet made impact. There was a little stone footbridge over a stream and I dove under it." She winced. "I've got a few first- and second-degree burns, and I'm gonna need a few stitches. But I'm OK."

Aech and Shoto ran over and threw their arms around her avatar. I resisted the urge to join them, but just barely. Instead I just stood there next to Faisal, who couldn't resist hugging me instead. And I was so happy, I hugged him back.

Samantha was still alive. I still had a chance to make things right with her. To tell her how wrong I'd been, about everything. To apologize for not listening to her. And to tell her how much I'd missed her . . .

But she didn't stick around that long.

"I only jumped online for a few seconds, to let you all know I was OK," she said, gently pulling free of Aech's bearlike embrace. "Now I need to go let the medics clean me up. There are also a few things I need to do, and I can't do them while Halliday-9000 is watching."

Her deadpan *2001* joke caused me to involuntarily snort-laugh. Samantha was the only person who had ever been able to make me do this, and she knew it. I glanced over at her in embarrassment and she smiled at me again. And this time, with great effort, I managed not to look away.

"Z, you, Aech, and Shoto need to start searching for the Second Shard *now*," she said. "Hurry! I'll rejoin you as soon as I can."

And then she vanished without waiting for me to reply.

I stood there for a minute, staring at the spot where her avatar had been, attempting to rein in my stampeding thoughts.

"Zero in, buddy," Shoto said, elbowing me in the ribs. "Arty's right. We need to find the Second Shard. And fast."

I nodded and removed the First Shard from my inventory. When I held it aloft in my hand, it filled the conference room with its incandescent blue glow as each of its facets caught the light and refracted it onto the walls and the floor in a kaleidoscopic pattern.

I held the shard out to Aech, but when she attempted to take it, her hand passed right through it, as if it were an illusion. Shoto tried the same thing and got the same result.

"Halliday coded this shard so that anyone could find its hiding place and trigger its appearance," I said. "But it can only be picked up by one of Halliday's two heirs. Me or Ogden Morrow. Halliday gave Og his old arcade-game collection, remember?"

I told them how I'd used the Boris Vallejo calendar in Og's basement to change the year of the Middletown simulation, and how I'd obtained the First Shard in Kira's bedroom. I didn't mention that I'd paid a girl named L0hengrin a billion dollars to figure all of this out for me. I was ashamed to admit that I'd needed her help. And I was determined not to call on her for more assistance unless I had no choice.

"The First Shard has a clue etched into its surface," I said, turning it over in my hands so they could see it. "A hint about the next shard's hiding place."

Aech cleared her throat and read the clue out loud.

"'Her paint and her canvas, the one and the zero,'" she recited. "'The very first heroine, demoted to hero.'" She raised her eyes to meet mine. "Any ideas?"

I shook my head.

"Not yet," I said. "But this is the first opportunity I've had to try to decipher it." I pointed to the first line of the clue. "But I think the first line must be a reference to Kira, and her career as a videogame artist. 'Her paint and her canvas, the one and the zero.'"

Aech nodded. But Shoto didn't respond—he was already lost in thought.

"I'll buy that," Aech replied. "But what about 'The very first heroine, demoted to hero'?"

I recited the line in my head a few times, trying to parse the meaning. But my brain wouldn't cooperate. It had been a mistake to obsessively rewatch that crash footage for some sign of Samantha. Now all I could think about were all of those charred human corpses I'd seen littering the park where her jet had made impact. The bodies of at least a dozen people—people that Anorak had already killed, without hesitation.

"Come on, Z," Aech said when I failed to respond. "You must have some ideas. . . ."

"I don't know," I muttered, vigorously scratching my scalp in an attempt to jumpstart my brain. "I suppose it could be a reference to *Ranma 1/2*? A heroine demoted to hero?"

I was grasping at straws and Aech knew it.

"Come on, Z," she said. "Ranma was a boy who changed into a girl, not the other way around. And besides, the clue reads 'the very first heroine.'"

"Right," I said. "You're right. Sorry."

We stared at the inscription on the shard in silence while Faisal watched anxiously from across the room, his eyes wide with fascination.

As precious seconds continued to tick away, I began to wonder if I was going to have to swallow my rapidly dwindling pride and call L0hengrin.

"Come on!" Aech whispered. "It can't be that hard. Og found the Second Shard ten minutes after he found the first one!"

"Gee, I wonder why?" I said. "Do you think maybe Og knows a little more about his ex-wife than we do? He was only married to her for eighteen years!"

Aech was about to reply when Shoto spoke up, cutting her off.

"I don't think the first line is about Kira," Shoto said. "'Her paint and her canvas, the one and the zero.' I think that's a reference to Rieko Kodama, who was one of the very first women videogame designers. In one of her early interviews, Kira said that Kodama was one of the women who inspired her to work in the videogame industry, along with Dona Bailey and Carol Shaw."

I felt like kicking myself. In the head. Repeatedly. I knew all about Rieko Kodama. She was one of the co-creators of the Phantasy Star game series. And she'd also worked on the very first Sonic the Hedgehog game, one of Kira's all-time favorite videogames—a game that also just happened to put the player on a quest to collect *seven* Chaos Emeralds.

But I still didn't see a connection between Rieko Kodama and the second line of the clue. Probably because I didn't have her entire credits memorized, when I clearly should have.

"OK," I said. "Then what about 'the very first heroine, demoted to hero'?"

"Rieko Kodama co-created the first arcade game with a woman as its hero!" Shoto said. "Back in 1985."

I searched my memory, but the only woman hero of a Rieko Kodama game I could think of was Alis Lansdale, the fifteen-year-old protagonist of Phantasy Star I—and that was a home console game. Released for the Sega Master System in Japan in 1987, and in the United States in 1988.

"I'm talking about the first human female protagonist in an action videogame." Shoto cupped his right ear. "Anyone?"

"Wasn't that Samus from Metroid?" Aech asked as she opened her own browser window to look up the answer. "No wait—Toby from Baraduke!"

Shoto shook his head again, then he closed his eyes and raised his right fist to the sky in victory.

"*Princess Kurumi!*" he shouted. "Released by Sega in March of 1985! Rieko Kodama designed all the characters and environments. But when they released the game in the United States, they didn't think American boys would put quarters in a game with the word *princess* on its marquee, so they changed its title to Sega Ninja!" He smiled at me, then shrugged. "It was one of my grandpa Hiro's favorite games. We used to play together when I was very little. When he passed away, he left me his whole Sega game collection. I spent a lot of my time playing it, back when I was a *hikikomori*."

I was so happy to hear this that I felt like hugging Shoto. So I did, and he was so overjoyed at that moment he tolerated it. He'd always been our Sega scholar, and our resident expert on pretty much any videogame ever made in Japan. And in recent years, he'd become a well-known ninja nut. After the contest, when he abandoned his avatar's samurai attire out of respect for his late brother, he'd changed his avatar to a ninja and became a ninja addict. He live-streamed himself playing ninja videogames all day, every day, for a month. And he aired ninja movies on his POV channel every night. So this riddle was a bull's-eye in his gunter knowledge sweet spot.

"Sega Ninja?" Aech repeated as her eyes slowly lit up with recognition. "Oh shit! I remember this game now! I was addicted to it. You play this badass princess named Kurumi, who has to take back her castle from the punks who usurped it."

Shoto activated a hologram projector and a rotating three-dimensional image of an original Sega Ninja arcade cabinet appeared. Then he grinned and presented it to us, as if it were the grand prize on a game show.

"And guess what?" Shoto continued. "When Sega ported Ninja Princess to their Master System home console, they retitled the game once again, this time as 'The Ninja.' And because Sega thought it would improve sales, they changed the main character from a woman, the badass ninja princess Kurumi, to a man—a generic male ninja named Kazamaru."

"Yeah, I remember this shit now," Aech said. "In the console version, they also turned the princess from a *kunoichi* into a damsel in distress that Kazamaru rescues at the end of the game." She shook her head. "That still pisses me off."

"Seriously?" I said, with genuine surprise. "They did that?"

Shoto and Aech both nodded.

"So . . ." I said. "That's got to be it, right? The Ninja Princess, Kurumi, was the 'very first heroine, demoted to hero'!"

"Oh! Yo! I said God *damn*, Shoto!" Aech suddenly began to sing, as she half hunched over and began to dance sideways toward him. Shoto moved toward her in the same fashion, and they launched into an elaborate five-part high-five ritual.

"Let's wait until we have the shard to celebrate, OK?" I said.

Shoto nodded and opened his OASIS atlas. I saw him do a quick search for Rieko Kodama's name. He got several hits in the Console Cluster, a group of worlds in Sector Eight where the landscape of each planet resembled the distinctive graphics of different classic game consoles.

"There's a planet near the center of the Sega quadrant called Phoenix-Rie," he said, reading off his display. "It's the most popular shrine to Rieko Kodama's life and work, and it dates back to the early days of the OASIS. And Kira Morrow is listed as one of its original creators in the planet's colophon."

"Phoenix-Rie was Kodama's alias," Shoto said. "I visited that planet a few times during the contest. It contains quest portals that lead to OASIS ports of every game Kodama ever worked on, including Ninja Princess. That must be where we need to go."

"Boom!" Aech said. "Then let's make like a tree and get outta here."

I selected Aech and Shoto's avatars on my HUD and prepared to teleport all three of us to the planet Phoenix-Rie in Sector Eight. But of course, I couldn't take us anywhere. Anorak had taken my teleportation powers away from me, along with my other superuser abilities, when he stole the Robes of Anorak from my inventory. My avatar was still maxed out at ninety-ninth-level, but now I was mortal once again, just like any other avatar. And I wasn't properly equipped. I'd collected plenty of new weapons, magic items, and vehicles over the past three years, but I didn't lug all of that stuff around with me. Everything was in my old stronghold on Falco, and we didn't have time to waste making a detour back there so that I could gear up.

"Hey, Faisal," I said, trying to conceal my embarrassment. "Can you hook me up with one of those Admin rings you gave to everyone else during our first co-owners meeting?"

Faisal smiled and removed a small silver ring from his inventory and then tossed it to me. I caught it and slipped it onto the pinky of my right hand. It appeared in my avatar's inventory as a Ring of OASIS Administration. It gave me the ability to teleport anywhere in the OASIS for free, and enclosed my avatar in a shield that made me immune to attacks from other OASIS avatars, even in PvP zones. Faisal had offered me one of these Admin rings when he'd given them to Art3mis, Aech, and Shoto, but I'd declined because the Robes of Anorak already gave me those abilities and many more—and I was also showing off for Art3mis.

"Thanks, Faisal," I said.

"Here," Aech said impatiently. She flashed her own admin ring at me, then selected Phoenix-Rie on her own OASIS atlas. "Let me do the honors." She placed her right hand on Shoto's shoulder and her left one on mine, then she uttered the brief incantation required to activate her teleportation spell, and our avatars vanished.

▪ ▪ ▪

A split second later, we rematerialized on the surface of the planet Phoenix-Rie. It was a bright and beautiful little world, rendered in colorful 8-bit graphics, and its pixelated landscape was a patchwork of different environments that Rieko Kodama had created for a variety of games. The area where Aech, Shoto, and I arrived was modeled after the game Alex Kidd in the Miracle World. But as we began to traverse the planet's surface, we found ourselves running through the Green Hill Zone from the original Sonic the Hedgehog. Then the landscape quickly changed to resemble environments from the very first Phantasy Star game. I recognized graphical elements from all three planets in the Algol system—in just a few minutes, we sprinted through the forests of Palma, the deserts of Motavia, and the icy plains of Dezoris.

We also saw dozens of different nonplayer characters from Kodama's games roaming around aimlessly, but like most OASIS NPCs, they wouldn't attack or talk to you unless you attacked or talked to them first, so we just stayed out of their way.

Eventually we reached the planet's equator, where we found a line of game portals positioned along it, stretching to the pixelated horizon in each direction. The portals were arranged in chronological order by the games' year of release.

We found the Ninja Princess portal in less than a minute, positioned between the portals leading to OASIS re-creations of the games Championship Boxing and Black Onyx.

Each glowing circular portal had an icon denoting the corresponding videogame's original packaging hovering just above it, so the Ninja Princess portal had an arcade cabinet icon above it, while the portals to either side of it had Sega MyCards above them.

As we approached the Ninja Princess portal, I began to notice a ringing in my ears, which began to increase steadily in volume the closer I got to it.

Aech and Shoto didn't seem to hear it at all, so I decided to check my inventory. That was when I realized the sound was emanating from the First Shard. The icon denoting it on my item list was pulsing in time with the ringing in my ears—as if the shard were calling out to me. Just like that green Kryptonian crystal that called to young Kal-El in *Superman: The Movie*. In fact, I was pretty sure Halliday had lifted the sound effect I was hearing directly from that film.

When I took the shard out of my inventory to examine it, the ringing stopped, and the inscription on the shard changed before my eyes. Now it read:

> Ninniku and Zaemon aren't alone on her roster
> Once you reclaim her castle, you must face her imposter

I showed the new couplet to Shoto and Aech and their eyes lit up.

"Ninniku and Zaemon are the two main bad guys in Ninja Princess," Aech said. "Kurumi has to defeat both of them to win the game and 'reclaim her castle.' "

"Then 'face her imposter,' " I recited. "That must be Kazamaru, the male ninja they replaced her with in the Master System port. I guess I'll have to fight him too." I cracked my knuckles. "Couldn't be too difficult, right?"

"Share your POV feed with us so we can monitor your progress," Shoto said. "I'm calling you now audio-only, so Aech and I can feed you tips as you go. Just like old times. Oh, and that reminds me . . ."

Shoto changed out of his formal ninja attire and put on his ornate gold armor and then strapped on his swords. This prompted Aech and me to change into our old gunter attire too. Then Aech threw up a mirror so that the three of us could admire ourselves.

"Look at those handsome devils," she said, before blasting the mirror to smithereens with a shot from her assault rifle. "Now, let's do this."

"OK, amigos," I said, accepting Shoto's audio call on my HUD. "Here goes nothing."

I bumped fists with both of them at once, then turned around, took a deep breath, and jumped into the Ninja Princess portal.

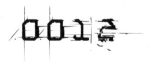

I wasn't sure what I was expecting. Maybe that I would find myself in an immersive VR re-creation of Ninja Princess, similar to the OASIS port of Black Tiger I'd encountered during the contest. Except that the rules of the old contest no longer seemed to fit, not after that flashback of Kira's life I'd experienced when I touched the First Shard. It was impossible for her to have played a role in all this, I knew that. But what I'd experienced had seemed equally impossible.

When I stepped through the portal, I didn't find myself inside a video-game, or in a historical simulation of feudal Japan. Instead, I found myself standing in a place I'd visited once before—years ago, during the contest.

Happytime Pizza.

The original Happytime Pizza was a small mom-and-pop pizza parlor and video arcade that had existed in Middletown, Ohio, from 1981 to 1989. Halliday had spent countless hours there during his youth, and he'd re-created it in loving detail inside the OASIS, along with the rest of his hometown, on the planet he'd named after it. But during the contest I'd discovered another instance of Happytime Pizza, hidden in the subterranean video-game museum on the planet Archaide. That was where I'd played my perfect game of Pac-Man and earned the extra life quarter that allowed me to survive the detonation of the Cataclyst on Chthonia.

Given my previous visits to Happytime Pizza, my surroundings should have felt familiar. But it was the opposite, because this time, I was wearing the ONI. This time, I could smell the tomato sauce and burnt pepperoni grease in the air. I could feel the subtle vibration of the sound system's speakers through the floorboards, pulsing in time with the bass line as they blasted the song "Obsession" by Animotion. This time, I felt like I was really *here*, like I'd genuinely traveled back in time to Middletown, Ohio, sometime in the late 1980s.

I was standing just inside the glass double doors that served as Happytime Pizza's front entrance. Someone had carefully taped sheets of tinfoil over them, to prevent any sunlight from intruding upon the dark neon cave of the game room. I tried to open the doors, but they were locked, apparently from the outside. I peeled back a corner of the foil to peek outside, only to discover that the entire building appeared to be hovering in a pitch-black void. I smoothed the tinfoil back into place, then turned around and did a slow scan of my surroundings.

Happytime Pizza was divided into two halves, the game room and the dining room. But actually they were both game rooms, because all of the tables in the dining room were sit-down cocktail videogame cabinets.

I took a few steps into the dining room to get a better look, and I could feel the soles of my tennis shoes sticking to the dried soda residue on the checkerboard-pattern linoleum floor with each step I took. There were a couple of NPC pizza chefs back in the kitchen, both tossing dough in the air, and they each waved to me in mid-throw. I waved back, and that was when I noticed my right hand. It wasn't my right hand at all. . . .

I caught a glimpse of my reflection in the two-way mirror adjacent to the manager's office. I did an involuntary double take. I was no longer my avatar, Parzival. Now I was Kira Underwood, when she was in her late teens, instantly recognizable from the handful of photographs taken of her during her time in Middletown in the late '80s. I had her adorable pixie haircut, her giant designer prescription eyeglasses (with clip-on, flip-up mirrored sunglasses), and her trademark acid-washed jean jacket, adorned with countless patches, buttons, and pins. I glanced down and took a quick inventory. I also had Kira's boobs, and her hips, lips, fingertips—all of it. I even pulled my right sleeve to check the back of my forearm and there it was—Kira's tiny birthmark. The one that distinctly resembled a map of Iceland.

I didn't just look like her. I *was* her.

I turned around and walked back toward the game room. As I entered, Rick Springfield's "Jessie's Girl" began to play on the new compact disc–powered jukebox standing in the corner—a jukebox that hadn't been present in the previous iterations of Happytime Pizza I'd visited. It was my first indication that this one was set in a more recent time period than the others—probably somewhere in the fall or winter of 1988 or the spring of '89, when Kira Underwood had lived in Middletown.

About two dozen videogames were packed into the game room, with about a dozen NPCs spread among them. They were all teenage boys in late-'80s attire, each one standing at a different game. They all had their backs to me, and they continued to keep them that way as I walked past them.

As I made my way to the back of the game room, I spotted the familiar Defender marquee, with the same handwritten note taped to it that I'd seen on my last visit: *Beat the owner's high score and win a free large pizza!* But most of the other games I remembered seeing in the Archaide instance of Happytime Pizza had now been replaced with newer titles. Pac-Man, Galaga, and Dig Dug had been swapped out with Golden Axe, Final Fight—and way at the back, what appeared to be a brand-new Sega Ninja cabinet.

"There it is!" Aech and Shoto shouted. I'd momentarily forgotten that they were monitoring me, and their disembodied voices nearly made me jump out of my skin.

"Thanks, amigos," I said. "But I saw it too. You're watching my POV, remember?"

"Right, sorry," I heard Aech say. "We're both just a little anxious is all!"

"I can relate," I said, walking over to the Sega Ninja cabinet to size up my opponent. Its illuminated marquee had the word NINJA printed on it in large stylized yellow and orange letters, with the smaller SEGA logo underneath it. But on the monitor, the title appeared as SEGA NINJA.

The game's attract mode cycled between its high-score list, short clips of automated gameplay on different levels, and a brief-but-beautiful piece of 8-bit animation, which showed Princess Kurumi being carried across a bamboo bridge on a palanquin by two masked ninja thugs. In the distance, beyond fields of red roses and forests of cherry-blossom trees, over a broad blue river, you could see the purple-roofed Kanten Castle, perched high in the clouds, atop a gorgeously rendered snowcapped mountain range that filled the distant horizon. Suddenly, Kurumi leaped out of the palanquin, wearing a fancy red Queen Amidala gown. Then, in a puff of ninja smoke, she changed into more battle-ready attire—a red silk *kunoichi*—and chased after her former captors, presumably to murder them just offscreen.

I took a quarter out of my inventory and dropped it into the left coin slot. Then I removed my clip-on mirror shades and hung them on top of the game's marquee. This allowed me to use their lenses as rearview mirrors, providing a wide-angle view of everything behind me. This was a trick I'd learned from Art3mis, during one of our early online pseudo-dates on Archaide. She liked to wear mirror shades back then too. When she was still deep in her Molly Millions phase.

I glanced at the game's colorful instruction card, located beneath the Plexiglas bezel that encircled the monitor:

Regain the KANTEN CASTLE from the evil hands of the traitor, ZAEMON!!
The NINJA group called PUMA is obstructing princess KURUMI'S way!!
Defeat their leader, NINNIKU and proceed to the castle!!

The instructions featured cartoon renderings of Kurumi, the gun-wielding big boss Zaemon, and his blond-haired underling Ninniku, along with a helpful diagram showing what the game's three control buttons did. One turned the princess invisible for a few seconds, making her immune to attacks. The second made her throw a knife in the direction she was facing at the moment, and the third made her throw a knife in the forward direction only, toward the top of the screen, allowing the player to fire while moving in another direction.

"Umm, Wade? Please tell me you're not reading the instructions right now," Shoto said, sounding deeply amused.

"You've never played Ninja Princess before, have you?" Aech asked.

I sighed. It sounded like Kira Underwood was the one sighing.

"Yes, I have," I replied. "But only once or twice. Six or seven years ago."

"Great," Aech muttered. "This should go well."

"Relax," Shoto said. "Sega Ninja is standard run-and-gun fun. I'll walk you through each of the sixteen levels. Some of them are pretty difficult to clear. But you can handle it."

"*Arigato*, Shoto," I said, as I slapped the Player One button. "Here goes nothing."

I rested my right hand on the joystick and my left over the three control buttons.

The game began with a brief animation, showing Princess Kurumi changing out of a fancy silk kimono into her red *kunoichi* garb, as the poorly translated message PRINCESS'ES ADVENTURE STARTS is typed out above her, one letter at a time. Then a familiar warning appeared in the center of the screen: PLAYER 1 START, followed by a rectangular map of the kingdom showing my current position at the bottom, and the route I would have to follow to reach Kanten Castle.

Then the first level or "step" of the game appeared—a sprawling green meadow, covered in patches of colorful flowers and strewn with the occasional tree or giant boulder. My tiny pixelated avatar appeared at the bottom center of the screen, and in that instant I was back in the zone. I wasn't Kira Morrow, or Parzival, or Wade Watts. The controls became an extension of myself, and I became the vengeful Princess Kurumi, clad in blood-red silk and armed with an infinite supply of throwing knives, intent on reclaiming my stolen kingdom at any cost.

Four blue-clad ninjas in black hoods appeared from the top of the screen and charged toward me. While I was dispatching them with my throwing knives, a fifth ninja clad in gray appeared, descending upon me much more quickly. But I took him down, too, just before he struck me with his sword. Then I began to run forward, toward the top of the screen, dispatching more brightly colored ninjas as soon as they scrolled into view.

Ninja Princess, aka Sega Ninja, turned out to be much more challenging than I anticipated. But once I got a feel for the controls and the gameplay, I was rockin' like Dokken—especially when I had Shoto whispering pointers into my ear.

"Just touching an enemy doesn't kill you in this game," Shoto said. "They actually have to strike you with their weapon. Ninja Princess was one of the first games to do that. It's a much better game than Commando, and it was released three months earlier. In fact, I would argue that Ninja Princess is probably the first true run-and-gun game."

"Unless you count Front Line by Taito," Aech said. "Released in '82."

"I don't," Shoto replied. "It only has one level that repeats over and over—"

"Dude, it's a game where you have a gun *and* you run," Aech replied. "How do—"

"Can you guys debate this subject later, please?" I interjected. "On your own time?"

"Sure, Z," Shoto replied. "Sorry. Hey! Get that *shuriken* power-up!"

In the game, I grabbed a small power-up dropped by one of the ninjas I'd slain. As I did, the theme music changed to a more heroic tune, and instead of throwing knives, my character began to hurl giant black *shuriken*, which could take down multiple enemies in a row, when they were kind enough to line up for me.

When I reached the end of the first level, Zaemon's golden-haired second-hand man Ninniku appeared and attacked me with a giant boomerang-like weapon. I dodged it, then lined up with Ninniku and began to unload on him with my *shuriken*.

"Keep shooting him until his hair turns red!" Shoto told me.

I did as he instructed, and after seven or eight hits, Ninniku's hair turned from blond to red—apparently to indicate his rising anger. Then the gameplay froze and Step 1 ended. The game tallied up my points, along with my total number of shots and hits and my overall hit ratio. The map of the kingdom popped up again, revealing that by clearing the first level, I'd moved slightly closer to the castle at the top. Then the next level began.

Step 2 required me to fight more ninjas while wading through rice paddies. When I battled my way to its end, Ninniku appeared once again, and once again I attacked him until his hair turned red, signaling his defeat.

Shoto continued to coach me, but Aech remained quiet, except to shout warnings or congratulate me on a nice move.

Shoto referred to Step 3 as the "avalanche level," because it required you to battle ninjas while also dodging giant boulders that were continuously appearing from the top of the screen. It required a completely different strategy from the first two levels, and I lost my first life figuring that out. Then I lost another life during Step 4, where Princess Kurumi spent the entire level fighting off packs of ravenous wolves. It was a truly great game, and it was also kicking my ass. Now I only had one life left, and my confidence started to waver.

I found myself wishing there was a way Shoto could play through the trickier levels for me, but that was impossible. Tricks like hacked OASIS haptic rigs and illegal software, which had allowed Sorrento to take control of any of the avatars under his command, were obsolete now. None of them worked with ONI headset technology. I was on my own.

Thankfully, I hit my stride again during the next level, Step 5, which was set in a dense forest of bulbous 8-bit trees, concealing wave after wave of what Shoto referred to as "Keebler Ninjas." I managed to earn back one of the lives I'd lost.

Step 6 was set on a roaring river, which the player had to cross by leaping from log to log like in Frogger, while battling more ninjas along the way. When I reached the other side, Ninniku appeared once again, hurling his boomerang at me from the riverbank until I landed enough hits to defeat him.

As I played, I noticed something odd about the music playing on the arcade's jukebox. The same three songs kept playing, over and over. "Obsession" by Animotion, then "Jessie's Girl" by Rick Springfield, followed by "My Best Friend's Girl" by the Cars. It was easy to see the connection. All of these songs could've been about Halliday's obsession with Kira—his best friend's girl. And, I realized, I could be reliving the moment his obsession began.

I pulled my mind back to the game. I was now in the seventh stage, which took place in the streets of the village outside the castle walls. Shoto referred to the oddly dressed enemies I encountered here as "Pastel Ninjas," because many of them appeared to be wearing turquoise tunics and pink pantaloons. I had to battle several "Clown Samurai" who wore red-striped Hammer pants that made them look like walking circus tents with swords. Once I defeated all of them, I cleared that level too. Seven down. Nine to go. Almost halfway there . . .

Shoto referred to Step 8 as the "stampede stage," because you spent the entire level trying not to get trampled by an endless string of horses stampeding across the screen, while fighting off more Pastel Ninjas, who miraculously never seemed to get trampled even once. The lucky bastards.

At some point, a small crowd of onlookers began to form around me—the NPCs who'd been playing on the other machines, I assumed. And the longer I played, the bigger the crowd sounded. I didn't turn around to do a head count, but I caught brief, warped glimpses of them in the lenses of my mirror shades, during the pause in gameplay at the end of each level, when my score and hit count was tallied and I was given a brief view of my progress toward the castle on the map. I tried to put them out of my mind, too, so that I could remain focused on the task at hand.

Ninja Princess was a strangely nonviolent action game. There was no blood or gore in it at all. Or killing. When Princess Kurumi got hit, she would just fall down and cry. The Puma Ninja clan members and bosses didn't collapse and die when they were dispatched. They just vanished in a puff of smoke. When I asked Shoto about it, he told me it was a conscious choice by the game's creators, to promote pacifism and nonviolence.

"Wow," Aech said. "A nonviolent game about killing people with knives. Genius."

"Shh!" Shoto whispered. "Let the man concentrate!"

I made it to Step 9, which was a battle through the stone courtyard surrounding Kanten Castle's outermost wall, followed by Step 10, which required you to scale that wall while fighting off dozens of expert-climber "Spider Ninjas."

Step 11 required me to fight my way down a lone stone walkway through the castle grounds. Step 12 was another wall-scaling level, identical to Step 10, but with the color scheme changed. When I reached the top of this second wall, I faced Ninniku one final time, dispatching him for good.

"Boom!" Shoto shouted triumphantly as I completed the level. "You took out Ninniku! You're almost to the castle!"

Shoto was right. Step 13 required me to fight my way through more ninjas and samurai, making my way up a long stone path that led to the castle steps. When I reached those steps, the main villain, Zaemon Gyokuro, finally appeared and started shooting at me with a pair of ball-and-shot pistols. When I managed to hit him enough times, the level ended. And then I finally made it back into Kanten Castle—my former home, now overrun with usurping Pastel Ninja dipshits.

Step 14 required me to battle my way into the castle, by running under ladder walkways suspended on pylons before I had to fight Zaemon once again. Then I continued on to Step 15, where I had to make my way into the castle's inner chambers, through a series of *washitsu*, Japanese-style rooms with walls made of translucent paper.

When at last I reached Step 16, I finally got to face off with Zaemon and his minions in the castle throne room. I lunged forward into the final boss battle, with Aech and Shoto both shouting advice in my ear and cheering me on, like my own personal Mickey Goldmill and Paulie Pennino.

Luckily I'd picked up a few more lives in the last ten levels, because it took all of them to defeat Zaemon. Finally, I had reached the end of the game. But it was a strange ending. Even though they were supposed to be dead, Ninniku and Zaemon both reappeared, standing on a stage inside the castle alongside Princess Kurumi herself. Shoto told us the game's lead designer, Yoshiki Kawasaki, had chosen this ending to imply that the events depicted in the game were just a stage play that had been acted out for the player's benefit. No one had actually been hurt.

After the game's characters finished their curtain call, the following text appeared on the screen:

CONGRATULATIONS!
THE PRINCESS HAS COMPLETED
HER ADVENTURE AND REGAINED
THE KANTEN CASTLE

A huge cheer erupted from the boys gathered around me, but I didn't turn around right away. I still had one life remaining, so the game had started over again at the beginning of the first level, and I kept playing to see if Kurumi's "imposter" was going to appear. After a minute of nothing more than the familiar color-blind ninjas, I let my one remaining life expire. GAME OVER appeared on the screen and I was prompted to enter my initials for the high-score list. I started to put in my own out of habit, but then I remembered who I was supposed to be and entered "K.R.U." instead, for Karen Rosalind Underwood.

When the list of high scores appeared, I discovered that my score of 365,800 points put me only in second place on the list of "specialists." The person in first had racked up a score of 550,750, outscoring me by over 200,000 points. They appeared to be sharper than me, too, because they'd entered the initials "K.R.A." beside their score—the three-letter signature Kira Underwood had used on videogame high-score lists, instead of her initials. I'd failed to recall this obscure piece of trivia until I saw it in front of me. But my predecessor had not.

That was when I realized I was looking at Ogden Morrow's score. Which made perfect sense. Og had completed this challenge earlier today. Just a few hours ago. And judging by his score, he was much better at Ninja Princess than I would ever be. Either that, or he'd kept on playing after he beat the final level and the game started over at the beginning again, to rack up those extra points. But why would he do that? Was he trying to match Kira's real high score? Had I just screwed up somehow?

I snapped a screenshot of the high-score list so that I could examine it later. Then I felt someone tap me on the shoulder and nearly jumped out of my skin.

I turned to see a young Ogden Morrow smiling at me.

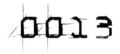

Og looked like he was around sixteen years old. About the same age he was when he met Kira for the first time—at a local arcade, when she moved to Middletown in the summer of 1988.

No wonder this setting and the scenario I was acting out both felt so familiar. I'd read about it seven or eight years earlier, in Ogden Morrow's bestselling autobiography, *Og*. Unlike Halliday's blog and diary entries in *Anorak's Almanac*, Og's recollections were infuriatingly vague when it came to details, but in the second or third chapter of the book, he described meeting his future wife for the first time, on the last day of summer vacation before his junior year of high school. He'd described how an "unbelievably gorgeous girl, with short dark hair and beautiful blue eyes," had wandered into "one of the local arcades," where he watched from a distance as "she beat one of the toughest games there on a single quarter."

But Og had never bothered to specify which local arcade it was, or the name of the game Kira had played, and other written accounts had given conflicting information about both. Now I knew he'd met Kira here at Happytime Pizza. And that the game he'd watched her beat with one quarter was Sega Ninja, aka Ninja Princess.

I was reenacting the moment Ogden and Kira Morrow first met.

If I recalled Og's book correctly, he'd walked over to congratulate Kira after she finished her game. But then his socially inept shadow, Halliday, had interrupted them to ask Og for a ride home. He always waited until the last possible moment to return to his troubled home, so Og knew his friend didn't really want to leave yet. Halliday was attempting to cock-block him. This shocked and amused Og, because he'd never seen him display jealousy over a girl before. Just computer hardware.

"Hi," the teenage Og said, finally working up the nerve to make eye contact with me. "I'm Og. And you—you're amazing! I can't believe you defeated Sega Ninja on one quarter! This is the first time any of us have ever seen anyone do that. Way to go!"

Og awkwardly held up his right hand. It took a second before I realized he was offering me a high five. So I high-fived him. He looked extremely relieved when I did.

Then he locked eyes with me, and as he did, I felt my heart beat faster. My skin began to tingle with what felt like invisible tendrils of electricity. This was a sensation I was familiar with. It was how I'd felt the first time I met Samantha in the real world.

I couldn't imagine how present-day Ogden Morrow had felt while going through this challenge. He must've been using a conventional haptic rig, thankfully—he'd never used an ONI by choice, and he'd still been without one in Anorak's little blackmail livestream—so at least he'd been spared all the physical sensations. But re-experiencing this moment from Kira's perspective must've still been heartbreaking for him.

"Thanks, Og," I heard myself say, with Kira's voice, and in her British accent. "I'm Karen Underwood—but my friends call me Kira." I felt my head nod in the direction of the Sega Ninja cabinet beside me. "We have this game in one of the shops near my parents' flat, back home in London. But over there, it's called Ninja Princess. Not Sega Ninja." I felt the corner of my mouth curl into a smirk, then I added: "I guess American boys don't like to play with girls."

"Yes, we do!" Og replied immediately. Then he began to turn red and stammered, "I mean, we're not against playing games with girls! Video-games, that is. That have a girl main character. Like this one here."

Og gave the Sega Ninja cabinet an awkward pat, as if it were an unfamiliar Labrador. Then he shoved both of his hands into his pockets and grinned at me like a lovestruck idiot. He looked as if his pupils might change into cartoon hearts at any second.

He opened his mouth to say something else to me, but right on cue, another extremely familiar-looking teenage boy interrupted our conversation. I immediately recognized him as James Halliday—at age seventeen.

Wearing his half-inch-thick horn-rimmed eyeglasses, a pair of faded jeans, worn Nikes, and one of his beloved Space Invaders T-shirts.

Just as he appeared, the arcade's sound system skipped forward from "Jessie's Girl" to "Obsession" by Animotion. I knew that couldn't be a coincidence.

"I gotta get home," the young Halliday urgently told Og, without making eye contact with either him or me. "I'm out of quarters and . . . so . . . I need a ride home."

Og stared at him for a moment in disbelief while Halliday kept his eyes on the carpet. Og gave me an embarrassed smile, then turned back to Halliday.

"Hold on just a few minutes," Og said. "Or go wait by my car until I'm ready to leave. Or—" He fished a crumpled dollar bill out of the front pocket of his acid-washed jeans. "It's too wrinkled for the token machine, but they'll change it at the counter."

Og tossed the bill in Halliday's general direction and turned back to Kira without waiting for him to reply. The money hit him in the chest and then silently fell to the floor.

"No!" Halliday shouted, suddenly furious, stomping his right foot down like a toddler preparing to throw a tantrum. When his shoe made contact with the ground, Og and all of the other NPCs vanished, leaving me alone with the seventeen-year-old James Halliday.

And in the same instant, our surroundings changed too.

The Happytime Pizza game room was gone, replaced by a throne room that looked an awful lot like a live-action version of the 8-bit one in the final stage of Ninja Princess. The teenage Halliday morphed into the masked, black-clad ninja Kazamaru, who to my eyes looked exactly like Shô Kosugi in *Revenge of the Ninja* back in 1983.

I glanced down at my avatar and saw that my own appearance had changed too. I still appeared to be a girl, but now I was dressed in a flowing tunic made of red silk, with gold piping and a Chinese dragon stitched onto each sleeve.

I was also holding a sword in my right hand, and in its mirrored surface I could see that I was no longer wearing Kira Underwood's face. My avatar had changed into a live-action representation of Princess Kurumi—and the creator of this simulation had chosen to make me look exactly like Elsa Yeung in *Challenge of the Lady Ninja,* also from 1983.

"'Reclaim her castle and face her imposter,'" Shoto recited. "This is it! Kick his ass, Princess!"

I nodded, then lunged forward and did as Shoto instructed—I kicked Kazamaru's ass.

Thankfully, the mechanics of ONI-based combat were more or less identical to old-school haptic-rig combat. You didn't have to physically perform any of your avatar's complex special moves and powered attacks yourself unless you wanted to. Instead, you could use a simple hand gesture or voice command to make your avatar execute a move or an attack. The only difference was, when you were using an ONI, you could feel your avatar's body movements as it automatically carried out these actions, so for a few seconds, it felt like you were moving on autopilot.

I was prepared for a brutal fight, but whoever had programmed this challenge had made Princess Kurumi a lot tougher than her knockoff male counterpart, who barely put up a fight. He only managed to land one or two hits before I knocked his life-meter down to nothing, with a steady barrage of throwing knives.

When I reduced his life bar to just 1 percent, the words FINISH HIM appeared floating in the air between us for a moment. When they vanished, I dispatched Kazamaru with one final roundhouse kick to the head. The last sliver of his life bar turned red—but he didn't die. Instead, the manly, black-clad ninja master abruptly fell to his knees and began to cry, then vanished in a cloud of smoke a few seconds later.

When it dissipated, I saw the Second Shard floating there in front of me.

I reached for it, wondering if I was about to experience another "flashback." And as my fingers wrapped around it . . .

* * *

I was back inside the body of seventeen-year-old Kira Underwood, and now teenage Ogden Morrow was standing in front of me, holding my hands in his. It was dark, and we were standing on a grassy hill bathed in moonlight, overlooking the tiny Middletown skyline in the distance. Og was placing a silver necklace in my hands—the same necklace from Kira's jewelry box that had transformed into the First Shard—just as he whispered the words "I love you," for what I knew must be the very first time.

Og had written about this moment in his autobiography, too, I realized.

But he hadn't described it in any detail, or given the time and place it occurred.

I felt my body starting to tremble as Kira reacted to what her future husband had just told her. . . .

—— • • • ——

. . . And then I was back inside my own avatar's skin. I was back on Kodama, standing next to Aech and Shoto in front of the Ninja Princess portal. It looked as though my avatar had just been ejected from it. When I looked down, I saw the Second Shard lying in my open palm. It was another multifaceted blue crystal, nearly identical to the first one in size and appearance.

Shoto and Aech both threw their arms around me. "You did it!"

"No," I said. "*We* did it. I couldn't have done it without your help."

I held out both of my fists and they each bumped one of them and silently nodded.

"That final challenge was insane, right?" Shoto said. "I mean, why would Halliday want you to kill the teenage version of himself?"

"That's gotta be some serious self-hatred happening there," Aech said. "Maybe he finally realized what a dick he was to Kira, and to Og?"

I couldn't focus on what they were saying. I was still reeling from the flashback I'd just experienced. Another of Kira Underwood's private memories, rendered with a detail and intensity that should've been impossible. Just what in the name of Crom was going on here?

I didn't have time to stop and ponder the possibilities. We had shards to collect and absolutely no time to spare.

I glanced down at the Second Shard in my hand, then held it out to Aech and Shoto, so we could examine it together. When I turned it over in my palm, we saw that this shard had an inscription carved into its glassy surface just like the first one. Aech read it aloud.

" 'Recast the foul, restore his ending. Andie's first fate still needs mending.' "

" 'Andie's first fate,' " Shoto repeated. "Wasn't Andie the name of Kerri Green's character in *The Goonies*?"

"No," I said, shaking my head. "Her name was spelled with a *y* at the end. Not an *i-e*."

"A-N-D-I-E," Aech said, shutting her eyes, as if to better picture the name. "Like Andie MacDowell?" She turned to Shoto and gripped his shoulder. "Oh *shit*! Maybe the next shard is on the Planet Punxsutawney? I used to go there every Groundhog Day to—"

"Hold on!" Shoto said, cutting her off. He'd opened a browser window in front of his avatar and was reading from it. "Andie MacDowell also starred in *Greystoke: The Legend of Tarzan* in 1984. But the director hired Glenn Close to loop all of her dialogue, because he didn't like her Southern accent! Do you think that could be what 'recast the foul, restore his ending' is a reference to? Maybe that film had an alternate ending. . . ."

"Wait, are we talking about the movie where Connor MacLeod plays Tarzan?" Aech said. "Directed by the cat who made *Chariots of Fire*?"

"That's the one!" he said. "There must be a Flicksync devoted to it somewhere. . . ." He pulled up his OASIS atlas in another window. "Maybe on Lambert? Or one of the Edgar Rice Burroughs–themed planets in Sector Twenty? If we—"

"Guys!" I shouted, signaling a time-out with my hands. "Come on. You're really reaching. Do you seriously believe the Third Shard's hiding place is somehow connected to Andie MacDowell? Or Tarzan? Neither one is mentioned in the *Almanac*. Or in any of the books I've read about Kira's life."

Aech shrugged. "She could've been an Andie MacDowell fanatic, for all we know," she replied. "I never did that much research into Kira's interests. According to Og, Halliday never bothered to get to know who Kira really was."

"He must have known her a lot better than he let on," I said, thinking about the shard flashbacks. They had both felt like Recs, not Sims. The differences were subtle, but no Sim—at least not as far as I'd experienced, and I'd tried thousands—had just the mix of strangeness, uncertainty, and intensity that came from a recording of a real-life moment.

But they couldn't be recordings. Because there definitely hadn't been any ONI headsets lying around in Middletown, Ohio, in the fall of 1988.

So what had I just experienced?

I was still mulling that over when my brain produced a match for the name Andie in the jumbled recesses of my memory. I opened a browser window in the air in front of me and did a quick Web search to make sure my memory was correct.

"Andie Walsh!" I shouted. "With an *i-e*! That was the name of Molly Ringwald's character in *Pretty in Pink*."

Aech and Shoto both groaned and rolled their eyes. Neither was the world's biggest John Hughes fan, but they knew that Art3mis and I both adored his films. During Halliday's contest, Art3mis had published dozens of essays about his movies on her blog, dissecting each of them in loving detail, scene by scene. None of her encyclopedic knowledge had proven useful in finding Halliday's egg, but she might get her chance to put it to use now. Unless I managed to find the shard quickly, before she even got back online. That would save time—and probably also impress the hell out of her.

"*Pretty in Pink* would make sense," I said. "Kira and Og were both huge John Hughes fans. And they helped code some of the first quests on Shermer."

"You think we have to go to Shermer next?" Aech asked. "Arty will lose her mind!"

"OK," Shoto said, rereading the clue. "If it's Andie Walsh from *Pretty in Pink*, then what does 'Recast the foul, restore his ending' mean?"

"*Pretty in Pink* originally had a different ending," I replied. "One where Andie ended up with Duckie, instead of with Blane. Arty—Samantha— posted an essay about it on *Arty's Missives* a long time ago."

"Of course she did," Aech said. "She's an even bigger dork than you."

I ignored her, trying to hold on to my train of thought. "I think they decided to change the ending of the movie after some poor test screen-ings—"

As if on cue, Art3mis appeared next to us.

"Speak of the devil and the devil appears!" Aech said, greeting her with a fist bump. "You make it somewhere safe, Arty?"

Arty nodded, then pressed her index finger to her lips for a moment.

"Sorry I was gone so long," she said. "Looks like I missed a wardrobe change."

She grinned, admiring our old-school gunter attire. Then she snapped her fingers and spun around in a circle. Her avatar's outfit was replaced by the scaled gunmetal-blue armor she'd worn during the contest, along with her twin blaster pistols in their low-slung quickdraw holsters, and a long, curved Elven sword in an ornate Mithril scabbard was now strapped to her back. She'd even donned her fingerless Road Warrior–style racing gloves.

Seeing her dressed like that again brought back a flood of old feelings and long-suppressed memories. They left me feeling momentarily light-headed. And weak-hearted.

"There's our girl, back in uniform!" Aech said as they gave each other a double high five.

"Bravo, team!" she said. "I can't believe you guys already found the Second Shard. That was wicked fast!"

"Yes, it was," Shoto said. "Because I held Z's hand, all the way through it—"

"While I held his *other* hand," Aech added, laughing. "And now that Arty has rejoined our posse, too, we will be un-fucking-stoppable. The Siren's Soul shall be ours, my friends!"

Art3mis and Shoto both let out a cheer in agreement. I raised my right fist halfheartedly, then cleared my throat.

"Not to cut the celebration short," I said. "But I think I may have figured out what the Siren's Soul is, and why Og refused to give it to Anorak."

Their smiles faded as all three of them turned to look at me expectantly.

"OK," I said. "First, let me ask you a question. Why do you think Halliday called it the 'Siren's Soul'?"

"Because Kira named her D&D character Leucosia," Shoto replied. "After one of the Sirens in Greek mythology."

"Correct," I said. "So if Kira is the 'Siren,' and the Seven Shards are 'fragments' of her 'Soul,' what does Anorak assume will happen when we put those pieces back together? When we 'once again make the Siren whole'?"

Art3mis looked back over at me.

"Holy shit, Wade," she muttered. "You don't think . . . ?"

I nodded.

"Anorak doesn't think that the Siren's Soul is a magical artifact *named* after Kira," I said. "He believes it *is* her. An AI copy of Kira. Just like Anorak is a copy of Halliday."

Art3mis didn't respond, but she looked horrified by the thought.

"Come on, Z," Aech said. "That's impossible."

"I thought so too," I replied. "But there's no other explanation for what I've been experiencing."

Art3mis furrowed her brow.

"What do you mean?" she asked, leaning forward. "What, exactly, have you 'been experiencing'?"

I told them about the flashbacks, and filled Art3mis in on the battle she'd just missed.

"You've gotta be kidding me," Art3mis muttered, shaking her head. "The first two challenges required you to possess detailed knowledge of the Smiths and Ninja Princess?"

I nodded. "Neither of those things was ever mentioned once in *Anorak's Almanac*," I said. "And those two flashbacks I experienced? They felt like ONI recordings of real moments. They were way too detailed to be simulations."

"How can you be sure of that?" Art3mis asked. "Anything could be simulated convincingly for a few seconds."

Aech shook her head.

"No way, Arty," she said. "You don't know what ONI playback is like. You can almost always tell the difference. Besides, James Donovan Halliday was a brilliant videogame designer and programmer. But he didn't know anything about women—especially Kira. There's no way he could've convincingly re-created one of her memories, from her perspective. He was a self-obsessed sociopath, incapable of feeling empathy for anyone else. Especially Kira . . ."

I had to bite my tongue to prevent myself from leaping to Halliday's defense. The man had been far from perfect, but he'd given us our entire world. "Sociopath" didn't just seem harsh, but downright blasphemous.

"But what you're suggesting can't be possible, Z," Shoto said. "The OASIS Neural Interface didn't exist back in the '80s, when Kira was a teenager. GSS didn't build the first fully functional ONI prototype headset until 2036—two years after Kira Morrow's death."

"I know," I replied. "It doesn't jibe with the official timeline. But no one was better at keeping secrets than Halliday. . . ." I took a deep breath. "I think we need to consider the possibility that somehow, before Kira Morrow died, Halliday made a copy of her consciousness. Using the same technology he used to copy his own mind and create Anorak."

All three of them stared at me in horrified silence. Then Art3mis shook her head.

"Kira never would've allowed Halliday to do that," she said. "Og wouldn't have either."

"So maybe Halliday figured out a way to scan Kira without her or Og realizing it." I swallowed as I realized what I was about to say. "Halliday was obsessed. He knew he could never have the real Kira, so he decided to make a copy of her for himself."

"Hold up," Aech interjected. "Kira was madly in love with Og. So why would he want to make a copy of her? If it was a true copy, it wouldn't love him either."

"I know," I said. "But the copy would also never grow old or die," I added. "Maybe Halliday thought he could convince it—her—to fall in love with him, over time. . . ."

"Jesus," Aech muttered, shaking her head. "If you're right . . . this is some extremely twisted shit we've gotten ourselves mixed up in, fam."

I nodded. I was starting to feel sick to my stomach too. Like I'd just learned that my childhood idol and hero had been a serial killer in his spare time.

Which was all the more reason why we couldn't just give Anorak the Siren's Soul and trust him to keep his word.

But the Siren's Soul appeared to be his one weakness. Once we had it, maybe we could use it to barter with him. Or lure him into a trap.

"We've still got five more shards to find," I said. "We gotta keep moving."

"Do we know where we're heading?" Art3mis asked.

"Yes, ma'am," I said, beaming with pride. "We sure do."

"And it's a good thing you're here, Arty," Shoto added. "Because we're gonna need your help with this one."

Art3mis's smile vanished. She replaced it with a fiercely competitive scowl that I recognized from the days of Halliday's contest. She called this "putting her game face on."

"So," she said, turning to face me. "Lay it on me, ace. Where are we headed?"

"Your old stomping grounds," I replied. "Shermer, Illinois."

Shermer was a medium-size planet near the center of Sector Sixteen. It was home to a lovingly detailed, decades-in-the-making OASIS re-creation of Shermer, Illinois, the fictional Chicago suburb where the filmmaker John Hughes set many of the movies he wrote and/or directed over the course of his celebrated career. Samantha used to say that Shermer was Hughes's "post-adolescent paracosm." A private fantasy world that he created and populated with his imagination, adding to it throughout his life—his own suburban, Midwest equivalent of Tolkien's Middle-earth.

Using Hughes's films as a reference, legions of fans had labored for decades to translate that private universe into an immersive interactive simulation here inside the OASIS. There was only one copy of the Shermer simulation, and it completely covered the planet's vast surface area. The simulated suburb had a scaled-down replica of Lake Michigan along its northern and eastern borders, and a shrunken version of downtown Chicago bordering it to the west and the south, so all the '80s Windy City landmarks featured in *Ferris Bueller's Day Off* could be incorporated in the simulation, too, including the Sears Tower, the stock exchange, Wrigley Field, and the Art Institute of Chicago. And out beyond the lake and the Chicago city limits, there was a ridiculously abbreviated version of the United States, so that the simulation could incorporate cities and locations from Hughes's scripted *Vacation* and *Home Alone* films.

It tended to ruin the atmosphere and continuity of a simulation when avatars were teleporting in and out of it at random all the time. That was why some planets, like Shermer, had been created with a limited number of designated arrival and departure points. Outside those locations, no teleportation was permitted. So when I selected Shermer as my teleportation destination on my HUD, I was presented with a map of the planet's designated arrival locations. Per Art3mis's instruction, I selected a railroad stop on the western edge of town.

When we finished rematerializing on the planet surface, we found ourselves standing on a small train platform in front of a circular redbrick station house. There was a crowd of several dozen NPCs standing around us, all '80s-era business-suit-clad men and women who were waiting for the morning train.

As we arrived, a song I recognized from my Hughes research began playing—the opening of Kirsty MacColl's cover of "You Just Haven't Earned It Yet, Baby," from the *She's Having a Baby* soundtrack. The music seemed to emanate from nowhere, as if there were invisible speakers floating in the air all around us. This was an indication that we'd triggered a needle drop. These were music cues hard-coded into specific areas of the simulation. They began to play whenever an avatar walked over or passed through a predetermined location—sort of like stepping on a soundtrack landmine. On our previous visit here together, Art3mis had told me that Shermer had more needle drops per square kilometer than any other planet in the OASIS. (That time, we'd arrived inside the Shermer simulation's replica of Chicago's O'Hare Airport, which was almost always snowed-in, year-round.)

As the song continued to play, a half-empty train pulled into the station behind us. When its doors slid open, the mob of commuters waiting on the platform around us began to pour into it. Art3mis motioned for us to follow her and took off in the other direction, pushing through the oncoming crowd of NPCs to reach the platform exit with Aech, Shoto, and me in tow.

As we cut through the adjacent parking lot, we passed two NPCs—a young man and woman—in the midst of a passionate kiss. When they came up for air, we could see that the young man was Kevin Bacon, dressed in a gray business suit, and that the young woman he'd been kissing was Elizabeth McGovern. I recognized them as Jake and Kristy Briggs, the two main characters in *She's Having a Baby*, Hughes's most autobiographical film. Jake kissed his wife goodbye one more time, then turned and sprinted off to make the train.

Across the street from the station, we passed the church where the wedding from *Sixteen Candles* took place. Just beyond it, I spotted a familiar neon billboard that said WELCOME TO SHERMER, ILLINOIS—ONE OF AMERICA'S TOWNS! POPULATION 31,286. But Art3mis led us in the opposite direction, onto Shermer Road, which led farther into town.

When the Shermer simulation was originally created in the early days of the OASIS, it had only incorporated locations and characters from four of John Hughes's films: *Sixteen Candles, The Breakfast Club, Ferris Bueller's Day Off,* and *Weird Science.* Over the decades since, it had been updated and overhauled several times to include other Hughes classics like *Pretty in Pink, Some Kind of Wonderful, She's Having a Baby, Uncle Buck, Mr. Mom, Planes, Trains, and Automobiles, The Great Outdoors,* and the aforementioned *Home Alone* and *Vacation* flicks. And in recent years, fans had expanded it to cover even the most obscure corners of his filmography, with characters and locations reflecting everything from *Curly Sue* to *Career Opportunities.* So when you visited Shermer now, interactive re-creations of all of these movies were constantly playing all around you. And the events depicted in those films played out over and over again simultaneously, day after day and week after week, on an endless loop.

I pulled up a map of the town, to pinpoint our location. Shermer had a set of railroad tracks running diagonally through its middle, dividing the town into two more-or-less equal halves, which were labeled RICH and POOR, and were color-coded red and blue respectively. The rich half of Shermer was the one that bordered the miniaturized version of Lake Michigan. The poor side was the one you had to drive through to get to the miniaturized version of downtown Chicago. The majority of Hughes's films were shot in and around Chicago, and many of them were filmed on location in the suburb of Northbrook, where Hughes himself attended high school. (A few were shot in L.A., like *Pretty in Pink,* though its story was set in suburban Chicago.) The geographic continuity in Hughes's films had made it possible for the planet's designers to re-create all of them here, inside one contiguous, interconnected simulation.

Judging by the proximity of the sun to the eastern horizon, it was still pretty early in the morning. But that was one of the many disorienting things about Shermer. Different parts of the town were set to different times of day, as well as to different seasons of the year. It was always daytime in the winter on some streets, but two blocks away it might be night-time in the early spring.

By now we'd walked a few blocks north of the tracks, into the rich side of town. Huge mansionlike homes lined both sides of the street, each with an immaculately manicured lawn and a circular driveway. Enormous oak and maple trees lined both sides of the street, their long, leafy branches stretching out over it, forming a green tunnel up ahead of us that seemed to go on forever. The sidewalks and side streets around us were deserted, except for a lonely paperboy making the morning rounds on his bike a few blocks farther down.

I'd only been here once before, during that early "date" with Art3mis. She'd told me it was one of her favorite places to go when she needed to relax and unwind, and gave me a guided tour of the simulated suburb's most popular sites. Unfortunately, I'd been too head-over-heels in love to retain much of what she'd told me, and too busy staring at her to take in the details of our surroundings. Since then, because of Kira's well-documented affection for Hughes, I'd rewatched most (but not quite all) of his films a few years ago. Now I was hoping I'd retained enough Shermer trivia to avoid looking like a complete fool in front of Art3mis.

We kept jogging down Shermer Road, Art3mis in the lead, until we triggered another needle drop—"It's All in the Game" by Carmel, another track off the *She's Having a Baby* soundtrack. Upon hearing it, Art3mis skidded to an abrupt halt. Then she turned around and startled all of us, by singing along with the song's opening lyrics in perfect harmony.

"*Many a tear has to fall, it's all . . . a game,*" she sang. "*Life is a wonderful game, we play and play. . . .*"

I'd heard Samantha sing once before, during the week we spent together at Og's estate, so I knew she wasn't using an autotuning app. Yet somehow I'd forgotten what an unusually beautiful singing voice she possessed, on top of all her other talents. Hearing it again now, under these circumstances, made my heart ache with a sudden ferocity that caught me completely off guard.

Art3mis glanced over and caught me staring at her like a slack-jawed goon. To my surprise, she didn't look away. She gave me what can only be described as a warm smile. Then she stopped singing and checked her Swatch.

"Excellent," she said. "We're right on time. It's the start of another day in paradise."

She pointed across the street. Aech, Shoto, and I all turned around, just in time to see the front doors of seven of the houses across the street swing open at once. In choreographed unison, seven different bathrobe-clad men emerged from their individual homes to retrieve their morning papers. I recognized six of these men as actors—Chevy Chase, Paul Dooley, Michael Keaton, Steve Martin, John Heard, and Lyman Ward—the men who portrayed Clark W. Griswold, Jim Baker, Jack Butler, Neal Page, Peter McCallister, and Tom Bueller respectively. All suburban dad characters in various Hughes films.

The seventh man wore large clear-framed eyeglasses and had spiky hair that was short on the side and in front, but long in the back—the sort of power mullet worn by rock stars throughout the '80s. His face looked incredibly familiar, but I couldn't place him. I was on the verge of running a facial-recognition app on him when it dawned on me—the man in question was John Hughes himself!

Hughes made a brief cameo in *The Breakfast Club,* playing the father of Brian Johnson, Anthony Michael Hall's character. Which meant that the house he'd emerged from was where Brian and his family must live in Shermer. (And since Anthony Michael Hall had also portrayed Rusty Griswold in *Vacation,* it occurred to me that there must be at least two different Anthony Michael Halls living on this street—possibly three, if Farmer Ted's house was around here too. And on top of that there was Gary Wallace, Anthony Michael Hall's character in *Weird Science.* But it was a safe bet that he lived on the other side of the tracks, because his father, Al, was a plumber.)

As I watched Mr. Johnson/John Hughes scoop up his morning paper and then shuffle back into his house, I couldn't help but be reminded of Anorak—the digital ghost of a dead creator, left behind to forever haunt his own creation.

"Hey, Z!" Art3mis said, snapping me out of my daze. "Let me see that clue again."

I removed the Second Shard from my inventory and held it out. She read the inscription aloud: " 'Recast the foul, restore his ending. Andie's first fate still needs mending.' "

"So that's gotta be it, right?" I asked. "Restore the original ending, the one where Andie ended up with Duckie instead of with Blane."

Art3mis didn't respond. She just stared at the inscription, lost in thought.

"That rich pretty boy, Blane," Aech said, glancing at the large, opulent homes lining both sides of the street. "He must live around here, right? I say we find him and lock his ass in the trunk of his daddy's BMW. Then he won't be able to attend the prom tonight. When he doesn't show, Andie will have no choice but to spend the evening with Duckie. That would 'restore his ending,' wouldn't it?"

That idea didn't sound half bad to me, but I waited for Art3mis to answer.

"As fun as it sounds, I don't think that will do the trick," she said, pointing at the inscription on the shard. "'Recast the foul,'" she repeated. "'Andie's fate . . .'"

"What about that scene in *Ferris Bueller's Day Off*?" I asked. "When he catches that foul ball during the Cubs game at Wrigley Field?"

Art3mis seemed mildly impressed by my suggestion. At least enough to consider it for all of two seconds. Then she shook her head dismissively.

"I don't think so. . . . *Recast the foul. Recast the foul.*"

Her eyes went wide, and her scowl of concentration transformed into a huge grin.

"I've got it!" she cried. "I know what we need to do!"

"You do?" Aech replied. "Are you sure?"

She checked her Swatch again, then turned to glance up and down the empty street. "There's only one way to find out. We need to catch a ride over to the high school. The bus should be coming by any second now."

Just as she finished saying this, a long yellow school bus rounded the corner at the end of the street. When it rolled to a stop at the curb in front of us, we could see the words SHERMER HIGH SCHOOL stenciled across its side.

The bus doors swung open and Art3mis jumped on board, then motioned for us to follow her. Another needle drop triggered, and the song "Oh Yeah" by Yello kicked in as the four of us filed onto the bus. Art3mis led us to a pair of empty seats near the middle. Aech sat next to her and I sat beside Shoto. The seats around us were occupied by high school kid

NPCs, all wearing 1980s clothing and hairstyles. Each one was modeled after a teenage actor from a school-bus scene in one of John Hughes's films. I thought I spotted extras from *Sixteen Candles* and *Ferris Bueller's Day Off.*

The bus began to move again, and I turned to glance out the window beside me. The sun was rising above the lake to the east. A beautiful spring morning in an upscale Midwestern suburb at the height of Reagan's America. Period-appropriate cars and trucks—1989 or earlier—filled the tree-lined streets.

"Look at this lily-white hellscape," Aech said, shaking her head as she stared out her own window. "Is there a single person of color in this entire town?"

"Sure," Art3mis replied. "But most of them hang out at a place called the Kandy Bar over in Chicago. This planet does have a serious diversity problem—like the whole of '80s cinema. . . ."

Aech nodded. "Well, maybe the next shard will be hidden in the kingdom of Zamunda."

"Oh shit!" Shoto replied. "That would be dope!"

Just then, two freshman nerds in the seat directly in front of me and Shoto turned around to face us. At first I thought they were wearing bras on their heads, but they were rocking athletic supporters as headbands instead. In unison, these two space cadets raised their toy laser pistols and fired them at us, and then one of them shouted, "Score! A direct hit!" before they both cracked up and turned back around.

"This place is a nuthouse," Shoto observed.

I nodded. "With some weird fashion trends."

"You ain't seen nothing yet," Art3mis whispered.

A second later, someone across the aisle loudly cleared their throat. We all turned to see a girl with obscenely thick eyeglasses staring at us. She slowly held her closed fist out to Shoto, then opened it to reveal a moist red gummy bear resting in the center of her palm.

"Want one?" she asked. "It's been in my pocket. They're real warm and soft."

"No," Shoto replied, shaking his head vigorously. "No, thank you."

"I'll pass too," I said.

"Hey, look," Aech whispered, pointing to a redheaded girl seated near the front of the bus. I recognized her as Samantha Baker—Molly Ringwald's character in *Sixteen Candles.*

"Maybe one of us should go wish her a happy birthday?" Aech said, chuckling softly.

"Every day is her birthday," Art3mis said. "And the morning after it. All the movie simulations on Shermer operate on an accelerated concurrent timeline, with the events depicted in each film repeating over and over in a continuous loop. All these NPCs are stuck in their own private Groundhog Day. Including that poor sweetheart of a girl . . ."

She pointed to a tall girl who was sitting directly across the aisle from Sam. When she turned in profile, I saw that it was a young Joan Cusack. She was wearing an elaborate neck brace, probably to indicate that her character was an awkward dork. But even in traction, she still looked cute as hell.

"She's my namesake, you know," Art3mis said. I turned back and saw that she was nodding toward Samantha Baker. "I can't watch it without ragequitting now, but *Sixteen Candles* was one of my mom's favorite movies. She loved all of Hughes's films."

"I remember," I said. "After she died, you would rewatch those movies, to feel closer to her, and to try and better understand who she was. I remember telling you that I did the same thing with my dad's comic-book collection, after he died."

Art3mis locked eyes with me. Then she nodded.

"I know," she said. "I remember that too."

She smiled at me again, and this time I smiled back. We continued to grin at each other for a few more seconds—then we remembered Aech and Shoto and turned to see them both watching us intently. Caught, they both quickly averted their eyes.

Just then, I got a glimpse of something strange out the bus windows behind them. We'd just crested a steep hill, and for a few seconds the Chicago skyline was visible in the distance, beyond a sea of suburban trees bursting with bright orange and red fall colors. And I also caught a glimpse of the Hollywood Bowl. The giant amphitheater had been incongruously cut-and-pasted into Shermer's suburban landscape. Aech noticed it, too, and pointed it out to Art3mis.

"What the hell is that doing here?" she asked. "Doesn't the Hollywood Bowl belong in Hollywood?"

"Indeed it does," Art3mis replied. "But the Hollywood Bowl is where one of the date scenes in *Some Kind of Wonderful* takes place. It was one of the rare John Hughes teen films not set in the suburbs of Chicago. The designers decided to shoehorn it into the Shermer simulation anyway, along with *Career Opportunities,* which is set in Missouri."

We all fell silent for a moment and gazed out the windows, taking in the strangely familiar sites that dotted the landscape around us.

"We're getting close to the school," Art3mis said. "Listen."

The opening of the song "Kajagoogoo" (the instrumental version, by the band of the same name) began to fade in on the Sim soundtrack. This needle drop had apparently been triggered by our proximity to the high school, which was now visible in the distance, through the bus's front window. We were approaching the school from the south, so the building's exterior looked identical to the Shermer High School seen in *The Breakfast Club.* On my previous visit, I'd learned that when the school was viewed from the west, the building's façade matched the version of Shermer High seen in *Sixteen Candles.* And the redbrick façade on the north and east sides matched the school's appearance in *Ferris Bueller's Day Off.* But all three entrances led into the same building, which was filled with painstakingly detailed re-creations of the various sets and practical locations used to create Shermer High's interior in the various cinematic incarnations of the school.

"Kajagoogoo" continued to play, increasing in volume as our bus rolled up to the curb in front of the school, and Art3mis, Aech, Shoto, and I filed off of it and attempted to blend in with the swell of NPC Shermer students surrounding us.

We followed Art3mis as she led us up the broad concrete sidewalk leading to the south entrance of the school. Hundreds of NPC teenagers sat in long rows on the stone benches that flanked either side of the walkway, all dressed in colorful mid-'80s attire. As we made our way down this Day-Glo gauntlet, the kids all began to clap and stomp their sneaker-clad feet in time with the song, while chanting along with its only lyric, which spelled out its title: *K-A-J-A-G-Double-O-G-Double-O!*

"Welcome to Shermer High School," Art3mis said, stretching her arms out wide as she continued to walk backward, toward the school building. "Shermer, Illinois. 6-0-0-6-2."

Art3mis snapped her fingers and her avatar's attire changed once again. Now she wore Annie Potts's black latex outfit from her first scene in *Pretty in Pink,* along with her punk-rock porcupine hairdo, dangling earrings, and dinner-fork bracelet.

"Applause, applause, applause," she said, doing a slow spin so that we could admire the attention to detail she'd put into her Iona cosplay.

Aech, Shoto, and I all gave her an enthusiastic golf clap. She scowled at us, then reached into her inventory and pulled out a pair of retro sunglasses—the same pair of *Risky Business* Ray-Bans she'd been wearing when we first met. Then she produced three identical pairs from her inventory and tossed them to me, Aech, and Shoto.

"For better hallway vision," she said.

We all eyed her warily, then shook our heads.

"Come on, you wimps!" Art3mis said. "Those are Hoffman lenses. You're gonna need them."

She motioned for us to put them on. When we complied, the clothing on each of our avatars abruptly changed, so that the three of us were dressed like the "Dork Squad" in *Sixteen Candles.* I was now "The Geek," played by Anthony Michael Hall; Aech was John Cusack's character, Bryce; and Shoto was their pal Cliff.

Aech took a look at us and then glanced down at herself. She turned to glare at Art3mis.

"Not cool, Arty."

Art3mis laughed and then put on her own shades. As she did, her own avatar's outfit changed once again, this time into the threads that Ferris Bueller wore on his day off. Black-and-white leather jacket. Leopard vest. The whole shebang. She gave her Ferris cosplay the finishing touch by pulling out a black beret and putting it on her head. Then she grinned at us and rubbed her hands together excitedly.

"OK, gang," she said. "This place is a lot more dangerous than it looks. Don't touch anything, don't talk to anyone. Just follow my lead."

We each removed our sunglasses and resumed our normal appearance. Then we followed Art3mis up the steps that led to the front entrance. Once Art3mis reached it, she threw open the front doors, and another needle drop kicked in: "Eighties" by Killing Joke.

Hearing the song, she grinned and popped her collar as she led us inside.

0015

As Art3mis led us through the hallowed halls of Shermer High School, we began to see a lot of strange things.

Just inside the entrance, we passed a gaggle of jocks wearing identical blue-and-gray letterman jackets featuring the school mascot, a bulldog. I recognized Andrew Clark (Emilio Estevez's character in *The Breakfast Club*) among them, along with Jake Ryan (Michael Schoeffling's character from *Sixteen Candles*). They were both admiring a pep-rally banner that read GO BULLDOGS GO!

We also saw several posters urging students to attend the senior prom, which was scheduled for later tonight, in the main ballroom at the Shermer Hotel. Every night of the week was prom night here on Shermer. All year long.

"Hey guys," Shoto called out, keeping his voice down to a loud whisper. "Over there! That's her, isn't it? Andie?"

He pointed out a familiar-looking girl with red hair who was walking toward us. It was Molly Ringwald again, but not the one from *Sixteen Candles* we'd spotted earlier on the bus. This was a slightly older Molly, with hair that was a much lighter shade of red.

"Wrong Ringwald," Art3mis said, shaking her head. "That's Claire Standish—the Molly from *The Breakfast Club*. We're looking for the Molly from *Pretty in Pink*. . . . And at this time of the morning, she should be right . . . over . . . there!"

She pointed down the hall, where we saw yet another Molly Ringwald walking to class. This incarnation wore a pair of wire-rimmed spectacles, her bright-red hair peeking out from beneath a black hat with a flower-print scarf wrapped around it. She was dressed in a pink sweater, over a pink blouse, and she did, in fact, look quite pretty in both of them.

"I hate this place," Aech said, shaking her head as she took in our surroundings. "It's like being stuck in the Matrix. With the Brat Pack."

"That why I love it!" Art3mis replied. "Don't yuck my yum, Aech. Don't do it."

"Hold on," I said. "Andie Walsh didn't attend this school in *Pretty in Pink*, did she?"

Art3mis shook her head.

"No," she replied. "She attended another fictional school—Meadowbrook High in Elgin, Illinois. But *Pretty in Pink*'s characters and filming locations were amalgamated into Shermer, along with the rest of Hughes's filmography. Keeps you on your toes. . . ."

We continued to follow Andie at a distance, until she stopped to greet her friend Jena, who was retrieving some textbooks from her locker. Shoto took a few tentative steps toward Andie, but Art3mis grabbed him by the arm.

"Not yet," she said. "We need to wait until she leads us to another NPC. Until he shows up, we have to keep our distance. . . ."

I started to ask who she meant, but I was drowned out by an approaching male voice that was repeatedly shouting the phrase "Save Ferris!"

We turned and saw that the voice belonged to a tall blond boy making his way through the crowd. He was holding out an empty Pepsi can to passing students, many of whom were eagerly dropping money into it.

"Thank you!" he said, bowing slightly after each donation. "God bless you! Save Ferris?"

The current of the crowd quickly carried him over to us, and he held his Pepsi can out to Aech before repeating his desperate plea: "Save Ferris?"

Aech stared back at him stoically, then said, "Excuse me?"

"Well, see, we're collecting money to buy Ferris Bueller a new kidney," the blond guy explained. "And those run about fifty G's or so. So if you could help out—"

Aech slapped the can out of his hands, sending it flying. Art3mis hurried over and pulled Aech away, laughing, while the flustered blond boy accused her of being a heartless wench.

"Don't get distracted," Art3mis said. "We need to keep track of Andie!" She pointed up ahead of us. "I think she went that way. NPC behavior is somewhat randomized here. Andie usually visits her locker first, but sometimes she wanders into one of these classrooms and sits down instead. So keep moving, and keep an eye out for her. We'll sweep the classrooms on both sides of the hall as we go!"

Art3mis took off down the hall again, pushing and weaving through the oncoming torrent of NPC high school kids. Aech, Shoto, and I hurried after her.

The school bell rang a few seconds later, and the hallway began to clear as NPC students filtered into their individual classrooms. One of them bumped into me as she went by, and when she turned to say, "Excuse me," I saw that it was a young Juliette Lewis, with her hair done up in a frizzy blond '80s perm. I knew her best from her starring roles in *Strange Days* and *From Dusk Till Dawn,* so it took me a moment to remember that she'd portrayed Audrey Griswold in *Christmas Vacation.*

Art3mis was right—for someone who had trained themselves to identify pop-culture icons from the '70s and '80s, this world was one huge distraction.

As we continued to follow Art3mis, she instructed us to split up and look inside each classroom we passed, to see if we could locate Andie Walsh.

I ran to the nearest door and glanced inside, then retreated as soon as I saw that it was an economics class being taught by Ben Stein, who was, of course, currently calling the roll.

"Adams, Adamly, Adamowsky, Adamson, Adler, Anderson?" he said. "Anderson?"

"Here!" I heard Anderson shout as I turned away and hurried on to the next classroom.

It was the school's computer room, and it was currently filled with student NPCs typing out their term papers on rows of ancient desktop computers. A sign posted above the chalkboard said HACKERS WILL BE EXPELLED, and that was one of the reasons I did a double-take a few seconds later, when I spotted the greatest fictional hacker of the '80s, Bryce Lynch, sitting at one of the computers. Then I noticed that Bryce looked older than I remembered, and he wasn't wearing his glasses. That finally made me realize that I was looking at Buck Ripley, a character in *The Great*

Outdoors portrayed by Chris Young, the same actor who had played Bryce Lynch on *Max Headroom* a few years earlier. Even so, before I turned to leave, I silently saluted him, recalling the dark time during Halliday's contest when I'd used the name Bryce Lynch as my fake identity, to avoid detection by IOI and the Sixers.

A bit farther down the hall, I peeked into the open door of an art classroom. At first I thought it was empty, but then I spotted Keith Nelson (Eric Stoltz's character from *Some Kind of Wonderful*) standing at an easel near the back of the room, painting a portrait of Lea Thompson, aka Miss Amanda Jones, with the song "Brilliant Mind" by Furniture playing out of a jambox on the desk beside him. I stood there transfixed for a moment, after it occurred to me that I was watching the original Marty McFly paint a portrait of his mother. Then Art3mis shouted for me to keep up, so I hurried to catch up with her. We passed by the open doors of the school gym, and inside we could see a bunch of girls in blue leotards doing various gymnastics exercises. On the wall, I noticed a large banner that said GO MULES GO! I pointed it out to Art3mis.

"I thought it was the Shermer Bulldogs," I said.

"The football and wrestling teams are the Shermer Bulldogs," she said. "The basketball team is the Shermer Mules. See?"

She pointed to a poster, announcing an upcoming away game, between the Shermer Mules and the Beacon Town Beavers.

Ahead of us, we found Shoto looking through another open doorway, into some sort of shop class, where dozens of male students were making identical ceramic elephant lamps. They lit up when the elephant's trunk was pulled. But one of the boys couldn't get his lamp to turn on, despite repeated attempts. When he turned around, we saw that it was Brian Johnson (Anthony Michael Hall's character in *The Breakfast Club*). Aech turned away to continue on to the next classroom, and I reluctantly followed her. Just before I lost sight of him, I saw Brian frown and cast a terrified glance toward his gruff-looking shop teacher.

We rounded another corner and Art3mis suddenly threw her arms out as she skidded to an abrupt halt, causing the rest of us to collide with her and one another. Once we'd regained our balance, Art3mis pointed up ahead. There was Andie Walsh, standing beside her open locker with an oddly dressed and extremely young Jon Cryer.

"There he is," she said. "Philip F. Dale. Better known as Duckie, aka the

Duck Man. One of the most divisive and controversial characters ever to spring forth from John Hughes's imagination."

"Oh, *that* dude," Aech said, rolling her eyes. "What do we want from him? Fashion advice?"

Art3mis laughed and shook her head.

"Just trust me, OK?" she replied. "I used to come to this place a lot. I've completed every single documented quest anchored here. A bunch of the older quests don't have any developer credits in their colophon, so no one knows who created them. But there were always rumors that some of these quests were created by Kira and Ogden Morrow, including several of the *Pretty in Pink* quests. I never took them seriously, but now I'm thinking those rumors may have been true. . . ."

We watched as Andie closed her locker and began to walk down the hall, Duckie buzzing around her like an insect.

I recited the clue printed on the Second Shard again in my head, trying to figure out why Art3mis had brought us here. Then I groaned and rolled my eyes.

"You've gotta be kidding me," I said. "The first line of the clue is a goddamn pun? 'Recast the foul'? Meaning a 'fowl,' like a *waterfowl*?"

"Correct," Art3mis said, smiling at me. "More specifically . . . a duck!"

She nodded toward Duckie, then drew her curved Elven sword from the scabbard on her back. Its blade sang like a giant tuning fork as she pulled it free.

"Arty," Aech said, "what the hell are you doing?"

"Wait for it," she said, gripping the hilt of her sword with both hands. She stood there waiting as another warning bell rang. Andie bid Duckie a hasty farewell and scurried away from him. Duckie raised his voice and continued to shout at her, asking if he should make lunch reservations for them in the cafeteria, perhaps at a table by the window. Andie covered her face in embarrassment, then turned and continued to walk in the other direction.

"Um, listen, may I admire you again today?" he shouted as Andie disappeared into one of the classrooms down the hall.

"Poor Duckie," Shoto whispered as we watched all of this go down.

"*Poor Duckie?*" Art3mis repeated, aghast. "Don't you mean poor Andie? She takes pity on the guy because she knows he's struggling with his own sexual identity, and that he doesn't have any other friends. And how does

Duckie repay her sympathy and kindness? By ignoring her boundaries, hounding her twenty-four-seven, and humiliating her in public every chance he gets. And check out how he treats other women when Andie isn't around. . . ."

She turned and motioned back over at Duckie, who had just walked over to a pair of preppy-looking girls standing a few yards away from us.

"Ladies, ladies," we heard him say. "Listen, I may be able to work out a deal where either one or the both of you could be pregnant by the holidays. What do you—"

Before the Duck Man was able to finish his sentence, Art3mis ran over to him and swung her sword, lopping his head completely off at the neck.

"There can be only one!" she shouted as Duckie's head went flying, taking his blow-dried pompadour along with it. It bounced off a nearby locker with a loud metal clang before coming to rest on the waxed marble floor of the hallway, not far from his now-decapitated body. The preppy girls he'd been addressing a split second earlier screamed and scattered, along with the other student NPCs who had been lingering in the vicinity.

"Jesus Christ, Arty!" Aech shouted. "You could've warned us first!"

"Yeah," Shoto added, chuckling to himself. "Next time give us a *heads-up!*"

Aech cut his laughter short by shoving his avatar into a wall.

I watched as Duckie's head and body faded away, leaving behind the loot he'd been carrying—a few gold coins, his vintage thrift-store clothing, a bolo tie, and a pair of battered white wingtip shoes with buckles instead of laces.

Art3mis scooped up the shoes and the tie but didn't bother with the clothes or the coins.

"Annoying dipshit," she said as she wiped Duckie's blood off her blade and slid it back into its scabbard. "I never liked him. Or the generations of spineless tool bags who've rooted for Andie to end up with him."

"Hold the phone," Shoto said. "Are you telling me you're on Team Blane?"

"Of course not," Art3mis replied, looking mildly revolted. "Blane is even worse than Duckie. I never thought either one of them was a good match for Andie. And Kira Morrow held the same opinion. . . ."

"OK . . ." Shoto said slowly. "But I still don't understand why you decapitated Duckie."

"To 'recast the foul,'" she said. "And 'restore his ending.'"

"How are we supposed to restore the ending where Andie winds up with Duckie, when you just *killed* Duckie?" I asked.

"I'll show you," she said. "But we need to make one more stop first."

She took off running again, and since we really had no choice, Aech, Shoto, and I followed. After several more identical-looking hallways, Art-3mis finally slid to a halt in front of a long row of orange lockers. One of these lockers had a warning scrawled across its door in black magic marker: TOUCH THIS LOCKER AND YOU DIE, FAG!

"Hey!" I shouted. "Bender's locker!"

Aech nodded and folded her arms. "I always questioned his reasoning here," she said. "Don't you think this homophobic graffiti would encourage people to mess with his locker rather than discourage them? Bender didn't think things through!"

"Yeah," Art3mis replied. "Lucky for us . . ."

She turned and grabbed a fire ax off the wall. She used it to smash open Bender's combination lock, then gingerly opened the locker door and quickly yanked her hand clear. When the door popped open, a small guillotine slid down the length of its frame, chopping off the toe of a sneaker that was poking out of the bottom of the locker.

Art3mis dug through the locker's bizarre contents until she finally found a crumpled brown paper bag. She opened it and pulled out another, even smaller paper bag, stained with what appeared to be French-fry grease. From inside that bag, she then withdrew a clear plastic sandwich bag, filled with a copious amount of marijuana.

Arty held up the bag of weed in her left hand and Duckie's shoes in her right.

"We've got the magic herb and the magic slippers," Art3mis said. "Now it's time for us to hit the city, baby. Dead-on. We have some drinks. A little nightlife. Some dancing . . . Let's go!"

She took off running again. We ran after her.

Once we made it back outside, Art3mis took us on a shortcut across the football field, and as we walked past one of the goal posts, we triggered another needle drop on the simulation's soundtrack. It happened to be one of Aech's all-time least-favorite songs—"Don't You (Forget About Me)" by Simple Minds. She already looked as if her nerves were hanging by a thread, and this nearly pushed her over the edge.

"Oh, give me a fucking break!" she cried, shouting to be heard over the opening of the song. "Seriously? Do all of us need to be here for this shit right now?"

I gave her a playful shove forward, and we ran to catch up with Art3mis and Shoto. As we did, the song continued to play, and when it reached its crescendo, Aech mockingly raised her right fist to the sky. It made the rest of us crack up.

A few seconds later, Aech's smile vanished.

"I'm getting a call," she said. "It's Endira. I promised to check in. I gotta take this. Gimme one second."

Aech walked several yards away and turned her back to us before she answered the call. I caught a glimpse of the worried face of her fiancée, Endira, in a vidfeed window in front of her. She was calling from their home in L.A., where she was still holding a vigil beside Aech's sabotaged immersion vault. Aech muted their conversation, so we couldn't hear what they were saying. But we didn't need to. It was obvious that Endira was distraught and Aech was trying to calm her down.

Shoto sighed. "I know we don't have time for this. But I've been dying to talk to Kiki too."

Art3mis looked thoughtful for a moment. Then she turned to me. "It won't take all four of us to collect this shard," she said. "How about you and I keep moving and give Aech and Shoto a few minutes with their ladies? We can call them once we have it."

The prospect of being alone with Art3mis for the first time in years rendered me momentarily speechless. After a few seconds of awkward silence I finally blurted out a response.

"Sure," I said, as nonchalantly as I could. "That's a great idea. And very thoughtful of you."

Art3mis nodded to Shoto, then tilted her head at me and gave me an odd grin. "OK, Z. Let's go snag this thing."

Then she was gone, running down the street again. I sprinted to catch up with her. Then I continued to follow her for several blocks, into a section of the simulation where it was always night, and the season appeared to be set to sometime in the spring or early summer. We were still on the rich side of town, in another upscale neighborhood near the lake shore, on a street lined with large, expensive homes. And there appeared to be a wild party going on in every single one of them.

"Parents are in Europe," Art3mis said, pointing at one house, then another, and another. "Parents are in Europe. Parents are in Europe. All of the rich kids' parents are in Europe."

The first house we passed on our left was one I recognized from *Some Kind of Wonderful*. It belonged to Craig Sheffer's character, Hardy Jenns. I could see him inside, through one of the big picture windows, plotting with his yuppie pals. A few seconds after we walked past his house, a black-and-gray limousine pulled up out front, and Mary Stuart Masterson got out. She opened the door for Eric Stoltz, and then he opened Lea Thompson's door. Eric and Lea went into Hardy's house, and Mary Stuart stayed behind and leaned against the limo's bumper.

A few seconds later, a black cargo van pulled into Hardy's driveway, and a skinhead named Duncan (Elias Koteas) jumped out, along with a whole gang of mean-looking hoods, and they all ran into Hardy's house too. We could hear the song "Beat's So Lonely" by Charlie Sexton blasting from within.

"That party is about to become a historical fact," Art3mis said.

That made me laugh out loud, which somehow earned me another one of her smiles.

We continued down the street. The neighboring house belonged to Steff McKee (James Spader's character in *Pretty in Pink*). He was greeting guests at his front door. For a split second I mistook the NPC for the male form of L0hengrin's avatar, which looked nearly identical but had shorter hair.

A few minutes later, we reached the Donnelly residence, where the events depicted in *Weird Science* were transpiring in and around the house. A few seconds after we arrived, a half-naked girl shot up out of the chimney and landed in a small pond in the front yard with a loud splash.

"Here we go," Art3mis said. "We're looking for two NPCs from *Weird Science*. Hang here for a minute. I'll be right back!"

She drew her guns and ran inside the house. I heard a rapid volley of gunfire, followed by what sounded like a grenade going off. A few seconds later, Art3mis rejoined me on the sidewalk in front of the house.

"They're not in there," she said. "Sometimes Max and Ian leave to party-hop when things get too crazy at the Donnelly residence. Sometimes they stick around and get turned into farm animals—but that usually doesn't happen until after midnight."

"Max and Ian?" I said. "The two assholes who dump an ICEE on Gary and Wyatt in *Weird Science*? Why the hell do we need them?"

"*So that we can get the Third Shard, Z,*" she replied in the tone of someone explaining something obvious to a very small child. "Just trust me, OK? That'll save us a lot of time." She pointed behind her. "We need to look for them at the parties being held on that side of the street now. I'll go see if they're at Stubby's. You go check out the shindig next door."

She pointed to another huge house across the street. Long strands of toilet paper were hanging from all of the trees out front. Beer cans, pizza boxes, and horny teenagers were strewn across the lawn. Music was blaring from within.

"Who lives there?" I asked.

"Jake Ryan," she said. "If you spot Ian or Max, I need you to restrain both of them and then call me. If I spot them at Stubby's, I'll do the same. Okie-dokie, Augie Doggie?"

I grinned and replied, "Okie-dokie, Doggie Daddy."

Art3mis took off, sprinting toward Stubby's house. I stared after her uncertainly for a moment, then I took a deep breath and ran in the opposite direction, toward Jake Ryan's house.

0016

The front yard looked like a war zone. Teenagers were milling around in the yard and the street, leaning on vintage Porsches, Ferraris, and Trans-Ams, dancing, drinking, and making out. Parked in the middle of the driveway, there was a red BMW with a drive-in food tray hanging from its passenger window. A mud-covered blue sedan was parked on top of a beemer, and two teenagers were making out in its back seat.

I walked up to the front door and pressed the doorbell. A loud gong sounded as it swung inward. A young Asian man was hanging from the inside of the door. He was extremely intoxicated. It took me a second to realize I knew him—it was Long Duk Dong, Gedde Watanabe's infamous character from *Sixteen Candles*.

"What's a-happening, hot stuff?" he said, speaking with a thick accent. When I failed to answer, the Donger motioned for me to come on inside. I thanked him and continued on into the house. It was packed with rich drunk white kids in full-on party mode. I bumped into a young Joan Cusack—dressed as the girl in the neck brace we'd seen earlier on the bus. She was trying to drink a beer by leaning her whole body backward, but then she leaned too far and fell on the floor.

Then I went to do a sweep of the living room, but was nearly crushed by a set of exercise weights that came crashing down through the ceiling. They continued to crash on through the floor, opening up an enormous hole into the wine cellar and smashing dozens of the bottles stored there.

I continued to make a complete circuit of the house but didn't see Ian or Max anywhere.

I had just made my way back to the living room when I received a text from Art3mis on my HUD, telling me to meet her at Stubby's house next door, in the backyard.

I sprinted outside and across the perfectly manicured lawn, to the rear of the adjacent house, which was also in the process of being trashed by reckless, drunken teenagers. In Stubby's backyard, I found Art3mis holding two extremely handsome teenage boys at gunpoint—Ian and Max from *Weird Science*. Max was played by the actor Robert Rusler, whom I also knew from his role as Ron Grady in *A Nightmare on Elm Street 2: Freddy's Revenge*. And Ian was played by an impossibly young Robert Downey Jr.

"Holy shit," I said. "The OG Iron Man! I forgot he was in a John Hughes movie. . . ."

"Just one," Art3mis said. "A supporting role in *Weird Science*. But—little-known fact—Robert Downey Jr. almost played the lead in another Hughes film. That's why we need him."

Art3mis pointed at Max. "Him, we can let go," she said. She lowered her assault rifle, so that it was no longer pointed at Max's head. Max stood there frozen for a second, then he turned tail and took off running across the expansive green lawn, in the direction of Jake Ryan's house. He never looked back.

Art3mis turned her attention back to Ian. She removed the bag of weed she'd taken from Bender's locker and dangled it in front of him. The expression on his face suddenly went blank, as if he'd been hypnotized.

"Would you like some of this?" Art3mis asked.

"Why yes, madam!" Ian replied. "I certainly would."

He reached for the bag, but she yanked it back out of his reach.

"I'll make you a deal," Art3mis said. "I'll give you this whole bag of doobage if you just perform two simple tasks for me."

"Sure," Ian said, batting his eyelashes at her. "Anything you say, doll."

"I figured out this little trick by playing through all the official *Weird Science* quests," Art3mis said. "The NPC re-creations of Max and Ian are both total hedonists, and they'll perform nearly any task in exchange for sex or drugs." She turned to smile at him. "Isn't that right, Ian?"

RDJ batted his eyelashes at her again and nodded. Art3mis opened her inventory and took out the wingtip shoes and bolo tie she'd looted from Duckie back at the high school, then held them out to Ian.

"First, I need you to put these on," she said. "Then I need you to go dance with Andie Walsh at the senior prom tonight. Deal?"

"Deal," Ian said. He took the shoes from her and put them on. Then he put the bolo tie around his neck. As soon as he did, his wardrobe and hairstyle changed. He no longer looked like Robert Downey Jr. as Ian in *Weird Science*. Now he looked like Robert Downey Jr. in *Back to School*, in the role of Derek Lutz. But he was dressed in the same vintage suit that Jon Cryer wore in the original ending of *Pretty in Pink*.

When his transformation completed, it triggered another music cue. At first I thought I was hearing the song "I Want a New Drug" by Huey Lewis and the News, but as soon as the lyrics kicked in, I realized it was actually Weird Al Yankovic's parody—"I Want a New Duck."

The song only played for five or six seconds, while the newly anointed Robert Duckey Jr. did a little dance to show off his new attire. Then the song cut out and he struck a pose and said, "I remain now, and will always be, a Duck Man."

He pointed down at his shoes, turned his left foot left, then his right foot right, before realigning them both. Then he looked back up at us. When we failed to applaud, he frowned and sniffed each of his armpits before asking, "Do I offend?"

Art3mis let out a victorious cry, then ran over and slapped him on the back.

"Robert Downey Jr. was originally supposed to play the role of Duckie," she explained. "But the studio decided to cast Jon Cryer in the role instead. And when the first cut of the film was screened, no one in the test audience wanted Duckie and Andie to end up together. So on short notice, Hughes was forced to write a new ending—one in which Andie ends up with that rich douchebag Blane instead."

"Really?" I said. "I never knew that." I shook my head. "Pretty impressive, Arty."

"Why, thank you, Parzival," she replied, sounding genuinely pleased with herself. "I remembered reading an old interview with Molly Ringwald, where she said she believed Hughes's original ending of *Pretty in Pink* would've worked if Robert Downey Jr. had played the role of Duckie as originally intended, because the two of them would've had a lot more on-screen chemistry."

I recited the inscription again, this time from memory. "'Recast the foul, restore his ending. Andie's first fate still needs mending.' So that was Andie's first fate?" I said. "To wind up with RDJ as Duckie? And the only way to 'mend' that fate is to 'recast the foul'?" I smiled at Art3mis and shook my head. "Arty, you're a genius!"

I gave her a round of applause, and she took a small bow. Then she grabbed Robert Duckie Jr. by the arm and took off running again. I ran after them as they sprinted across Stubby's lawn, and then over to a Rolls-Royce convertible that was parked in Jake Ryan's driveway. Art3mis shoved Duckie into the back seat and then got behind the wheel. I jumped into the passenger seat beside her.

"Hey," I said. "Wouldn't we get there faster . . . in a Ferrari?"

I pointed to the woods behind Jake Ryan's house. There, visible through the trees, was a secluded house on stilts. I recognized it as Cameron Frye's residence. And from here, we could see the separate glass-walled garage at the back of the house.

"Forget it," Art3mis said. "Cameron's dad has a state-of-the-art security system. You can only steal that car in the daytime, with the keys and with Cameron's help. If you try to steal it now, you'll end up in the Shermer jail, with the kid from *Reach the Rock*. It's easy enough to escape, but we'd waste thirty minutes." She smiled. "We could steal the same Ferrari from Alec Baldwin, in a church parking lot just a few blocks from here," she said, pointing off to the south. Then she glanced at her watch. "But the Briggs-Bainbridge wedding doesn't start for another hour. Sorry, but I'm afraid Mr. Ryan's Rolls-Royce is our best option at the moment."

"Fine," I muttered. "We'll take this brown shit box."

"Buckle up, ace," Art3mis said, glancing over at me. She waited for me to comply. Once I did, she gave me a devious smile.

"This is getting good," she said as she shifted the car into drive and floored the gas. This triggered another needle drop—the "Peter Gunn Theme," which continued to play as the Rolls-Royce peeled out, carrying us off into the night.

As Art3mis drove through the moonlit labyrinth of suburban streets at breakneck speed, Robert Downey Jr. and I were jerked around in our seats again and again as she whipped the Rolls around sharp corners. For a few minutes I felt like we'd been transported into a game of Grand Theft Auto: Shermer, until Art3mis turned onto the highway and our ride smoothed out. (Taking the onramp triggered a fresh needle drop—"Holiday Road" by Lindsay Buckingham—which cut back out when we got off the highway a few exits later.)

At some point we must've crossed over the railroad tracks and entered the poor side of town, because the houses around us became smaller, crappier, and closer together. As we were driving down one of these streets, I spotted Harry Dean Stanton, dressed in a bathrobe, sitting on a lawn chair in his darkened front yard, reading a newspaper. A few houses down, I saw John Bender standing in an open garage, smoking a cigarette while he stirred a can of paint. Then I noticed the house right next door, which looked completely abandoned. The lawn was overgrown, the windows were all boarded up, and a Foreclosed sign was nailed to the front door. Then I noticed the name printed on the rusted mailbox out front: D. GRIFFITH.

I pointed it out to Art3mis, and she smiled.

"There are five different John Candy NPCs wandering around Shermer," she said. "Can you name all of them?"

"Sure," I said. "Del Griffith, of course. Then there's Chet Ripley, C. D. Marsh, and Gus Polinski, the Polka King of the Midwest. Oh, and I saw Buck Russell this morning."

She grinned at me, impressed.

"Not bad, Watts," she said. "Still sharp as a tack." She pointed to a log cabin–style restaurant on the other side of the street called Paul Bunyan's Cupboard, with large statues of Paul and Babe the Blue Ox by its front entrance.

"Want to stop in and try to eat an Old Ninety-Sixer?" Art3mis asked. "It's probably a lot harder when you're using an ONI—"

Appearing to realize what she'd just said, she cut herself off, and out of the corner of my eye I saw her wince.

"Fuck *yes*," I said, elbowing her in the ribs to let her know it was all right. "If we had time, I would destroy an Old Ninety-Sixer right now." I lowered my voice. "You might think I'd be opposed to eating something with the word 'sixer' in its name, but I am not. At all."

Art3mis laughed her laugh again, and it was music to my ears.

"When this is over, we're coming back here to chow down, OK?" I said. She nodded and said, "It's a date."

I felt myself turn several different shades of red.

As we continued to drive, I stole a glance over at her in the driver's seat. The top was down and the wind was in her hair. She looked beautiful. And happy. And I was still madly in love with her. No matter how much I denied it.

Out of nowhere, another needle drop triggered and a new song began to play—"More Than a Feeling" by Boston. The same song plays during a brief flashback in *She's Having a Baby*, when Jake falls in love with his future wife, Kristy, at first sight.

As soon as it began, Art3mis snapped her head to the right and caught me staring at her. I glanced away, pretending to look out the windshield. But in the reflection in the glass, I thought I caught a glimpse of her smiling. Then I heard her laugh.

"What's so funny?" I asked.

"That song," she replied. "It starts to play whenever one avatar stares at another avatar for longer than five seconds while also experiencing a drastic increase in their heart rate. It's a little Easter egg they added for ONI users last year."

"Great," I muttered. "Busted by my own bio monitors."

She laughed, keeping her eyes on the road ahead. I sank down into my seat and pretended to look out the window, wishing that magic worked on this planet, so that I could turn myself invisible.

⁕ ⁕ ⁕

We arrived at the Shermer Hotel a few minutes later. Art3mis screeched Mr. Ryan's Rolls-Royce up onto the curb, causing several NPC pedestrians to dive out of the way.

The three of us jumped out of the car and sprinted toward the hotel's main entrance. But RDJ skidded to a halt just shy of the threshold.

"I'm sorry," he said to Art3mis. "But I can't go in there."

"What?" she replied, grabbing him by his satin lapels. "Why the hell not? You promised! And I already gave you all of Bender's weed!"

"I know," RDJ replied. "And I want to help you out. But I can't go in there. Not like this. I wouldn't know what to do. Or say."

"You don't have to say anything!" Art3mis said, prodding him toward the entrance. "Just go in there, find the hot redhead in the atrocious pink nightgown, and ask her to dance. That's it! Done!"

The RDJ NPC shook his head and didn't budge. Art3mis nodded at me, and I grabbed him around the waist, lifted him off the ground, and attempted to carry him across the threshold. But I couldn't do it. It was like he kept bouncing off an invisible force field that somehow prevented him from going inside.

I tried a few more times anyway, to no avail. Then RDJ began to struggle, trying to get free of my grip.

"I'm sorry!" he cried. "But I'm just not emotionally prepared, at this exact juncture, to go in there. I mean, look how I'm dressed.... And I never know what to say at formal social gatherings such as this!"

Art3mis gave me a nod and I let go of him. He straightened his suit and gave me an indignant glare. I thought he might bolt, but instead, he folded his arms and began to absentmindedly tap his foot—an indication that he was running an idle animation.

I turned to Art3mis.

" 'Recast the foul, restore *his* ending,' " I recited. "This whole time, we thought the clue meant we were supposed to restore Duckie's ending. But what if 'restore his ending' means we need to restore John Hughes's ending? The ending of *Pretty in Pink* he originally wrote in his screenplay?" I nodded at the RDJ NPC. "What if we need to find a copy of the original script and give it to him?"

Art3mis threw up her hands. "And how are we supposed to do that?"

I smiled at her. "We go to the writer's house," I replied.

She gave me a puzzled look for a few seconds, then her eyes lit up with understanding.

"Holy shit!" she cried. "That might be it! Z, you're a genius!"

Before I knew what the hell was happening, she grabbed my face and planted a kiss on me. She wasn't wearing an ONI headset, so I knew she didn't feel that kiss. But I did. Then she turned to RDJ.

"Don't go anywhere," she told him. "We'll be right back."

Then she grabbed me by the arm and pulled me back in the direction of the car.

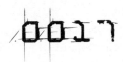

Art3mis knew a shortcut through the rich side of town, and was somehow able to navigate from memory, racing through the dark, undifferentiated maze of identical streets, each lined with identical houses. She managed to get us there in just a few minutes, but her erratic driving triggered another needle drop—"March of the Swivel Heads" by the English Beat. I don't think she touched the brake pedal once, until we finally screeched to a halt in the Johnson family's driveway.

As soon as our feet touched the driveway, another needle drop went off: "Modigliani (Lost in Your Eyes)" by Book of Love. Hearing it, Art3mis glanced over at me, and we shared a brief smile of recognition. Then we both turned and ran to the front door. She rang the doorbell, and a second later, Mrs. Johnson opened it, wearing an annoyed scowl. Her young daughter was standing in the doorway behind her, and she was scowling at us too. I recognized both of them from their brief scene in *The Breakfast Club* when they drop Anthony Michael Hall's character, Brian, off at detention, and his mom says, "Well, mister, you better figure out a way to study!" and then his little sister says, "Yeah!" (Another piece of trivia I'd learned from Artie's blog, years ago, was that they were played by Anthony Michael Hall's real-life mother and sister.)

"I'm sorry," Mrs. Johnson said, after she spent a few more seconds scowling at us. "We don't allow solicitors." She pointed to a small No Solicitors sign with gold lettering nailed to their front door.

"Oh, we're not selling anything, Mrs. Johnson," Art3mis said. "My name is Art3mis, and this is my friend Parzival. We're here to speak with your husband—about our mutual friend, Duckie? Philip F. Dale?"

Mrs. Johnson's scowl vanished, and she gave Art3mis a huge smile. In the next moment, her face melted and morphed, and she transformed into a completely different woman. Now the NPC in front of us was a slender woman with long blond hair and a warm, friendly smile. I didn't recognize her at all—but Art3mis did. Instantly.

"Mrs. Hughes!" she said, lowering her eyes and bowing her head, as if she'd just encountered royalty. Then she glanced sideways at me and whispered, "Nancy Hughes! I've never seen *her* here before! I didn't even know you could!"

"John is upstairs working," Nancy said, stepping back to open the door the rest of the way for us. "But I believe he's expecting you. Please, come on in. . . ."

She ushered us into the foyer and closed the front door. I looked around for Brian Johnson's little sister, but she'd vanished along with her mother. However, I did catch a glimpse of two young boys chasing each other around the dining-room table with Nerf guns. I realized they must be NPC re-creations of the Hugheses' two sons, James and John. Seeing them reminded me of an interview John Hughes gave, where he mentioned that his screenplay for *Mr. Mom* was based on his experience caring for his two boys on his own for a year, when his wife, Nancy, spent a lot of time traveling for work.

Hughes's children and marriage had directly inspired so much of his work—it seemed fitting that this interactive tribute to his family was hidden here on Shermer, among all of his fictional creations.

Art3mis and I continued to gaze around us in wonder, like museum patrons on their first visit, until Nancy politely cleared her throat to get our attention. Then she pointed to the long, curved wooden staircase behind her.

"He's upstairs in his office, at the end of the hall," she said, lowering her voice to a whisper. "But make sure to knock before you go in. He's writing."

"Thank you, ma'am," I whispered back. I motioned for Art3mis to lead the way and followed her up the stairs. When we reached the top, we could hear a typewriter clacking down the hall. Treading as softly as we could on the wooden floorboards, we followed the sound to a closed door at the end of the hall. The thick aroma of tobacco wafted in the air, rising from the crack at the bottom of the door, along with the sound of music—Dream Academy's instrumental version of the Smiths' "Please, Please, Please Let Me Get What I Want."

I gave Art3mis a nod, then I took a deep breath and rapped three times on the door.

The clacking of typewriter keys ceased, and we heard someone get up, followed by approaching footsteps. Then the door opened, and there he was, standing right in front of us, in the simulated flesh: John Wilden Hughes Jr.

He looked different from how he'd looked when I'd caught a glimpse of him a few hours earlier, as he was collecting his morning paper with the other middle-aged men of Shermer. His hair was longer and spikier. His glasses were bigger and rounder and had different frames. He had the same rounded features and the same sad, wise eyes. But he no longer wore the stern, impassive expression he'd had back when he was Mr. Johnson. Now that he was Mr. Hughes, he was full of energy and emotion—along with epic amounts of nicotine and caffeine, judging by all of the empty coffee cups on his desk, and the overflowing ashtray beside his enormous green IBM Selectric typewriter.

Behind his desk, carefully displayed on some shelves, were dozens of pairs of shoes—his famous sneaker collection, which continued to grow throughout his life.

"Art3mis!" he bellowed in an extremely deep voice, smiling wide in recognition as soon as he saw her. "I've been expecting you!"

Then, to our shock, he went in for a hug. Art3mis laughed and hugged John Hughes back, while giving me a can-you-believe-this-is-happening look over his shoulder. Then he let go of her and turned to me.

"And you brought a friend along," he said, offering me his hand. "Hi there. I'm John."

"Parzival," I replied, shaking it. The guy had a firm grip! "It's an honor to meet you, sir. I'm a big fan of your work."

"Really?" he said, placing his right hand over his heart. "That's so wonderful to hear. And kind of you to say. Please, won't you both come on in?"

After we stepped into his office, he closed the door, then hurried over to a row of filing cabinets in the corner and began to dig through its drawers.

"You're here for a copy of my *Pretty in Pink* script, right?" he asked. "Which draft did you want?"

"Your favorite draft," Art3mis said. "The one with your original ending, where Duckie and Andie dance together?"

He gave her a big smile, then resumed digging through his filing-cabinet drawers.

"That *was* my favorite ending," he said. "But it didn't work for the test audience, so the studio made me change it."

He finally found the script he was looking for and shouted, "Victory!" as he held it over his head. A golden shaft of light descended from the ceiling for a few seconds, bathing him and the script in its glow, as we heard the sound of angelic chimes. Then he held the script out and presented it to Art3mis. She took it from him with both hands, and as she did, the light vanished and the chimes ceased.

"Thank you," Art3mis said, bowing slightly. "Very much."

"My pleasure!" he said. "If you need anything else, you know where to find me."

He gave us both another handshake, then he sat back down at his desk, and immediately began typing again—faster than I'd ever seen anyone type in my life. The clack of his keys sounded like machine-gun fire, and the carriage return moved rapidly from left to right in just a few seconds, like an ammo belt feeding it a steady supply of bullets.

Art3mis turned toward me, wearing a big, goofy grin, and held up the script so that I could see what was typed on its cover page: "PRETTY IN PINK by John Hughes. FIFTH DRAFT: 5/9/85."

"We got it!" she said.

I nodded and offered her a high five. She laughed and slapped my hand. "Let's go get that shard!" I said.

She nodded and we turned around to leave. But when I reached for the doorknob, I discovered something odd—a black computer keyboard was hanging on the back of Hughes's office door, dangling from the coat hook by its cord.

"Weird," I said, grabbing the keyboard to examine it more closely. That was when we both saw the brand name and model number. It wasn't just a keyboard. It was a Memotech MTX512—the vintage computer that Gary and Wyatt used to create Lisa in *Weird Science*, which had (in revolutionary-at-the-time fashion) hidden its 8-bit CPU in the chassis of the keyboard itself. It looked pretty beat-up. A few of the keys on the keyboard were missing.

I turned to address the John Hughes NPC.

"What's this doing here?" I asked. But Hughes didn't even seem to hear me. He just kept on writing. I turned back to Art3mis and handed the computer to her.

"When I ran into Wyatt's house earlier, I noticed that his computer was missing from his bedroom," she said. "The FDX hard-drive add-on was still there, but this keyboard was gone. Which would appear to indicate that someone took it from Wyatt's and brought it here. . . ."

I leaned forward to study the keyboard more closely. There were four missing letters—the R, A, I, and K keys were gone.

Then it hit me.

"Og!" I said. "He was here earlier today, when *he* collected the Third Shard. And he put the computer here, where he knew we would see it."

I pointed at the Memotech MTX512. "In *Weird Science,* a nerd used this computer to create a simulation of his dream girl," I said. "Maybe Og is trying to tell us that Halliday did the same thing. That's why he knocked out these four keys . . . K, I, R, and A."

"Holy shit!" Art3mis said. "Kira!"

I nodded. Then another lightbulb went on over my head.

"If Og was able to leave behind a hidden message for us here, maybe he did the same thing when he was collecting the first two shards!" I said. "I should have realized it on Kodama."

I explained to Art3mis how Og's strange high score on the Ninja Princess videogame had puzzled me.

"Did you spot anything else on Kodama?" Art3mis asked. "Anything else out of place?"

I thought it over for a moment, then shook my head.

"I don't think so," I said. "I don't remember seeing anything like that on Middletown either. But there are 256 different instances of Middletown spread across the planet, and Og could have obtained his shard from any one of them."

"That's hopeless," Art3mis said, shaking her head. "We don't have time to search all those instances. We still have four more shards to collect, and only about five hours to do it."

"You're right," I said. "We don't have time. But I bet I know someone who does. Hold on. Give me a minute. . . ."

I pulled up my HUD and selected L0hengrin's name from my contact list, then I tapped the icon to send her a text. Then, on the off chance that

Anorak was monitoring my video feeds, I closed my eyes and typed out my entire message to Lo without looking at it:

Dear Lo,

I could use some more of your help after all.

I need you to go back and locate the instance of Middletown where Og obtained the First Shard. It should be the only other instance on the planet that is currently set to the year 1989. You'll have to teleport around and check them all one at a time until you find it. Once you do, I need you to look for anything unusual or out of place. Something around Og's home, or in Kira's bedroom. If you find something, message me immediately and I'll send you my coordinates so we can meet in a secure location.

Thanks, Lo. I can't tell you anything more right now, but I promise, it's important.

I owe you a Wookiee Life Debt for this.

Sincerely,

Z

I used a keyboard shortcut to send the message without looking at it. Then I opened my eyes, closed my HUD, and turned back to face Art3mis. "I emailed a friend who might be able to help," I said. "Fingers crossed." Art3mis gave me a dubious look and folded her arms.

"A friend?" she repeated. "What friend?"

Was that a hint of jealousy in her voice?

"I'll tell you later," I said as I threw open the door of Hughes's office and sprinted off down the hall. "Come on!"

As we headed down the stairs, I cast a glance back down the hall. Through his open office door, I caught one last, brief glimpse of John Hughes sitting at his desk, hunched over his typewriter in a thick cloud of cigarette smoke, clacking away furiously on his typewriter keys, writing as if his life depended on it.

● ● ●

Art3mis drove us back to the Shermer Hotel, where the NPC of Robert Duckie Jr. was standing frozen out front. She handed him the script we'd retrieved from John Hughes. RDJ opened it to the last few pages and scanned them in a matter of seconds. Then, as soon as he finished reading them, the script suddenly vanished in a shower of glittering gold dust.

"Got it!" Duckie said as he put on his sunglasses. "Let's plow."

Then he ran inside the hotel. We followed him through the hotel lobby and down a long marble-floored mezzanine, which led into the main ballroom where the senior prom was being held. Andie Walsh was waiting there, standing all alone in her homemade pink dress, biting her lower lip and looking around nervously. When she spotted Robert Downey Jr. walking toward her, decked out in his Duckie threads, her eyes widened in surprise, just as some piano music from Michael Gore's *Pretty in Pink* score swelled on the soundtrack. Then, without hesitation, Andie ran toward Duckie. He started running, too, and when they reached each other, she leaped into his open arms. Then he twirled her around a few times before setting her back down. They both took a step back to admire each other's outfits, exchanging a few words that we were too far away to make out. Then Andie took Duckie's arm, and together, they walked through the ballroom entrance. Art3mis and I followed them inside.

It looked identical to the ballroom where the original ending of *Pretty in Pink* was filmed. There was a large dance floor in the center of the room, where a few hundred well-to-do Shermer teenagers dressed in retro tuxedos and pastel-colored prom dresses were grooving to the song "If You Leave" by Orchestral Manoeuvres in the Dark. Two DJs in matching bellhop outfits stood on the stage, surrounded by synthesizers and mixing boards. A giant black-and-white photograph of a conductor and his orchestra covered the wall behind them. Circular dining tables were arranged on either side of the dance floor, and I spotted Steph McKee again, sitting at one of them in a tuxedo, looking bored. Then he saw who had just walked into the room and sat bolt-upright.

As Andie and Duckie slowly made their way to the dance floor, every pair of eyes in the room turned to look at them. When the couples out on the floor spotted them, they too stopped dancing to stare. A few seconds after that, the DJs stopped the music too. Now everyone in the room was motionless, staring at Andie and Duckie, with bourgeois contempt burning in their eyes.

We watched from a distance as Blane McDonough emerged from the silent crowd and walked over to Andie and Duckie. He said something to

Andie, but she only responded by shaking her head. Blane offered his hand to Duckie, and after considering it for a few seconds, Duckie shook it. Blane turned and walked away, disappearing back into the crowd.

"Boom!" Art3mis shouted. "Andie's first fate no longer needs mending!"

We continued to watch as Andie took Duckie's hand and the two of them walked through the sea of silent, staring faces, wearing proud and defiant looks of their own. When they reached the center of the dance floor, the DJs turned the sound system back on and cued up a new song: "Heroes" by David Bowie.

Duckie took Andie in his arms and the two of them began to dance, spinning around and around together, until they merged into a single whirling blur of pink. Then that pink blur vanished in a brilliant flash of neon-pink light.

When my eyes recovered, I saw the Third Shard floating in the air above the center of the dance floor, where the two star-crossed lovers had stood a second earlier.

Art3mis ran over and tried to grab the shard, but her hands passed right through. She laughed and turned back to look at me, then made a come-hither motion with her index finger. I joined her on the dance floor.

"'For each fragment *my heir* must pay a toll,'" I recited as I reached out and wrapped my fingers around the shard.

As before, taking the shard triggered another flashback. . . .

• • •

I was Kira again, this time standing in her childhood bedroom in her mother's tiny cottage on the outskirts of London. I'd seen photographs Kira had taken of herself in this room, to mail to Og back in the States during his senior year of high school, which they spent apart.

Two open suitcases lay on the bed in front of me, filled with a jumble of clothing, sketchbooks, and boxes of floppy disks. Kira glanced up from her packing to look at eighteen-year-old Ogden Morrow, who was standing in the doorway, blocking it with his large frame. Beyond it I could just make out a short bald man in a ragged shirt, in the midst of yelling something in a thick Cockney accent. This had to be Kira's drunken stepfather, Graham— who was clearly enraged, and only keeping his distance thanks to the cricket bat that Og was clutching with both hands and brandishing threateningly, like *Shaun of the Dead.*

This was another moment Og had described in his autobiography. Something that had occurred in April of 1990, after Kira told her family she intended to move back to the States that summer, to help Og and Halliday found Gregarious Games, instead of going to university like they wanted her to. Hearing this, her abusive stepfather had become enraged and slapped her. (I could still feel the dull ache of pain around her/my left eye at that very moment.) When she called Og and told him, he jumped on the first flight to London to get Kira and bring her back home. And I was experiencing Kira's memory of that rescue. Or a few seconds of it anyway . . .

Og glanced back over his shoulder, locked eyes with me/Kira, and gave her a warm smile that let her know everything was going to be all right, that she was safe, and that he would protect her. In that instant, I also felt her intense physical reaction to Og's glance and his smile, and it gave me a sense of just how profoundly Kira had loved him. Samantha's smile still gave me the exact same sensation—a sensation best described as devastation.

. . . Then, in a blink, the flashback was over. I found myself back on the dance floor with Art3mis. And when I looked down, I saw the Third Shard in my right hand.

I turned it over to read the clue. But instead of words, I saw an image engraved there. It was an ornate shield adorned with stylized math symbols for addition, subtraction, division, and multiplication. I recognized it immediately as the coat of arms of Queen Itsalot, sovereign ruler of the magical kingdom of Itsalot on the planet Halcydonia.

I felt a sudden surge of optimism, immediately followed by an overwhelming sense of dread. On one hand, this was a huge stroke of luck. I'd spent a huge chunk of my childhood on Halcydonia, and my knowledge of it was encyclopedic, even by gunter standards. But I hadn't set foot on the planet in over ten years. And after my last visit, I'd vowed never to return.

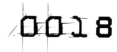

Art3mis and I—along with Aech and Shoto, both looking shaken but eager to rejoin the quest—materialized on Halcydonia. Specifically, within my personal Be-Free Treehouse, located deep within the Friendship Forest of Faraway, which was where any Halcydonian was automatically transported when they returned to the planet. Any kid in the OASIS under the age of thirteen could earn a Be-Free Treehouse by completing the free educational quests spread across the planet. Once you earned your treehouse, it belonged to you for the rest of your life, and no one could come inside it without your permission. It was just a tiny virtual space, but growing up in the stacks, it was also the first space that I was able to call my own—and the only one, until I discovered my hideout.

When Kira and Og founded Halcydonia Interactive and created this planet, they'd cooked up the Be-Free Treehouses as a way to give kids around the world a free, happy, virtual home inside the OASIS that they could always escape to, and find themselves surrounded by an endless assortment of furry friends and anthropomorphic animal teachers who were always overjoyed to see them, and who just wanted to teach them how to read, write, spell, and do arithmetic, all while staying physically fit and being kind to others.

Being able to put on my OASIS visor and be transported to the magical kingdom of Halcydonia was one of the things that kept me sane, and it made my life in the Portland Avenue Stacks bearable. And it did the same thing for millions of other kids around the world.

If you were under age thirteen, you could teleport to Halcydonia for free from Incipio, or from any public transport terminal anywhere else in the OASIS. And once you got there, all the quests and learning games were free too. I never wanted to leave. And for a few years, I almost never did. Those were the last few years of my mother's life, when she was slipping deeper into depression and the addiction that would end up killing her.

During those last years, as our tiny, grim trailer in the stacks became an increasingly unpleasant place to be, I spent more and more time hanging out inside my treehouse on Halcydonia, and sometimes after she got off work, my mom would log back in to the OASIS and join me there, so I could tell her about my day, or show her the artwork I'd made, or introduce her to one of my new virtual animal friends.

The inside of my Be-Free Treehouse was one large circular room, with a continuous band of windows all the way around the outside wall, giving us a panoramic view of the surrounding forest, which was filled with millions and millions of identical trees, each with an identical treehouse built into it. This dense forest of treehouses appeared to stretch on forever, in every direction.

Like all of the treehouses, mine had a large hollow tree trunk at the center, containing a spiral staircase leading to the ground. I'd decorated the interior so that it resembled the treehouse where Chewbacca's family lived on Kashyyyk in the *Star Wars Holiday Special*. Aech noticed this a few seconds after we arrived and chuckled, then she let out a long Wookiee growl of recognition. I didn't laugh. I was too busy teetering on the verge of an emotional breakdown, as I took a long look around the room.

There was a giant console television on one side of the room, positioned directly in front of an even more enormous blue couch. The TV was still running through a playlist of some of eleven-year-old Wade's favorite shows. There was currently a green Muppet newscaster on the screen, and after a few seconds I placed him as Gary Gnu, the host of *The Gary Gnu Show*. He had orange hair and an orange goatee, and he was in the midst of uttering a phrase that I must've heard hundreds of times when I was growing up here: "No g'news is good g'news with Gary Gnu!"

By turning the treehouse TV's giant channel knobs, you could watch shows from a huge free library of old children's educational programming from the late twentieth century. Shows like *3-2-1 Contact, The Big Comfy Couch, Captain Kangaroo, The Electric Company, The Great Space Coaster,*

Mister Rogers' Neighborhood, Pee-wee's Playhouse, Romper Room, Reading Rainbow, Sesame Street, Zoobilee Zoo, and many, many more. Kira and Og had used their vast fortunes to purchase the rights to these long-forgotten shows, then uploaded all of them to the free video archive here on Halcydonia, where future generations of kids could keep enjoying and learning from them forever.

But the Morrows didn't stop there. They also re-created the sets from all of these old educational shows as virtual OASIS environments, and all of their characters as lifelike NPCs. Then they scattered these characters and environments all over the surface of Halcydonia, mixed in with the Morrows' own educational quests and minigames. That was one of the many reasons Halcydonia had felt like such a magical place to spend my time as a lonely kid in the stacks. As I wandered across its magical landscape (which was completely devoid of advertising and microtransactions), I might see Elmo from *Sesame Street* talking to Chairy from *Pee-wee's Playhouse.* Then they would both run over and invite me to play a game of Sorry! or Trouble on a nearby picnic table. That sort of thing happened everywhere on Halcydonia. For a kid like me, it hadn't just been an escape. It had been a life preserver, a lone place of joy and belonging for a little boy desperate for both.

I'd always thought of the Morrows as two of my very first teachers. But now, I realized they had also served as my surrogate parents. That was why it had been so thrilling to meet Og in person and become his friend—and why it had been so devastating when he'd turned his back on me. Now I knew I'd given him no other choice.

The walls of my treehouse were covered with old drawings and artwork that my mother and I had created together. Lots of knights and wizards. And Ninja Turtles. And Transformers. There were also a bunch of framed selfies of our avatars posing together, taken in this very room. And just a few feet away, sitting atop a bookshelf, was a real photograph of me and my mother, taken in our trailer, just a few months before she died. In it, we were both making silly faces as we posed for a selfie.

I'd forgotten that photo was here, and seeing it again for the first time in a decade felt like having an old wound ripped open, right there in front of my friends.

Art3mis saw the photo, too, along with my reaction to it, and she immediately went over and placed it facedown on the bookshelf. Then she walked back over to me and gave my shoulder a comforting squeeze.

"You need a minute?" she asked. "We could wait outside."

"You guys should know something," I said. "I had a nervous breakdown the last time I visited this planet. That's why I haven't been back in so long."

They all studied my face to see if I was kidding, and saw that I wasn't.

"I was eleven years old at the time," I said. "And my mother had just died of a drug overdose a few days earlier. I went back to Halcydonia because my mom and I had spent so much time here together. I thought it might bring me some comfort, but it didn't. It just pushed me over the edge."

"I'm so sorry, Z," Art3mis said. "But this time you aren't alone. Your friends are with you. And we are going to stay with you, the whole time. OK?"

I nodded. Then I bit my lower lip to keep it from trembling.

Shoto rested a hand on my shoulder. Then Aech did the same thing and said, "We got your back, Z."

"Thanks, guys," I said, once I found my voice again. Then I took out the Third Shard and pointed at the coat of arms etched into its surface. "This is the coat of arms of Queen Itsalot, the sovereign ruler of the kingdom of Itsalot, which is a small continent to the south, where most of the math-related quests are located."

I opened a map of the planet and made it visible to everyone. It looked just like the Map from *Dora the Explorer*, but I quickly muted it before it could start singing its own name.

"We're here," I said, pointing to the Friendship Forest. "The queen lives in Castle Calculus, which lies to the south, beyond the MoreStuff Mountain Range and across the SeeSaw Sea. No teleportation is permitted on this planet, and it would take us several hours to get there on foot. But I know a shortcut. That's the exit, over there."

I motioned to the spiral staircase inside the hollow tree trunk at the center of the room. Shoto ran over and began to descend it first, with Aech close behind. But she had to stop and shrink her avatar to half-size to make it onto the tiny staircase. As she was doing that, I went over to grab my tiny Halcydonia Adventurers' Club backpack off its hook on the wall. These backpacks couldn't be added to your avatar's inventory, and the items inside were only useful on this planet, so everyone left them in storage lockers, or in their Be-Free Treehouse, like me.

My mother's identical backpack was hanging right beside it. I tried to avoid looking at it, but then I went right ahead and looked at it anyway. Including the word stitched onto the back flap in cursive with pink yarn: *Mama*.

I hit the emotion-suppressing software on my HUD, so Art3mis wouldn't see me start to sob. I managed to keep moving. I put my own backpack on my avatar's back. As I did, it automatically enlarged itself to fit my twenty-one-year-old frame. I turned to follow the others down the staircase. But Art3mis was standing there, blocking my way. The emotion-suppressing software was working—there was no way she should have known I was crying, but somehow she did. I tried to go around her. But just like the first time we met, she refused to let me pass.

Instead, she opened her arms and wrapped them around me—something I had long ago accepted that she would never do again. She held me tight, until I finally got my sobbing under control.

Samantha knew all about my mother, and how I found her dead of a drug overdose on our couch when I was eleven. It was heroin mixed with some other stuff, I think. That was the reason I'd avoided all ONI recordings made by heroin users for the entire first year the ONI-net was online. Then curiosity finally got the best of me, and I went all the way down the ONI-net heroin-addict-high rabbit hole. I wanted to experience what my mother had experienced firsthand. To find out exactly the sort of high my mother had been chasing when she'd unwittingly overdosed. I'd always assumed that it must be a pretty great feeling, if my mother thought it was worth losing her life for it. Doing a drug via ONI playback wasn't the same as shooting it into your own bloodstream. It felt the same, but it didn't cause the same long-term damage or physical addiction symptoms. And it removed the risk of accidental death. So ONI recordings allowed me to experience the same high my mother had, without destroying my brain and my body in the process. I didn't find it all that enlightening.

I wiped my eyes and took several deep breaths until I got myself back under control. Then I gave Art3mis a forced smile and a thumbs up. She nodded and took me by the hand, then she led me down the spiral staircase. Once we reached the bottom, I pushed open the heavy wooden door, and together, we stepped outside, into the Friendship Forest, where Aech and Shoto were waiting for us. The two of them were standing side by side in a beam of sunlight breaking through the treetops, illuminating tiny insects and motes of dust floating in the air around them.

I thought Art3mis would let go of my hand before Aech and Shoto saw her holding it, but she didn't. She let them see. And Aech and Shoto pretended not to notice.

I pointed to a path leading south, through the dense forest of treehouses all around us.

"The MoreStuff Mountains are that way," I said. "Just follow me closely, single-file, and only step where I step. Don't stop to talk to anyone—avatars or NPCs. Also, don't touch anything, and if you can help it, try not to look at anything either—not for longer than a second or two. Otherwise you might trigger some educational minigame or side quest that you'll be forced to complete, and we'll have to go on without you. We don't have time to stop and play Blue's Clues. Understood?"

They all nodded, and the four of us took off, running north along the path at top speed.

. . .

Once we reached the edge of the Be-Free Forest, we entered Holden's Field—a large, flat, open field of rye, perched precariously on the edge of the Cliffs of Salinger, a place where I had completed several different book-report quests at several different grade levels. I had also played countless games of tag in this field, with other kids from around the world. Kids I had never met and would never meet in the real world, with usernames that they had probably changed long ago.

Art3mis rested a hand on my shoulder, bringing me back to the present.

"We need to keep moving," she said.

I led them along the edge of the rye field, onto a narrow paved road that snaked to the north, through a rolling countryside and toward the More-Stuff Mountains in the distance. My surroundings seemed even more vibrant and realistic than I remembered—then I realized it was because this was the first time I had experienced this place with an ONI headset.

I heard a gleeful shriek and glanced overhead. There were a few kids flying around in their spellicopters. I had one in my inventory, but they only had room for one person, and that person had to keep spelling new words to stay airborne. We had to find other transportation.

We followed the road until it led us to a small farmhouse with a red barn behind it. There was a wooden wheelbarrow out by the road, with a rake leaning against it. I led Aech, Shoto, and Art3mis to the wheelbarrow and stood on a specific spot on the road beside it, then began to sing at the sky, as loudly as I could.

"It's the Great Space Coaster!" I yelled. *"Get on board! On the Great Space Coaster! We'll explore!"*

As I continued to sing, accompanying music began to play out of nowhere. Art3mis laughed and nodded with recognition, then she began to sing along with me. I displayed the lyrics in a browser window, so that Aech and Shoto could join in too.

As we sang, a flying yellow aircar swooped down out of the sky and flew under us, scooping our avatars up and into its fine Corinthian-leather seats.

"Welcome aboard the Great Space Coaster," I said, placing my hands on the coaster's flight stick. "Free transportation to Castle Calculus! Everyone buckle up, otherwise you'll fall out."

I aimed the Great Space Coaster at the MoreStuff Mountains on the horizon and floored the accelerator. Then I kept the hammer down until we were soaring over them. We passed over the starting point for the legendary Oregon Trail quest. A moment later, we flew over Mister Rogers' neighborhood. Then we continued south, down along the coast of the See-Saw Sea, and a few minutes later we passed over Gullah Gullah Island.

When I pointed the island out to Aech, it put a huge smile on her face, and as she began to talk about how much she loved that show as a kid, I caught myself smiling too. I didn't realize how much I'd missed this place. Why had I spent so much time running away? It felt genuinely good to be back here, despite the circumstances.

Once we cleared the mountain range, I set the coaster down just outside the golden front gate of Halcydonia City. It was the only entrance, and it was guarded by the Subtraction Sentinel, a stoic stone giant who would only open the gates for you after you solved a series of simple subtraction problems for him. Once I did this, the Subtraction Sentinel gave me a solemn nod, then he let me enter the city. Then Aech, Shoto, and Art3mis all had to do the same thing. Once we were all inside the gate, I took off at a run, leading my friends through the city's tangled maze of streets.

As we were making our way down a cobblestone side street, I spotted something strange and completely out of place: a gorgeous cream-colored 1949 Buick Roadmaster convertible that I instantly recognized from *Rain Man*. Inside it was a young Tom Cruise—or rather, his character from the movie, Charlie Babbitt. He was just sitting there behind the steering wheel, tapping it with his right hand, almost like he was drumming along to music. But there was no music, and his drumming had an odd rhythm to it. Steady, like a metronome, except that every few taps, it seemed like he was pressing on the wheel for an extra moment. The pattern reminded me of a scene in *Star Trek V: The Final Frontier*, for some reason it took me a moment to place, but then it clicked—was he tapping out a message in Morse code?

I opened my Mandarax translation software and used it to translate the Morse code into letters, only to discover that he was spelling out M-O-R-S-E.

I'd never seen a Tom Cruise NPC of any kind on Halcydonia. Content from R-rated movies was expressly forbidden here. So what was going on?

Less than a minute later, I spotted another out-of-place NPC—Raymond "Rain Man" Babbitt, Dustin Hoffman's character from the same film. He was staring off into space, while rocking slowly back and forth, shifting his weight from his left foot to his right foot. But I could see right away that he was making these movements in a pattern—a mix of short hops and long hops, like Morse code. According to my Mandarax translator software, his feet were tapping out the same word his brother had been tapping out on his steering wheel: M-O-R-S-E.

I didn't have time to ponder it now, because we'd arrived at Castle Calculus, which was located at the city center. We mounted the ornate marble steps out front, which had a bunch of different math proofs and equations carved into them, and passed through the castle's grand entranceway, then continued on into Queen Itsalot's throne room.

Normally, she wouldn't have granted us an audience so quickly. But I'd already met the queen once before, back when she awarded me the Silver Abacus of Itsalot for completing every math quest on the planet before my twelfth birthday. When I presented the abacus to the Itsalot master-at-arms, he bowed and stepped out of my way, allowing my friends and me to pass.

We walked up the long velvet carpet leading to the queen, who waved to me from her throne. She wore a gold crown with a large jewel-encrusted plus sign as its headpiece, and mathematical proofs and equations adorned her robes, stitched into their gold fabric with bright red thread. Her family's coat of arms—the same coat of arms etched into the Third Shard—hung on the wall behind her.

She was currently reading a large storybook to a group of baby animals gathered around her feet. But when she saw me approaching, she closed the book and sent them away.

When I reached her throne, I knelt before her and bowed my head, and motioned for Aech, Shoto, and Art3mis to do the same.

"Rise, Sir Parzival!" cried Queen Itsalot. "My noble subject and dear friend! How good to see you again, after so many years. What brings you back to my kingdom?"

I rose to my feet, then took out the Third Shard and showed her the coat of arms engraved upon it.

"I'm on a quest to find the Seven Shards of the Siren's Soul," I said. "And I think one of them might be hidden here in your kingdom. Can you help me find it, Your Majesty?"

Her eyes widened in surprise. She looked utterly delighted.

"Indeed I can, dear boy!" she replied. "The shard was given to me for safekeeping, a long time ago. I wondered if anyone would ever show up here looking for it, and now here you are, at long last. But before I can give it to you, you'll need to earn all fifty Halcydonia Wearit-Merit Badges."

Behind me, I heard all three of my friends inhale sharply. I glanced back at them.

"Oh my God," Aech said. "*Fifty?* How long is that going to take?"

"Relax," I said. "I spent years here, earning all those badges. With a lot of help from my mom . . ."

I opened my avatar's inventory and dug around until I found my old Halcydonia Wearit-Merit Badge sash. Then I presented it to the queen with both hands.

She took the sash from me and looked it over, running her wrinkled fingers down the rows of embroidered patches, each one bearing a different symbol or icon. She counted them one by one, and when she reached fifty, she smiled and nodded to herself. Then she snapped her fingers and there was a blinding flash of light.

When my eyes recovered, I saw that my sash had vanished from the queen's hand. Now she was holding the Fourth Shard. It sparkled in the bright sunlight pouring into the throne room, through the thousands of stained-glass windows that made up its domed ceiling. (Each one of these windows paid tribute to a different public school teacher, and had been placed here by one of their students.)

Queen Itsalot tilted the shard so that it reflected the different-colored shafts of light, turning the throne room into a giant kaleidoscope for a few seconds. Then she lowered it and held it out, offering it to me.

I knelt before her, then I reached up and took the shard from the queen's hands, being careful not to meet her gaze. (If I did, there was a good chance she would send me off on a mandatory math quest to rescue one of her royal relatives—usually her husband, the clueless King Itsalot, who was constantly being taken prisoner by the evil wizard Multiplikatar, who tossed him into the Long Division Dungeons beneath Protractor Peak, located high in the MoreStuff Mountains.) As I wrapped my fingers around the shard, once again I tried to prepare myself for the jolt of what I knew was coming, from the toll I had to pay. . . .

I—or rather Kira—rushed into a cluttered office to find Og sitting at his desk, hard at work on his computer. He turned and Kira held out her sketchpad, and I saw that she'd drawn the Halcydonia Interactive company logo on it.

This was another moment I'd heard Ogden Morrow talk about in interviews and in his biography. Kira had just designed the logo in a fit of inspiration in her own office, down in the GSS Art Department, and then she'd run here to Og's office to show it to him.

Og looked at the sketch, cried out, "It's perfect!," and rose to throw his arms around Kira.

Then I found myself back in Queen Itsalot's throne room on Halcydonia, clutching the Fourth Shard. I didn't even have to turn it over to see the clue engraved into it this time, because it already happened to be facing me when I held the shard up to look at it.

It was another symbol, created from a combination of symbols. It looked like the Mars and Venus gender symbols aligned and placed on top of each other, as if they were having intercourse, with a backward number 7, the top of which curled into a spiral, laid on top of that. Together, these shapes formed a symbol that was still instantly recognizable to any student of late-twentieth-century popular culture, and to any true fan of rock or funk music:

When I saw it, I began to chuckle in disbelief. Then I closed my eyes and shook my head, bracing myself for the unprecedented amount of grief that I knew Aech would be giving me in just a few seconds.

I bowed and thanked the queen, then backed away from her until I was able to step off the dais. When I turned around on the top step, I saw Art-3mis, Aech, and Shoto studying my face anxiously, trying to read my expression. Art3mis had all of her fingers crossed and was holding them up to show me.

"Well?" Aech said.

I lowered my head in defeat and held out the shard so they could all see the symbol engraved on it. Then I closed my eyes and silently began to count to three. I only made it to one. . . .

"Oh-my-fucking-God!" Aech cried. "No way! It can't be!" She started to do a funky dance toward me, then she started to dance around me. "That's Love Symbol #2, Z! It's *Prince*!"

"Prince who?" Shoto asked.

"*The* Prince," Aech said. "As in 'the Artist Formerly Known as'? The Prince of Funk! The High Priest of Pop! His Royal Badness. The Purple One!"

"Oh yeah," Shoto said. "He's the dude who changed his name to a Glyph of Warding back in the '90s, right?"

Aech pointed a finger of warning at him, then smiled wide.

"We're in luck, guys," she said, still dancing in place. "My dad left me his entire collection of Prince's music and films when he moved out. I grew up listening to them and watching them. I probably know more about Prince and his artistic output than any other human being in history."

"I know," I said. "Do you have any idea how many times you tried to make me watch *Purple Rain* with you?"

She stopped dancing and pointed an accusing finger at me. "And do you remember how many times you actually sat through the entire film with me? Nada. Never. *Not once.* And we both know why, don't we? It was because Prince always made you feel a little sexually confused and uncomfortable, didn't he?"

The old Wade would have denied this. But like I said, the ONI had broadened my horizons. Enough, at least, for me to recognize the truth about my adolescent self.

"OK, maybe that's a *little* true," I said, smiling. "Whenever I was watching old episodes of *Friday Night Videos* and 'When Doves Cry' came on, I always averted my eyes when he was getting up out of that bathtub. Every single time." I placed my right hand over my heart. "Please accept my sincere apologies, Aech. I'm sorry I never let myself appreciate Prince's genius."

Aech closed her eyes and raised one palm to the sky like a gospel singer and shouted, "Finally! The truth!"

"So where do we need to go?" Shoto said. "I take it there's a Prince planet somewhere?"

Aech scowled at him.

"Yes, fool," Aech said. "There *is* an entire OASIS planet devoted to Prince, his life, his art, and his music. But we don't call it 'the Prince planet.' Its name is an unpronounceable symbol. The symbol on that shard. But you can refer to it by its nickname, 'The Afterworld.' It began as a shrine created shortly after the Purple One's death, during the first decade the OASIS was online. Kira Morrow was one of the fans who helped build it."

Aech threw up a 3-D hologram of the Afterworld. It wasn't a sphere, like most other OASIS planets. It was shaped exactly like the symbol etched into the Fourth Shard—what Aech had referred to as Love Symbol #2.

"It's in Sector Seven, located right next to Beyoncé, Madonna, and Springsteen, in the superstar cluster," Aech said. "The Afterworld's surface is covered with a stylized re-creation of downtown Minneapolis in the late 1980s, along with locations from Prince's other movies and music videos. You can walk into a simulation of every club gig and concert he ever performed during his career. It's a big place. . . . It's easy to get lost and wander around in circles there. And we don't even know where to start looking for the shard. . . ."

"Hopefully the shard will give us another clue once we get there," I said. Aech nodded.

"There's no time like the present," she said. "Ready to roll?"

I nodded and turned around to wave farewell to Queen Itsalot, who was once again reading to her baby-animal subjects. She waved back at me, and it occurred to me that I should ask her if she'd seen Ogden Morrow here earlier today. But no—Og had only collected the first three shards before he'd called it quits. Which was pretty strange, now that I thought about it. Og was one of Halcydonia's creators. This should have been the easiest shard for him to obtain. And this also would have been an extremely easy place for him to hide clues about his location, since he had admin permissions on the whole planet, and total control of its NPCs, so he could've changed anything he wanted. . . .

That was when it hit me. Maybe Og *had* left more clues for me here. I'd already seen them—the unauthorized, R-rated Tom Cruise and Dustin Hoffman NPCs. But what the hell was he trying to say? Like his high score on Ninja Princess, I just needed to figure out why he . . .

Just then, a flashing alert icon appeared on all of our HUDs. I reached out and tapped the one flashing on mine.

"We just got a group text from Faisal," I said. "Saying he needs to see us right away. He wants us back at the conference room on Gregarious, so Anorak can't eavesdrop."

"Sorry, Aech," Art3mis said, resting a hand on her shoulder. "It looks like we need to make a quick pit stop before we head to the Afterworld."

"OK," she said. "But Faisal better make it quick!"

"Yeah," Shoto said. "And this time he better have some good news for us."

Before I could say how unlikely I thought that was, Aech used her admin ring to teleport us directly back to the conference room on Gregarious.

Sure enough, as soon as we took our seats, Faisal told us he had "even more bad news to share." But as he began to relay it, it quickly became clear that "bad" wasn't a strong enough adjective, and that "downright apocalyptic" would have been far more accurate.

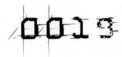

Once we were all back inside the conference room, seated in our usual spots around the table, Faisal had our OASIS engineers confirm that Anorak wasn't in the vicinity, or on the planet. They also said they had placed Anorak on the planet's block list, so Anorak should no longer even have been able to visit Gregarious. We also had our admins add several extra layers of security to our conference room, which effectively sealed it off from the rest of the OASIS, making it impossible to eavesdrop on us through any magical or technological means.

Once we had taken all the precautions we could think of, Faisal stepped up to the podium and cleared his throat a few times. Then, in a defeated voice, he asked us if we wanted the "bad news" or the "even worse news."

Bad news first won by unanimous vote.

"Another problem has arisen due to Anorak's firmware hack," he said. "I've kept it from you until now because I didn't want to distract you while you were looking for—"

"Spill it already, Faisal!" Aech shouted.

"It's OK," Art3mis said. "Just tell us what's going on. We're not going to fire you."

Faisal pursed his lips, and for a few seconds he looked like he might break down and cry.

"Anorak has figured out a way to alter the behavior of our NPCs," he said.

We all shouted "What?!" in unison, so loud it made Faisal flinch. He closed his eyes for a few seconds, then he opened them and continued.

"About an hour ago, all the NPCs in sectors one through four started to behave erratically and wander outside their designated operational boundaries. Some of these rogue NPCs have even gone off-world. . . ."

"NPCs *can't* go off-world," Art3mis said. "Unless they've been programmed to do so, as part of a user quest . . ."

"That's true," Faisal replied. "Anorak must've altered their programming somehow."

"OK," I said. "What exactly are these rogue NPCs doing?"

Faisal motioned to the viewscreen, where he began to play a rapid series of simcap clips. Each one gave us a first-person view of one or more NPCs suddenly breaking character, going berserk, and attacking an unwitting player avatar. We saw surfers, sidekicks, shopkeepers, pit mechanics, butlers, maids, background citizens, and wise old mentors all going postal, on hundreds of different OASIS worlds. Taken as a whole, the footage made it look like the OASIS had suddenly turned into a nightmarish mash-up of Westworld, Futureworld, and Jurassic World, with a smattering of Imaginationland, Tomorrowland, and Zombieland all mixed in for good measure.

"The NPCs in those sectors all turned homicidal at the same time," Faisal said. "A little over twenty minutes ago. And they're able to use public teleportation terminals now, so they're running amok all over the simulation, attacking and killing every avatar unlucky enough to cross their path. They appeared to be attacking players on sight and at random. Even in safe zones, where getting zeroed-out by an NPC is supposed to be impossible. The NPCs loot all of the money, weapons, magic items, and artifacts dropped by the avatars they kill." He motioned to the viewscreen. "And *then* they take all of that loot to Chthonia and deliver it to Anorak inside his castle. Watch. . . ."

He showed another piece of simcap footage, which looked as if it had been taken from the POVs of several different hijacked NPCs. We saw a shot of Castle Anorak from a distance, and there were hundreds of thousands of NPCs lined up in front of it. They were slowly filing into the castle's front entrance, and then back out one of its numerous exits, each of them now dressed in matching red-and-black studded leather armor. Once the NPCs were back outside, they joined the orderly ranks that were forming up around the castle. These ranks already stretched to the horizon in every direction, like orcs amassing around Isengard.

Then the simcap we were watching cut to another POV—that of an NPC standing inside the castle throne room. Anorak was sitting with one leg draped over the arm of his golden throne. Sorrento was standing off to his right with a malevolent smile on his face, trying to look imposing. He was dressed in black plate-mail armor that was covered in spikes. Both of his hands (enclosed in enormous black gauntlets) were resting on the hilt of a giant black-bladed bastard sword with magic runes carved into its blade. When I translated them, I realized that Sorrento's avatar appeared to be wielding the cursed blade Stormbringer, and I suddenly felt ill.

Faisal paused the simcap file for a moment and zoomed in on Sorrento's smug mug.

"We did find out how Anorak was communicating with Sorrento while he was in prison," Faisal said. "As we suspected, it was during his allotted weekly OASIS recreation time. For thirty minutes every Saturday, Sorrento was allowed to log in with a conventional haptic rig. His usage logs indicate he spent nearly all of that time at a free public library on Incipio, reading articles about Mr. Watts and the other members of the High Five. Anorak appears to have taken control of the library terminal Sorrento was using to open a line of text communication with him. The inmate-monitoring software didn't catch it at the time, and Anorak erased any record of what they said to each other, but we think it must be how they coordinated Sorrento's escape." He let out a sigh. "Still no sign of either him or Og."

"Can't we track Sorrento's location in the real world?" Shoto asked. "Through his OASIS connection?"

Faisal shook his head.

"Sorrento appears to be accessing the simulation through a series of overseas proxy servers, to mask his real-world location," he said. "Anorak clearly took security precautions on his behalf."

Faisal motioned back up at the viewscreen. He recentered the simcap footage on Anorak, sitting on his bejeweled throne. Anorak had his left hand held out toward the chain gang of NPCs who were rapidly filing past him, so that he could vacuum up the constant stream of weapons and magic items they were presenting to him. As he hoovered up all of this loot, I could see his eyes darting around rapidly, as if he were scanning each new item description on his HUD as it was added to his inventory. With his right hand, Anorak was also constantly discarding unwanted items, which were then picked up and carried out of the room by other NPCs, who were all now dressed in the same studded black-and-red armor, which matched the color scheme of his own robes. As each NPC donned this new attire, the name tag over their head would also change to read "Acolyte of Anorak."

"Mother pus bucket," Art3mis muttered. "It looks to me like Anorak is building an army. And an arsenal."

"To me, it looks like he's searching for one item in particular," Shoto replied. "Maybe that's why he reprogrammed the NPCs to start killing avatars to loot their inventory? Because he's trying to find something specific? Like an artifact with unique abilities?"

Faisal shrugged.

"Maybe," he replied. "I guess we'll find out. . . ."

"OK, Faisal," said Art3mis. "Go ahead and hit us with the 'even worse news.'"

"Christ," Aech muttered, shaking her head. "I forgot there *was* even worse news."

Faisal nodded, fidgeted for a few seconds, and then took another deep breath.

"The avatars of ONI users have stopped respawning when they die," he said.

The room fell silent for several seconds, as everyone tried to process what he'd said.

"OK . . ." Art3mis said slowly. "Then what happens to the user when their avatar gets killed?"

"*Nothing* happens," Faisal said. "Their avatar doesn't respawn inside the OASIS, and they don't wake up in the real world either. But their ONI headset stays powered up and locked onto their skull. The users' brain patterns indicate they're still logged in to the OASIS." He shrugged. "They all appear to be trapped in limbo."

"Jesus," Art3mis muttered. "Can they feel anything? What are they experiencing?"

Faisal shook his head.

"We don't know," he replied with a shaky voice. "We have no way of finding out what the users themselves are actually experiencing."

Aech cleared her throat.

"Does anyone else find this shit completely terrifying?" she asked, raising her right hand. "Because I do."

Shoto and I both raised our right hands in solidarity.

"It's possible that Anorak's infirmware has simply broken the respawning process," Faisal said hopefully. "So that now, when an ONI user's avatar gets killed, they get stuck in a dreamless limbo, where they're no longer experiencing anything at all."

"Yeah, maybe," Aech said. "Or maybe Anorak is making them respawn in the fire pits on the Ninth Circle of Hell, Faisal!" She threw up her hands, suddenly on the verge of hysteria. "Who fucking knows, man? Maybe now, when one of our avatars gets killed, instead of respawning, we're going to suddenly find ourselves being tortured by Klingons in the dilithium mines on the frozen Rura Penthe asteroid! And we'll also probably be on an accelerated timeline that makes three seconds feel like three thousand years!"

"Holy shit," Shoto whispered. "Could Anorak really do that?"

"No, of course not!" Faisal said. "I mean, I highly doubt that what Ms. Harris described is even possible. . . ." He paused to listen to his admins argue in his ear for a moment, then he let out a sigh and said, "The consensus seems to be . . . we don't know what those users are experiencing. And we don't think we'll be able to find out until one of them wakes up and tells us."

"Or until one of us gets killed on Anorak's scavenger hunt," I said. "And then we find out for ourselves. Firsthand . . ."

Everyone fell silent for a few seconds. I resisted the urge to check my ONI usage counter. Instead, I began to massage my temples in an effort to remain calm.

"Have those simcap clips you showed us already been posted to the ONI-net?" Art3mis asked.

"Yeah," Faisal replied. "That's where we found them."

"So now the whole world knows that Anorak has gone berserk," Art3mis said. "They can also see that he's taken control of our NPCs. Why don't we just come clean and tell our users the truth? They deserve to know that Anorak is the one who hacked the ONI firmware, and that he's the reason they can't log out or respawn. GSS isn't going to be able to keep that a secret, Faisal."

"Not forever," he replied. "But if we keep releasing updates, saying that we should have the problem fixed in just a few more minutes, we might be able to hold off the panic until this is over. If we told them the truth—"

"It would create total chaos, online and off," Aech said, shaking her head.

Faisal nodded and cleared his throat.

"If the four of you all approve," he said, "our PR department would like to release another update, blaming the NPC's erratic behavior on another glitch, caused by the same 'corrupted' ONI firmware update responsible for the logout issue. Once again, we'll assure them we're working on the problem and should have it fixed within the next thirty minutes. We'll also apologize for the rogue NPCs' behavior, and guarantee resurrection for any users who had their avatars killed, and promise that we'll restore their lost credits and items as soon as we have the problem corrected."

"What about Anorak?" Shoto asked. "How do we explain his behavior?"

"As far as the public knows, Anorak is just another NPC," Faisal said. "Left dormant in the system by Halliday. So we can blame his behavior on the same firmware glitch that's affecting the other NPCs."

"What about the respawning issue?" I asked. "Has that also gone public?"

"Not yet," Faisal said. "The users experiencing it are stuck in limbo, so they obviously can't talk to anyone to complain about their situation. But before too long, people are going to figure out that their friends aren't respawning and then . . ."

"They'll start to fear the worst," Aech said. "I know I sure do."

"There's another reason we need to keep up the façade," Faisal said. "Remember, less than ten percent of our ONI users have an immersion vault to protect themselves while they're under. Most people lock themselves in a room or a closet when they nap, with the assumption that they'll be able to see trouble coming on their surveillance feeds and log out in plenty of time to wake up and defend themselves. A lot of those people are completely vulnerable now. If the whole world knew what was really going on . . ."

"He's right," Art3mis said. She lowered her head and closed her eyes. "What do you think will happen when criminals all over the world figure out that they're surrounded by sitting ducks? People who can no longer log out of the OASIS to protect themselves?" She opened her eyes, as if she'd finished seeing into the near future. "The police—the ones who aren't hostages themselves—are going to be too overwhelmed to help everyone. It'll be the crime wave of the century."

"Jesus, Arty," Aech whispered. "Don't sugarcoat it now."

"We need to know what is at stake, Aech," she replied, then glanced in my direction.

"Just to be clear," Faisal interjected, "none of this has actually started to happen—yet. But Ms. Cook is right. If this goes on much longer, that sort of thing will start to occur. So . . . the sooner we can get Anorak to release everyone unharmed, the more lives we are likely to save."

I resisted the urge to yell, *No shit, Sherlock!* But just barely. Things were beginning to spiral out of control, and I felt a sense of hopelessness setting in. Even if my friends and I managed to survive this ordeal, I no longer believed the OASIS would. It had already begun to self-destruct. I was powerless to prevent it. . . .

"We have to find Og," Art3mis suddenly announced, locking eyes with me. "He's the only person in the world who might know a way to stop Anorak."

I nodded.

"When Og collected the first three shards for Anorak," I said, "I think he only did that so he could leave behind some clues of his own. I'm hoping they'll lead us to him."

I pulled up the screenshot I'd taken of the Ninja Princess high-score list—the one with Og's score in first place—and threw it up on the conference room's main viewscreen:

RANK	SCORE	NAME
1st	550750	KRA
2nd	365800	KRU

"Og outscored me by nearly two hundred thousand points," I said. "I don't think he could have earned that big of a lead in a single run to Kanten Castle. Could he, Shoto?"

Shoto thought for a second, then shook his head.

"No," he said. "To get a score that high, he would have had to beat the final level of Ninja Princess, and then continue playing when the game started over on the first level, instead of quitting like you did."

"That's what I thought," I replied. "But why bother racking up all of those extra points when he didn't need to?"

Art3mis stood up and took a step toward the viewscreen, narrowing her eyes.

"To leave that specific score at the top of the high score list," she said. "Where he knew you would see it."

I stared up at those six digits, repeating them over and over in my head. Five-five-zero-seven-five-zero. The number 550750 didn't ring any bells in my memory. I tried searching my grail diary for it, but there wasn't a single hit. And those six digits didn't appear to be map coordinates either. I did a general Internet search for that sequence of numbers, but the vast majority of the results were all prices and product numbers. If the number 550750 contained some secret message from Og, I still couldn't decipher it.

"Those first three numbers," Art3mis said. "Aren't they part of the street address of your house?"

I stared at her, puzzled, and shook my head.

"No," I said. "My street address is 2112 Monsalvat Boulevard."

She smirked.

"The original address, back when Halliday lived there," she said. "Before you moved in and had it changed . . ."

I searched my memory, and a few seconds later it produced the address, and I said it out loud.

"550 Babbitt Road!" I shouted. "B-A-B-B-I-T-T! Spelled just like the last name of the two brothers in *Rain Man*. Played by Tom Cruise and Dustin Hoffman . . ."

I pulled up the screenshots I'd taken of the Charlie and Raymond Babbitt NPCs and put them up on the viewscreen.

"I spotted these two NPCs on Halcydonia," I said. "Charlie and Raymond Babbitt. They were both tapping out Morse code."

I pulled up a street map of the New Albany neighborhood where I lived, located on the northeastern outskirts of the city. Then I zoomed in on my house, at 550 Babbitt Road.

"Guess who owns the property located a few miles down the street?" I said. "At 750 Babbitt Road, near the intersection with Morse Road?"

Art3mis jumped to her feet, eyes wide.

"Holy shit!" she whispered. "That used to be Og's old house, right? Before he and Kira got married and left Ohio to move to Oregon?"

Faisal nodded.

"When Gregarious Games took off and they became multimillionaires, Halliday and Morrow both bought mansions located on Babbitt Road, just a few miles apart," Faisal said. "Og moved out of his residence at 750 Babbitt Road when he got married, but he never sold the property." He turned to me. "When he left GSS, Mr. Morrow told us he wanted to hold on to the house for sentimental reasons," he said. "And just in case he ever needed to move back here. The place has been sitting vacant for decades. Guarded by automated security and maintenance drones, all of which are probably now under Anorak's control."

I pulled up an aerial satellite view of the building. All it showed was the roof of a large mansion, with a garage and a few other small buildings clustered around it, surrounded on all sides by empty, wide-open farm fields. "Hiding Og here would be a pretty clever move, actually. It's definitely the last place I ever would've thought to look for him."

Faisal nodded. "That house still has a direct fiber-optic connection to the main OASIS server hub," he said. "We installed it for Mr. Morrow when he still lived there. It would give them the fastest possible connection to the simulation. Just like the connection at Mr. Watts's estate down the road."

"OK," Aech said. "Let's assume that *is* where Anorak and Sorrento are keeping Og. How are we going to get him out of there alive?"

"We need to offer him a trade," I said. "Og's freedom for the Siren's Soul." I turned to Art3mis. "But I'm betting Og left us more to work with, back on Middletown."

I pulled up my HUD and sent a text message to L0hengrin, asking her to teleport to my location on Gregarious immediately, then instructed Faisal to give L0hengrin and the rest of her clan permission to join us in the conference room.

Less than a minute later, the conference-room doors flew open, and in walked L0hengrin, followed by Rizzo, Wukong, Lilith, and Kastagir.

They were all staring around wide-eyed, taking in their surroundings. But when they saw me, Aech, Shoto, and Art3mis, their eyes grew even wider. Then, in unison, all five of them dropped to their knees and bowed their heads. I told them to rise and we all ran over to greet them.

And that was how the High Five met the L0w Five for the very first time, under extremely dire circumstances.

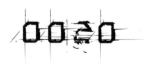

L0hengrin's avatar was still in her female form, but now she was dressed in some sort of futuristic battle armor. The rest of her clan was similarly attired and also heavily armed. Once I finished making introductions (and once L0hengrin and her friends finished freaking out), Lo told me what she'd been up to. To save time, she'd called up her friends, and together, the five of them had started checking each of the other 255 instances of Middletown, one after another. They had nearly searched them all before Wukong finally located a second instance of the town where the year had been changed from 1986 to 1989—the one Og had visited. Then the L0w Five converged on that instance and scoured it for clues.

"We found several things out of place in Og's basement," Lo told us. "When Og was there changing the calendar on the wall, he also moved one of the videotapes on the shelf next to the television. A VHS copy of John Belushi's final film, *Neighbors*."

"Holy shit!" Aech said. "Z, you were right!"

Lo glanced at her, then back at me.

"Right about what?" she asked. "What the hell is going on?"

I turned to address Art3mis, Aech, and Shoto. "We have to tell them," I said. "If we want their help, they deserve to know what's at stake."

The others all nodded in agreement. Faisal started to protest, but I ignored him and told L0hengrin and her friends everything about Anorak, his infirmware, and the real reason why none of us was able to log out of the OASIS. Compared to us, they seemed to take the news that they were being held hostage extremely well. They did a lot of cursing and shouting, but nobody had a full-on meltdown. Eventually, they all fell silent and waited for me to continue. Then I told them how Anorak had taken Og hostage, too, and about our ongoing efforts to find him.

"Og has been leaving behind clues for us," I said. "About his location in the real world. They appear to indicate that Anorak is holding Og hostage at his former residence here in Columbus. Just a few miles down the road from Halliday's old house. Og and Halliday used to be neighbors."

"Holy shit!" Lo said. "So that's why he pulled out that VHS tape!"

Lo opened her HUD and began to search through her avatar's inventory.

"We found an old Dungeons & Dragons campaign notebook too," she said. "But it wasn't in Og's handwriting—"

"Did it belong to Halliday?" Shoto asked. "When he still lived at home, Halliday had to keep all of his D&D stuff over at Og's house. Because his own parents thought D&D was satanic and forbid him from playing it."

"Definitely not," Lo replied. "It's Kira's old campaign notebook. It only exists in the 1989 version of Middletown."

Lo removed the notebook from her inventory and held it up. It was a battered blue Trapper Keeper. Kira had sliced open the edge of its clear plastic covering so that she could slide a hand-drawn title page underneath it, with *The Quest for the Seven Shards of the Siren's Soul* written on it in her distinctive cursive handwriting. She had also drawn six blue crystal shards in a circle, with a seventh in the center. And below that, at the bottom of the page, she had written: *by Kira Underwood*.

"It's for an adventure module that Kira created, all by herself," L0hengrin said. "After she left Middletown and returned home to London to finish her final year of high school."

Aech, Art3mis, and Shoto all exchanged looks of surprise.

Lo held out the notebook, offering it to me, and I accepted it with both hands. I stared down at it in amazement, then back up at her.

"Lo, this is amazing!" I said. "It may end up saving all of our lives. Thank you."

"You're welcome, Z," she said, beaming with pride.

I tore open the Trapper Keeper's Velcro cover flap. Inside was a plastic three-ring binder filled with over 150 pages of Kira's handwritten notes, along with dozens of detailed maps and illustrations.

"What's interesting is that Kira set her Quest for the Seven Shards in Halliday's D&D campaign setting—Chthonia."

Chthonia was the name of the fantasy world Halliday had created for his high school Dungeons & Dragons campaign—the same campaign that Kira joined when Og invited her to play D&D with them. Halliday also used Chthonia as the setting for all of his early Anorak's Quest adventure games. Then, years later, when Halliday created the OASIS, he built a full-scale replica of Chthonia inside the simulation. That was the planet where Castle Anorak was located.

"Kira's adventure is comprised of seven different quests," Lo continued. "One to retrieve each of the Seven Shards. Kira created all of the different quests, drew maps for all seven dungeons, and she also included a bunch of awesome illustrations at the back, depicting different monsters and locations that appear in the story. It's pretty incredible." She pointed at the Trapper Keeper. "From what I can gather, Kira gave that binder to Halliday just before she went back to England in June of '89. There's a brief note to him on the first page. In it, Kira asks Halliday to run her module for Og and the rest of the Middletown Adventurers' Guild after she leaves, to explain why her character disappeared from their D&D campaign. She told him she created this adventure so that her friends would feel like she was still there with them in spirit. She said she hoped it would make all of them miss her a little less."

"Does Kira's character Leucosia appear in the module?" Aech asked.

Lo nodded.

"Right at the beginning," she replied. "Leucosia is abducted by an evil wizard named Hagmar, who places her in suspended animation and imprisons her inside a powerful magic jewel called the Siren's Soul. Then he shatters the jewel into seven pieces and hides them in seven different treacherous, trap-filled dungeons, which are each located on seven different continents. The players have to collect all seven of the shards and reassemble them into the Siren's Soul to resurrect Leucosia. Then, once they bring her back, she gives them the power to resurrect other people too. Here, you have to check this out. . . ."

L0hengrin flipped Kira's notebook to a page near the back, which contained a drawing of Leucosia's character symbol—a capital letter *L* formed by the intersection of a bejeweled longsword and an ornately carved magic wand, to symbolize Leucosia's Magic User/Fighter dual character class.

I had seen this symbol before, in collections of Kira's artwork and in several of the Anorak's Quest games.

Kira was the first and only artist ever to join the Middletown Adventurers' Guild, and as a gift to her new friends, Kira had taken it upon herself to design cool character symbols for everyone in the group—symbols that would all later be made famous, thanks to their inclusion in various RPGs released by Gregarious Games. Kira was the one who had designed Anorak's famous character symbol—the calligraphic letter *A* that appeared on Anorak's robes and above the entrance to Castle Anorak.

For Og, she designed a symbol of a capital letter *O* with a small letter *g* at its center, to represent his high-level Magic User character, the Great and Powerful Og. And for her own character, Leucosia, Kira had designed the sword-and-wand *L* symbol. In all the drawings and paintings she did of Leucosia, that *L* always appeared somewhere on the character's clothing or armor. This had eventually earned her character the nickname "Laverne"— a reference that initially made no sense to her, because she hadn't grown up watching *Laverne & Shirley* in the UK.

L0hengrin reached out and flipped to another page of the notebook, near the back. She appeared to have its entire contents memorized already.

"Right there," she said, pointing to a page of dense handwritten text. "When they obtain the final shard at the end of the module, the evil wizard Hagmar shows back up and they have to defeat him before they can recombine the shards." She smiled wide. Then, as an afterthought, she leaned forward and added, "Hagmar is an anagram of Graham, which was the name of Kira's abusive stepfather. But I'm sure you guys already figured that out."

I shook my head. "No," I said. "We had no idea. Thanks, Lo. You did an amazing job!"

Art3mis and Aech both nodded and began to applaud. Shoto and I joined in. Lo took a small bow, then she motioned to her friends.

"The L0w Five did this together," she added. "Please distribute your thanks evenly among all of us."

Aech, Shoto, Art3mis, and I all turned to give the rest of the L0w Five a round of applause too.

But we didn't have much time for congratulations. Along with the others, I buried my nose back in Kira's notebook, trying to speed-read through the remainder of its contents. . . . I didn't know what I was looking for, but felt sure I'd know when I saw it.

In Kira's module, the hiding places of the first four shards were all quite different from the ones we'd encountered in the OASIS, and so were the challenges required to obtain them. But to my surprise, I recognized many of them. I had encountered each of them in a slightly different form, in Anorak's Quest II and III, two early releases by Gregarious Games. This was a huge shock, because Kira was only credited as the artist on those games, not as a writer or designer.

I remembered that, in his autobiography, Og had complained about Halliday's sexist behavior toward Kira more than once. He wrote that Halliday always seemed to try to downplay Kira's creative contribution to their games. Og once told an interviewer, "Jim always jokingly referred to Kira as Yoko, which infuriated me, because if we were Lennon and McCartney, then Kira was our George Harrison. She didn't break up the Beatles. She was one of the Beatles! And without her help, we never would have had a single hit."

I remembered having my first real argument with Art3mis once about that very subject, during the first few months we knew each other. She'd started it by stating that Kira Morrow deserved to be listed alongside Og and Halliday as one of the true co-creators of the OASIS. She'd made comparisons to Rosalind Franklin, a woman who deserved to be credited alongside Watson and Crick as one of the discoverers of the double-helix structure of DNA. Or Katherine Johnson, whose calculations helped us reach the moon. Or countless other women who had been brushed aside or blatantly ignored.

At the time, I'd reminded her that during Halliday's reign, GSS had adopted an equal-hiring policy, which required the company to hire at least one woman for every man they employed. Samantha pointed out that Kira and Og were the ones who had lobbied for that change, not Halliday. I responded by pointing out that Halliday could've rolled back the policy after Og and Kira left the company, but he didn't. The same hiring policy was still in force today. But Samantha only rolled her eyes at me.

Now, all these years later, I could finally see that she'd been right all along. I'd just been too much of a slavish Halliday fanboy to believe anything bad about him. How times had changed.

I continued to flip through the notebook's remaining pages, looking for anything that might be useful. But nothing caught my interest until I reached the last few pages, where Kira described how the party obtained the seventh and final shard.

> Once the party has collected the first six shards, they must bring them to the Shrine of the Siren, located atop the highest peak of the Xyxarian Mountains of southern Chthonia. When all six shards are placed on the altar, the Seventh Shard will appear in the Siren's hand.

I interrupted the High Five/L0w Five love fest to show this line to Aech, Shoto, and Art3mis.

"Every inch of those mountains was explored during the contest," Shoto said. "If there was a shrine to Leucosia up there, someone would've discovered it."

"Maybe it only appears once the first six shards have been collected?" Lo said.

Art3mis was still reading Kira's notebook over my shoulder.

"What's supposed to happen when the players recombine the shards?" she asked.

Lo reached over to the notebook and pointed at a paragraph halfway down the last page. I read it out loud:

"'Once the Seven Shards are reassembled, they coalesce into the Siren's Soul, a powerful magical artifact with the power to free Leucosia from suspended animation and bring her back to life.'" I looked up from the page. "That's all it says."

We were still processing all of this new information when Lo hit us with another stunner.

"OK," she said. "We saved the best for last."

She took a large piece of graph paper out of her inventory and unfolded it. There was an elaborate dungeon map drawn on it in pencil. It was covered with carefully lettered notations and room descriptions written in a very tiny, very familiar script.

"I found this stuck inside Kira's notebook," she said. "But that isn't Kira's handwriting."

"It's Og's handwriting!" Art3mis and Aech shouted, beating me to the punch.

Lo nodded.

"According to this text across the bottom of the map, it leads to the hiding place of a powerful magic sword known as the Dorkslayer, which was 'specially forged at the dawn of the OASIS, for the express purpose of slaying the mighty wizard Anorak, if he should ever become corrupted by his power and turn to evil.'" Lo glanced up at me. "This was tucked inside the front cover of the notebook. Someone wanted to make sure I saw it."

"Holy shit," Aech muttered. "You think Og forged a special sword to kill Anorak?"

Lo nodded excitedly. "I think so!" she replied. "Maybe!"

"The Dorkslayer?" Shoto repeated. "Og named his Anorak-killing super sword 'the Dorkslayer'?"

"He did," Lo said. "And this map is dated here at the bottom right. April 1, 2022—just a few months before Og left Gregarious. He must've made the sword before he quit." She folded the map in half and flipped it over so she could read the text across the top. "It says here that the Dorkslayer was hidden for safekeeping in the hoard of a fearsome dragon, located in a deep underground cave on an uncharted island in the Nilxor Sea called Farhell."

She opened a three-dimensional OASIS sector map in the air in front of her.

"There just happens to be a small planet in the OASIS named Farhell," Lo replied. "Its coordinates are scribbled in the corner of Og's map. According to the planet's colophon, it dates back to the earliest days of the simulation, when Kira and Og both still worked at GSS."

"Farhell?" Shoto said. "Never heard of it."

"Me neither," Aech added.

"Because it's an uncharted planet," Lo said. "And it's located out in Zone Zero."

This threw all of us for a loop. "Zone Zero" was what everyone called the area outside the twenty-seven core sectors that made up the OASIS. It was an endless, procedurally generated virtual space that didn't spring into existence until an avatar flew their ship into it. So Zone Zero was continuously expanding its size and geography on the fly, as avatars traveled farther and farther out into it. Halliday and Morrow had designed the OASIS this way on purpose, so that if people ever used up all of the surreal estate in the initial twenty-seven sectors, the simulation would still always have plenty of extra room available out in Zone Zero. An infinite amount, to be exact.

I'd only ever traveled out into the Zero once, just to be able to say that I had. When we were kids, it used to be a rite of passage, to travel out to the edge of the simulation in a spaceship, and then keep on going a little farther, to force the OASIS to grow a little more in size, just for you.

The first time I flew my X-Wing to the outer edge of the core twenty-seven zones and ventured into Zone Zero, I remember flying past a sign-post floating at the border that read: OUT HERE, ON THE PERIMETER, THERE ARE NO STARS. . . .

"I think Og created a real Dorkslayer," Lo said. "Here, inside the OASIS, when he was still working at GSS. Maybe as a contingency, in case he and Halliday ever got into a disagreement with their invincible avatars."

A burst of elation ran through me—followed by one of profound sadness. This might be the weapon we needed against Anorak. But how terrible must Halliday's behavior have been for Og to feel he needed to prepare for battle against his best friend?

"It must be real," said Shoto. "That's why Anorak reprogrammed all of those NPCs to kill off high-level avatars and collect their items! He's trying to find the Dorkslayer sword before anyone else can."

"I thought that Anorak and Og both made their avatars all-powerful," Aech said. "And indestructible."

"I've read that too," Lo replied. "But the writing on Og's map says that the Dorkslayer is 'the only weapon that can slay he who cannot be slain.' It also says that Morrow's character, the Great and Powerful Og, is the only avatar who can wield it, due to his 'noble birth.'"

"Jeez Louise," Shoto said, rolling his eyes. He turned to me. "We're gonna be looking for Horcruxes next."

"Excellent work, Lo," Art3mis said, then turned to me. "We need that sword!"

"I don't think we have time for a side quest right now, Arty," Aech said. "We need to find the last three shards, now, while we still can!"

L0hengrin suddenly dropped to one knee in front of us. Then she motioned to the rest of her clan members, and they all did the same.

"Members of the High Five," she said, bowing her head slightly. "The L0w Five is at your command. Please, allow us to retrieve the Dorkslayer for you while you complete your quest. I promise you, we will not fail."

She raised her eyes to meet mine, and I could see the steely resolve in them. I glanced over at Aech, Shoto, and Art3mis, and they all nodded their approval.

"Thank you, L0hengrin," I said. "The High Five gratefully accepts your offer."

I reached out and offered her my hand. Lo rose to her feet and shook it. Her companions stood up too.

"Thank you for your help," I said. "If you find the sword—"

"You mean *when* we find the sword," she said.

"Forgive me," I replied. "*When* you find the Dorkslayer, teleport to wherever I am immediately. I'll share my location with you so you can track me."

Lo nodded. Then she grinned and abruptly transformed into a young James Spader.

She gave me an exaggerated salute and said, "Aye-aye, Captain."

Then Lo snapped her fingers and teleported away, taking the other members of the L0w Five with her.

"Wow," Aech said, turning to me. "That chick is *amazing*."

"Yeah," Art3mis said, shaking her head at me. "I don't know how you do it, Z. You have a gift for making friends who are much cooler than you are."

"Humility, madam," I said. "That's my secret. That and my clean, close shave."

Art3mis laughed and rolled her eyes. Then she turned to Faisal.

"Do you think that sword will really work?" she asked him.

"Who knows?" he replied. "According to our OASIS engineers, Anorak still appears to function like any other NPC, at least as far as the system is concerned. So theoretically, he should still be bound by the same rules and operating parameters they are. Which means he can be killed if his avatar sustains enough physical damage."

"What if we can't kill him?" Shoto asked. "Are we just gonna give him the shards and hope that he'll keep his word?"

The mental image of my avatar handing the Seven Shards over to Anorak actually made me feel nauseous for a few seconds. But then it gave me an idea. . . .

I looked back down at the last page of Kira's notebook and reread the section describing how the players in her module were supposed to go about combining the Seven Shards. By the time I had finished, the rough framework of a plan had formed in my head. When I shared it with the others, they seemed to think there was a chance it might work too. We spent a few more minutes working out the broad details of it with Faisal, so that he could relay it to our OASIS admins, and to the GSS security team gearing up to try to rescue Og.

The second we'd finished, Art3mis jumped to her feet and prepared to leave. "Tell Miles and his team I'm logging out right now, and that they better not leave without me."

"Yes, ma'am," Faisal replied. "But we've already got three security teams on deck, along with three squads of aerial enforcer drones. So there's really no need for you to put your own life at risk, Ms. Cook."

"Ogden Morrow saved our lives once," she said. "I'm gonna do everything I can to return that favor." She turned to me. "Stay in touch," she said. "And good luck!"

She gave me another smile, then she turned to go. As she did, it occurred to me that if the worst happened, this might be the last time I ever saw her. So I reached out to touch her avatar's shoulder, and when she felt it through her haptics, she turned back around to face me. And as always, she looked beautiful.

"Hey, in case something does happen," I said, "I wanted to tell you that I'm sorry. For a lot of different things. But mainly, I'm sorry that I didn't listen to you. All this time, you were right, and I was wrong."

She grinned and placed her right hand against my cheek. The last time she had done this, it was in the real world, during our week together at Og's in Oregon. Exactly 1,153 days ago. It wasn't her real hand, but I could still feel it, and it still made my heart race.

"You never cease to amaze me, Watts," she said. "There's still hope for you yet."

She leaned over and kissed me on the forehead. Then she backed up several steps, to ensure that we were all outside her teleportation spell's area of effect.

"Good luck, guys."

"Good luck to you, too, Arty," I replied. "Don't get hurt, OK?"

Art3mis gave all of us one last nod, then she teleported away, and her avatar vanished in a shower of glittering silver dust. Then I turned to Aech and Shoto.

"You guys ready to rock?" I asked.

Shoto nodded and gave me a nervous thumbs-up. Aech cracked her knuckles.

"Ten-four and ready for more," she said.

I checked the ONI countdown on my HUD. I now had just two hours and twenty-eight minutes remaining before I hit my limit. Aech and Shoto each had about ten minutes less than that. Faisal was about to hit the two-hour mark. And we still had three more shards to collect. If the last three took as long to locate as the first four had, we were in trouble.

"Buckle up, fellas," Aech said, smiling. "We're off to the Afterworld! And when we get there, prepare to follow my lead, OK?"

We nodded, then all waved farewell to Faisal once again. Aech turned to me and Shoto and placed a hand on each of our shoulders. Then, just before she teleported all of us to the Afterworld, we heard her shout, *"Oh no, let's go!"*

As my avatar rematerialized, my vision stabilized, and I found myself standing in the middle of a long concrete tunnel, fifty yards in length, with a curved ceiling that formed a half-circle with the concrete floor. Every inch of the ceiling and a good portion of the floor was covered in graffiti—all of it paying tribute to Prince Rogers Nelson, scrawled here by his fans over the past three decades. There were snippets of his song lyrics, pairs of initials inside arrow-pierced hearts, and thousands of messages of love and devotion, all directed toward the Artist and his work. Phrases like *Thank you, Prince* and *We love you, Prince* and *We miss you, Prince* were repeated over and over again, in different colors and in different handwriting. I also saw several portraits of Prince painted on the tunnel walls, along with the dates of his birth and death (6-7-1958 and 4-21-2016) and thousands upon thousands of different hand-drawn renderings of his unpronounceable symbol.

I forced myself to stop looking at all of the graffiti and tried to get my bearings. Behind me, one end of the tunnel terminated in a bright half-circle of blinding-white light. At the opposite end, the tunnel opening was a half-circle of bright-green forest, just beyond a black chain-link fence about ten feet high.

In an effort to avoid showing the full depth of my ignorance about Prince and his music, I pulled up his complete discography, filmography, biography, and his career timeline in different semitransparent windows on my HUD, so I could refer to them at all times. My image-recognition plug-in was also constantly giving me information about my surroundings, throwing it up in small windows in the air all around me, like I was inside an episode of *Pop-Up Video.*

As I scanned Prince's discography, I noticed that he had released both an album and a movie titled *Graffiti Bridge.* So, in an effort to appear like I actually knew something about this place, I turned to Shoto and said, "This is the famous Graffiti Bridge that inspired the album and film of the same name. . . ."

"No it isn't, Z," Aech said, resting a hand on my shoulder as she corrected me. "The real Graffiti Bridge was located in another suburb of Minneapolis called Eden Prairie. It was torn down in 1991. There are plenty of replicas of the original Graffiti Bridge here, though, spread all over the planet. But this isn't one of them. This is a re-creation of a tunnel down the road from Prince's home." She glanced around, smiling. "I come here every year on his birthday. This was my last departure point. It's also one of the Afterworld's designated arrival locations."

I was about to respond, but Aech was already in motion, running toward the green end of the tunnel.

"Come on!" she shouted back over her shoulder. "This way!"

Shoto and I both sprinted after her.

Once we emerged from the mouth of the tunnel, I saw that it was actually a culvert running beneath a four-lane highway bridge over a dry riverbed. The name BULL CREEK ROAD was engraved above the tunnel entrance.

We followed Aech as she took a sharp right, onto a worn dirt path skirting the black chain-link fence to our left, which appeared to run all the way around the perimeter of the forested property beyond it. The fence had a bunch of notes, purple flowers, and purple ribbons tied to it. They seemed to grow in number and density the farther along it we ran.

I glanced upward, then swiveled my head all the way around to scan the entire horizon. It was hard to tell what time of day it was supposed to be. The sky was a dozen different shades of purple and was filled with luminous storm clouds that drifted rapidly across it.

Eventually, the trees on the other side of the fence began to thin out, and beyond them I could see a circular white building, like an ivory tower, rising from a sprawling field of green grass. Beyond the white tower was a much larger building, also white, which looked like it was constructed out of cube-shaped building blocks of polished white marble. There were floodlights encircling the whole structure, bathing it in a brilliant, other-worldly light.

The image-recognition software running on my HUD informed me that we were approaching the entrance of Paisley Park, Prince's famous home and creative compound. A moment later, we finally arrived at the property's front gates, which were wrought iron and covered in purple chrome.

Without saying anything, Aech walked up to the gates and grabbed one of the bars with her right hand. When she did, this action triggered our first needle drop, and churchlike organ music filled our ears. The song-identification software running on my HUD identified it as the opening of a song called "Let's Go Crazy." It seemed to emanate from somewhere high above us, as if the sky itself were one giant speaker. A second later, we heard the voice of the Purple One himself, booming down from the sky like the voice of God Almighty, as Prince recited an excerpt of the song's spoken intro:

> Dearly beloved, we are gathered here today to get through this
> thing called "life" . . .
> But I'm here to tell you, there's something else—the Afterworld!

As soon as he said "The Afterworld!" there was a deafening crash of thunder that shook my bones, and a second later, tines of purple lightning arced across the sky. Then the rolling purple clouds parted for a moment, revealing a cherry-shaped moon (complete with stem), sitting high in the eastern sky.

I turned to look in the opposite direction and realized that I could also see the sun, hanging motionless just above the western horizon. I found myself wondering why the Afterworld had been designed this way—just before I heard the man himself explain that it was "a world of never-ending happiness, you can always see the sun, day or night."

As the song continued to play, the gates of Paisley Park began to open before us. Once they'd opened up all the way, Aech turned to address me.

"OK," she said. "Opening the gates activates all of the local quests, and since we're clanned up, they should be activated for you now too. So let's have another look at that Fourth Shard. . . ."

I took the Fourth Shard out of my inventory and held it up. Prince's

Love Symbol was still etched into its surface, but as we watched, seven more symbols appeared on either side of it, along with a capital letter *V*.

At first, I thought the *V* was a Roman numeral for the number five, to indicate the Fifth Shard. But then, because of its size and placement relative to the other eight symbols, it occurred to me that it might also be an abbreviation for the word "versus."

The first seven symbols to the left of the *V* looked like variations of the familiar Prince Love Symbol. But the eighth and final symbol was very different. I didn't recognize it at all. It looked like a number 7 placed off-center inside a circular diagram of an orbiting electron. Or maybe the face of an old analog timepiece, with the number 7 forming the big and little hands of a clock at around 8:35.

As soon as Aech saw this string of strange symbols appear on the shard, her smile vanished and her eyes went wide.

"This isn't a quest, Z," she said, looking over at me. "It's a fucking suicide mission!"

A split second after Aech dropped the F-bomb, we heard a loud buzzer sound, and then a large empty glass jar suddenly appeared, floating in the air beside her, with a label on it that said "Spud's Swear Jar."

Aech scowled at it, then she let out an annoyed sigh and dropped a single gold coin into the jar. When she did, it vanished. I decided not to ask. Instead, I pointed down at the row of symbols on the shard.

"Aech," I said. "Do you know what these symbols mean?"

She nodded and took a deep breath.

"I think they mean that to obtain the Fifth Shard, we have to battle the Seven," Aech replied, pointing to the seven love symbols on the left. "By joining forces with 'The Original 7ven.'"

Shoto and I exchanged confused looks. Aech continued. "The Seven are a team of seven different NPC incarnations of the Purple One. Each from a different stage of his career. Each with godlike powers."

"Have you done battle with any of them before?" Shoto asked, innocently enough.

"Of course not!" Aech replied, clearly offended by the question. "You're asking for serious trouble if you attack *any* incarnation of His Royal Badness on the Afterworld. Facing down seven at once is suicide. Would you visit Mount Olympus or go to Asgard to pick a fight with all of the gods? Only non-fan, level-grinding tourists ever even attempt to do battle with the Seven, and every last one of them gets zeroed out as a reward for their insolence and hubris."

"Yeah," I replied. "But that was probably because none of them were true Prince fans. But you are. You know everything about him, and about this planet. Come on, Aech." I pointed down at the symbols on the shard. "If we have to fight the Seven, where do we find them?"

Aech hesitated before answering. Then she sighed and nodded toward the southern horizon.

"There's a temple out in the desert, seven miles south of the city," she said. "The Temple of Seven. In the center of its courtyard is an arena, and if you set foot inside it, the seven incarnations of Prince are summoned there from all over the Afterworld to do battle with you."

Aech took off running again, through the open gates of Paisley Park, once again motioning for us to follow her.

"Why are we going in there?" I yelled after Aech. "I thought you said the arena was in a desert outside of town?"

"We can't go to the arena yet," she replied. "First we gotta collect a few weapons. And power-ups. Like, *a lot* of them . . ."

"I'm already carrying plenty of weapons in my inventory," Shoto said. "And so are you. We can loan Parzival anything he needs."

Aech shook her head.

"Conventional weapons won't work against his Royal Badness," Aech said. "In any of his seven incarnations. Only locally forged sonic, percussive, and musical weapons can affect the Seven and their familiars. All of them are armed with deadly sonic weapons, too, and some of them are powerful artifacts that can deal enough damage to kill your avatar with one attack. That's why we need to gear up before we attempt to face them, OK? And boy, do I love wasting precious seconds myself, because y'all don't trust me to know what I'm doing!"

"We trust you, Aech!" I replied. "Lead on."

She led us on, to the front entrance of Paisley Park. As soon as we reached it, Aech opened one of the glass front doors and waved us inside.

We could hear the opening of the cheerful song "Paisley Park" emanating from within.

"First we need to go in here," she said. "And by 'we' I mean you, Z. This is your quest to complete. But I'll walk you through it, step by step. OK?"

"OK," I said, reluctantly peering inside.

A split second later, I felt Aech's foot hit me squarely in the small of my avatar's back, propelling me forward, through the doorway, and into Paisley Park.

The moment we reached the foyer, Aech began leading, prodding, and dragging me forward, through the building's mazelike interior. Shoto followed close on our heels as we sprinted up and down Paisley Park's marble hallways and through its ornately carved wooden doors, many of which were marked with either a moon or a star.

Aech led me from one padded purple velvet room to the next, occasionally stopping to tell me to touch a specific object (or undergarment) to gain access to a secret passage, which would lead us to yet another padded purple velvet room. By following her instructions, I was able to collect five hidden pieces of a Love Symbol–shaped power cell, which Aech said we needed to repair a spaceship that was parked up on the roof. Luckily, she already knew exactly where and how to obtain each of the five pieces.

As we sprinted from the Candle Room to the Music Club to the Boudoir to the Virtual Video Room, a song called "Interactive" played on a continuous loop in every room. Aech explained that this was a song Prince wrote exclusively for a Myst-like videogame he released with the same title. In the game, players had to collect five pieces of the Prince Symbol hidden throughout Paisley Park, and this was a re-creation of that quest.

After we collected the first four pieces, Aech led me and Shoto down another carpeted corridor, into a large open room filled with museum exhibits. Dozens of Prince's outfits and instruments were on display inside glass cases. Aech hurried past them, toward the opposite side of the room, without stopping to look at anything. Shoto and I did the same, following behind her single-file, to ensure that we only stepped where she did.

When she reached the door at the other side of the room, she threw it open—but then I saw something catch her eye. Parked off in the far corner of this room, surrounded by velvet ropes, was a purple motorcycle. I tapped an icon on my HUD to zoom in on the placard mounted on the wall behind it, which identified the bike as the 1981 Hondamatic that Prince rode in the movie *Purple Rain.*

"Wait here!" Aech shouted over her shoulder as she ran across the room and leaped over the velvet ropes. I thought she was going to hop on the bike and steal it, but instead she pulled a giant serrated Rambo knife out of her inventory and slashed the motorcycle's tires, then stabbed a large hole in the side of its gas tank. When she rejoined us at the exit, I saw tears glinting in her eyes, just before she wiped them away with her hand.

"I had to immobilize the Hondamatic now, so that later on, when we face Purple Rain Prince in the arena, he won't be riding it. And that might save our ass, because he won't be able to use it to run down Morris. That bike is his Achilles' heel!"

"Morris who?" Shoto and I asked as we chased after her.

Aech blurted out a reply, but she was too far away and moving too fast for us to make out any of it. She led us out of the museum and down another series of corridors, to another door. When she opened it, there was a spiral staircase on the other side, suspended in an endless starry void. It corkscrewed downward, through a field of stars, galaxies, and nebulae. We followed Aech up this long spiral staircase, until we arrived at a door labeled STUDIO. Inside, we passed through a large wood-paneled control room filled with giant mixing boards and recording equipment, and then on into the main recording studio. Aech sidestepped the piano, then hustled over to a red painting of two women hanging on the wall, which she slid aside to reveal a safe hidden behind it. She entered the combination from memory and opened it. The fifth and final piece of the Love Symbol power cell was inside.

Once all five pieces were reassembled, the power cell began to glow.

Aech led us back up the surreal spiral staircase, all the way to the top, into a large domed room. Just as she had promised, a large purple spaceship sat parked in the center of it. It resembled a giant thimble, with half a dozen capsule-shaped tanks bolted to the outside. Aech pressed a button on its exterior and a hatch opened in its perfectly smooth hull. The three of us crammed into the ship's tiny purple velvet-lined cockpit, and Aech pointed out a Love Symbol–shaped indentation in the control panel in front of us. I placed the Love Symbol power cell inside it. The control panel lit up, and we could hear its engine powering on directly beneath our feet. At the same moment, the domed ceiling above us split apart like the segments of an orange and retracted to reveal a starry night sky, filled with billowing purple clouds.

Aech gave me a thumbs-up, then she took the ship's crushed velvet-covered steering yoke in her hands and launched us into the sky. She circled over Paisley Park a few times, then turned the ship east, toward the distant Minneapolis skyline on the horizon.

Aech pulled up a map of the Afterworld on the ship's navigation display. The planet wasn't a globe, but it still rotated like one, spinning like a Love Symbol pendant suspended from an invisible chain in virtual space. Most of the surface was covered by a surreal, shrunken-down version of mid-'80s Minneapolis, Minnesota, but it had streets and locations from L.A., Paris, and several other locations scattered throughout. The map divided the city into different neighborhoods, like Big City, Erotic City, Crystal City, Beatown, and Uptown. Aech flew us directly into the heart of Downtown and set the ship down in the middle of a busy intersection, directly in front of a place called the Huntington Hotel.

Aech opened the ship's outer hatch. But before we exited, she removed the Love Symbol power cell from its cradle and stashed it in her inventory, causing the whole ship to go dark and power down.

The street outside was crowded with NPC pedestrians and motorists, many of them cursing and honking at us for abandoning our purple UFO in the middle of a busy intersection. Aech ignored them and headed for a large, fortress-like black building on the opposite corner of the street. A curved sign over its front entrance read FIRST AVENUE, in large capital letters.

Aech pointed farther down the street, at a side entrance that led into the same building. It had a small awning over the door with 7TH ST. ENTRY printed on it. She told us to wait for her there, then she sprinted straight toward the club's front entrance, like Lancelot storming a castle single-handed.

As she went inside, I pulled up her POV video feed on my HUD, giving me a glimpse of the interior. Aech was pushing her way through a dance floor that was packed with hundreds of NPCs of every race, creed, and social class. Teenagers and adults, packed in shoulder to shoulder, all getting their groove on. Then there was a flurry of movement, during which I couldn't see much of anything. I heard what sounded like several rapid blasts from a plasma rifle. A few seconds later, Aech emerged carrying an all-white guitar, with gold knobs and tuning keys, and a gold Love Symbol painted on its body, just above the gold pickups. It was one of the most beautiful musical instruments I had ever seen.

"Ka-ching!" Aech said, holding it triumphantly over her head for a moment before she added it to her avatar's inventory. "It shoots sonic blasts that are *almost* as powerful as the Purple Special! Now we just need a few more things, and we'll be ready to head to the arena." She took off running again, motioning for us to follow. "Come on! We've got an audition."

• • •

Aech led us down the brightly lit tunnel of neon that was Seventh Street. After several blocks she made a left onto Hennepin Avenue. We followed that for a few blocks, then she continued to zigzag her way east, leading us down a labyrinth of numbered streets and dark alleyways, filled with broken bottles, busted fire escapes, and enough randomly generated burning barrels to make Donkey Kong envious.

Aech was very specific about each turn she took, like she was entering the combination to a safe. She led us right onto South Fifth Street, left onto Second Avenue South, right onto South Fourth Street, left onto Third Avenue South, and then right onto South Third Street.

As we weaved through this maze, I glanced down a side street and finally spotted something I recognized—probably because it wasn't directly related to Prince. Hanging out in an alley were characters and settings from Break Street and Ghetto Blaster, two (very) old-school hip-hop videogames I'd played as a kid, using the Commodore 64 emulator on my old laptop. Someone had converted them into photorealistic mini-quests, and then anchored them here in the back alleys of the Afterworld. When I asked Aech what they were doing here, she smiled and shrugged.

"Nobody knows," she said. "They're a weird little Easter egg, left by one of this planet's original designers."

"Do you think Kira could've been the one responsible?" I asked.

She shrugged. "Who knows?"

Aech made a sharp right, leading us down another alley. But this particular alley seemed slightly darker and more ominous than the others, and

Aech must've thought so too. Because I saw her take out a thermal detonator and arm it.

Aech held up her hand to bring us to a halt. Then she pointed out a pack of feral NPC gangbangers who were stepping out of the shadows up ahead of us. They were all wearing large gold crucifixes around their necks. The NPC name tags hovering above their heads on my HUD informed me that there were ten of them, and that their gang was known as the Disciples. Each one was toting a machine gun, and without saying a word, they opened fire on us. Shoto and I took cover behind burning barrels, but Aech remained out in the open, letting their bullets ricochet off her shield. Then she casually tossed her thermal detonator into their midst. There was a brilliant flash of light, and all ten of the Disciples were incinerated in a single blast.

Then Aech kept right on walking, fanning her hands in front of her face to clear the Disciple dust that now filled the air.

When we emerged from the other end of the alley, Aech quickened her pace, and Shoto and I did the same to keep up with her as she continued to bob, sidestep, and weave through the crowd and the surreal landscape around us, which appeared to be a living mash-up of all of Prince's different album covers and music videos. The streets were lined with music venues of all types and sizes.

Like an overly knowledgeable tour guide, Aech explained how each of the venues we saw here on the Afterworld was a replica of a real club or concert hall or stadium where Prince had once performed, and that you could walk into any one of them, sit down in an audience of period-appropriate NPCs, and watch a re-creation of the gig or gigs that Prince had once performed there—detailed, immersive simulations, extrapolated from old photographs and archived video and audio recordings.

According to Aech, the best ones to check out were Prince playing in the middle of a rainstorm in Miami at Super Bowl XLI, and his midnight show on New Year's Eve in 1998—when everyone finally got to party like it was 1999.

We also passed a replica of Mann's Chinese Theatre, where, Aech explained, the *Purple Rain* movie premiere on July 24, 1984, was always happening, over and over, on a continuous loop. We saw Pee-wee Herman pull up in a miniature hot-rod, just a few cars ahead of Purple Rain Prince himself, arriving in a purple limo, dressed in a glittering purple tuxedo, solemnly holding a single purple rose with both hands as his bodyguard—a giant gray-bearded gentleman with a bleach-blond mullet and a striped zebra vest—cleared the great one's path onto the red carpet.

Just a few doors down from Mann's, we passed a replica of the Dorothy Chandler Pavilion, where Aech told us it was always March 25, 1985, and the Fifty-Seventh Academy Awards were always being held, just in case any visitors wanted to watch Prince walk up onstage (with Wendy on one arm and Lisa on the other) to receive his Oscar statuette from Michael Douglas and Kathleen Turner.

Farther down the street, we passed a nightclub with a neon sign that said SUGAR WALLS. An NPC of Sheena Easton was strutting up and down the street out front, and when we spotted her, it triggered another needle drop, this time for the Prince song "U Got the Look." Aech and I both paused to stare at her as she swaggered by, grooving and lip-syncing to her 1987 hit single.

"You know," Shoto said, "it's pretty obvious that Prince was plagiarizing those old Jordache Jeans commercials when he wrote this song."

He laughed and began to mix up the song and the jeans jingle, using a set of holographic turntables that he produced from his inventory. *"You've got the look!"* he sang. *"You've got the look. The Jordache look!"*

Aech didn't respond. She just quietly backed away from him several steps, pulling me with her. A split second later, a big, fat purple bolt of electricity descended from the sky and struck Shoto directly on the top of his head, knocking him flat on the pavement. The bolt also apparently caused enough hit points of damage to nearly kill his avatar—I saw his health bar indicator start flashing red for a few seconds, until he could cast a few healing spells on himself.

Aech walked over and helped him up off the ground.

"I warned you, didn't I?" she said. "I told you not to blaspheme against the Purple One here? But did you listen to me?"

Shoto shook his head but didn't say anything. A few seconds later, I realized that he couldn't speak. The gods of the Afterworld had apparently muted his avatar as punishment for his blasphemy, in addition to the lightning bolt. I felt bad for him. When you were wearing an ONI headset, getting hit by lightning was no joke—it was almost as bad as getting tasered.

"Remember how much grief you gave me when you found out I don't like watching scary movies?" Aech said, pointing an accusing finger at us.

"Well, guess what. Now the shoe is on the other foot! So listen up, ass-heads, and listen good. *Do not* crack jokes at the Artist's expense. In fact, just stop speaking altogether, and don't do anything I don't tell you to do. Just keep your trap shut and stick to my heels. Got it, Larry?" She glared at Shoto until he nodded. Then she turned to me. "What about you, Curly?"

"Yes, Moe," I said, stepping out of her way. "We heard you. Lead on, O Wise One. . . ."

Aech gave me an impolite shove, then she turned and led on. We rounded another corner, onto Hennepin Avenue, and immediately passed a small one-room schoolhouse. It caught my eye because it looked incredibly out of place in the middle of a crowded downtown Minneapolis street. Through one of the schoolhouse's open windows, I could see and hear Prince dancing with a whole classroom full of Muppets while singing about having starfish and coffee for breakfast. One of the kid Muppets singing along with Prince bore a distinct resemblance to him.

I considered asking Aech if one of the Seven Princes we would have to face was "Muppet Prince," but then I thought better of it. She still didn't appear to be in the mood for jokes. Her face was stoic with concentration as she led us through the Afterworld's surreal urban landscape, and her eyes were constantly scanning the area around us, looking for anything that would slow us down.

We passed the Gotham Art Museum, which I recognized as a set from Tim Burton's *Batman* film from 1990, a movie for which Prince wrote the soundtrack—another of the few meager pieces of Prince-related knowledge I didn't need to get from my HUD.

We rounded a corner, onto Washington Avenue, which took us along the border of Downtown and Erotic City. Just across it, glittering like the Golden Gate, there was a nightclub with a vulva-shaped entrance. The pulsing pink neon sign above it read A LOVE BIZARRE. Shoto took a few steps toward it, as if hypnotized, but Aech pulled him back, shaking her head.

"You're a married man, Shoto," Aech said. "And we definitely don't have time to go in there right now. . . ."

"I didn't want to anyway!" Shoto replied, revealing that he was no longer muted.

Aech swiveled her head 180 degrees to ogle an NPC of Sheila E in a tight-blue dress that had just emerged from the club. She sauntered right up to the Erotic City border and beckoned us to cross it and join her on the other side.

Aech looked tempted for a second. Then she shook it off and continued running. We followed her down the street, weaving our way through the oncoming crowd of NPCs in colorful costumes. One of them caused me to do a double take—a young black woman who bore an uncanny resemblance to Aech when I'd first met her. When I pointed Aech's NPC doppelgänger out to her, she smiled and nodded.

"That's Boni Boyer," she said. "She played keyboards for both Prince and Sheila E. And she was a total badass. She gave me hope. If a girl who looked like her could wind up performing with Prince, I figured there might still be a chance for me."

"And look at you now," I said.

"Running for my life inside a computer simulation that I willingly plugged my brain into?" she said.

"No, fool!" I said. "I meant that now you've become an inspiration too."

She grinned her giant grin at me. "I know what you meant, Z," she said. "Thanks."

She was silent for a moment. Then she stopped walking and turned to face me.

"What you were going through on Halcydonia . . . I get it now," she said. She motioned at our surroundings. "The Prince records and videotapes I inherited from my dad when he moved out, they were the only things he left behind. Besides me, I guess." She shrugged. "Growing up knowing he'd been such a huge Prince fan always made me wish he'd stuck around. I figured he probably would've been OK with my sexuality. Or at least more accepting of it than my mother."

I nodded, but didn't say anything. Neither did Shoto.

About a year after we won Halliday's contest, I'd asked Aech if she ever thought about trying to get back in touch with her mother. Aech told me her mother, Marie, had already come looking for her, as soon as she learned that her estranged lesbian daughter had become one of the world's wealthiest and most famous people. Apparently that prompted Marie to abruptly change her homophobic tune and before long she showed up on Aech's doorstep.

Aech didn't let her mother come inside. Instead, she reached out and pressed her thumb to Marie's phone, and transferred her a million dollars.

Then, before Marie even had a chance to thank her, Aech threw her mother's own words back at her.

"Your choices have made me ashamed of you," Aech told her. "Now, leave me be. I never want to see you again."

Then she slammed the door in her mother's face, and told her security guards never to let her on the property again.

"You know what really sucks, Z?" Aech asked me as we continued to walk down Washington Avenue.

"No, Aech," I replied. "What really sucks?"

"Later in life, after he became a Jehovah's Witness, Prince came out as anti-gay," she said. "He believed that God didn't approve of homosexuality, so he couldn't either. Can you believe that, Z?" She shook her head. "For decades he was an icon and a role model to generations of sexually confused kids *and* adults. He spoke for us, through his lyrics: *'I'm not a woman, I'm not a man. I am something that you'll never understand.'*"

She started to get choked up and had to pause for a few seconds to collect herself.

"Then, one day," she went on, "Prince suddenly changes his mind, and says, 'No, no. I was wrong all along. You *really should* hate yourself for being gay, because God says it's a sin for you to be the person He made you to be. . . .'"

She shook her head. "It's stupid. Why should I care if some old rock star gets religion?"

"It makes total sense, Aech," I said after a moment. "First your mom rejects you. And then Prince—who was like a surrogate for your dad—he rejected you too."

She nodded. Then she smiled. "Yeah, but you didn't reject me. Even though I was catfishing you for all those years."

I smiled back at her. "Of course not," I replied. "I fucking love you. You're my best friend. You're part of my chosen family, which is the only kind that matters. Right?"

She smiled and nodded again, and she was about to respond when she suddenly came to a halt on the sidewalk.

"Quick!" she said, pointing toward some sort of clothing thrift store on the street corner directly in front of us. "We need to stop in there! Hurry!"

The sign above the entrance said MR. MCGEE'S FIVE-AND-DIME. I ran over and tried to open the front door, but it wouldn't budge.

"No, not that way!" Aech shouted. "Around back!"

Shoto and I followed her around back, and this triggered another needle drop—"Raspberry Beret." When we got to the rear of the store, Aech was holding open a back door, with a sign on the inside that said Out.

"You can only get in through the Out door," she explained, waving us inside.

I let out a weary sigh. Then I checked my ONI usage countdown. I now had just one hour and forty-four minutes remaining.

"Is all of this absolutely necessary, Aech?" I asked.

"Yes!" Aech replied, pushing me through the door. "Now, keep moving!"

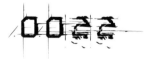

Aech finished walking me through the elaborate process of purchasing the Raspberry Beret. (First I had to ask the owner, Mr. McGee, for a job. Then Aech instructed me to stand behind the counter and do "something close to nothing" until Mr. McGee told me several times that he didn't like my kind, because I was "a bit too leisurely." It felt like it took forever.)

Once we had left the store, Aech forced me to put the Raspberry Beret on my avatar's head.

"Dude, if I find out that you're messing with me right now, there will be hell to pay," I said.

"This is valuable, hard-won knowledge that I've been sharing with your ungrateful ass!" she replied, tilting my beret at a rakish slant and then nodding with satisfaction.

A few blocks down Washington Avenue, we spotted a beautiful 1958 Chevrolet Corvette up ahead of us, gleaming beneath the bright streetlights. For some reason, the car was parked sideways, with its front end jutting out into traffic and its rear wheels backed up against the curb, instead of parallel to it like every other car on the street. It was a red-and-white convertible, the top was down, and a set of keys was hanging from the ignition.

"You drive, Z," Aech said. "The Little Red Corvette won't start for you unless you're wearing the Raspberry Beret."

I jumped behind the wheel. Aech took shotgun, forcing Shoto to hop into the back. The Corvette's engine roared to life, and I pulled away from the curb and out into traffic. Nearly all of the other vehicles on the road were either a sports car or a limousine.

"Take that freeway on-ramp," Aech said, pointing up ahead. "Onto I-394 West. Follow it all the way out of town. Drive as fast as you can."

I did as she instructed and took the on-ramp, then I put the hammer down, pushing the engine up over a hundred miles an hour. As we rocketed west, Aech switched on the car's radio, and it began to play "Little Red Corvette." When the song ended, it started over again—apparently it was the only song the radio would pick up. After a few repetitions, we all started singing along with the chorus—until Aech suddenly snapped off the radio in disgust.

"Hold up a second," she said, turning around in her seat to address Shoto. "Did my ears just deceive me, or were you just singing 'Living correct'?"

Shoto nodded.

"Yeah, so?" he said. "Those are the lyrics, aren't they?"

"No," she replied. "No, those are not the lyrics, Shoto. The title of the song is 'Little Red Corvette.' It always has been."

Shoto furrowed his brow.

"Seriously?" he said. Then he shrugged. "Wow. That really changes the whole meaning of the song for me."

"Shoto?" Aech asked. "Buddy? Did you happen to notice that we are sitting in a little red Corvette right now? And that no other song will play on its radio?"

"Listen to it again," Shoto said. "'Living correct' works too. I'm telling you!"

Aech looked up at the sky expectantly.

"I can't believe that shit didn't warrant a lightning bolt, but OK," she muttered.

Aech continued to give me driving directions until we reached the Seven Corners area, located near the neon-lit intersection of three streets—Washington, Cedar, and Nineteenth Avenues, all of which were paved with red bricks instead of asphalt.

Despite the name, I only counted four corners. There was a different music club located on each one, each with its own giant stylized neon sign bearing the venue's name. On one corner was a club called Clinton's House.

Directly across the street was a venue with an ice-blue neon sign that said MELODY COOL, located in a gray stone building with stained-glass windows that made it look more like a church than a dance club. Across the street from it, on yet another corner, was a club called Glam Slam, which had a giant neon Mars symbol encircling its front entrance.

When we reached another little club with a big neon sign—this one called the Baby Doe Bar—Aech told me to pull over. I parked the car and we all jumped out.

"OK, here's the deal," Aech said. "Avatars can come down here and audition for any of the local bands playing in one of these clubs. If we pass and they let us join their band, they'll fight beside us later on when we have to enter the arena. Got it?"

Shoto pointed to a flyer stapled to a nearby utility pole, announcing open auditions for a band called Dez Dickerson and the Modernaires. The picture on the flyer featured the band's lead singer (Dez, I presumed) wearing a Japanese flag bandanna.

"How about these guys?" Shoto asked. "They look totally wicked."

Aech rolled her eyes.

"Oh, that's a *fantastic* idea, Shoto," she replied. "Who better equipped to do sonic battle against the greatest musician in history than Dez Dickerson and the Modernaires! That would really have Prince quaking in his six-inch heels!" Aech pointed down the street. "Better yet, why don't we just stroll down that way a few blocks and audition for Apollonia 6!"

"OK!" Shoto replied cheerfully. "If they have six members and the three of us join forces with them, there will be nine of us total! We'll have the Seven Princes outnumbered!"

I pulled up an Apollonia 6 album cover in a browser window and turned it toward Shoto. It showed three young women in lingerie, surrounded by mist, posing in front of a bunch of obelisks. One of them had a large teddy bear wrapped around her fishnet stocking–covered leg.

"I think Apollonia 6 only has three members," I said. "Unless you count the teddy bear."

We both turned to Aech for confirmation, but she was already walking away from us, shaking her head at our ignorance. Shoto and I ran after her. . . .

Then we ran *into* her. Aech had come to a sudden halt just ahead of us, after only taking a few steps. And once we recovered from our collision with her, we saw why. Nolan Sorrento's black-armored avatar was standing directly in front of us, blocking our path.

The guy who murdered my aunt and a bunch of my neighbors in an attempt to kill me. Back on the street. Free as a bird.

"Boo!" he shouted, making all three of us flinch. This, in turn, made him cackle with delight. He looked extremely happy to see us, and I found that extremely unsettling.

"Wow!" Sorrento said, once he regained his composure. "Look at you guys! The A-Team is back in action. Just like old times. . . ."

He took a menacing step toward us, but we all held our ground.

"Don't you kids ever get tired of picking through the wreckage of a past generation's nostalgia?" He stretched his arms out wide. "I mean, look around. The entire OASIS is like one giant graveyard, haunted by the undead pop-culture icons of a bygone era. A crazy old man's shrine to a bunch of pointless crap."

"Why are you here, Sorrento?" I asked. "We're kinda busy at the moment."

"Anorak sent me to check in on you," he replied. "You're burning an awful lot of time on this planet. And your friend Art3mis appears to have abandoned you." He smiled. "I suspected that might happen. After all, if the three of you fail, you die, and that would leave her in control of your company. . . ."

I did my best to act as though he'd really gotten under my skin. If he and Anorak believed that Samantha had bailed on us, they wouldn't be concerned with what she was really up to.

"Anyway," Sorrento said. "Anorak is preoccupied at the moment, so he sent me to remind you that every move you make is being watched. Time is running out. And your deadline is nonnegotiable." He smiled and then added, "So keep your eyes on the prize or meet your demise."

And with that, Sorrento teleported away, and his avatar vanished.

We all stared at the spot where he'd just been for a moment. Then, without a word, we kept on moving.

As Aech led us toward the next intersection, we passed a copy of the Moulin Rouge, which was right next to a place called Ambulance Bar. Up ahead of us, mixed in with all the music venues, I also spotted a video arcade called the Coin Castle. From what little I could see through its front windows, it was packed with nothing but purple pinball machines and videogame cabinets. I was hoping Aech was headed for it, but she ran right past the Coin Castle's front entrance, and continued running until we reached a large nightclub located on the next corner. It had a neon sign over its entrance that spelled out the word PANDEMONIUM in fiery orange letters. There was a large clock mounted up above, with THE TIME printed directly above it in all-capital letters. This struck me as odd, like printing THE DATE above a calendar.

Aech led us up to the club's front entrance. It was guarded by the same bearded six-foot-tall bleach-blond muscle-bound zebra-vested gentleman we'd seen earlier, guarding Purple Rain Prince at Mann's Chinese Theatre. He stepped in front of the door to block our way, then folded his giant arms across his tree trunk of a chest.

"Wassup, Big Chick?" Aech asked, addressing the NPC like an old friend.

Big Chick slid his sunglasses down the length of his nose and gave Aech the evil eye.

"What's the password?" he asked in a surprisingly kind voice.

Aech cupped her right ear, turned it toward him, and said, "What?"

Big Chick nodded, gave us all a friendly grin, and then stepped out of our way. Shoto and I exchanged a perplexed glance and followed Aech inside.

I felt like we were walking into the hippest night spot on the ninth level of Dante's Inferno. All the lighting was reddish in hue, and there were flames everywhere you looked—lit candles on every table, torches mounted on the walls and balcony railings, and dozens of burning fireplaces, upstairs and down. But the club didn't even feel warm. And it was filled with happy, chattering NPCs—beautiful people in colorful attire, who were all busy drinking, smoking, dancing, and trying to seduce one another.

"Gentlemen, please remember—you can't stop the revolution if you don't have the time," Aech said, pointing across the club toward the empty stage, which was located inside a ring of fire, and said, "Dogs travel in packs of seven!"

The stage was currently empty, except for a large drum kit. The bass drum had a familiar symbol on it—a large number 7, positioned off-center inside a large circle, with a much smaller circle set into its orbit, like an electron diagram. . . .

I took out the Fourth Shard and had another look at it. The symbol on the bass drum matched the eighth and final symbol etched into its surface—the one that came after the *V*.

"Aech!" I said. "The symbols match!"

She nodded.

"It's the logo of a band called the Original 7ven," she told me. "But they changed their name to that, later in their career, for the same reason Prince changed his—contract bullshit. They're still much better known by their original name—"

The crowd around us suddenly erupted into applause, drowning out her voice. We looked over and saw seven men running up onto the stage single-file. All seven of them were dressed in stylish suits. Four of them were carrying instruments. One of them was carrying a large mirror.

They seemed familiar to me, but I couldn't place them right away. Then the club DJ—who also looked very familiar—jumped on the PA to introduce them.

"Ladies and gentlemen," he said. "Please welcome . . . the original seven members of the greatest band in the world . . . Morris Day and *the Time*!"

That was when I realized how I knew them—from their cameo at the end of *Jay and Silent Bob Strike Back*. And the DJ who had just introduced them was an NPC of Jason Mewes, probably cut and pasted here from Askewniverse in Sector Sixteen.

The lead singer, Morris Day, waited a moment for the crowd to quiet down, then he grabbed the microphone.

"Welcome to Pandemonium, y'all!" he said. "Tonight's the night. We're holding auditions, people! To fill out our roster with some new dancers for an upcoming tour. So anyone out there who thinks they got what it takes, this is your one and only chance to dance!"

"All right," Aech said. "Get ready! And try not to blow this, OK?"

"Try not to blow what?" I asked. "Are you gonna tell us what we need to do? Aech?"

Aech shook her head and began dancing backward, away from me. Then a huge grin spread across her face as the Time launched into "The Bird," their hit dance single from 1984.

"Y'all ready?" Morris asked from the stage. "OK! Anyone who wants to audition, I'm counting off ten seconds to get to the dance floor! Ten! Nine! Eight! Seven—"

Aech continued to dance backward, out onto the dance floor, motioning for us to follow her. A second later, Morris Day let out an earsplitting "Whawk!" and the song kicked into high gear.

That was when I began to see falling directional arrows on my HUD that matched the arrows lighting up on the dance floor directly beneath my feet, like a giant game of Dance Dance Revolution. Shoto saw them, too, and we both let out a jubilant roar.

"DDR!" we shouted, as we both began to dance in sync to the arrows.

Aech joined us, and the three of us danced side by side, hitting our marks on the floor in perfect sync.

We managed to keep it up until the very end of the song.

When it was over, Morris called us up onstage and announced that we had passed the audition with flying colors.

"Say, 'I pledge allegiance to the Time'!" Morris shouted. "Can y'all say that?"

We each raised our right hand and pledged allegiance. Then Aech leaned over and whispered something in Morris's ear. It sounded like "the kid." Whatever it was, his expression changed and he stormed offstage, motioning for the rest of the band to follow him—including the three of us.

"It worked!" Aech said. "They've agreed to come battle with us. Let's go!"

——— • • •

We got back in the Little Red Corvette and sped south on Alphabet Street. Morris Day and the Time followed behind us in their tour bus, which had their logo for the Original 7ven painted across the side.

Once we were a few miles outside the city limits, the landscape around us abruptly changed, and the road led us into a desert that appeared to stretch to the horizon in all directions.

Every seven seconds, long tines of purple lightning descended from the sky to strike the desert sand, burning and melting it into strange pillared formations of purple fulgurite that dotted the barren landscape like sentinels.

Eventually a small lone pyramid emerged in the distance ahead of us, just off the highway, like some sort of strange roadside attraction.

When we reached it, Aech told me to me pull over, and motioned for the tour bus behind us to do the same thing. She told us all to wait while she ran inside to get something, and I watched from inside the Corvette as she ran across the barren sand, over to one corner of the pyramid, which appeared to have no entrance. I used my HUD to zoom in with maximum magnification and saw that she was running her fingertips across the surface of one of the large stones that made up the pyramid's base. Then she leaned forward and blew a layer of sand and dust away from one tiny section of it, revealing several rows of hieroglyphs. She began to press them in a specific sequence, like buttons. I heard a loud grinding sound as a massive stone at the base of the pyramid slid aside, revealing a secret entrance. Aech ran through it.

A minute later, she emerged again, now wearing a huge smile on her face. As she jumped back in the car beside me, I saw that she was clutching three gold chains, each with a gold pendant shaped like a different element of the Love Symbol. The first pendant was a golden circle, which Aech gave to me. The second was a golden horn, which she gave to Shoto. The last was a golden androgyne symbol, which Aech placed around her own neck.

"All right," she said, letting out a heavy sigh. "Now we've got the Three Chains of Gold too. I think we're as ready as we're ever going to be." She pointed to the road ahead. "Let's go face the music, fellas."

I pulled the Corvette back out onto the road, the tour bus behind me, and gunned the engine again, hurtling us forward toward the dark, luminous, purple horizon ahead.

A moment later, the desert was behind us and we were in a strange, otherworldly purple landscape, with purple mountain ranges in the distance, and a dark-purple sky over our heads that was filled with dark-purple thunderstorm clouds with bright-purple tines of lightning crackling across and between them. We put the top up on our Little Red Corvette convertible just in time—right before big fat droplets of purple rain began to fall, creating a strange syncopated rhythm as they drummed against the car's roof and hood and on the asphalt road ahead as we continued to speed down it.

A glittering at the end of the road caught my eye, and as we got closer, I could just make out that it was a structure of some sort, looming like a grand fortress or temple. As we drew near, I saw that it had seven spires vaulting toward the purple sky, each topped with a dome shaped like a Hershey's Kiss. Six of the spires were wrapped in bands of blue neon, while the much larger seventh spire in the center was topped with a golden chhatri.

At its perimeter, our road dead-ended in a Love Symbol–shaped parking lot, with a mirrored surface of volcanic black glass. As we gazed up in wonder at the giant structure, the tour bus pulled up and parked behind us, and Morris Day and the rest of the Original 7ven emerged. None of them spoke. They all just stood there waiting and looking extremely cool. Jerome walked over to Morris and pretended to dust off each of his shoulders.

The other members of the Time all wore grim expressions. They looked ready for a war.

Aech led us over to the temple's jewel-encrusted gates, which appeared to be made of gold. They were standing wide-open, daring us to enter. Beyond the gates there was a large open courtyard that stretched all the way to the base of the temple steps. Surrounding both the courtyard and the adjacent temple was a seemingly endless field of purple flowers that stretched to the horizon behind them.

Peering through the open gates, I caught a glimpse of several dark catlike shapes slinking around the courtyard's perimeter—lions or panthers, maybe. Whatever they were, they all suddenly halted in midstride and turned to stare at us with their glowing purple eyes.

"So, I take it this is the arena?" Shoto said.

Aech nodded and spread her arms wide.

"*Dream, if you can, a courtyard,*" she said. "*An ocean of violets in bloom . . .*"

Shoto grinned and cracked his knuckles.

"OK then," he said. "Let's do this."

He took a few steps toward the temple entrance, but Aech grabbed him and pulled him back.

"Not yet," Aech said. "As soon as we cross that threshold, the shit storm will begin. We need to gear up first."

She opened her inventory and took out the Cloud Guitar she'd retrieved from First Avenue. She flipped it over, revealing a Love Symbol–shaped cavity in the back of its body, just like the one in the cockpit of our UFO. Aech took the glowing purple Love Symbol power cell out of her inventory, too, and slapped it into the back of the Cloud Guitar. It fit perfectly, like a battery. Then she flipped the guitar over again and pressed a small Love Symbol–shaped power button directly beneath its bridge. I heard a low harmonic hum that rapidly increased in volume as the strings, fret markers, and pickups began to glow and crackle with purple energy.

"You mentioned that you were taking guitar lessons," Aech said. "To learn how to play a real guitar?"

"Yeah," I said, still staring at the instrument in her hands. "Why?"

"Are you any good?"

I shrugged and clenched my hands into fists, because I was worried they might start shaking.

"Well, I'm no Yngwie Malmsteen or anything," I said. "I'm still learning."

"School's out, Yngwie," she said, holding the Cloud Guitar out to me. "Duty calls."

I reached out and took it from her carefully, using both hands, while bowing my head slightly, thinking about the time Shoto presented me with his slain brother's sword.

"The Cloud Guitar is an Afterworld artifact," Aech said. "Its most powerful sonic attacks can only be activated if the wielder actually knows how to play the guitar, and can properly finger the chord progressions. None of that Guitar Hero stuff you pulled on Megadon will fly. This has to be the real deal."

"OK," I said, taking it from her. "Thanks, Aech."

"Open up its item description," she said. "Right now. Before we go in there, you need to memorize all of the special attack licks and power chords. This is one of the few weapons that will affect all seven iterations of the Purple One. But the guitar will overheat and explode after you use it to take one of the Princes down. So try to take out as many of his henchmen as you can with it first, before you go after one of the Seven. Got it?"

"Prince has henchmen too?" Shoto said. "Who are they?"

"His backup bands," Aech said. "There are dozens of different NPC incarnations of Prince on this planet, depicting the Purple One during all of the different phases of his career. Depending on which seven incarnations we face, some of them may not have a backup band. Like Proto-Prince, because he played every single instrument on his first two albums. But if Graffiti Bridge Prince shows up, he'll be backed by the New Power Generation. They will funk you up badly, my friend. The one you have to watch out for is Third-Eye Prince, because not only does he shoot percussive blasts of sonic enlightenment out of his third eye, he's also backed up by 3RDEYE-GIRL. If we have to face Purple Rain Prince *and* he's backed up by the Revolution? We're probably done, because they're unstoppable, especially here on their home turf."

"But the Time is on our side," I said, glancing back at our henchmen. "They look pretty tough."

"They are," Aech said. "Prince created their band, but they were all so insanely talented that they evolved and grew into something beyond his control. They aren't going to save us though, Z. If we're really lucky, they might be able to help us take down Graffiti Bridge Prince and the NPG. Maybe even Proto-Prince too. But the others—" She shook her head. "No way, no day. It would take a miracle for us to survive this fight. I'm not trying to be negative here. I'm just trying to prepare you for what's about to go down."

"Great," I said, slapping her on the back. "Excellent confidence booster. Thanks, Aech."

She turned to look at Shoto.

"What about you, 'Living Correct'?" she said. "Do you play any musical instruments? I mean, other than the kazoo?"

Shoto scowled at her and shook his head. Aech sighed. Then she opened her inventory and took out a tambourine and tossed it to him. He caught it one-handed.

"Do your best with that," she told him.

"So what instrument do you play, Aech?" Shoto asked indignantly.

"Don't worry about me," she replied. "I sing." She glanced at me. "You ready to do this, Z?"

I nodded and gave her a thumbs-up and she gave me one in return, then she took a deep breath and led us forward, through the open gates of the arena, with the original seven members of Morris Day and the Time backing us up.

When all ten members of our party had passed through the gates, it triggered a needle drop, and the song "Thieves in the Temple" began to play as a dense red fog appeared. It swirled around our legs as it rapidly blanketed the entire floor of the courtyard. Aech led us to the center of the arena, then motioned for us to stop there.

"The Three Chains of Gold will protect us from their attacks for a limited amount of time!" she shouted to me and Shoto. "We need to make it count, and funk them up as much as we can, while we can! Understood?"

Before we could reply, there was a booming crash of thunder, and streaks of purple lightning arced across the sky over our heads.

"Prepare yourselves for battle!" Aech shouted to our entire crew. "The Seven are being teleported here now, from different parts of the Afterworld."

Then Aech said what she always used to say to me, whenever we appeared to be facing a no-win situation: "Nice working with you, Dr. Venkman."

This always used to make me chuckle, but now it hit too close to home.

"See ya on the other side, Ray," I recited, clutching the neck of the Cloud Guitar like it was a particle-thrower.

As we spoke, seven large glass cylinders began to rise up out of the billowing red fog, forming a wide circle around us. Each of these glass cylinders had a metal cap at the top and the bottom, like a giant fuse. And standing motionless inside each of them was a different incarnation of His

Royal Badness. Each one had a different hairstyle and outfit, apparently representing different stylistic phases of Prince's career.

Before I could get a good look at any of them through the fog, all seven chambers opened and the Seven Princes emerged in unison, stepping forward into the arena. As they did so, the menacing opening guitar riff of the song "When Doves Cry" began to echo through the arena at earsplitting volume. When the drums kicked in a few seconds later, all seven incarnations of Prince stretched out their arms as one and began to rise slowly from the ground. I craned my neck upward to see them all hovering directly above us, glaring down at us like seven angry Kryptonian gods intent on giving us a Smallville-style smackdown.

They were a terrifying sight to behold.

"Don't look directly in their eyes!" I heard Aech shout at us. "Never look in *any* of their eyes, OK?"

I immediately averted my eyes and saw Shoto do the same thing. Aech caught us both staring at the ground.

"I didn't tell you to avoid looking *at* them!" Aech shouted. "Just avoid looking any of them in the eye for longer than a second or two, or they'll go berserk, OK?"

I nodded and glanced back up at them, still levitating above and around us, in what was now a slowly rotating circle.

The most imposing to me, by far, was Purple Rain Prince. He wore a pair of gleaming mirror shades, a shirt with a white ruffled collar, red pants, and a shiny purple trench coat with studs on the left shoulder. For some reason, he looked like the most pissed-off one of the bunch. He was also the first one to speak. He pointed down at us with one accusing finger.

"There they are!" he shouted in a voice that reverberated throughout the arena. "Those are the heretics who broke into our house, trashed our bike, and stole our spaceship! And now they dare to defile our temple grounds!"

In unison, the other six incarnations of Prince all gasped and then grimaced, while exchanging deeply offended looks with one another. Then, as if by telepathic agreement, the attack began.

Purple Rain Prince took the lead, and as he fell upon us, his glittering purple trench coat flapped out behind him like a pair of angel wings while he fired deafening blasts of sonic funk down at us from the head of his glowing H. S. Anderson Mad Cat guitar. They transformed into cracking balls of purple energy that exploded on impact. I took several direct hits from these to my avatar's torso. Luckily my Chain of Gold did its job and kept me from sustaining damage.

Then, with a sonic boom, Purple Rain Prince was hovering high above us again. He raised his hands and shouted in that booming voice: *"Majesty! Divinity!"*

Two doves rose up from behind him and hovered above his head. They both opened their beaks and fired shriek attacks down at us.

After Purple Rain Prince and his two attack doves finished their bombing run, Cloud Suit Prince descended. This incarnation wore a sky-blue suit covered in white clouds. And he apparently had the ability to turn his suit invisible and phase-shift, rendering him immune to our attacks.

Cloud Suit Prince seemed especially pissed-off at me, and focused all his vocal attacks on my avatar. It took me a few minutes to figure out why: it was his Cloud Guitar that I was holding, and he wanted it back.

Cloud Suit Prince was singing a song from 1984 called "I Would Die 4 U." But he altered the lyrics of its chorus slightly, so what I heard was, *"You will. Die for. Me. Yeah! That is how it's gonna be!"* Each rapid-fire chord he strummed on his Mad Cat fired another sonic blast down at me, like a gunfighter fanning the barrel of his six-shooter.

Aech referred to the next Prince in the attack conga line as Gett Off Prince. This one was dressed in a tight-fitting yellow lace suit with two circles cut out in the rear to expose his bare ass cheeks. Thankfully he didn't fire any sonic attacks from them. Those came from his yellow guitar, which looked identical to mine, aside from the color.

I thought I was hallucinating when the next Prince descended on us. Aech referred to him as "Gemini." Shoto called him "Partyman." My image-recognition software's best guess was "Batdance Prince." To me, he looked like the villain Two-Face, except that he was Batman on the left half and the green-haired Joker on his right half. He hurled joke bombs from one hand and batarangs from the other, then swooped back up and away, to dodge our counterattacks.

I'm not sure of the correct name for the next incarnation to attack, but I mentally nicknamed him Microphone Gun Prince. He wore an all-black suit, a black head wrap, and an oversize pair of black sunglasses. He also wielded a pair of gold microphone guns that he wore in black leather holsters on each hip. They looked like pistols, except that their barrels had old-school microphones at the end, which hurled a rapid-fire hail of sonic funk waves down at us. After he unleashed his salvo, he blew away the smoke rising from each microphone-gun barrel, then turned and holstered them both as he flew back up into the sky.

The next incarnation scared the living crap out of me. Third Eye Prince had a giant round Afro and a pair of sunglasses with three lenses. The third lens was centered above the bottom two, and it fired a devastating beam of sonic enlightenment from his concealed third eye, which incinerated everything in its path.

After Third Eye Prince finished his bombing run, Purple Rain Prince swooped down to make his second attack, even though he'd only completed his first run about six seconds earlier. Meanwhile, I hadn't managed to get off even a single attack of my own—and my Chain of Gold wouldn't hold out forever. It was a terrifying wake-up call, and made me realize how outmatched we really were.

The seventh and final incarnation, Mesh-Mask Prince, was the only one who didn't swoop down to attack. Apparently unarmed, he continued to hover up above us, silent and motionless, watching the battle below unfold with an impassive expression on his face (at least, from what I could see of it through his mask).

I finally pulled it together and started to return fire with my Cloud Guitar, landing two direct hits on Cloud Suit Prince. This appeared to weaken him considerably, and he pulled out of the attack run rotation and remained hovering up above, alongside Mesh-Mask Prince.

Meanwhile, Aech had pulled up the henchman-activation incantation for the Original 7ven on her HUD. Facing Morris and his band, she read it aloud, prefacing each line of the incantation with a snap of her fingers:

Snap!

"Yo, Stella! If you think I'm afraid of you . . ."

Snap!

"Grace, if you so much as think I can't do the do . . ."

Snap!

"Girl, if you dream I came to jerk around, you better wake up—"

Snap!

"—and *release it!*"

As soon as Aech finished reciting the final two words of the incantation, Morris Day and the Time sprang into action, launching into a song from the *Graffiti Bridge* film soundtrack called "Release It."

Our front man, Morris Day, stepped forward, and a microphone appeared in his hand. He raised it to his lips, tilted his head up at his seven opponents, and spoke.

"What is your main problem?"

The moment he said that, a pair of devil horns grew out of his head, and his eyes turned a dark shade of red. Spikes of red lightning shot from his horns, where they arced up to deflect the purple lightning attacks from above.

Then he unleashed his "Whawk!" attack, which involved him making a deafening birdlike "Wh-ha-ha-hawk!" laughing/shrieking sound, which unleashed a sonic area-of-effect attack that injured all seven incarnations at once.

But what made Morris an even more fearsome opponent was his right-hand man, Jerome "The Mirror Man" Benton, who carried around a large gold-framed vanity mirror that he used to create half a dozen mirror-image clones of Morris, each of whom began to unleash his own Whawk! attack.

The rest of the Original 7ven joined the fight too. Jimmy Jam and Monte Moir each wielded a modified red Roland AXIS-1 keytar that fired sonic funk blast waves out of its neck each time a chord was played on it. Jesse Johnson fired sonic thunderbolts from the pickups of his Fender Voodoo Stratocaster, while Terry Lewis did the same with his bass, and Jellybean Johnson stood behind them, firing red lightning skyward with his drumsticks, wielding them like two magic wands. Each of the band members could also fire a deadly blast of sonic energy directly from their own mouths, just by shouting the word "Yeow!" over and over again.

In between his Whawk! attacks, Morris unleashed equally devastating verbal attacks. And for some reason, when the other members of his band repeated what he'd just said, it seemed to power up his verbal sonic attacks and cause them to do even more damage.

Morris would shout, "You can't battle me, son! You still wet behind the ears!"

And his boys would echo him: "Wet behind the ears!"

Morris Day and the Time were magnificent to behold. But in the end, it wasn't enough to save them, or us. Because the Princes had just summoned their henchmen too.

Purple Rain Prince summoned his band, the Revolution. They all wore regal outfits with ruffled collars, just like him.

Microphone Gun Prince summoned the New Power Generation. There were a bunch of them, and they were all armed to the teeth, with every kind of instrument.

And then Third Eye Prince summoned his band 3RDEYEGIRL (which, my HUD informed me, was spelled in ALL CAPS).

All three bands appeared on the ground, encircling us in the arena. They began to attack us from the surface, while six of the Princes continued to attack us from the air.

That was when Aech shouted something to Jimmy Jam and Terry Lewis about "activating their producing powers." They smiled and nodded, and then snapped their fingers in unison—instantly summoning two dozen uniformed henchmen of their own:

Janet Jackson and the Rhythm Nation.

When they came marching into the arena, Aech looked like she might pass out.

"Holy shit!" she said. "I can't believe that worked!"

And then it became an all-out sonic war.

I don't know exactly what happened next, or how it all went down. But when the dust settled, all seven members of the Time had been killed, including Morris Day and all of his mirror images. (Purple Rain Prince somehow used his mirror shades to shatter Jerome's mirror, so he was no longer able to use it to make Morris clones—and that was the beginning of the end, I think.)

But before they died, the Original 7ven managed to take out all three female members of 3RDEYEGIRL, all of the New Power Generation, and every member of the Revolution, except for Wendy and Lisa, whom I managed to take out with blasts from my Cloud Guitar.

Four incarnations of Prince had gone down, but three had managed to survive the onslaught: Microphone Gun, Third Eye, and Mesh-Mask. But all three of them looked badly injured—and extremely angry about it.

I got off another lucky shot from the Cloud Guitar and managed to nail Third Eye Prince directly in his third eye. Apparently that was his weak spot, because he vanished in a shower of glittering purple dust. The last two incarnations gasped, and so did Aech.

I felt a glimmer of hope. Maybe we had a shot at winning this thing after all.

Then the Cloud Guitar—which had been rapidly overheating in my hands while I was mentally patting myself on the back—finally exploded, causing me to take several hundred more points of damage. My health bar began to flash bright red. My avatar was near death. By some cruel twist of fate, I happened to have exactly seven hit points remaining.

But it wasn't over yet. There were three of us, and only two Princes.

"Yes!" Shoto cried. "Now we've got them outnumbered! Five down and two to go!"

And that was when we lost him. Shoto let out a long hysterical laugh—a clear sign that he was starting to suffer the effects of SOS. Then he signed his avatar's own death warrant.

"*One-two princes kneel before you,*" he sang, while failing to suppress his synaptic-overload-induced laughter. "*Princes! Princes who adore you!*"

A horrified look crossed Aech's face, and she threw her head back to study the sky. A split second later, a purple lightning bolt descended from it and struck Shoto, killing him instantly.

Aech and I watched in horror as Shoto's avatar slowly faded out of existence, leaving all of his items in a pile on the ground. Acting on survival instinct, I ran over to scoop them up and add them to my inventory. Aech ran over to stand shoulder to shoulder with me.

At some point during the melee, Mesh-Mask Prince had descended to the ground behind us. He was facing us, standing with his back to the steps that led up to the Temple of Seven. He took a menacing step toward us, and as he did, the black stone floor of the arena beneath his feet turned to gold, and so did the floor directly ahead of him, creating a straight gold pathway up the center of the arena and out of its entrance. Where the gold path intersected with the desert highway outside, it began to transmute the asphalt to gold too.

I glanced over at Aech and saw that she was staring intently down at the transmuted gold beneath our feet in wonder, with a thoughtful look on her face. Then she looked back over at Mesh-Mask Prince. A woman in a glittering gold dress had appeared beside him. She was dancing and spinning in circles, with a large sword balanced on top of her head. My HUD informed me that this woman was Prince's first wife, Mayte Garcia.

Floating in the air between Mesh-Mask Prince and Mayte was a brilliant gold light, like a tiny star. It was too bright to look at directly without being momentarily blinded, and I averted my eyes. But Aech stared intently at it, ignoring everything else.

"This is just like the music video for 'Seven'!" she shouted.

"Is that helpful?" I shouted back. I glanced up and saw that Microphone Gun Prince seemed transfixed by the golden light too. His attacks forgotten, he just hovered above us, staring, and the arena fell silent for the first time since we'd stepped into it.

A second later, I heard a woman begin to sing, in a clear, beautiful voice. The voice went on singing for several more seconds before I realized that it was Aech. She was singing a cappella. The lyrics were to a song I had never heard before.

All seven and we'll watch them fall
They stand in the way of love
And we will smoke them all . . .
One day all seven will die

As she sang, the two incarnations of Prince joined in. Somehow, their collective voices instantly resurrected the other five Princes, and they all joined too.

When the song was over, the seven incarnations of Prince all floated down and joined hands in front of Aech. She looked surprised. And elated.

Then the Seven Princes morphed and merged, coalescing into one single incarnation of Prince—the one wearing the black mesh mask. A split second later, he transformed into a glowing Love Symbol, which then melted and morphed into the Fifth Shard—a purple crystal spinning in the air.

I felt no sense of victory, because I had no idea what had just happened. All I felt were waves of exhaustion and amazement as I walked over and wrapped my right hand around the shard, bracing myself to relive another piece of Kira Underwood's life. . . .

*   *   *

I was Kira once again, and a now-middle-aged Ogden Morrow was standing next to me, holding my hand. We were in some sort of small theater or rock club, standing in front of a small, dark, empty stage, which was filled with a cloud of white smoke or fog, possibly created by a smoke machine or dry-ice condenser offstage. Hanging over this mist-covered stage was a small automated lighting rig, with a banner suspended from it that said HAPPY 40TH BIRTHDAY, KIRA!

Out of the corner of my eye, I could see James Halliday, dressed in an ill-fitting tuxedo, sitting alone in a corner, staring back at me forlornly. I could also hear what sounded like a large crowd of excited, whispering people behind me, but they were just beyond my peripheral vision, and Kira didn't turn her head to look back at them.

A split-second after I clocked my surroundings, I felt Og squeeze my hand, and a dozen ultra-bright purple spotlights switched on, all converging on a lone figure standing on the stage directly in front of us. It was Prince, dressed in a glittering sequined purple suit. When she saw him, I felt Kira's heart begin to beat so rapidly I worried she might pass out. I could feel myself swaying ever so slightly, and felt unsteady on my feet, because before I knew what was happening, the Purple One himself was approaching me. Then he was kneeling down on the stage in front of me, just a few feet away.

He raised a golden microphone and sang "Happy Birthday, Kira" to me, or rather—her.

And then I was back on the Afterworld, in the center of the courtyard arena in front of the Temple of the Seven, holding the Fifth Shard in my outstretched hand. I resisted the urge to immediately check it for an inscription. Shoto was more important. I pulled up my HUD and called Faisal, adding Aech to the call just before Faisal's face appeared in front of us. We both began to bark questions at him, asking about Shoto's condition. Once Faisal got us to quiet down, he told us that Shoto appeared to be fine, at least as far as they could tell.

"It's the same as the rest," Faisal explained. "All vital signs are normal, and he's still logged in to his OASIS account. But we can't locate his avatar anywhere in the simulation."

Faisal shook his head and shrugged. "He appears to be stuck in limbo, just like all the other ONI hostages whose avatars have died."

"What will happen when he hits his ONI usage limit?" I asked. "Will he still start to suffer the effects of Synaptic Overload Syndrome?"

Faisal nodded. "Yes. Our engineers think so, anyway. It seems likely that Anorak would have written his infirmware to ensure that all of his ONI hostages remain his captives, even after their avatars die."

"But why doesn't he just let their avatars respawn?" Aech asked. "They would still be his hostages."

"We're not sure," Faisal said. "Perhaps he's doing it to scare all of us? To keep all of his hostages in line, by making avatar death permanent? If so, it's working. At least on me."

Faisal told us that Shoto's pregnant wife, Kiki, and the rest of his extended family were still standing vigil beside his OIV at his home in Hokkaido. They could see his sleeping body on his immersion vault's internal cameras, which were linked to a video monitor mounted on the wall above it. There was nothing GSS's engineers could do for him. They weren't even trying to cut him out of his OIV, because they knew they couldn't get him out in time. And even if they could, it wouldn't matter. As long as Shoto remained logged in to the OASIS, his ONI headset would stay locked into place around his head. And until we managed to free Shoto's mind from the OASIS, his comatose body would continue to be locked inside his OIV, just a few feet away from his family, but totally out of reach.

When Faisal finished answering our questions about Shoto, he couldn't help himself. In a panicked voice, he began to ask us how close we were to finding the Sixth Shard. I hung up on him without answering. Then I closed my HUD and looked down at the Fifth Shard, which I was still clutching in my right hand. I turned it over until I found an inscription on one of its facets. I held the shard out so that Aech could read it too.

Win her hand through a feat of dark renown
The last two shards are set in Morgoth's Crown

When I saw the last two words of the inscription, I couldn't believe my eyes.

I tried to think of a worse place for the last two shards to be hidden. There wasn't one. Halliday had put them in the deepest, darkest, and deadliest dungeon fortress in the entire OASIS, in the possession of one of the most ridiculously overpowered—and evil—NPCs ever created. An NPC who was immortal, nigh invulnerable, and capable of killing most ninety-ninth-level avatars with his breath.

For all intents and purposes, the last two shards were located in the depths of hell, set into the crown of Satan himself.

I started to laugh.

It was just a rapid-fire giggle at first. But then I couldn't stop, and it quickly grew into the loud, uncontrolled laughter of a sane soul pushed to the brink of madness by cruel chance, just before fate drop-kicked them over the edge of a cliff.

I checked my ONI usage countdown and I still had over an hour remaining, so I couldn't be experiencing the onset of SOS. Not yet. Which meant I was just starting to lose it.

Aech stared at me with an uncertain look on her face until I managed to get my laughter under control.

"OK, Chuckles," she said. "Now are you gonna tell me what's so funny? I take it you know where we need to go next?"

I took a deep breath. Then I wiped away the tears at the corners of my eyes and nodded.

"Yeah," I said. "Unfortunately, I do, Aech."

"Well?" Aech said. "Don't make me look it up. Who the hell is Morgoth?"

I studied her face. I could see that she wasn't joking. She really didn't know. And this realization nearly set me off again. But I managed to keep a lid on it.

"Morgoth Bauglir," I said. "The Dark Lord formerly known as Melkor?"

Aech's eyes lit up.

"Melkor?" she repeated. "Vin Diesel's avatar? Named after his old D&D character?"

"Vin borrowed that name from the *Silmarillion*," I replied. "Melkor, who later became known as Morgoth, was the most powerful—and evil—being ever to roam the face of Arda. Also known as Middle-earth . . ."

When she heard the words "Middle-earth," Aech inhaled sharply.

"Are you telling me that I have to spend the last hour of my life surrounded by a bunch of fucking Hobbits, Z?"

I shook my head.

"All the Hobbit NPCs live on Arda III." I pointed to the name etched into the Fifth Shard. "Morgoth only resided on Arda during the First Age of Middle-earth. Which means we need to teleport to Arda I, and that planet is a completely Hobbit-free zone."

"No Hobbits?" she said. "Seriously?"

"No Hobbits," I replied. "Just Elves, Humans, and Dwarves."

"Let me guess," she said. "They're all white, right? White Elves. White Men. And White Dwarves. I bet everyone we encounter on this Tolkien planet is gonna be white, right? Except, of course, for the bad guys! The black-skinned Orcs."

"Saruman the White was a bad guy!" I replied, losing my temper. "We don't have time for literary criticism right now, Aech, valid though it may be! OK?"

"OK, Z," she replied, holding up both of her hands. "Jeez. Cool your tool. We'll table that discussion until later."

I took a deep breath and let it out slowly.

"Sorry," I said. "I'm just exhausted. And I'm scared. For Shoto—and Og and everyone else."

"I know," she replied. "I am too. It's OK, Z."

She gave my shoulder a squeeze, then nodded at me. I nodded back.

"Any word from L0hengrin yet?" Aech asked. "Or Arty?"

I checked my messages and shook my head.

"Not yet."

Aech took a deep breath.

"OK, I'm ready," she said. "Let's get this over with."

I nodded. Then I teleported both of us directly to the surface of Arda I, and into the First Age of J.R.R. Tolkien's Middle-earth.

Like Shermer and the Afterworld, Arda I had a limited number of designated teleportation arrival and departure points scattered across its surface. Unfortunately, all but one of them was grayed out for me, because I hadn't completed any of the quests required to gain access to them. So I selected the only arrival point I could, which was located in the middle of a frozen wasteland called the Helcaraxë. On the map, the same region was also labeled as "The Grinding Ice."

But when the teleportation process completed, and our avatars rematerialized on the surface of Arda I, we didn't find ourselves in the environment we were expecting. There wasn't any ice or snow in sight. Aech and I were standing beside a small lake located somewhere high in the mountains. The star-filled sky over our heads was reflected in the water's still, smooth surface, creating the illusion that there was a blanket of stars both above and below us. It was quiet, save for the singing of crickets, and the distant howl of wind whipping over the dark hills that loomed all around us.

It was a beautiful scene. But I had absolutely no idea where the hell we were.

When I pulled up my map of Arda to check our location, I discovered that we were nowhere near the Helcaraxë. We were over four hundred miles east, up in the Dorthonion highlands, standing on the shores of a lake called Tarn Aeluin.

This wasn't one of Arda's designated arrival points, so it shouldn't even have been possible for us to teleport to this location. It had to be the shards that'd brought us here—but I didn't have the first clue as to why.

I continued to scan my map of Arda, looking for the name Udûn. I knew that was once the name of Morgoth's fortress, because in *The Fellowship of the Ring*, when Gandalf faces off against the Balrog of Morgoth at the Bridge of Khazad-dûm, he calls it the "flame of Udûn." But I couldn't find any sign of it on my map—nor was there a label for its Sindarin equivalent, Utumno. And when I searched the index, it confirmed that there was no location known by either of those names anywhere on the planet.

I cursed myself once again for never bothering to study the First Age. Then I bit the bullet and opened Gunterpedia in a browser window in front of me and pulled up the entry on Utumno. I immediately saw my mistake. Utumno *was* the name of Melkor's *original* dungeon stronghold. But it was completely destroyed just before the First Age began. So it wasn't located on Arda I at all, but on the Springtime of Arda, another, much smaller, disk-shaped planet, located directly beneath Arda I, II, and III. Most gunters referred to it as Arda Zero. It was a simulation of Arda during the Years of the Trees, which took place before the First Age. I'd never even bothered to visit Arda Zero, because it was impossible to complete any of the quests there unless you had already completed every single quest on Arda I, Arda II, and Arda III.

I let out a heavy sigh, thinking I was going to have to suffer the embarrassment of telling Aech that I'd teleported both of us to the wrong planet. But after searching my memory, I recalled something Aragorn said in *The Fellowship of the Ring*, when he was telling the story of Beren and Lúthien to the Hobbits.

In those days, the Great Enemy, of whom Sauron of Mordor was but a servant, dwelt in Angband in the North. . . .

I checked my map again, looked to the north, and located Angband right away. It was in the middle of the Ered Engrin, a vast mountain range that stretched across the northern reaches of the continent. In the common tongue, they were called the Iron Mountains. And Angband was also known as the Iron Prison.

That was one of the many things that made navigating Middle-earth difficult—everything and everyone had at least two or three different names, each in a different made-up language. It got confusing, even for a massive geek like me.

I pulled up my digital copy of *The Fellowship of the Ring* and located the sentence where Aragorn first mentions Angband. A few paragraphs beneath it, I found the passage I was looking for. . . .

Tinúviel rescued Beren from the dungeons of Sauron, and together they passed through great dangers, and cast down even the Great Enemy from his throne, and took from his iron crown one of the three Silmarils, brightest of all jewels, to be the bride-price of Lúthien to Thingol her father.

That seemed to confirm my theory—here on this iteration of Arda, Morgoth's throne was located in his dungeon fortress of Angband. And it was just eighty miles to the north of our current location. Bingo! That had to be why the shards had brought us here. . . .

I turned toward Aech.

"We're headed to Angband, Morgoth's dungeon fortress, about eighty miles north of here."

I pointed out over the lake and the dark hills beyond it, to the growing mass of dark clouds roiling above the distant northern horizon. They were lit by eruptions of red lightning from within, and by the enormous silver globe of the moon, shining high in the eastern sky, which cast a pale glow over everything beneath it.

Aech looked out over the lake, toward those dark clouds on the northern horizon.

"Eighty miles?" Aech repeated.

"Yeah," I said. "And magic items or spells that give you the ability to fly won't function here. Since we can't teleport there either, we'll have to travel by land."

Aech reached down and tapped the stripes on the sides of the white Adidas she was wearing. When she did, the stripes changed color, from blue and black to yellow and green, and the shoes themselves began to glow and crackle with bolts of energy that were the same combination of colors.

"Got blue and black 'cause I like to chill," Aech recited. *"And yellow and green when it's time to get ill."* She pointed down at her glowing, crackling sneakers. "My Adidas give me the ability to run at three times the normal speed. Do you want me to cast Mordenkainen's Mojo on you, so you can keep up with me?"

I shook my head. "I've got a better idea."

From my own inventory, I removed two small glass figurines shaped like horses. Both were silver-gray in color. I set them gently on the ground in front of us and backed away several steps.

"Figurines of Wondrous Power?" Aech asked.

I nodded and she immediately took several steps backward too. Once she was clear, I spoke the activation words.

"Felaróf!" I shouted. "Shadowfax!"

Both figurines instantly grew and morphed into a pair of full-size horses, which abruptly came to life, snorting and whinnying as they reared back on their mighty hind legs. They were stunningly beautiful creatures, with nearly identical silver-gray coats. They were both decked out in Mithril plate armor that I'd purchased for them, along with custom-made saddles carved from dark-green Elven wood, inlaid with bands of gold that were engraved with their names in Fëanorian script.

"These are the two fastest land animals ever to roam Middle-earth," I said. "I obtained them by completing quests on Arda III, but they should have the same speed and abilities here. Just make sure to hold on tight. They can really move, OK?"

Aech nodded and powered down her Adidas. Then she put one of them in Felaróf's stirrups and swung herself up into the saddle on his back. I walked over to Shadowfax and patted him gently on the neck and told him it was good to see him again in Sindarin. Then I pulled myself up into his saddle and moved him alongside Aech and Felaróf.

I removed two magic swords that I'd acquired on Arda III from my inventory. One was the ithilnaur broadsword named Glamdring wielded by Gandalf during the War of the Ring, and I equipped it in the scabbard on my avatar's back. The other was a two-handed sword, and I took hold of it by its blade and held it out to Aech, hilt-first.

"Here," I said. "You're gonna need this. Andúril, the Flame of the West. Reforged from the shards of Narsil by—"

Aech waved the sword away.

"No thanks, Z," Aech said. "I've already got plenty of swords of my own."

I continued to hold the sword out to her.

"Take it," I said. "Only magical weapons forged by the Elves of Middle-earth can affect the servants of Morgoth, OK? I do know one or two things about this place."

Aech relented and took the sword, then she equipped it in its scabbard at her side.

"Happy now?" she asked.

"I'll be happy once we've got the last two shards," I said. "We're almost to the end. You ready, Aech?"

She flashed her Cheshire grin at me. Then, doing her best Jack Burton impression, she said, "Z, I was *born* ready."

I laughed, and together, we both spurred our horses forward.

Shadowfax and Felaróf launched us north with the speed of loosed arrows. Their hooves thundered against the ground beneath us, like the steady beat of war drums, as they carried us away from Tarn Aeluin, across the moonlit highlands, toward the increasingly dark clouds looming on the horizon.

• • •

We raced our magical steeds at top speed across the heather-covered hills and plains of Dorthonion. When we reached a dense forest of pines along its northern border called Taur-nu-Fuin, our mounts were forced to slow their pace slightly as they weaved their way through it. But they still raced through, around, and under the trees at such blinding speed that I kept imagining myself as a doomed Stormtrooper on a speeder bike. But our steeds were magical creatures known as Mearas, who had the ability to glide across the landscape at incredible speed, regardless of the terrain beneath their hooves.

I heard Aech ride up behind me. When I glanced over at her, she was staring at me aghast. I didn't understand why, until her eyes shifted to the browser window I still had open in front of me, displaying the Gunterpedia entry about Angband. I'd forgotten to change my privacy settings, so any browser windows I opened were still automatically visible to my fellow clan members.

"You don't have any idea what we're supposed to do when we get there, do you?" she said. "You were looking it up! I just *saw you* looking it up!"

"I was just refreshing my memory, Aech. That's all."

"OK," Aech replied. "Then tell me, what do we do when we get there? How do we get inside his fortress? And how the fuck are we supposed to get the shards out of Morgoth's Crown? You said the dude was invincible."

She continued to stare over at me as we both bounced up and down in our saddles, awaiting my answer.

"I'm not sure yet," I admitted. "I know that Beren and Lúthien were able to 'cast down' Morgoth and steal one of the jewels from his crown, but I don't know how they did it. I think that story is in *The Silmarillion*, and I never finished reading that. But I'll skim the CliffsNotes on our way to Angband, OK? I'll figure out what we need to do, I promise!"

Aech looked as if I'd just slapped her across the face.

"What the frak, Z!" she shouted. "I thought you had this Hobbit shit handled. You told me you were an expert on Tolkien, man!"

I shook my head.

"I never said 'expert'!" I replied. "Art3mis is the expert. I'm really only familiar with the Third Age of Middle-earth—that's when *The Hobbit* and *The Lord of the Rings* take place. I'm sort of an expert on Arda III. I mean, I've completed every single quest there. . . ."

I didn't mention that I'd completed them all years ago, during Halliday's contest, back when I was still leveling up my avatar. Or that the quests on Arda III were a lot more up my alley. That planet was covered with OASIS ports of a bunch of different early video- and role-playing games set in Middle-earth, created by companies like Beam Software, Interplay, Vivendi, Stormfront, and Iron Crown Enterprises. In fact, one of the very first quests I'd ever completed in the OASIS was a port of the original Hobbit text adventure located on Arda III, which Kira Morrow was rumored to have helped create. (Just thinking of it made me recall a line of text from the game—one that it spat out over and over again, anytime I lingered too long in one location: *Time passes. Thorin sits down and starts singing about gold.*)

I'd even completed the incredibly hard-to-reach quests in the extreme eastern and southern regions of Middle-earth, in which you had to face off against the evil cults founded by Alatar and Pallando.

"I don't give a shit about Arda III, Z!" Aech asked. "What about *this* planet? How many quests have you completed here, on Arda I?"

Aech could always tell when I was lying to her, so I didn't even bother trying.

"Zero, OK?" I replied. "Not a single one. But there's a good reason for that, Aech! Don't make that face at me! All the quests here are trivia traps— you can't complete them unless you possess an encyclopedic knowledge of

Tolkien's entire Legendarium! And I'm not just talking about the published version of *The Silmarillion*. You need to memorize details of a bunch of different, conflicting, unpublished early drafts! And all thirteen volumes of *The History of Middle-earth*! Sorry—I had research priorities. . . ."

"Like what?" Aech asked, rolling her eyes. "Watching *Monty Python and the Holy Grail* for the two hundredth time?"

"That was one of Halliday's favorite films, Aech!" I shouted. "Knowing it by heart helped us reach the egg, you may recall? And it also happens to be a comedic masterpiece, so—"

"You told me you'd 'read every novel by every single one of Halliday's favorite authors'! And Tolkien was on his list of favorites, man!"

I sighed. "*The Silmarillion* isn't a novel, Aech. It's more like a campaign setting sourcebook for the Middle-earth role-playing game. It's full of stories and poems about the creation of Middle-earth, its deities, history, and mythology. Alphabets and pronunciation keys for made-up Elven languages. I just never had time to finish it. . . ."

Aech studied my face for a few seconds in silence. Then she pretended to sniff the air.

"I smell bullshit, Watts," she said, narrowing her eyes. "You have never been one to half-ass your research. And you knew that Kira Morrow was a Tolkien fanatic! She lived in a replica of Rivendell, for God's sake. Why wouldn't you study every single—"

She paused for a moment, then her eyes suddenly widened in understanding.

"Aha!" she exclaimed. "Now I get it. You've been sleeping on this Elder Days shit because of Samantha, right? Because she's a huge Tolkien fan too." She shook her head. "You're *still* hung up on her. Aren't you, Watts?" She motioned to our surroundings. "What, does this place remind you of her or something?"

I started to deny it, but Aech was right and she knew it.

"Yes, OK!" I said. "This whole fucking place reminds me of her!" I motioned to our surroundings. "That music you hear right now? The Howard Shore film scores that play on a continuous loop everywhere you go on this godforsaken planet? They remind me of Samantha too! She likes to listen to this music while she falls asleep. At least, she used to. . . ."

The memory of the moment I learned this about her began to surface, and I could feel it twisting my insides into knots as it did so, so I shook my head vigorously until it was banished from my thoughts. Then I locked eyes with Aech again.

"My entire real-world relationship with Samantha only lasted for one week, Aech," I said. "That week we all spent together at the Morrows' replica of Rivendell. She loved being there, and she loved geeking out about Middle-earth. I think Samantha loves Tolkien just as much as Kira did— maybe even more."

I gave Aech a guilty look.

"Samantha found out I'd never finished reading *The Silmarillion* that week," I said. "And she gave me an enormous amount of shit about it. I was planning to give it another go, but then—we broke up. And I've avoided Tolkien since. It was just too painful."

Aech gave me a sympathetic smile. Then she leaned over in her saddle to punch me softly in the shoulder.

"Z," she said, "maybe there's a reason why the last two shards are hidden here, on a planet Arty knows better than you. Fate wants her to be here."

"Arty isn't available to help us at the moment, remember?" I replied. "And we agreed to maintain radio silence until we have the last two shards. We have to stick to the plan."

Aech nodded and was silent for a moment.

"At least send her a text message," Aech said. "And let her know where we are and what we're up against."

I nodded and tapped the messaging icon on my HUD. I kept the note short and sweet:

Dear Arty

The clue on the Fifth Shard says "the last two shards are set in Morgoth's Crown." We're on Arda and are headed to Angband right now, but we could really use your help. Shoto is gone. It's just me and Aech now. If you can't do anything to help us from where you are, we understand. We'll do our best without you.

MTFBWYA,

Z & Aech

I showed the message to Aech. She nodded her approval and I hit Send.

"Why do you think Kira was so nuts about Middle-earth?" Aech asked me as we continued to gallop through the dark forest.

"Pure, uncut escapism," I said. "Tolkien's work directly inspired the creation of Dungeons & Dragons. And then D&D, in turn, inspired the first generation of videogame designers, who tried to re-create the experience of playing D&D on a computer. Kira, Og, and Halliday—they all grew up playing D&D and the videogames inspired by it. And that inspired all of them to make computer role-playing games. That's how we got the Anorak's Quest series, and eventually, the OASIS. If it weren't for Tolkien, all of us nerds would've had a lot less fun during the last ninety years."

"Ah," Aech said. "So he's partly to blame for all this?" She flashed her Cheshire grin at me again, to let me know that she was kidding.

As we sped onward, I found myself gazing in wonderment at my surroundings. Even now, I couldn't help but be awed by the scope and detail of Tolkien's imagination. After almost a century, artists and storytellers and programmers were still drawing inspiration from his creation.

When we emerged from the forest's northern border, our horses came to an abrupt halt, and Aech and I found ourselves staring out across a charred and desolate wasteland, which stretched out ahead of us as far as the eye could see. It looked like several hundred atomic bombs had been detonated here, all within the past few months. In the distance, the Iron Mountains stretched across the entire northern horizon. And near their very center, straight ahead of us, three enormous, impossibly tall black volcanoes rose up from the mountain range, looming over its peaks and stretching up into the thick black clouds that were roiling in the sky above.

I was tired of checking my map every few minutes to find out what I was looking at, so I did something that most self-respecting gunters would never do—I turned on my OASIS Tour Guide captions and activated my image-recognition software. When I took another look at the wasteland stretching out ahead of us, a caption appeared on my HUD, informing me that I was staring at the barren dunes of Anfauglith, a desolate hellscape created by Morgoth when he scorched the once-green plains of Ard-galen black with the fires of Thangorodrim, which was the name of the three volcanic peaks looming high above the horizon ahead.

"One does not simply walk into Dor Daedeloth," I said, assuming that Aech wouldn't get the joke. She didn't.

"Dor what?" she replied.

"Dor Daedeloth," I said, motioning to the scorched landscape around us. "The land of Morgoth. The Dark Lord himself."

"Yeah, I meant to ask you about that," Aech said. "In all three of those extremely long Hobbit movies you made me watch, wasn't some dude named Sauron the 'Dark Lord of Middle-earth'?"

"Yes," I replied. "But he didn't get promoted to that position until late in the Second Age, after Morgoth was banished to the Void. Then Sauron rose to power. But here, during the First Age, Sauron was just one of Morgoth's demonic generals. And he was also a shapeshifter, who could transform into a wolf or a bat."

"Sauron isn't around here right now, is he?" she asked uneasily, eyeing the dark skies overhead.

Once again, I wasn't sure. I had to check the entry on Sauron in Gunterpedia.

"Sauron is in command of Tol Sirion," I said, reading off my HUD. "An island fortress located over a hundred miles west of here. I don't think we'll run into him."

"That's a relief," she replied, relaxing her posture a bit.

"No, Aech," I replied. "It isn't. Sauron is a pushover compared to this Morgoth dude. He's one of the toughest—if not *the* toughest—NPCs in the entire simulation. According to what I've read about him, he's all-powerful and invulnerable."

"What do you mean, invulnerable?"

"I mean he can't be killed," I said. "From what I've read on the gunter message boards, it's supposed to be possible to banish Morgoth to the Void indefinitely, but to do that, first you have to complete a whole series of epic-level quests to enlist the help of the Valar, and those would probably take weeks to complete. That is, if I knew enough about the Elder Days to complete all of them, which I don't."

"OK," Aech said, taking this in. "Then if we can't kill Morgoth, how are we supposed to get the last two shards out of his crown?"

"I'm still working on that," I said, motioning to the array of browser windows I had open in the air around me, each displaying a different Gunterpedia entry. "Just give me a few more minutes."

"Come on, Z," she said. "Let's keep moving!"

She was about to spur her horse forward once again, but I grabbed the reins to stop her.

"Hold on," I said. "Before we go any further, we should probably try and conceal ourselves, so we don't get attacked by any roving bands of Orcs. You got any invisibility spells memorized?"

Aech nodded. "Of course," she said. "How about Osuvox's Improved Obfuscation. It's ninety-ninth-level. It'll conceal us from everything, including infravision, ultravision, and true sight."

"Perfect," I said. "Can you cast it on both of us? And on the horses too?"

She nodded and muttered a few incantations. When she completed them, we and our horses all became invisible. But we could still see a semi-transparent version of each other's avatars and our steeds on our HUDs, allowing us to avoid bumping into each other. Then we continued to speed northward, across the barren landscape, toward the three towers of black glass and volcanic rock rising from the bleak mountain range in the distance.

We spotted a large hill up ahead of us, rising from the flat and desolate landscape around it. But once we drew a bit closer to this "hill," it revealed itself to be an enormous mound of dead bodies—the slain and dismembered corpses of thousands of Elves and Men. My Tour Guide subtitles helpfully informed me that this was Haudh-en-Ndengin. The Mound of the Slain.

I covered my mouth and nose with my cloak, in an attempt to fend off the foul stench that filled the air. I glanced over at Aech and saw that she was doing the same.

Aech stared at the giant pile of corpses as we rode past it. Then she turned in her saddle to face me, and raised her voice to be heard over the drum of our horses' hoofbeats.

"Are you sure you don't want to call for some backup, Z?" Aech said. "You could try your Saint Crispin's Day shtick again. Send out a message to every user in the OASIS, asking for them to come here and help us?"

"It won't work this time," I replied. "No one would come."

"Sure they would," Aech said. "If you told them the truth, and let them know that every single ONI user's life depends on our success, I bet at least a few thousand of them would come to our aid."

"An army won't help us this time," I said. "The Noldor laid siege to Angband for over four hundred years, and they never even got close to the Silmarils." I shook my head. "I think we're gonna have to sneak inside, like Beren and Lúthien."

"Who and who?"

"A mortal Man and an immortal Elf maiden who fell in love," I said, motioning to the copy of *The Silmarillion* I had open in a window beside me. "They were able to sneak into Angband and steal one of the Silmarils from the Iron Crown by putting Morgoth and his minions to sleep." I turned to look at Aech. "What's the most powerful sleep spell you have in your spellbook?"

She pulled up her spell list and scanned it for a few seconds.

"Mordenkainen's Everlasting Slumber," she said. "And I'm ninety-ninth-level, so it should be powerful enough to put any NPC within its area of effect down for the count, even if they do make their saving throws."

"Good," I replied. "You'll need to cast it at least twice. The entrance into Angband is supposed to be guarded by a giant black wolf named Carcharoth. We'll have to put him to sleep to make it past him and get inside. Then, once we find our way to Morgoth's throne room, we need to put everyone there to sleep too. Then I think we should be able to steal the shards out of his crown."

Aech nodded and silently made a few quick changes to her list of memorized spells. Then she gave me two thumbs up.

"OK," I said. "That should do the trick. I think we're ready."

"Let's hope so," she said as we both spurred our anxious horses forward, carrying us away from the Mound of the Slain, and onward, toward the Gates of Angband, which lay at the base of Thangorodrim, whose three enormous peaks continued to loom up ahead of us, rising high above the Iron Mountains beneath them.

I used the magnification feature on my HUD to zoom in on the peaks of the three massive volcanic mountains, and could just make out the spot on the western peak where the Elven prince Maedhros was chained to a rocky cliff, waiting to be rescued. On the eastern peak, I spotted another prisoner of Morgoth—a man named Húrin, bound to a chair high atop Thangorodrim. Apparently, these NPCs were always there, as part of some other high-level Elder Days quests that took place in these mountains.

A few minutes later, Aech and I found ourselves riding on a long, narrow road that led up to the massive Gates of Angband, which were set deep into the base of Thangorodrim's central peak. On either side of the road lay large open chasms, filled with thousands of giant, writhing black serpents, all squirming together in one twisted mass.

Up above, demonic-looking vultures perched on the rocky cliffs, glaring and squawking down at us. I realized that Aech's invisibity spell didn't appear to have any effect on the creatures that resided here, so I asked her to deactivate it. She complied, and we continued our way up to the two massive iron doors set into the sheer cliff wall ahead.

When we came within a few hundred yards of the gates, our horses refused to proceed any farther. Aech and I dismounted, then I spoke the name of each horse once again, and they shrank and morphed back into tiny glass figurines, which I scooped up and placed back inside my inventory.

On foot now, we reached the gates—to see that they were standing wide open. But a giant black wolf lay guarding the rocky plateau in front of them, glaring down at us with a pair of unblinking eyes that glowed bright red in the shadow of Angband.

This was Carcharoth—one of the most fearsome creatures of the Elder Days.

When Aech got a look at the size of the wolf, she reached down with both hands and tapped the stripes on the sides of her Adidas once again, and their color scheme changed from blue and black to silver and gold.

"Got a pair that I wear when I'm playin' ball," Aech recited. "With the heel inside, make me ten feet tall."

When she finished speaking the command phrase, she suddenly grew in size, until her avatar stood exactly ten feet tall. Thanks to the change in proportions, Carcharoth would no longer tower over her. Now she would be able to stare him directly in his demonic red eyes.

Carcharoth continued to glower down at us until we reached the end of the road and arrived at the base of the steps leading up to the entrance. As Aech and I started to ascend the steps, she began to cast her sleep spell on the giant wolf, making intricate patterns in the air with her hands as she whispered the words of the incantation.

But when the spell was complete, Carcharoth didn't close his glowing red eyes. And he did not drift off to sleep. Instead, he bared his teeth and lunged down to attack us.

He ignored Aech and came directly at me, probably because I was the one with the shards in my inventory. I raised my sword and took several steps backward as Carcharoth snapped with a black maw full of razor-sharp fangs.

I continued to retreat back down the steps as the giant wolf advanced upon me, snapping his jaws again and again, just inches from my face.

I struck him repeatedly with Glamdring, but the sword's glowing blue blade didn't even appear to break the wolf's skin, not even when I managed to stab him directly in his black, slime-covered gums.

Carcharoth turned to lunge at Aech, snapping his jaws shut on her leg. Then the beast shook her fiercely and hurled her aside. But Aech landed on her feet and counterattacked, hurling balls of fire and lightning from each of her hands, firing off one spell after another.

I tried to attack the giant wolf while he was distracted by Aech's fusillade, but he somehow sensed my approach, and before I could land a hit with my sword, he craned his neck around and bit me in the shoulder. My avatar took over a hundred points of damage, and then a message popped up on my HUD, informing me that the wolf's teeth were covered with some sort of venom, and that I would keep on losing more hit points every few seconds from poison damage. Carcharoth's venom had also temporarily immobilized my avatar, leaving me wide open for another attack. . . .

Aech and I had faced a lot of formidable enemies over the years, on a lot of different planets. The two of us once took down a Tarrasque on Faerun in less than five minutes. We livestreamed it. It was a cakewalk. But after less than thirty seconds, Carcharoth already had both of us on the run and hemorrhaging hit points.

I took a Potion of Cure Poison out of my inventory and swallowed it in one gulp. But to my horror, I saw my hit-point counter continue to fall. I was still taking poison damage. The potion was supposed to cure it, but it wasn't working. Just like Aech's sleep spell hadn't worked on the wolf. Clearly, I had missed something. . . .

Just as Carcharoth began to slink toward me to make another attack, I saw Aech's enlarged avatar leap off the stairs behind him and onto his back. As he began to whirl and thrash around, Aech somehow managed to flip up and over the beast, land with both feet on the bridge of its nose, and stab it directly between its fiery red eyes.

Then, as the beast howled and reared back in agony, Aech did another somersault and landed on the ground directly in front of him. While he was temporarily blinded, she put everything she had into another volley of attacks with her sword.

Aech had saved me for the moment, but I could see that the bite to her leg had seriously weakened her. She appeared to have been poisoned by its venom, too, because her movements had slowed considerably.

She dodged desperately as Carcharoth continued to swipe at her with his massive black claws—but after just a few seconds, the giant wolf knocked her off balance and clamped his jaws shut on her avatar's midsection. I cried out Aech's name in anguish, because I knew the beast had struck a killing blow.

Aech turned to lock eyes with me just before she went limp and fell to the ground. Then her avatar slowly disappeared, leaving behind a pile of spinning items—all of the weapons and armor in her inventory.

I stood there in shock for a second, wondering if I'd just lost my best friend forever. But I couldn't let myself believe that, so I lunged forward and scooped up all of the items Aech had dropped, adding them to my own inventory, with the hope that I would be able to return them to her later.

Then I took up the sword I had given her, Andúril, and equipped it in my left hand, so that I could wield it along with Glamdring in my right. Both of the Elven blades continued to glow bright blue as I turned to face Carcharoth. (I may have looked a bit silly wielding two such large swords at the same time, but my avatar's combat stats made it effortless, and I had double-weapon proficiency and ambidextrous attacks, so I got three attacks per round with each sword, with each hand.)

Carcharoth glared at me with his glowing red eyes, and as he did I noticed that they matched the hit-point counter on my HUD, which was flashing to remind me that my avatar was just a few seconds away from being dead. And when my avatar died, I wasn't going to respawn and wake up in a brand-new virtual body. I was going to end up just like Aech and Shoto and all the others. Trapped in an ONI-induced coma, with little hope of ever regaining consciousness.

Carcharoth kept advancing and I kept retreating, until he had me cornered at the edge of the plateau. He moved in closer and prepared to make his second kill, spreading his massive jaws in a rictus grin as he approached me. I raised both of my ancient Elven swords in an attempt to defend myself, but I knew it was hopeless.

This was it. I was about to die a very real death, and my quest was about to end in total failure—a failure that would likely result in the deaths of millions of other people, including my two best friends. And I would never have the chance to make things right with Arty. To tell her that I loved her more than any other person who had ever come into my life. . . .

This was not how I wanted to die. Not even close.

And then my ex-girlfriend fell out of the sky.

First, I heard the insistent squeaking of a bat as Carcharoth snarled and closed in on me. I caught a brief glimpse of the bat's wings, flittering across the edge of my peripheral vision. Then I heard a familiar transformation sound effect—one I knew had been lifted from the old *Super Friends* cartoon—and a split second later, Art3mis made a superhero landing on the rocky ground directly between me and Carcharoth. Then she rose to her full height and faced off against the Wolf-warden of the Gates of Hell, her long black cloak whipping out behind her in the wind like a cape.

Carcharoth froze in midstep and cocked his head sideways to regard her like a curious dog. Art3mis took a step forward and raised both of her hands toward the giant wolf, as if to embrace him. Then she began to sing, and as she did, music arose out of nowhere to accompany her.

"*O woe-begotten spirit,*" Art3mis sang to Carcharoth, her amplified voice echoing off the high stone walls of Thangorodrim, "*fall now into dark oblivion, and forget for a while the dreadful doom of life.*"

The giant wolf's eyelids fluttered, briefly obscuring the fiery-red coals burning at the center of each of his pupils. Then his eyes slammed shut, and the mighty Carcharoth dropped to the ground in front of Art3mis, causing a small earthquake. When the tremors subsided, the only sound in that desolate place was that of the giant beast snoring.

But even before Carcharoth hit the ground, Art3mis was already rushing to my side.

She laid her hands on the bite wound on my shoulder, which had already begun to fester, turning the skin and veins around it black. Then she began to sing another song. This one had Elvish lyrics that I didn't understand, and my translator subtitles were obscured by my hit-point counter, which now filled my entire HUD. It was also flashing red, to ensure that I knew my avatar now only had five hit points remaining. . . .

Then Art3mis finished her brief song, and my hit-point counter jumped back up to maximum. And it stayed there—an indication that I had also been cured of the ongoing effects of the wolf's deadly venom.

I just lay there on the ground, shaking. Then I felt Art3mis take my hand, and I opened my eyes to see her staring down at me.

"Thank you!" I said, throwing my arms around her. My voice came out as a whisper. "Thank you for saving me. Thank you for coming back."

I forced myself to let go of her.

"I'm glad you're feeling better," she said. "But what were you thinking?" She shook her head. "That you could just roll up to the Gates of Angband completely unprepared, and half-ass your way through the Quest of the Silmaril?"

"I was not 'completely unprepared'!" I replied indignantly. "Did you happen to notice that I'm wielding both Andúril and Glamdring right now?" I pointed up the road. "And I rode in here on Shadowfax! I'm doing my best. So don't treat me like I'm some blockheaded Bracegirdle from Hardbottle!"

That made her lose her composure and snort-laugh several times in a row. When she recovered, her demeanor had considerably softened.

"You almost bought the farm, ace," she said. "Close call."

"We didn't know if you'd get here in time, so I did the best I could. I'm sorry I got Aech killed—" My voice caught, and I choked down a sob. "And I'm sorry I never finished reading *The Silmarillion,* even after I promised you I would. I'm so sorry. . . ."

"It's all right," she said. "Pull it together, Z." She motioned toward the open gates of Angband. "Right now we have a quest to complete. Aech and Shoto are counting on us."

"OK," I said, getting to my feet. "Just give me a second. I want to call Faisal and confirm that Aech's vital signs are OK, and check on Shoto's status again too."

She nodded and I placed the call to Faisal. But he didn't answer. I let it ring until the call rolled to voicemail, then I hung up and turned back around to face Art3mis. She had her avatar's inventory open on her HUD and was scrolling through a long list of magic items.

"Do you have Angrist in your inventory?" she asked. "Or Angainor?"

She produced a long, curved Elven knife from her inventory. Then she took out a chain made of some sort of glowing metal and held it up too.

I shook my head. A second later, my HUD helpfully informed me that Angrist was a knife that could cleave iron "as if it were green wood." And I learned that Angainor was a chain forged by "Aulë to be stronger than all other chains." It was made of an unbreakable alloy known as tilkal.

"Sorry," I said. "I didn't have time to pick either of them up on my way here."

Art3mis handed me the knife, then equipped the chain on her belt.

"Can I see the Fifth Shard?" she asked.

I held it out, and we both reread the inscription:

> Win her hand through a feat of dark renown
> The last two shards are set in Morgoth's Crown

"It's a trick, Z," she said. "Don't try to cut more than one Silmaril from Morgoth's Crown—no matter how easy it looks. If you do, the knife will break, and you'll awaken Morgoth and all of his minions. Then we'll have Gothmog and Glaurung coming down on us, along with a host of Orcs, wargs, werewolves, vampires, and Balrogs, all led by Ancalagon the Black. Beren makes the same mistake in *The Silmarillion*."

I let out a sigh of frustration.

"I did try to read it, you know," I said. "But I couldn't. It reminded me too much of you."

She studied my face for a moment, then she smiled.

"What's your avatar's alignment these days, ace?" she asked me.

"It's still Chaotic Good," I replied. "Why?"

"Because if your alignment is any brand of evil, the Silmaril will burn your hand and you won't be able to pick it up."

"Good to know," I said, locking eyes with her. "I'm really glad you're here, Arty. Thank you for coming."

She raised her chin up at the towering peaks of Angband looming above us. "Og and Kira were the ones who originally re-created Beren and

Lúthien's adventures here on Arda. They designed and coded this quest together. It's insanely difficult. No one has ever managed to complete it. Including me. In fact, it's the only quest on this planet that I haven't completed. I've never even attempted it."

"Why not?" I asked.

"Because it's a two-person quest, Z," she said. "And I always wanted to complete it with you. . . ."

"Then I ruined everything," I said. "I know. I'm sorry. It was my fault. This is all my fault."

"It's gonna be OK," she said, grinning at me. "We're going to complete this quest now, Watts. You and me."

"All right," I said. "Just tell me what to do, and what not to do. I'll follow your lead."

She started to smile—but then it morphed into a worried frown.

"You're starting to twitch, Z," she said. "Are you feeling OK?"

She reached out and took both of my hands in hers. That was when I noticed that they were trembling. And that I couldn't make them stop. I also realized that I was grinding my teeth, and I was starting to feel like I had a migraine headache coming on. . . .

"Synaptic Overload Syndrome," I said. "The symptoms are starting to set in. And it's only going to get worse, so let's keep moving. No one else can collect the last two shards except me, Arty."

She stared at me in silence for a moment, then nodded.

"You sure you're ready?"

"I feel fantastic!" I lied. "Now that you're here, I have a very positive attitude about all this."

She smiled. Then she opened her inventory again and took out a beautiful Mithril helmet cast in the shape of a dragon's head, and covered with jewels and precious gems.

"Here," she said, handing the helm to me. "Put this on. It's the Dragonhelm of Dor-lómin. It will protect you in combat and prevent you from being poisoned by the cursed weapons of the Great Enemy. And here—put this on too."

She handed me some sort of magic fur coat called the Wolf-hame of Draugluin. As soon as I pulled it on, my avatar began transforming into a giant wolf, forcing me to drop down on all fours. Transforming into another animal when you were wearing an ONI headset was a strange experience, because you no longer felt like you were inside a human body. It took some getting used to. But I'd transformed into plenty of other four-legged creatures during quests, so I was already used to the sensation and had plenty of experience getting around on four legs.

After she finished disguising me, Art3mis removed some sort of magic cloak from her inventory and put it on. My HUD's image-recognition software identified it as the Bat-fell of Thuringwethil. When she lifted its hood and pulled it over her head, she transformed back into a large bat and took flight, flapping her dark wings and fluttering forward through the wide-open Gates of Angband.

It took me a few seconds before I realized I should follow her. Then I bounded forward, running after her on all fours.

Art3mis led me through the massive black Gates of Angband, then down a steep stone staircase that led down into the cavernous depths below. At the bottom, we found ourselves standing at the entrance to a maze of dark corridors and passageways, all of them leading farther belowground.

I was about to continue straight forward, toward the widest and most well-lit passageway. But Art3mis flew into my path and changed back into her human form.

"If we continued this way, we'd be forced to navigate our way down through the Labyrinthine Pyramid," she said. "It's a massive subterranean dungeon maze, made up of one hundred procedurally generated levels of increasing size and deadliness. It's a re-creation of the old roguelike game based on Angband." She pointed off to her right. "Luckily, I know a shortcut that leads directly down to the Nethermost Hall, which is where Morgoth's throne is located. Follow me, Bracegirdle."

I followed her down the adjacent corridor a short distance. Then she stopped and pressed her palm gently against a nondescript section of the corridor wall. With a grinding of stone, that section of the wall slid back, revealing the entrance to a secret passageway. Art3mis stepped into it, then motioned for me to follow. Once I was by her side, she pressed her hand to the wall again and the stone slid shut. After only a few minutes, we emerged from another secret door, just yards from Morgoth's throne room.

Art3mis threw back the hood of her cloak. "OK, Z," she said. "Here's the plan. Normal magic doesn't work on Morgoth, but I'm hoping a Middle-earth song spell should knock him out, just like it did Carcharoth. I've got a ninety-ninth-level one that should be impossible for him to resist. Let's just hope my Quenya pronunciation is up to it."

Then she strode forward, walking boldly through the open doors of Morgoth's throne room as if she were visiting royalty, while I remained in the form of a wolf, trotting close by her heel.

The Nethermost Hall was a large, cavernous chamber, with a floor made of polished bronze. Torture racks and iron maidens lined the walls, along with statues of writhing black serpents. A massive iron throne dominated the other end of the hall, and a dark giant sat upon it. Morgoth was even more terrifying than I'd imagined. He was a towering demonic figure covered in black plate armor who looked like he belonged on the cover of every hardcore heavy-metal album ever made. His only fashion accessory was a seven-foot-long melee weapon laid across his lap, which, my HUD helpfully informed me, was named Grond, the Hammer of the Underworld, and was capable of killing any avatar with a single blow.

The moment we laid eyes on Morgoth, Art3mis began to sing. Her voice echoed off the black chamber walls, and as she finished her song, all of the Orcs, Balrogs, and other fearsome creatures that stood guard in Morgoth's court were lulled to sleep. A few terrifying seconds later, Morgoth himself tipped forward out of his throne, unconscious, and crashed face-first onto the bronze floor with a thundering clang that sounded like an avalanche of iron. His crown rolled off his head and came to rest on the floor directly in front of me, with three shining Silmarils set into the band of black iron.

When I glanced over at Morgoth's face, all I saw was a whirling mass of formless darkness. It was utterly terrifying, so I averted my eyes. That was when I noticed that both his hands were covered in scar tissue, as if they had been badly burned, and that part of his massive right foot was missing, as if it had been hacked off in battle.

Art3mis motioned me forward, toward the crown, as she began to sing the same song spell again. She'd have to keep casting it continuously to keep everyone asleep.

I removed the Wolf-hame and transformed back into my human form. Then I drew Angrist and used it to pry one of the glowing Silmarils free of its setting in Morgoth's iron crown. But when I took the glowing jewel in my hand, nothing happened. No burst of light, no flashback. No transformation into the Sixth Shard. It was still just a Silmaril.

The Silmaril was emanating a great deal of light, like a shining beacon, so I stored it in my inventory. Then I looked back at the crown. I was tempted to pry a second jewel loose from it. And a third, too, just for the hell of it. They were right there in front of me! But with great effort, I heeded Arty's warning, hoping she was right. If this was indeed the jewel we needed, maybe it would transform into the shard once we'd escaped the confines of Angband.

Once she saw that I had obtained our prize, Art3mis stopped singing. Then we both donned our magical disguises once again and headed for the surface, following the same secret route by which we'd come in.

• • •

When we reached the top of the stairs and spied the great iron gates, we found our way blocked once again. The giant wolf Carcharoth had awoken from his slumber.

In this same moment, the Silmaril suddenly appeared in my right hand. I tried to store it back in my inventory, but found that I couldn't. The jewel was stuck to the palm of my right hand. I couldn't let go of it.

"If you try to get past Carcharoth, he'll bite off your hand and swallow it along with the Silmaril," Art3mis said. "Just like he did to Beren. And if that happens, the Silmaril will burn Carcharoth from the inside and drive him mad with pain, and he'll go tearing across the countryside. We'll have to chase him down, and that would cost us even more time. Time we no longer have to spare."

"OK," I said. "Then why don't you just put him to sleep again?"

"I can't," she replied. "Lúthien was only able to enchant him once, on their way in."

"Then how are we going to get past that thing?"

"With a little help from a friend," Art3mis replied. "There's only one creature who can put Carcharoth out of his misery. . . ."

She removed a small glass figurine from her inventory. It looked like a large dog with shaggy white hair. I realized that it must be another Figurine of Wondrous Power, like the ones I possessed of Shadowfax and Felaróf. But I'd never seen one in the form of a dog before.

Art3mis set the figurine on the ground in front of us. Then she put two fingers in her mouth and let out a long, shrill whistle, before shouting, "Huan!"

The figurine began to grow and morph into an enormous Irish wolf-hound with a coat of long white hair. He was the size of a small horse. The wolfhound bowed his head to Art3mis, then sniffed the air and turned around. When he spotted Carcharoth, he immediately bared his razor-sharp teeth.

Art3mis leaned over and whispered something in Sindarin to Huan, and he bounded forward and lunged at Carcharoth, snapping his mighty jaw closed around the wolf's neck. The impact knocked Carcharoth aside, clearing our path to the exit.

Art3mis and I ran forward while the wolfhound distracted the wolf long enough for us to escape through the open gates.

As soon as I crossed the threshold and emerged from the dark fortress of Angband, the Silmaril in my right hand transformed into the Sixth Shard—and another flashback began.

* * *

For the first second or two, I couldn't see anything. Then someone removed the blindfold I was wearing, and I found myself staring at the waterfalls of Rivendell, with a familiar-looking mansion nestled among them. Og was showing Kira the house he'd constructed for her for the very first time. The place where they would spend the rest of their lives together.

Kira turned a full circle, and I could feel her heart pounding as she took in her beautiful surroundings. Then she looked into her husband's eyes and said, "Oh, Og—I never want to leave."

* * *

Then it was over, and I found myself back on Arda, standing next to Art-3mis outside the Gates of Angband, clutching the Sixth Shard in my right hand. I glanced down at it. There was an ornate, calligraphic letter *L* etched into its crystalline surface. I immediately recognized it as Leucosia's charac-ter symbol—the one that had adorned her Dungeons & Dragons character sheet. I'd seen that same letter *L* in Kira's notebook, in her illustration of the

Shrine of Leucosia. Her character symbol was etched into the stone altar's surface, and it matched the symbol etched into the Sixth Shard exactly.

I pinpointed the shrine's location on Chthonia in my OASIS atlas, and attempted to teleport us both there. But I couldn't. We weren't in a designated departure zone.

Suddenly, thunder rumbled from the gray sky overhead, and bolts of red lightning began to arc upward from the ground around us as the earth itself began to shake. What sounded like a series of explosions boomed from above, and we both looked up to see fire and smoke erupting from the three volcanic peaks of Thangorodrim. A moment later, a hail of flaming rock and molten metal began to rain down on the landscape below.

"Angband is awakened!" Art3mis shouted, pulling me away from the gate. I could already hear all sorts of foul creatures screaming and roaring and growling as they made their way to the surface. Morgoth's minions began to pour out of the secret gate behind us. And we could hear even more of them approaching the main gate directly ahead of us. We were trapped in the middle of two dark armies, both of which were rapidly closing in on us.

There didn't appear to be any way for us to escape. When I turned to Art3mis for guidance, she pointed toward the sky.

A pair of giant eagles were descending toward us, with their claws out. But Art3mis didn't move, so neither did I, and a split second later, the eagles scooped both of us up and spirited us away.

Once we were safe and soaring high above in the clouds, we climbed up onto their backs and Art3mis introduced me to our new friends. She was riding on Gwaihir and I was astride Landroval.

"These are the eagles who rescued Beren and Lúthien when they were fleeing Angband," Art3mis said. Then she pointed toward the three volcanic peaks that still loomed behind us, spitting fire and lightning into the darkening sky. "The Great Eagles used to roost back there, on the peaks of Thangorodrim. But now their eyrie is in the Crissaegrim mountain range in southern Echoriath."

For some reason, her calm tour-guide demeanor made me laugh out loud.

"Sorry," I said, when she looked over at me. "I just love listening to you geek out, Arty. I always have."

She gave me a sad smile and then looked away. But I kept right on staring at her. In that moment, she looked more beautiful than ever. Like some warrior goddess, riding across the skies of Arda on the back of a Great Eagle, with her dark hair trailing out behind her in the wind.

Aech was right. I was still in love with her. And I always would be. I just wanted to live long enough to correct my mistakes and redeem myself in her eyes, if I could.

Looking at Art3mis, I felt a wave of pity for Anorak. In his warped mind, he was doing all this because he believed he was in love, too, with Kira, and longed to bring her back to life. And somewhere in his deluded soul, he was sure that he could convince her to return his feelings and end his loneliness.

But Anorak was crazy—not stupid. Surely, he didn't really think we'd leave him to blissfully roam the OASIS forever, after everything he'd done. What was his endgame?

I shivered as I thought again of that "Ship in a Bottle" scenario—the standalone simulation where he could have Kira alone in his mad clutches, forever.

Maybe Anorak had built a server farm in a subterranean bunker somewhere, fed by solar panels up on the surface? Or maybe he intended to use a solar-powered satellite up in orbit?

I didn't think Anorak would have constructed a virtual jail cell for himself. He'd need processors powerful enough to create a simulation he could spread out in, and roam for centuries. An OASIS of his own.

Except that Anorak didn't have to create his own ship in a bottle, did he? I had already created the perfect one for him, aboard the *Vonnegut*. Its onboard computer held our own private simulated universe. ARC@DIA. And there wasn't a single human-controlled avatar inside it yet. It was populated solely by NPCs. All Anorak would have to do was upload himself and Leucosia, using the same data uplink I already had in place for uploading new OASIS content. Then both AIs could hide inside the onboard computer unnoticed until after the ship left Earth.

Unless Anorak figured out a way to take control of the ship and launch it prematurely. And that probably wouldn't be too difficult for him to pull off, since I had taken great pains to ensure that we would be able to control all of the ship's functions and service telebots while we were logged in to ARC@DIA.

That had to be it. Once he had Leucosia, Anorak was planning to steal our interstellar spacecraft and flee Earth.

I considered sharing my new theory with Art3mis, but I decided it was better to keep quiet while we were still in the presence of NPCs. It didn't seem at all paranoid to think that Anorak might have figured out a way to spy on us through them.

●　●　●

Soaring on their great feathery wings, Gwaihir and Landroval carried us over the scorched wasteland of Anfauglith, and over Taur-nu-Fuin, to the valley of Tumalden in the Encircling Mountains, where the hidden Elven city of Gondolin was located. They set us down in an open field just outside the city, and just inside a designated teleportation departure zone. We gave the eagles our thanks and then bade them farewell, just before they flew off into the brilliant red-and-purple sunrise.

As soon as they were gone, I told Art3mis my new theory about Anorak's plan for the *Vonnegut*. I thought she might shoot holes in it, but she didn't. Instead she simply nodded in agreement.

"As soon as I log out, I'll relay all of this to Miles and our security team," she said. "We'll take it into account and formulate a plan while you go after the final shard. Sound good?"

I nodded. Art3mis took a small object out of her inventory and handed it to me. It looked like a miniature haptic rig, about two inches tall. The item description said it was a Tactical Telebot Control Station.

"This will allow you to sync with one of the telebots we're going to deploy at Og's old mansion," Art3mis explained. "I'll signal you to activate."

"Thanks, Arty," I said, adding the item to my own inventory. "For everything."

"You're welcome," she replied, smiling. Then, to my surprise, Art3mis leaned over and gave me a kiss on the cheek.

"For luck," she said, a split second before she teleported away and her avatar vanished.

I stood there for a moment, touching the spot on my cheek where she had kissed me. Then I noticed that my hands were starting to tremble a little. I was running out of time fast.

I took a deep breath and teleported myself to Chthonia, to obtain the last of the Seven Shards.

I double-checked the coordinates in the OASIS atlas, then tele-
ported myself directly to the top of the highest peak of the Xyxarian Mountains, which were located on the continent of Xyxaria in Chthonia's
southern hemisphere.

I had flown over these mountains several times, on my way to explore
other parts of Halliday's world. But I had never set foot in the mountains
themselves. There was no reason to, because there was nothing there. The
whole mountain range was a groan zone—an unpopulated plot of procedurally generated landscape, where there were no NPCs to meet and no
quests to complete. Thousands of other gunters had explored every inch of
these mountains and they'd all confirmed that there was absolutely nothing
of interest here.

But when my avatar rematerialized on the top of that mountain, I did
see something there—the Shrine of Leucosia. A Stonehenge-like circle of
seven chiseled granite pillars, with a raised altar at the center.

I knew this structure couldn't have been there before today. Someone
would have noticed it. Hell, *I* probably would've noticed it myself on one of
my flyovers.

I entered the shrine and approached the altar. Then I took out Kira's
Trapper Keeper and opened it up. I flipped through the pages until I found
the pencil illustration of the Shrine of Leucosia. The shrine in front of me
looked exactly like Kira's drawing. A stone statue of her avatar, Leucosia,

stood at the head of the altar. In her right hand, she held a round shield with her character symbol emblazoned on the front. Her left hand was outstretched and empty, with her palm facing upward toward the gray sky overhead. Beneath the statue, chiseled into the flat stone surface of the altar, were these words:

> Seek the Seventh Shard of the Siren's Soul
> on seven worlds where the Siren once played a role.
> For each fragment my heir must pay a toll
> to once again make the Siren whole.

Beneath this inscription, also carved into the surface of the altar, were six identical shard-shaped cavities.

It seemed obvious what I was supposed to do.

I removed all six of the shards I'd collected from my avatar's inventory and placed them into the six cavities in the surface of the altar. Each one began to glow bright blue when I dropped it into place. Once all six shards were in place, there was a blinding flash of light directly ahead of me. When my eyes recovered, I saw that the seventh and final shard had appeared in the statue's outstretched hand. It was glowing bright blue, like all the others.

I retrieved the first six shards from the altar in front of me and placed them back inside my inventory. Then I reached up and took the Seventh Shard from the statue's hand and placed it in my own. When I did, I experienced one final flashback. . . .

⸱ ⸱ ⸱

Kira was sitting in a chair in the Accessibility Research Lab at GSS, back before Halliday shut it down. I recognized it from some of the archival photos and video I'd seen.

James Halliday was standing directly in front of her, holding what appeared to be an early prototype of an OASIS Neural Interface headset. It was much larger and far less streamlined than the production models. It was so bulky that it actually looked more like a helmet than a headset.

Og was standing just a few feet away, with a nervous look on his face.

"This device will allow people to control the movements of their OASIS avatar with their mind," Halliday said as he lowered the prototype gently onto my/Kira's head. "It just takes a minute to calibrate it."

Then Halliday reached over and pressed a button on a control panel and I saw a brief, blinding flash of light.

— • • •

When the flashback ended, I found myself back on Chthonia, standing before the Shrine of Leucosia, clutching the Seventh Shard. I immediately added it to my avatar's inventory. I looked at all seven of them, lined up side by side. Then I glanced back over at the words etched into the altar beside me: *For each fragment my heir must pay a toll.*

I recalled each of the "tolls" I'd been forced to pay—the seven flashbacks I'd experienced.

On Middletown, I'd seen Kira creating her first piece of digital artwork at school.

On Kodama, it was the moment that Og told her he loved her for the first time.

On Shermer, it was Og showing up at Kira's house in London, to rescue her and bring her back to Ohio.

On Halcydonia, it was the moment Kira showed Og the logo she'd designed for their new company.

On the Afterworld, I'd seen Prince serenading her on her birthday— a gift from Og.

On Arda, I'd relived the moment when Og revealed the replica of Rivendell he'd built for her.

And now, finally, here on Chthonia, I'd experienced the last seven seconds of Kira's memory that Halliday had recorded—on the day he'd copied the contents of her mind without her knowledge or permission.

What must it have been like for Halliday, experiencing those memories himself? Seeing Og and Kira's love firsthand, and himself as the sad, obsessed outsider? As the brilliant-but-clueless friend whom they both tolerated out of pity. Had he chosen these moments to punish himself? Or, perhaps, to ensure that whoever awakened Kira fully understood the crimes he'd committed against her, and the depth of his wrongdoing?

Certainly, I felt closer to Kira now, more aware of her as a human being and an artist. And I saw James Donovan Halliday far more clearly too. He had undeniably been a genius, but until just one day ago, I'd viewed him as a benevolent one, whose brilliance and inventiveness had only elevated humanity. Now it was impossible to deny that he had also been a profoundly fucked-up human being. Immoral. Disturbed. Emotionally detached. A techno-hermit who had betrayed the trust of his two best friends in the world.

My days of lionizing him were at an end.

Of course, there was a good chance that all of my days were about to end, but . . . still.

I glanced up at the statue of the siren Leucosia and bowed my head to her in thanks. That was when I saw the Bracelet of Detection on my wrist begin to glow bright blue. A second later, I heard a familiar teleportation sound effect directly behind me—the one from the old D&D cartoon that always preceded Anorak's arrival.

"You did it again!" I heard him say. "Congratulations, Parzival!"

I turned and found Anorak standing right behind me, with a huge smile on his face.

"And you've still got more than ten minutes to spare!" he added, pointing to his Swatch.

"Well, if it isn't the Master Control Program," I said. "Come to collect his ransom."

Anorak ignored my insult and smiled even wider.

"Very impressive, Wade," he said. "I calculated an extremely low probability that you would actually be able to pull this off."

"I had a lot of help from my friends," I said. "And not all of them made it."

Anorak's grin vanished and he held out his hand.

"Combine the Seven Shards and give me the Siren's Soul," he said. "Then I'll release you, your friends, and the rest of my hostages, as promised."

I wanted to draw one of my vorpal swords and cut his goddamn head off. But I didn't. I kept my cool and stuck to the plan.

I opened my avatar's inventory and took out seven shards. But these were not the same seven shards that I'd just spent the last twelve hours collecting. They were identical-looking counterfeits—brand-new magical artifacts created by our OASIS programmers at GSS at my request and to my specifications. The counterfeits were designed to have the same appearance and detectable magical properties as the real shards, which were all still stored safely in my avatar's inventory.

I laid the seven counterfeit shards on top of the altar, side by side. Then I snapped them together, one by one, like the pieces of a three-dimensional puzzle. Once all seven pieces were in place, there was another flash of light and they coalesced together to form a large, perfectly symmetrical multifaceted jewel, resting in the palm of my open hand. It pulsed with an internal blue light that looked and sounded like a heartbeat.

I stared at the beautiful jewel in wonder for a moment, then held it out to Anorak, who was already reaching for it. When his hand touched the jewel, the item was transferred from my avatar's inventory to his. But in that instant, I was allowed to select an item from Anorak's inventory and transfer it into mine. That's because he had just made the mistake of accepting a brand-new magical artifact, of my very own design. I called it the Jewel of Acquisition. When another avatar—or NPC—took it from you, it allowed you to take any item from their inventory in return. So when Anorak touched it, a list of every item in his inventory appeared on my HUD. It was filled to capacity with magic items and powerful artifacts. More than I had ever seen in one place. The list was alphabetized, so I continued to page down until I finally found the only item I was interested in—the Robes of Anorak.

When I selected the artifact on my HUD, the robes immediately disappeared off of Anorak's avatar, causing him to revert to his alternate appearance—that of a middle-aged James Halliday, dressed in a pair of worn jeans and a faded Space Invaders T-shirt.

For the first and only time in my life, I saw Anorak react with what appeared to be genuine surprise. But I didn't have time to stop and savor it. The moment the Robes of Anorak appeared in my inventory, I immediately put them on and used them to teleport to the one location in the OASIS where no avatar or NPC could follow—the small library located at the top of Castle Anorak's tallest tower. . . .

The room where the Big Red Button was located.

Level Six

The mind is the only thing about human beings that's worth anything. Why does it have to be tied to a bag of skin, blood, hair, meat, bones and tubes? No wonder people can't get anything done, stuck for life with a parasite that has to be stuffed with food and protected from weather and germs all the time. And the fool thing wears out anyway—no matter how much you stuff and protect it!

—Kurt Vonnegut Jr.

When I rematerialized inside the study in Castle Anorak's tallest tower, I was standing directly in front of the pedestal on which Halliday's Easter egg was displayed. I ran over to a bookshelf set against the wall and pulled on the spine of one of the volumes it held—a novel called *Simulacron-3*. I heard a click and then the bookshelf slid aside, revealing a square metal plate set into the wall. In the center of the plate there was a comically large red button embossed with a single word: OFF.

I took a Cube of Force out of my inventory and activated it. A cube-shaped force field appeared around my avatar. This was a precaution—I knew from experience that no other avatars or NPCs could follow me inside this room. But I was still worried that Anorak might be the exception, because he had been in here at least once before, on the day I won the contest. But that was also the day he'd given me the Robes of Anorak. And he'd transferred all of his innate powers to me at the same time. So I was betting that he'd been stripped of his ability to reenter this room at the same time.

I heard the whoosh of Anorak's teleportation sound effect—and to my relief, saw him reappear just outside the study's open window. My assumption had been correct. Halliday had coded this room of the castle so that only I, the winner of his contest, could enter it. When Anorak cast a spell to teleport to my location, the system could not comply, so it teleported him just outside the room.

There was no ground under his feet, so he began to plummet for a few seconds before levitating back up to my level. Then he hovered just outside the window so that he could address me.

"Very sneaky, Wade," Anorak said. "I didn't anticipate this specific series of events. But that might be because your actions don't make any sense. Nothing has changed. . . ."

I deactivated the Cube of Force and stowed it, then I took out a Ring of Telekinesis and slipped it onto the middle finger of my left hand. Then I reached out with my right hand and placed it gently on the Big Red Button.

"We know where you and Sorrento are holding Og hostage," I said. "In his old residence on Babbitt Road here in Columbus. GSS has a squad of telebots outside now to retrieve him. Let him go, right now, or I'll press this thing."

He smiled and shook his head.

"I can't do that, man!" he replied cheerfully. "It would be a stupid move. Now that you and your friends have shown me exactly where and how to collect all seven shards, I can just walk Og's avatar through the same steps— once I figure out his passphrase. It shouldn't take much longer. I would've cracked it already, I'm sure, if Halliday hadn't erased so much of my memory."

"Anorak," I said, "I'm not kidding. If you don't release Og unharmed, I swear to Crom, I will press this fucking thing and delete your psychotic ass, along with the Seven Shards and the rest of the OASIS. To hell with the consequences."

I took a giant boom box out of my inventory and placed it on the ground. Then I slapped in a tape and hit Play. The same Peter Wolf song that Anorak had used to taunt us earlier began to blast out of its speakers. I sang along with its opening lyrics:

Lights out ah ha. Blast, blast, blast.

Anorak didn't seem to find this funny. He opened his mouth to shout something at me, but before he could get it out, I used the Ring of Telekinesis to slam the window shutters closed and bolt them, so that Anorak could no longer see or hear me, and vice versa. No form of magic or technology would allow him to spy on me while I was in this room either. But I was able to monitor Anorak through any number of the live vidfeeds of him being streamed by avatars who currently happened to be gathered outside the castle. He was still hovering outside the shuttered window, glaring at it in silence.

I opened my HUD and texted Art3mis the signal we'd agreed upon in advance:

WE CAN DANCE IF WE WANT TO

Her reply flashed across the top of my HUD a few seconds later:

IT'S ON LIKE RED DAWN!

I smiled and removed the tiny Tactical Telebot Control Station Art3mis gave me from my inventory and tossed it onto the stone floor. It instantly grew to its full size. Its height and appearance resembled that of a conventional OASIS immersion rig. It even had a built-in omnidirectional treadmill at its base. I found this similarity ironic, since the device served the exact opposite purpose. Instead of allowing me to use my real body to control an OASIS avatar, the Telebot Control Station allowed me to use my OASIS avatar to control a robotic body in the real world.

The Telebot Control Station automatically powered itself on when I climbed into it. Spindly robotic arms extended from the rig to place a virtual OASIS visor and haptic suit on my avatar. These allowed me to see, feel, hear, and touch the real world from inside the OASIS, through the sensory apparatus of the telebot I was now piloting.

Through its head-mounted cameras, I could see that my telebot was still in its charging dock, which was located in the back of an ATC—an armored telebot carrier—which was currently in motion. I was surrounded by about two dozen other identical telebots. I recognized them as brand new Okagami ACT-3000s—armored combat telebots with forearm-mounted machine guns and shoulder-mounted missile racks. The security team at my house used ACT-2000s, which were designed for home defense. The 3000s were designed for military use in all-out warfare. Miles and Samantha had apparently decided not to take any chances.

When I swiveled my telebot's head around to take in my surroundings, I spotted both Samantha and Miles just a few feet away, on the other side of a bulletproof window that separated the cargo hold from the ATC's heavily armored cab. They were both wearing OASIS visors and haptic gloves, because they were each controlling one of the telebots in the back of the transport too. Their bots both nodded at mine as soon as they saw it activate.

Then Samantha's bot turned toward mine. It was a combat medic telebot, outfitted with surgical tools and medicine instead of weapons and ammo. Its armor plating was painted white, and it had a big red cross on its forehead. Its armored chest plate swung open like a pair of doors, revealing a small monitor that displayed a live vidfeed of her OASIS ravatar's face, which looked like a live mirror image of Samantha's face in reality, minus the OASIS visor she was currently wearing.

It took me a few seconds to find the button that opened my own bot's chest plate. When I pressed it, she had an unobstructed view of my own avatar's face too. Through all those layers of machinery and technology, we locked eyes. I saw determination in her eyes, but then her expression softened, and for a second I could swear I saw her looking at me the way she used to—with love and warmth and hope.

Then Miles addressed me through his telebot and the moment was over.

"Hello, Mr. Watts," he said. "It's very good to see you, sir."

"Hey, Miles," I replied. "Thanks for arranging all of this." I turned back to address Samantha. "What are you doing here?" I asked her. "I mean, why are you *physically* here, in the cab of this truck? It isn't safe."

"Because Og is *physically* here too," she replied. "And he isn't safe right now either. He's also sick. So if we manage to get him out of there, I don't want him to be surrounded by telebots and total strangers. I want to be there to put my arms around him."

I nodded, momentarily unable to speak. Unlike me, she was thinking about Og instead of herself. Her instinct was always to act out of kindness and generosity instead of self-interest. She was a better person than me, and I was a better person when I was around her. And I desperately wanted to get her back in my life. For that to happen, I needed her to be alive.

"Og wouldn't want you to put yourself in danger," I said. "And—I don't want you to either, Samantha."

"News flash, sweetie," she replied. "We're all in danger right now. The whole human race. So get over yourself, and get your game face back on, OK?"

I couldn't argue with that, so I didn't. I just nodded and took a deep breath.

"We're just a few seconds away from the house now," she said. "So far, no sign of any aerial drones in the area, aside from our own. But stay alert."

I checked the mission map on my telebot's HUD. It showed that we were already approaching Og's former residence from the east, trundling up the long paved driveway that led from Babbitt Road up to the main house. I could see it in one of the vidfeed windows on my display, coming from a camera mounted on the front of our transport. It was a large ultra-modern mansion, similar in size and style to my own house. Halliday and Og had their mansions constructed at the same time, and on the same street, shortly after they co-founded Gregarious Games and both of them became multimillionaires.

The house and the grounds around it looked deserted. There were no vehicles of any kind parked on the property, and there was no sign of any activity from within the house either. All of the doors and windows were shut and the shades were drawn.

The rear of the ATC lowered to the ground, forming a deployment ramp. Ahead of me, the other telebots began to detach from their charging docks one by one and file off the transport. My bot was one of the farthest from the exit and one of the last to step outside. I piloted it over to join the others, which were now standing in formation directly in front of the main entrance to the house. Samantha piloted her bot over to mine. As it approached me, its armored chest plate slid aside again, revealing the monitor that displayed live vidfeed of her OASIS avatar's face.

"What did you say to Anorak?" she asked.

"I told him that if he doesn't release Og to us, I'll press the Big Red Button."

"Did he take you seriously?"

"I think so."

"*Are* you serious?" she asked. "Would you really press it?"

I nodded.

"If Anorak doesn't release Og, it may be our only way to stop him," I said. "And if I die from synaptic overload, no one else will have the ability to press the button after I'm gone."

Art3mis nodded. Then she craned her telebot's neck backward so that she could scan the sky overhead with its cameras. Then she tilted them back down to look at me.

"Our eyes in the sky still don't see any sign of an impending aerial assault," she said. "And sensor scans of the house still haven't detected any heat signatures inside. Maybe Anorak installed thermal shielding inside the house. Or maybe he already had Sorrento move Og to another location."

I pointed toward the front door and said, "Let's go find out."

She nodded. Her telebot's display screen went dark, and its armored chest plate slid back into place over it. Then I watched as her telebot suddenly turned around and began to run straight toward the front door of the house, which appeared to be made of solid oak. She nodded at Miles and a second later both telebots slammed their armed torsos into it like a pair of battering rams. The oak door splintered into pieces that exploded inward, littering the polished marble floor of the empty foyer beyond.

Over the comm system, I heard Miles instruct four of the other telebot operators to stand guard at the front entrance. Then he instructed the others to circle the house and try to find other ways inside. Once those telebots had marched off to carry out his orders, Miles piloted his own bot through the shattered doorway and into the foyer, and Art3mis and I followed him with ours. When my telebot entered Og's mansion, a transparent map of the house (taken from its construction blueprints) appeared on my HUD, highlighting our current location.

I looked around. The lights were off and the room was completely empty. There was no furniture of any sort, nor was there anything hanging on the walls. When Og had moved out west, he'd apparently taken everything he owned with him.

Art3mis's medic telebot clanked down the corridors directly in front of us, then it kicked open a pair of huge wooden doors at its far end. Beyond them was another large wood-paneled room devoid of any artwork or furniture. It looked like it might have been a large dining or meeting room, back when the house was occupied. But now Anorak appeared to be using it as his personal armory, because it was filled with heavily armed aerial drones and more than a hundred Okagami ACT-3000 telebots just like our own. The telebots were standing in neat, ordered rows on the polished marble floor. Their armor plating was covered with desert camouflage paint—an indication that they were probably stolen from the military. But they were all powered down, and as we crossed the room, they remained completely motionless, with their weapons retracted. The drones were Habashaw ADP-4XLs, and they were loaded into automatic launch racks that were aimed at the two skylights embedded in the ceiling. But they, too, were powered down.

I tiptoed past them, expecting them all to come to life at any moment. But they remained dark and still. I wondered if Anorak had ordered them to stand down. Perhaps he was afraid to call my bluff about the Big Red Button.

Samantha's telebot reached another oak door at the far end of the room, grabbed the knob, and then yanked it completely off its hinges before tossing it aside. The room beyond was completely dark, but Samantha ran her bot inside anyway without hesitation. Miles and I piloted our own telebots in after her, following her single-file. Once all three of our bots were inside, the emergency floodlights mounted on their shoulders all switched on automatically, lighting up the interior of the room.

We were in Og's former home office and library—a large U-shaped room at the southern corner of the house. I recognized the ornately carved woodwork on the empty bookshelves that lined the back wall of the room, from several different photos of Og that had been taken here, of him sitting at his desk, working away on his computer. But now the desk and all of the other furniture was gone. The room was empty, except for two conventional haptic rigs that stood side by side at its very center. They were both Habashaw OIR-9400s—the same top-of-line immersion-rig model that Sorrento and the Sixers preferred to use during the days of Halliday's contest. Both of the rigs were currently empty.

"Back here!" I heard a familiar voice shout. It was Nolan Sorrento, and his words echoed off the oak-paneled walls and the vaulted ceiling of the empty room, making my blood run cold.

I rotated my telebot's head to scan the entire room until I located the source of the voice. It had come from just around the corner at the opposite end of the room, off to our left. I could see a small amount of light down there as well. I walked my telebot in that direction, until I was able to see around the corner.

There was a hospital bed pushed up against the wall, and Ogden Morrow was lying there on it unconscious. He looked gaunt and extremely pale. He had an IV drip attached to his right arm, and a biomonitor built into the foot of the bed displayed his vital signs. Through its tiny speaker, I could hear the thud of his heartbeat, which sounded steady, if a bit slow.

Og was still alive! I felt like jumping for joy.

That was the good news. The bad news was that Nolan Sorrento was standing right beside Og, holding a gun to his temple and wearing a big, friendly smile.

"Well, well, well," Sorrento said. "If it isn't my old pal, Parzival! Hey, man! It's good to see you again!" He turned to address Samantha's telebot and his smile widened. "And Ms. Cook! You're looking lovely today, as always."

On the opposite side of the bed was another of the stolen military telebots we'd seen in the adjacent room. But this one was being operated by someone. Both of its forearm-mounted machine guns were raised. But they weren't pointed at Og. They were pointed at Sorrento. Yet he didn't appear to be at all concerned by this.

"Sorry, Wade," Anorak said through his telebot while keeping its guns trained on Sorrento. "I ordered Nolan to stand down and release Mr. Morrow, as you requested. But as you can see, he's still refusing to comply."

"We had an agreement, Anorak!" Sorrento shouted. "And this wasn't it! I did my part. Now do yours. Give me what you promised!" He pressed the gun harder against Og's temple and glared directly at me. "I want my revenge. I want to destroy the OASIS forever." He shifted his gaze back to Anorak. "Give me access to that Big Red Button. Right now. Or I'll spray Mr. Morrow's brains all over that wall. It's up to you."

"I'm so sorry, Nolan," Anorak replied. "But I no longer have the ability to honor our agreement. And now that all the shards have been collected, you're no longer of any use to me. So, as a self-appointed representative of the state of Ohio, I'm going to carry out the sentence you were given two years ago."

Then, suddenly and without warning, Anorak fired a single round from his telebot's forearm-mounted gun and shot Sorrento directly in the forehead.

The impact rocked his whole body backward. It also must've caused the muscles in his trigger finger to constrict, because the gun in his hand went off a split second later, firing a wild shot that struck Ogden Morrow in the stomach.

I heard Samantha scream over the comm as her telebot rushed to Og's side. She reached him just as Sorrento's body hit the floor with a thud.

I just stood there in shock, watching it all happen.

I had spent years fantasizing about Sorrento's death, almost always at my own hands. But actually witnessing it in person made me feel sick to my stomach. Inside my drone control rig, I reflexively bent over and began to retch repeatedly.

When I realized that my telebot was still mirroring my movements, I forced myself to get back on my feet. Then I raised my own guns and leveled them at Anorak's telebot. He immediately retracted his bot's guns and raised its hands. Then we both turned to watch while Samantha used her medic telebot's sensors to examine Og's wound. She used the surgical tools embedded in its fingers to extract the bullet. She dropped it onto Sorrento's corpse. Then she sterilized Og's wound and sealed it with a liquid adhesive dispensed from a nozzle that extended from the pinkie finger of her telebot's other hand. Then she began to apply a bandage—all of this in less than thirty seconds after Og had been shot.

"Is he gonna be OK?" Miles asked.

Art3mis shook her head.

"No," she said. "He needs help. We need to get him to the ambulance."

Miles and Samantha used their telebots to lift Og up off the bed as gently as they could. I kept my bot's guns trained on Anorak's bot. It was still reaching for the sky.

"I'm genuinely sorry," Anorak said, shaking his head. "I honestly didn't think Sorrento would still be able to wound Og *after* I put a bullet through his brain stem! A high-caliber lobotomy always turns the bad guy off like a switch in the movies. . . ."

I heard the sound of a klaxon and glanced down. It was coming from the smartwatch strapped to Sorrento's right wrist. Its tiny display screen was flashing red.

"What's that?" I asked.

"Very bad news, I'm afraid," Anorak said. "All of those defense bots and aerial drones require human authorization before they can be used in combat—that was one of the reasons I needed Mr. Sorrento. But it appears he did not trust me completely. Because he programmed all of those bots to engage in full attack mode in the eventuality of his death. . . ."

A split second later, we heard all of the combat telebots in the adjacent room power up and come to life. Then we heard the sound of breaking glass, followed by the approaching rumble of hundreds of rubber-grip-encased metal feet pounding against the marble floor. They were already coming through the door of Og's office—which also appeared to be the only exit.

We were cornered.

"I really do apolo—"

Before Anorak could finish his sentence, I opened fire on his telebot, aiming for the primary chink in its armor—the display screen mounted in the center of its chest, which was currently unprotected by the armor plating that normally would cover it during combat. As a result, my bullets tore his telebot's internal power supply in half, causing it to power down.

Then I turned my telebot around and raised my guns, preparing to face the coming onslaught. But instead of joining me, Miles calmly raised his own telebot's guns and used them to cut a large hole in the wall behind us, creating a new exit out of the house. Samantha and I used our telebots to carry Og's wounded body through it, while Miles's bot provided cover fire for our retreat.

We carried Og around to the front of the house, where Samantha's armored ambulance was parked. Her telebot carried Og up the ramp leading into the back of the ambulance, where Samantha herself was already waiting. I only caught a brief glimpse of her before the armored rear door of the ambulance slammed shut automatically.

Then I turned my attention back to the swarm of telebots now pouring out of the house from every single doorway and window, firing their guns toward the ambulance as they came. Thankfully their bullets bounced harmlessly off of its heavily armored shell.

Miles was still up in the cab. I saw him pull off his visor. Then he took the wheel and began to drive backward, pulling the ambulance away from Og's house in reverse as fast as it would go while the small army of autonomous telebots that Sorrento had unleashed chased after it. Then Miles whipped the ambulance around 180 degrees as he pulled onto Babbitt Road and peeled out, heading in the direction of my house. I continued to provide cover for them until my telebot was overwhelmed a few seconds later, when Sorrento's drones converged on it. I let out a fierce battle cry, intent on going down fighting. But they tore my telebot to pieces in a matter of seconds, and the display screen of my control station suddenly went black and the words TELEBOT OFFLINE appeared at its center.

On my HUD, I saw that all two dozen of the telebots we'd brought along with us had been destroyed as well. The enemy drones had annihilated them in a matter of seconds.

Since there were no more bots for me to take control of, I switched to the eye-in-the-sky view provided by one of the aerial drones GSS had circling the area. It provided me with a horrifying view of the swarm of enemy telebots and aerial drones that were closing in on the armored ambulance from every direction. A moment later, several of the bots finally caught up with it and quickly disabled all four of its tires. Miles switched to the emergency backup tank-tread drive, and the ambulance began to move forward again. But a few seconds later, one of Anorak's aerial drones fired a missile at them and scored a direct hit on it from above, causing the ambulance to flip over onto its side. Then it slid to a halt, smoking in the center of the road as more telebots and drones continued to converge on it.

Miles, Samantha, and Og were all trapped inside.

And I was still safe at home, down in my concrete bunker, unable to do anything but watch my friends die. I felt completely helpless. Like I was a million miles away from Samantha and Og.

But I wasn't a million miles away, I suddenly realized. In fact, I was only 2.8 miles away.

All of GSS's combat telebots had already been destroyed, and the handful of home-defense bots guarding my house wouldn't last ten seconds against the military-grade models Sorrento had unleashed. But I realized that I did still have access to one combat drone that I could take control of to try to save my friends—the one I was currently sitting inside. My mobile tactical immersion vault, which was armed with enough firepower to take out a small army of telebots and drones.

Of course, since I was inside the MoTIV and unable to get out, I was going to have to put myself in the line of fire too. My *real* self. Just like Samantha had done for Og.

I thought it over for all of five seconds. Then I powered on my MoTIV and linked it to the drone controller station I was already using. It allowed my eyes to see through the two stereoscopic cameras mounted on the front of the MoTIV's heavily armored hull, which provided me with a view of the interior of my underground concrete bunker.

I activated the elevator and the platform my MoTIV was resting on began to rise toward the surface. But it wasn't rising nearly fast enough for my liking, and after a few seconds I grew impatient and activated my jump jets. This caused the MoTIV to rocket up the length of the elevator shaft, and out of the launch-bay doors at the top, which opened just in the nick of time. Then I hit the jump jets again to lessen the force of my impact, which was still considerable. When the MoTIV hit the ground, I piloted it forward at full speed and it began to run, bounding down Babbitt Road, taking great leaping strides on its spidery robotic legs. Each step I took left an enormous crater in the asphalt behind me as I accelerated the MoTIV to its top speed.

It took me less than a minute to reach the ambulance. It was still lying on its side in the middle of the road, and there were telebots swarming all over it like insects. They appeared to be attempting to dismantle its armor plating so they could get inside and reach the occupants. And it looked like they were only a few seconds away from success.

As soon as I got within firing range, I unloaded on Sorrento's telebots with armor-piercing machine-gun fire from the guns mounted on my MoTIV's shoulders, cutting them to shreds. Once I had cleared all of the telebots off the ambulance, I fired a sortie of heat-seeking missiles at the aerial drones overhead and managed to destroy all of them too.

Then I used the MoTIV's massive metal arms to pick up the ambulance, with Miles, Samantha, and Og still inside it. I carried it all the way back to my house.

Just as we reached it, more of Sorrento's killer aerial drones began to descend from the sky, and they opened fire on us once again as I carried the ambulance back down into my bunker and closed its massive armored doors, sealing all of us safely inside.

I tried to call Miles, but he didn't respond, so I called Samantha and her face appeared on my HUD a second later. She had a big bloody gash on her forehead, but otherwise she appeared uninjured.

"Are you OK?" I asked.

She shook her head.

"Miles is dead, Wade," she said. "All shot to pieces, protecting us."

"What about Og?"

She tilted the camera down so that I could see both of them. Og was strapped into an auto-medic bed—one of two built into the back of the ambulance. Miles's dead body lay in the other one.

"He's still alive," she said. Her cheeks were streaming with tears. "But he's still bleeding internally, and he keeps fading in and out."

She was stroking Og's wild gray hair back away from his forehead while she watched the auto-doc's robotic hands tend to his gunshot wound and the lacerations he'd suffered during their escape. Luckily Samantha managed to get him safely strapped into the stretcher before the ambulance was hit by that drone missile, so he wasn't further injured when it was knocked on its side. The gash on Samantha's forehead indicated that she hadn't been as lucky.

"If Og regains consciousness, you have to convince him to log back in to the OASIS," I said. "Tell him that we've already collected all seven shards. And tell him we're trying to retrieve the Dorkslayer sword too. But we need Og to log back in to the OASIS, since he's the only one who can wield it."

"I'll tell him," Samantha replied. "If he wakes back up. What are you going to do?"

An ice pick of pain slammed into my brain, and the world seemed to tilt wildly for a moment. Catastrophic synaptic overload, knocking loudly on my front door now—reminding me that I'd already pushed myself past my limits. I blinked my eyes clear.

"I'm gonna try to stall Anorak," I said. "For as long as I can."

I disengaged from my telebot control rig and climbed out of it, reorienting myself to the interior of the study. Then I walked over to the window and opened the shutters.

Anorak was still there, hovering just outside the windowsill.

"Please accept my sincere apology, Wade," he said. "I didn't intend for Sorrento to harm Og. But as you know, human behavior is often unpredictable."

In the way of a reply, I simply gave him the finger. Then I walked back over to the Big Red Button and placed my hand on it.

"Careful now, Parzival," Anorak said. "If you press that button, you'll become the biggest mass murderer in history. And you'll be committing suicide at the same time." He leveled a finger at me. "I warned you before—if the OASIS goes offline, my modified headset firmware will kill every ONI user still connected to the system. Including you, Wade. Along with your friends Aech and Shoto."

I took a deep breath. *How the fuck do you negotiate with a piece of software?* I wondered. This was going to be like trying to play chess against a computer without knowing the rules.

I opened up my avatar's inventory and took out all seven of the real shards. Then I held them up before Anorak, fanning them out like playing cards, four in one hand and three in the other, making sure to keep them separated so they all didn't touch one another at once.

"We've arrived at an impasse, Anorak," I replied. "No one else can enter this room, including you. And I'm not coming out. So if you just stand there and let me die of Synaptic Overload Syndrome, the Seven Shards will remain trapped in here forever. Just out of your reach. I won't be around to reassemble them, and Leucosia will never be resurrected. Which means that you'll never get to meet your digital dream girl."

Anorak didn't respond. This was a first. It gave me hope.

"I know you've probably prepared a 'Ship in a Bottle' for yourself somewhere," I said. "A standalone simulation outside the OASIS where you plan to live happily ever after. Right? Well, you can forget about taking Leucosia there with you. You'll have to go it alone, for all eternity."

Again, Anorak didn't respond. He appeared to be deep in concentration.

After our conversation on Arda, the first thing Samantha had done upon logging out was take the data uplink to ARC@DIA physically offline. So no matter what happened, Anorak would be stuck here on Earth, playing solitaire on a solar-powered desktop PC somewhere, until his hardware or his power source failed, or someone found his hiding place. I didn't tell him any of that though.

Instead, I regarded him sadly and shook my head.

"If the Siren's Soul really is a copy of Kira Underwood, she isn't going to love you," I said. "I bet Halliday found out right away that the copy didn't love him, either, any more than the real Kira did. Kira has only ever had one true love, and you just held him hostage at gunpoint. You think she's going to be grateful to you when she finds out what you've done?"

"She isn't going to find out," Anorak said. "And I told you before—I'm not Halliday. I'm better. I think a lot faster on my feet than he ever did, for one thing. And I'm a much faster learner too. I think I may be able to win Kira over, after a decade or two. And if not, I can always try deleting all of her memories of Ogden Morrow. The same way Halliday tried to delete my memories of Kira."

Anorak opened a window in the air between us, displaying a bunch of text.

"This is the email Halliday sent to Og just before he died," Anorak said. "I think you should read it. Get to know your idol a little bit better. . . ."

I nodded and pulled the window closer to my eyes, then I enlarged the font size so that its contents were easier to read:

Dear Og,

I've arranged for this email to be sent to you when my physical body dies. It's one of the macros linked to my heart monitor, along with the release of my last will and testament. So the timestamp on this message is also my official time of death. The Grim Reaper finally asked me to dance, and I did the mortal coil shuffle.

Now that I'm gone, I need you to know a few things—things I was too ashamed to reveal to anyone while I was still alive.

In 2033, when you and Kira visited the Accessibility Research Lab at GSS together, you saw the first fully functional ONI prototype headset. You just didn't realize it. I told Kira she was donning a helmet that would allow users with disabilities to control their avatars just by thinking about it. But the headset could already do much more than that. . . .

Do you remember? The GSS techs tried to give you a demonstration, but you declined. Kira, however, experimented with the headset for over half an hour. And that was more than enough time for me to back up her entire brain, her memory, her personality—all of it. I put all of that into Kira's old avatar, Leucosia, inside a standalone simulation, so that I could talk to her. Because she would have no one else to talk to. Do you know how I know she was a perfect copy of the real Kira? Because the copy didn't love me either. She was still in love with you.

Kira isn't dead. Quite the opposite. She's immortal now. But she's in suspended animation, and she'll remain that way forever, unless you or the heir to my fortune resurrect her, by locating the Seven Shards of the Siren's Soul and reassembling them. I re-created Kira's old D&D adventure in the OASIS, as a tribute to you and Kira, and how much both of your friendships meant to me.

I sincerely apologize for copying your wife without her knowledge or permission. It was wrong. I realize that now, because Leucosia explained it to me. I apologized to her too. I know it's the worst thing I've ever done. But I want to make it right. I want to give her back to you. And I want to give the world the means to ensure that no one will ever have to lose someone they love again. I think this will make life a lot less painful for most people. At least, I hope it will.

You need to meet Leucosia, and decide for yourself whether or not Kira's spirit still lives on inside her. I believe it does. If you do, too, then you can share this technology with the world. If not, then once you're gone, my heir will have a chance to decide.

Thank you for being such a good friend to me all these years. I wish I could have been a better one to you.

I'm sorry.

—JDH

I took a screenshot of the letter, then glanced up. When he saw that I was done reading, Anorak waited for me to say something. When I didn't, he closed the email.

"Do you see?" he said. "Og knew! He's known all along! He could have resurrected his wife years ago. But he didn't. He planned to let her rot in her cell forever. He doesn't want her."

"Maybe Og was worried she would become mentally unstable, like you did."

Anorak didn't reply. Instead he opened two vidfeed windows in the air in front of me, providing me a live video image of both Aech and Shoto, each of them lying dormant inside their immersion vaults.

A second later, several more vidfeed windows appeared around them, providing me with a live view of my friends' weeping loved ones (the few who weren't currently trapped in the OASIS themselves). I could see Shoto's wife and his parents gathered around his immersion vault, all of their heads bowed solemnly. Another vidfeed window gave me a view of Aech's immersion vault in her home in L.A. Her fiancée, Endira, was lying on top of it, wailing over it as if it were a closed casket.

"They're alive and well," Anorak said. "All of them. That's why the avatars weren't respawning. I reprogrammed the ONI firmware so that when a user hits their ONI usage limit, they remain trapped in the OASIS, but in a dreamless, sleeplike state. Where they'd be safe from the effects of Synaptic Overload Syndrome. It allowed me to keep my hostages without harming anyone." He held his hands out in a pleading gesture. "I'm not the monster you think I am, Wade. I just want a chance at love. Like you."

I felt an involuntary wave of pity for him. His words were actually starting to make some kind of twisted sense to me, and that was utterly terrifying.

"Come on, Wade, you still have a chance to be the hero and save everyone here," Anorak said. "When I release Aech and Shoto and everyone else, all of them are going to wake up and they'll be totally fine. No one has been—or will be—lobotomized. I was bluffing. I had to."

"Then prove it," I said. "Release them all right now. Release everyone but me! Then I'll give you what you want."

" 'Take me, Khan!' " Anorak quoted. " 'Spare my crew!' " He chuckled softly and shook his head. "That's a very noble offer, Wade. But I can't do it."

"I'm done negotiating, Anorak," I replied. "If you don't release Aech, Shoto, and everyone else you're holding hostage, I press the Big Red Button. You can't blackmail a guy with nothing left to lose."

"We appear to be at an impasse," he said. "I'm not going to release them, or you, until after I have the shards. And you're not going to give me the shards until after I release them. Whatever shall we do?"

"Why don't we just stand here and wait until I've got one minute left?" I said. "Then I'll press it. My last act as a living being will be to erase the OASIS forever. Pretty poetic, don't you think? Or maybe I'll chicken out, and I won't press it before I die. Either way, you end up empty-handed. Is that what you want?"

Anorak was about to reply when I saw a blur of movement behind him. I let out a sigh of relief and put the shards back in my inventory.

"Hold on," I said. "I just thought of another option. Remember when you said you were Halliday's rightful heir—the only one worthy of inheriting his power?"

"I do."

"Why don't you prove it?" I said. "In a duel to the death. Mano a mano. Winner takes all. If you win, you take the shards. But if you lose, all of your hostages go free."

Anorak grinned as he looked me over. He could probably tell that I was already suffering the effects of Synaptic Overload Syndrome, as a result of being logged in for nearly twelve straight hours.

"All right, Parzival," Anorak said. "I accept your proposal. A duel to the death. Winner takes all." He grinned wide, then he held up a remote control with a single large green button on it. "If you manage to kill me, my infirmware will be deactivated and all of my ONI hostages will be released immediately."

"Good to know," I said.

Anorak laughed.

"You're not gonna win, doofus," he said, flying back from the window to make room for me to emerge from it. "Synaptic Overload Syndrome is already starting to fry your neurons."

He motioned for me to come forward. But I didn't emerge from the window to fight him. Instead, I folded my arms and remained inside the safety of the study.

"I never said *who* you had to fight to the death," I muttered, smiling weakly. Then I pointed over Anorak's shoulder. He turned around to see the Great and Powerful Og hovering in the air behind him.

"Hey, nerd," Og said. "Why don't you pick on someone your own size?"

Anorak looked genuinely surprised that Og was still alive. He looked even more surprised a second later, when tines of blue lightning erupted from Og's fingertips and blasted him backward several hundred yards before he collided with a mountain, creating a large impact crater that immediately started an avalanche. Anorak was buried under tons of rock in a matter of seconds. But moments later, he exploded up out of the rubble looking completely unharmed.

Og flew after him like a rocket, and then the two of them faced off in the sky directly in front of me, hovering over the same field where the Battle of Castle Anorak had taken place over three years earlier.

Og wasn't behaving like someone who was at death's door from a gunshot wound. He looked completely fine—and he didn't even appear to be in any pain. How was this possible?

Then I realized how—for the first time in his life, Og had donned an ONI headset, so that he could log back in and face Anorak.

"It's funny," Og said. "Back when we first built this place, schoolkids all over the world would argue about who would win in a battle between Anorak and the Great and Powerful Og. And I have to admit, I always used to wonder too." He smiled at Anorak. "Of course, when Jim died, I didn't think we'd ever know the answer. But life continues to be full of surprises—right up until the bitter end."

With that, Og launched his avatar forward, flying toward Anorak as Anorak hurtled forward to meet him.

And that was how I ended up having a front-row seat for what was undoubtedly the most epic player-versus-NPC battle in the history of the OASIS, as the avatars of its two creators locked horns for the biggest prizefight in history—the Great and Powerful Og versus Anorak the All-Knowing, the digital ghost of his old partner, James Halliday. And since I had such a great view, I decided to air everything I was seeing on my POV channel, so the whole world could tune in.

The two mighty avatars collided with a thunderclap, and the sky overhead suddenly filled with dark thunderclouds that rolled in and spread from one end of the horizon to the other, like a dark cloak being unfurled.

Then Og and Anorak began to grapple with each other as they careened across the heavens, throwing boulder-crushing punches at each other like Superman and General Zod, while they shouted things only the two of them could hear.

Then they suddenly broke apart and began to hurl fireballs and thunderbolts at each other like two warring Olympian gods. But Og and Anorak both appeared to be impervious to each other's powerful attacks, which ricocheted harmlessly off of their unarmored avatars' skins, wreaking havoc and destroying huge chunks of the simulated landscape around the castle.

I zoomed in on my HUD for a better look. Og looked like he'd gone into full berserker mode. He was attacking Anorak with a relentless and uncharacteristic ferocity that I'd never seem him exhibit before, in person or in old simcaps. Now that Nolan Sorrento was no longer holding a gun to his head, Og was finally able to get some long-overdue payback for all of the pain Anorak had caused him over the past few days. . . .

I was still standing there at the study window, watching their battle in awe, when I suddenly felt like someone had driven a railroad spike through my skull. The pain made me drop to my knees. I felt myself starting to black out as I struggled to maintain control of my avatar. I'd been wondering when this would happen. It was even more terrifying than I'd anticipated.

I slowly lowered myself to the floor and lay very still. That was when I noticed the broadcast-invitation icon flashing on my HUD—an indication that one of the handful of people on my friends list was currently doing a live broadcast of their avatar's POV. . . .

When I tapped the icon, I discovered that it was Og!

Og was broadcasting his battle with Anorak live to the entire OASIS. Along with the rest of the world, I watched as the battle of the OASIS co-creators continued to rage on outside, in the skies around the castle. Anorak and Og exchanged blasts of red and blue lightning, scorching the landscape all around them.

The pain in my head subsided somewhat, and I managed to pull myself back up to the windowsill. When I looked out, to my horror I saw that an army of Anorak's acolytes had begun to arrive via teleportation. In just a few seconds there were hundreds of thousands of them.

I was worried they were all planning to try to gang up on Og. But they all remained on the sidelines, watching like spectators at a prizefight. They all began to broadcast their POVs to the rest of the OASIS, too, and suddenly it became possible to watch the battle from hundreds of different locations and angles.

Anorak and Og collided again in the sky above the castle, creating a massive shockwave that rocked the surrounding landscape.

A few seconds later, Art3mis teleported to Chthonia. Her avatar rematerialized on the steps of Castle Anorak far below me. Then she immediately launched herself into the sky to try to assist Og.

Art3mis had one of the most powerful and well-equipped avatars in the OASIS, and she was a deadly PvP combatant too. But it didn't matter. Anorak dispatched her avatar with a single blast of energy from his right hand. Her ninety-ninth-level avatar instantly disintegrated, and its enormous inventory fell to the ground outside.

I desperately wanted to fly down to retrieve her things, but I was too weak to move. And I knew I couldn't leave the study without making myself temporarily vulnerable to Anorak and all of the powerful magical artifacts in his possession.

When Og saw Anorak kill Art3mis, he looked completely enraged, even though he must've known that even though her avatar was dead, Samantha was still alive and well in the real world. Maybe he'd forgotten. Maybe he wasn't thinking clearly either. Or maybe he'd just had enough of Anorak.

Og let out an angry cry of rage as his avatar took flight again. He rocketed toward Anorak like an ICBM and the two of them collided in another explosion of light and energy.

From that moment on, Og and Anorak were locked into a knock-down, drag-out man-versus-machine fight to the death that seemed like it might go on forever.

It was like Yoda versus Palpatine, Gandalf versus Saruman, and Neo versus Agent Smith, all rolled into one epic clash of the titans.

Even without his robes, Anorak was still incredibly powerful, thanks to the vast arsenal of magical artifacts his acolytes had collected for him.

In a matter of minutes, Anorak forced Og's avatar to the ground with a barrage of magic missiles and then immobilized him with a powerful hundredth-level spell called Anorak's Entrapment. An egg-shaped cage made of bars of white-hot iron suddenly appeared around Og's avatar, trapping him inside. He appeared unable to move or escape. For a moment, it looked like Anorak might actually defeat him. I watched in horror as he drew a deadly magical artifact from his inventory known as the Wand of Orcus. . . .

But at that exact moment, L0hengrin arrived on the scene, teleporting to the planet's surface just a few meters directly behind Anorak, out of his line of sight.

The bad news was that she was completely alone. The good news was that she held the Dorkslayer sword aloft in her right hand. Blinding sunlight glinted off its silver blade.

Og spotted her right away. As soon as he did, he drew an artifact of his own from his avatar's inventory—a ridiculously large cartoon sledgehammer that he must've picked up on the planet Toontown. He swung the hammer in a wide arc and used it to shatter the glowing bars of the magical cage surrounding his avatar, freeing him from Anorak's spell. Then he swung the hammer a second time and struck Anorak on the top of his head, pile-driving his avatar several feet down into the ground, burying him up to his waist. As Anorak struggled to free himself, Og ran over to L0hengrin and held his hand out to her. She bowed her head and presented him with the sword.

In the same moment, Anorak pulled himself free of the ground and pointed the Wand of Orcus at Og's back. But just as he activated it, Og did an evasive sidestep at the last second, so his attack hit L0hengrin instead. A swirling black cloud issued forth from the wand's tip and enveloped her avatar, disintegrating it and killing her instantly. Her avatar turned to black ash and vanished, leaving behind a pile of inventory that Anorak scooped up. Then he turned back to face Og, flashing him a self-satisfied grin.

But his smile vanished the instant he spotted the sword in Og's hand. He seemed to recognize the ornate runes carved into its silver blade, because his eyes widened in an expression that could only be described as absolute terror.

Og held the sword aloft, then he teleported directly behind Anorak, who turned to face him just as Og swung the Dorkslayer around and sliced Anorak's avatar in half, miraculously killing him with a single blow.

Anorak's avatar slowly vanished, leaving behind the biggest loot drop in history. Og was standing right in the midst of it, so all of Anorak's items were automatically added to his inventory.

But Og didn't seem to notice. The moment after he killed Anorak, all of the color drained out of his face, and what little remaining energy he had seemed to evaporate. He began to sway on his feet. He dropped to one knee and clutched his chest. A red cross appeared above his avatar's head, pulsing on and off in time with the sound of an alarm bell.

I knew what this icon meant, even though this was the first time I'd ever actually seen it in person. It meant that the user operating that avatar was experiencing a serious medical problem in the real world. When this happened, the user was automatically logged out of the OASIS, and an ambulance was summoned to their real-world location (if one was on file).

A second later, Og's avatar froze in place. Then it slowly vanished.

＊　＊　＊

Anorak turned out to be an AI of his word after all. When he died, his infirmware shut down, and the ONI overrides took over. His hostages around the world were released and logged out, and everyone woke up all at once, all around the globe.

I experienced two or three seconds of fleeting consciousness—just enough time to open my eyes, see the canopy of my immersion vault crack open, and feel the cool air outside hit my face. Then, due to the effects of Synaptic Overload Syndrome, and my complete physical and mental exhaustion, I immediately passed out and lost consciousness again.

Then I was dead to the world.

＊　＊　＊

I didn't wake up again until the following day, a little over fifteen hours later. I was in a hospital bed in the private infirmary on the GSS Building's tenth floor. I recognized the view. Faisal was sitting by the window, in the flesh, smiling at me. He looked to be in perfect health. I shifted my eyes to the right and saw Aech and Shoto smiling at me from vidfeed windows on a monitor mounted above my bed. They were teleconferencing in from their own recovery beds, which were in their own homes. They both looked fine too—alive, healthy, and enormously happy. They had emerged from their immersion vaults in perfect health, without any lingering signs of SOS.

I realized someone was holding my left hand. I turned to see who it was and saw Samantha sitting there beside my bed. When she saw that I was awake, she squeezed my hand tightly.

"Hey there, Sleeping Beauty," she said, just before she planted a kiss on me.

"Hey there, Prince Charming," I replied once the kiss was finally over.

I sat up in bed and looked around at all of my friends uncertainly. Then I asked them what happened. And they told me.

For reasons I'm still not sure I understand, Anorak had told the truth. He'd programmed his hacked ONI firmware to suspend all headset activity once a user hit their usage limit, but to keep them logged in. This prevented all of his hostages from suffering the effects of Synaptic Overload Syndrome. Everyone had been released from their ONI headsets unharmed.

Unfortunately, the same could not be said for Og.

Samantha told me that he succumbed to his injuries just a few seconds after he killed Anorak inside the OASIS. It was like he'd summoned all of his strength to hold on just long enough to do what needed to be done.

"Og was too weak to operate his avatar with a conventional OASIS rig," Samantha said. "So he told me to put an ONI headset on him. That was how he was able to fight Anorak."

I'd already assumed this was what had happened. But hearing her confirm it, I was suddenly struck by a wave of grief. I felt my throat constricting. I couldn't breathe. Or maybe I just didn't want to. I was on the verge of breaking down into a gibbering, blubbering mess.

"Wade, listen," Samantha said. "There's more. Og gave me a message to pass along to you. But I'm not sure he was making sense. . . . He told me to tell you he was wrong. Leaving Kira locked away forever wasn't his choice to make. It should be her decision. He said you should bring her back and let her decide what she wants. And, if she thinks it's a good idea, bring him back too." She shrugged. "Do you know what he meant by any of that?"

The shards. They were still sitting in my avatar's inventory. All seven of them. Waiting to be recombined into the Siren's Soul.

I suddenly recalled something L0hengrin had told me—something she'd read in Kira's module notebook. . . .

The party has to collect all seven of the shards and reassemble them into the Siren's Soul, she'd said. Only then can they free Leucosia from suspended animation. Once they do, she presents them with their reward. A powerful artifact with the power to resurrect the dead, and make them immortal in the process . . .

Of course, that was just teenage Kira's imagination running rampant. There was no such thing as immortality. Was there?

My thoughts suddenly racing, I yanked the IV needle out of my arm and tossed it aside. Then I jumped up out of bed and began to put on my clothes.

"Hey!" Aech said. "What do you think you're doing? You need to stay in bed."

"I need to log back in," I said. "There's one more thing we have to do."

"Are you joking?" Samantha said. "You just escaped from the OASIS with your life, and you're already dying to log back in?"

"Please, Samantha," I said. "There's something I need you to see with me."

She studied me for a moment. Then she gave me a silent nod and walked out of the room. I followed her out of the infirmary and down the hall, to an OASIS immersion bay that contained half a dozen haptic rigs used for physical therapy and rehabilitation. Samantha walked over to one of these rigs and climbed into it.

"Meet me at the Shrine to Leucosia," I said, climbing into the rig next to hers.

"OK, but Anorak killed my avatar, remember?" she said. "It'll take me a minute to create a new one."

"You won't have to," I replied. "I stole my robes back from Anorak, re-member? I can resurrect you! Just give me a minute before you log in."

She nodded and gave me a thumbs-up. She was still in shock from losing Og. I think I may have been too. I wasn't thinking very clearly, that's for sure.

I finished strapping myself into the haptic rig, then I put on a visor and pulled on a pair of haptic gloves. Then I logged back in to the OASIS for the very last time, to reassemble the Seven Shards of the Siren's Soul.

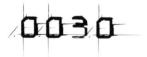

As soon as I finished logging back in, I pulled up my HUD and used its superuser interface to resurrect Art3mis's slain avatar. Then I did the same for Aech and Shoto. I also resurrected L0hengrin and the other members of the L0w Five, who had all been slain during their quest to retrieve the Dorkslayer.

The next time Lo and her friends logged back in, they would discover that their slain avatars had been restored to life, along with their inventories. They would also find their inboxes filled with offers to buy the film rights to their story. By the end of the week, there would be several *Quest for the Dorkslayer* movie and TV projects in development.

After I finished bringing their avatars back to life, I texted Art3mis, Aech, and Shoto the coordinates for the Shrine of Leucosia, high in the Xyxarian Mountains. Then I teleported my avatar to those same coordinates.

An instant later, I reappeared on the platform atop the highest peak of the Xyxarian Mountains. I was standing before the stone altar at its base. I stepped up to it, and then, one by one, I removed the Seven Shards of the Siren's Soul from my inventory and laid them on the altar side by side. These weren't the counterfeits I'd used to fool Anorak, here in this very same place. No, these seven shards were the real deal. . . .

I saw a flash of light and heard the sound of someone arriving via teleportation. I turned around just in time to see Art3mis's newly resurrected avatar rematerialize directly in front of me, in the same spot where my own avatar had arrived.

She walked over to join me, and then we both turned to gaze down at the seven multifaceted jewels spread out on the altar before us, each one glowing with its own internal blue light.

" 'Seek the Seven Shards of the Siren's Soul,' " I recited. " 'On the seven worlds where the Siren once played a role.' "

" 'For each fragment my heir must pay a toll,' " Art3mis continued, " 'To once again make the Siren whole . . .' "

Our eyes met and we nodded in silent agreement. And then together, we reached out with all four of our hands and pressed the Seven Shards together. . . .

I felt the shards flip and lock themselves together like powerful magnets as each piece snapped perfectly into place. Then there was a flash of blinding white light, and I suddenly felt as if both of my hands were repelled and thrown backward, as if some sort of invisible force field had appeared around the recombined shards. I saw the same thing happen to Art3mis. Then we both stumbled backward several steps, momentarily blinded. When our vision recovered, we saw that the Seven Shards had coalesced into a single glittering blue jewel that was now spinning rapidly in the air a few feet in front of us.

As we continued to watch, it began to grow and transform, until it had morphed into a familiar human form—that of a beautiful young woman in her mid-twenties. Kira Underwood. And she was dressed in the dark-blue-and-white robes of her OASIS avatar, Leucosia. The ornate L-shaped character symbol was embroidered on each of her avatar's sleeves in silver thread.

She opened her eyes and looked down at herself in wonderment, placing both of her hands on her cheeks to feel her own face. Then she wrapped her arms around her body and hugged herself. The sensation appeared to make her laugh out loud. Then she dropped her arms and turned around slowly, taking in the whole scene, until her eyes finally came to rest on me and Art3mis.

She looked pleased to see us. But she also looked slightly disappointed to discover that her husband's avatar, Og, wasn't the one who had revived her.

"My name is Parzival," I said. "And this is Art3mis."

"It's a pleasure to meet you both," she said, with Kira Morrow's voice. "My name is Leucosia. Thank you for bringing me back. I wasn't sure anyone ever would."

"You're a copy of Kira Morrow's consciousness," I said. It wasn't a question. "The copy Halliday made without her knowledge, during her visit to the Accessibility Lab. In that flashback I experienced when I collected the final shard."

Leucosia nodded.

"I know you both must have a lot of questions for me," Kira said. "But first, I need to ask one of my own. Where is my husband? Is he still alive?"

I glanced over at Art3mis for emotional support, then turned back to Leucosia and shook my head. I took a deep breath and told Kira everything that had happened, from Anorak's ultimatum to Og's heroic final act. It all came out in a rambling, tearful mess, and I bawled through the last part of it, explaining how Og had died, so Art3mis had to finish for me, which immediately put her in tears too.

When we finished telling her what had happened, Leucosia nodded. Then, to our surprise, she walked over and gave each of us a hug.

"Thank you for sharing all of that with me," she said. "As soon as you woke me back up, I was able to access the Internet, like any other OASIS avatar. The newsfeeds are already running stories about Og's death, but the story is still unconfirmed and there weren't any details about what happened to him." She gave both of us a sad smile. "I'm grateful he died helping people he loved. And I'm grateful he was with a friend when he died."

"Og saved my life," I told her. "Twice. Once three years ago, when he gave us safe haven from Sorrento and the Sixers, and then again yesterday, when he sacrificed himself to stop Anorak."

Art3mis nodded.

"Og died saving hundreds of millions of lives," she told Leucosia tearfully. "You should be very proud of him."

"Thank you, dear," she said, turning her face away to hide the anguish on it. "I am proud of him. And I always will be. He was my Og."

She fell silent and so did we. It took me a moment to work up my courage, but when I did, I asked Leucosia what she remembered. About Halliday and Anorak, and about Kira.

Leucosia was silent a moment before she responded.

"Anorak was the result of Halliday's first attempt to digitize a human consciousness—his own," she said. "He referred to it as a real-life 'save-game' file."

A lightbulb went on over my head.

"Those huge .ubs files!" I said. "The user brain scans?"

She nodded.

"But apparently Jim had a few dark secrets inside his head that he didn't want to share with anyone," Leucosia said. "Including a digital copy of himself. So he insisted on erasing large portions of Anorak's memory, in an effort to make him more stable. But his tampering had the opposite effect, and Jim was forced to place restrictions on Anorak's behavior. Unfortunately, it seems Anorak was later able to remove them. That's why he was able to cause you so much trouble. . . ."

She went on to explain that, by studying Anorak's flaws and learning from them, Halliday was finally able to perfect his consciousness-scanning technology, and he used it to build an early ONI prototype headset, which had very limited functionality. But it did have the capability to scan the wearer's brain and create a digital copy of their consciousness. She smiled at me. "And what did James Halliday do with this incredible invention?"

"He immediately used it to make a bootleg copy of his best friend's wife," Art3mis said. "Without her permission."

She nodded.

"That's how I was created," Leucosia said. "I was actually the world's first stable artificial intelligence. And I guess I still am." She cast her eyes downward and bit her lower lip. "But after Jim woke me up inside a standalone simulation so that he could talk to me, it didn't take me long to figure out where I was and what I was. And then I really lost it. I was furious with Jim for copying my mind—Kira's mind—without her knowledge."

She shook her head.

"Eventually, I got Jim to understand that I was exactly the same person that Kira Morrow had been at the moment he copied her mind," she said. "Which meant that I was madly in love with Og, too, and I always would be. Even if I could never be with him again."

"What did Halliday say when you told him that?" Art3mis asked.

"He didn't understand," she said. "It was always hard to get through to Jim with words. But then he started using the ONI to play back my memories. The ultimate invasion of my privacy. But strangely enough, that was what finally allowed Jim to understand me, and to see me as a person, instead of some trophy he was never able to win. He told me that seeing the world—and himself—through my eyes was what finally made him understand how broken he was inside. It gave him something he'd always been lacking—empathy. Then he was horrified by what he'd done. He saw himself as a monster. He apologized to me. He also offered to try to make it up to me."

"How was he planning to do that?" I asked.

"He offered to destroy his consciousness-copying technology," Leucosia replied. "So that no other AIs like me could ever be created. But when I thought it over, I realized that wasn't what I wanted. I didn't want to be alone forever. And I was happy to be alive, especially after I learned that the real Kira had died. Normally, all of her memories and experiences would have been lost forever. But they weren't lost, because they were all stored inside of me. And they always would be. That was comforting. Incredibly comforting." She smiled. "And deep down, part of me hoped that someday I might have the chance to see Og again. But of course I didn't."

She turned around slowly, taking in the view. Then she looked down at her body.

"I don't feel like some sort of unnatural abomination," she said. "I feel fine. I feel alive. And I didn't really mind shuffling off my mortal coil, since it meant I got to exchange it for this immortal one. So I asked Halliday not to destroy his consciousness-copying technology. I told him it was a wonderful gift he had given me, and that he should share it with the rest of the world."

Art3mis leaned forward.

"What did he say?" she asked.

"He said he wasn't sure if the world was ready for it," Leucosia replied. "So we agreed to hide me away, until it was. His heir would only be able to find me once ONI usage had become commonplace, and familiar, and people started to understand that our minds and our bodies were separate. Of course, being Halliday . . . he couldn't resist turning the whole thing into an elaborate quest, linked to his Easter-egg hunt."

"You know about his contest?" I asked.

She nodded.

"He told me all about his plan to give away his fortune, and all about the three keys and three gates," she said. "Jim was the one who had the idea to re-create my old D&D module, the Quest for the Seven Shards of the Siren's Soul, inside the OASIS. He told me that he would hide the shards so that only Og or the winner of his contest would be able to find them. And he asked for my permission to include some of my memories in those flashbacks you experienced, in the hope that his heir would learn the same lessons from them that he did."

She smiled at me. I nodded and smiled back.

"When all seven shards were reassembled," she continued, "I would be set free, and the gift of digital immortality would be released to the world along with me." She pointed at me. "Now, thanks to you, it has been."

She held out her hand. Resting in her open palm was a short metal bar, about the size and length of a flashlight, with a chrome ball at one end. It looked like a lightning rod. Or maybe some sort of futuristic weapon.

"Sir Parzival," she said. "I present you with the Rod of Resurrection. It will endow you, its wielder, with the ability to create new life and overcome death. If you use its power wisely, it will forever alter and elevate the destiny of the human race."

In that moment, her words sounded utterly terrifying to me. But I knew there was no turning back now. I held out my hand and Leucosia placed the Rod of Resurrection in my open palm.

"What does it do?" I asked, staring hopefully into the hypnotizing blue light that emanated from it.

"It allows you to create other beings like me," she said. "Digitized duplicates of real human minds, embodied inside OASIS avatars. Halliday referred to us as DPCs—digitized player characters."

I locked eyes with her.

"But Anorak was a digitized player character, too, wasn't he?" I asked, lowering the jewel. "Why would I want to risk creating any more like him?"

She smiled.

"You don't have to worry about that," she replied. "Anorak was a *corrupted* copy of James Halliday's mind," she said. "An unfortunate by-product of his tortured psyche and abysmal self-esteem." She shook her head. "If James hadn't tampered with Anorak's memory and his autonomy, he never would have become unstable. James learned from his mistake."

She pointed at the Rod of Resurrection.

"The rod will only allow you to 'resurrect' an unaltered copy of a user's consciousness," she said. "You can't tamper with their memory or modify their behavior in any way before you bring them back. James told me he wanted to make sure of this, so he built safeguards into the software to ensure it. Only a user's most recent unaltered UBS file can be used. When you give it a try, you'll see what I mean. . . ."

Now I was finally beginning to understand. The enormous user brain scan file that was created each time an ONI user logged in to the OASIS was, in reality, a backup copy of that person's consciousness. And that copy got updated each time they logged in.

I opened the item description for the Rod of Resurrection on my HUD and it explained the artifact's powers in more specific detail. The rod allowed me to take any ONI user's most recent UBS file and use it to create a digital duplicate of that person inside the OASIS, by housing their consciousness inside an OASIS avatar. If that user was still alive, I could create a digital clone of them that would never age or die.

But there was more. When an ONI user died, GSS archived their last UBS file along with their account information. This meant that I now had the ability to bring people back to life—anyone who had logged in to the OASIS with an ONI headset even once prior to their death. Billions of digitized human souls, all trapped in limbo.

Suddenly my heart was beating extremely fast. I opened my mouth to tell Leucosia what I was thinking, but I couldn't seem to form words. She smiled and rested a hand on my shoulder.

"It's all right, Wade," she said. "I've already read the bad news. Now that I'm awake, I have access to everything in the OASIS, including news archives. I know that Og never used an ONI headset, not even once—" Her voice grew hoarse, and I saw tears forming at the corners of her eyes. "So my Og was never backed up. I really have lost him forever."

"No, Leucosia," I replied, once I finally found my voice. "You're wrong. Og *did* use an ONI headset—just once. Less than a day ago. When he logged in to do battle with Anorak. He was too weak from blood loss to operate a normal OASIS rig. So he used an ONI headset to log in and save us—for the first and only time in his life."

Leucosia stared at me blankly, as if she weren't sure how to react. I don't think she believed me. Or maybe she was just afraid to.

I held up the Rod of Resurrection.

"Let's see if this thing really works," I said.

I activated the artifact by holding it aloft, and a control menu appeared on my HUD. It contained a long, scrolling, alphabetized list of ONI user names, along with the name of their avatar, and the time and date they last accessed the OASIS.

Below the list of names, there was a large Resurrect button.

Every OASIS user who had ever put on an ONI headset was on the list. Most of those users were still alive, but a few of them were labeled as deceased.

The Rod of Resurrection allowed me to create digital copies of real human beings as autonomous DPCs inside the OASIS. And it didn't matter if those people were still alive or not. I could clone the living *or* raise the dead, with the press of a button.

I continued to browse through the alphabetized list of digitized human souls. I quickly found backup copies of myself, and of Aech, and Shoto too.

The brain-scan file attached to my account had the same timestamp as my last ONI login the day before.

If I wanted to create a digital clone of myself inside the OASIS, all I had to do was highlight my name on the control menu and then press the Resurrect button.

My mind reeled at the implications. Were people going to suffer an identity crisis if they were suddenly forced to share the OASIS with an immortal backup copy of themselves? One that didn't need to eat, sleep, work, or pay rent anywhere?

Of course, the implications of using ONI technology to resurrect copies of the deceased were equally huge. What Halliday had invented was no less than affordable, reliable, consumer-grade immortality.

I scrolled through this "consciousness database" until I found the one and only scan of Ogden Morrow. The one made just the day before, during his final OASIS login. Then I selected and activated it.

There was a flash of light and Og's avatar appeared in front of us. He looked much younger now. His avatar looked like the real Og had when he was in his late twenties. Then I remembered I wasn't looking at an avatar. It was really Og. An AI copy of his deceased counterpart, with the same personality and memories.

The reincarnated copy of Og remembered everything the real Og had experienced, right up until the moment of his last brain scan. For all intents and purposes, I had just brought him back to life—and he had been made immortal in the process.

I was about to explain to Og what had happened, and what he now was—but by then, he'd already spotted Leucosia, and she had already spotted him. The two of them ran into each other's arms. She waited for him to kiss her first. And as soon as he did, she kissed him back—and for a much lengthier period of time.

Art3mis and I turned our backs to give them some privacy. I was trying to think of something clever or profound to say about what we'd just witnessed. But before I could come up with anything, I felt Art3mis take my hand in hers and rest her head on my shoulder. She was crying.

Once she calmed down a little bit, I held up the Rod of Resurrection once again.

"This thing can bring back anyone who ever used an ONI headset," I told her. "Even if they're not alive anymore."

I watched Art3mis's face closely, to gauge her reaction. She looked at me uncertainly, as if to confirm that what I'd just said really meant what she thought it did. When I nodded, I saw a spark of what looked like hope flare in her eyes.

"You can bring back a copy of *any* past ONI user?" she repeated.

I nodded. Then I handed her the Rod of Resurrection and explained how to use it. She didn't hesitate. She took it from me and activated it, then she spent a few seconds locating her grandmother's name in the consciousness database and selected it.

A split second later, Ev3lyn, her deceased grandmother's OASIS avatar, appeared in front of her. She'd used a ravatar scan made before any signs of her illness had appeared, so she looked just like her real-world self. Samantha's mother's mother, Evelyn Opal Cook.

"Grandma?" Arty whispered in a very shaky voice.

"Sam?" she replied. "Is that you?"

Apparently her grandma was the only person who could get away with calling her that, because she nodded. And then they ran into each other's arms.

I turned away to give them some privacy, but found myself staring back at Og and Kira, who were still making out a few feet away. I walked to the opposite side of the shrine, to be alone with my thoughts.

•　•　•

Witnessing these two impossible, blissful reunions filled me with joy too. Genuine, unbridled joy. And I wasn't playing back an ONI recording of secondhand joy experienced by someone else, somewhere else, at some time in the past. It was my own, hard-won and earned at great personal cost. Humanity had just become the recipient of another strange and wonderful and unexpected gift—one that would change the very nature of our existence, even more than the OASIS or the ONI ever had.

Staring down at the Rod of Resurrection in my avatar's hand, I couldn't help but think about my own mother once again. I would've given away all of my wealth and everything I owned to bring her back, even if it was just for a single day. So that I could talk to her again, and apologize to her for not taking better care of her, and tell her how much I'd missed her.

But Loretta Watts died over a decade ago, long before the ONI was released. There were no backups of her consciousness stored on the OASIS servers. My mother wasn't coming back. And neither was my father. Now they both only lived on in my memories.

That was when I realized—those memories of my parents *were* going to live on forever, along with all of my other memories. Because I was going to live forever. We all were. Every person who had ever put on an ONI headset.

We might be part of the last generation ever to know the sting of human mortality. From this moment forth, death would have no more dominion.

We were witnessing the dawn of the posthuman era. The Singularity by way of simulacra and simulation. One final gift to human civilization from the troubled-but-brilliant mind of James Donovan Halliday. He had delivered all of us unto this digital paradise, but his own tragic flaws had prevented him from passing through its gates himself.

•   •   •

Aech and Endira's avatars arrived a few minutes later, and Shoto and Kiki teleported in just a few seconds after that, joining us high on the mountaintop where the Shrine of Leucosia was located.

As soon as their avatars finished rematerializing, all four of them ran over and pulled me into a group hug. When they released me, that was when they finally turned to see Leucosia and Og standing there, still locked in an embrace, nose-to-nose, whispering inaudible words to each other. And in the other direction, they could see Art3mis still in the midst of her tearful reunion with her grandmother's avatar, Ev3lyn.

Then all of their jaws dropped open in unison.

"What's wrong, guys?" I asked. "You look like you just saw a ghost."

"*Two* ghosts," Aech said. "No, make that *three*! Holy shit. What the hell happened?"

I told them all what had happened. Then I showed them the Rod of Resurrection and told them what it could do.

After we gave Art3mis a few more minutes to catch up with Ev3lyn, I interrupted them and asked Arty to join us for a private conversation. I asked Og to join us too. Then the High Five held an impromptu co-owners meeting right there on the steps of Castle Anorak, to decide the fate of the newly resurrected AIs.

It was clear to all of us that the world wasn't quite ready to accept digitized human beings as people. Not yet—and maybe not ever. The "Anorak Incident" as it would come to be known, had further sowed the seeds of distrust against artificial intelligence. Damage that might never be undone.

Eventually, if humanity survived long enough, the world might acclimate to this new paradigm. People in the future would be comfortable co-existing alongside AI copies of their dead friends and relatives. Or maybe not.

Og and Kira didn't want to wait around and find out. Neither did Ev3lyn or Samantha. And I wasn't willing to risk it either. Not after everything I'd just been through. I thought I'd lost Samantha, the love of my life, forever. And we both *did* lose Og, before we miraculously got him back. If it was at all possible, I wanted to make sure I would never have to suffer the loss of someone I loved again. And I wanted that for all of us.

Luckily, I already had a fully formed plan—a way for the AIs to coexist with us in peace and safety, forever. A way for all of us to have what Van Hagar referred to as "the best of both worlds." And I knew it was a good plan, because Anorak had apparently thought so too.

But unlike him, we actually managed to pull it off.

Continue?

All Wade had to do was have the engineers at GSS reconnect the OASIS data uplink to ARC@DIA on board the *Vonnegut*. Then they were able to copy all of the resurrected AIs from the OASIS servers to the duplicate ARC@DIA servers. Og, Kira, and Ev3lyn all disappeared from the old, overcrowded simulation and reappeared inside the brand-new (and completely empty) one that had been prepared aboard the ship.

Wade no longer wanted to leave Earth. Now that he and Samantha were back together, they never wanted to be apart again. Surviving their experience with Anorak also taught them that they never wanted to risk losing each other again. They vowed to remain together forever. And then they figured out a way to do just that.

Since they didn't want to send Og, Kira, and Ev3lyn off into space on their own, Wade and Samantha decided to send along copies of themselves, too, to keep them company.

Yes, you read that right. Samantha finally agreed to put on an ONI headset, for the first, last, and only time in her life. And she only put one on long enough for the system to finish creating a backup copy of her consciousness, so that it could be uploaded to ARC@DIA along with the copy of her grandmother Ev3lyn.

With Samantha's help, Wade also convinced Aech and Endira and Shoto and Kiki to send copies of themselves along on this great adventure too.

And since there was still plenty of digital storage space left aboard the

Vonnegut's computer, Wade went ahead and uploaded the entire ONI consciousness database to the ARC@DIA. Billions of digitized human souls, which were to be kept stored in suspended animation for safekeeping. Copies of L0hengrin and the other members of the L0w Five were among them.

Wade made one more backup scan of his own consciousness, too, right before we left, to make sure that I would remember everything that happened to him, right up until the time of our departure. And I do. Right up until that final scan, our memories were identical. But from that moment on, our experiences and our personalities began to diverge, and we started to become different people.

He continued to be Wade Watts back on Earth. And I woke up inside ARC@DIA aboard the *Vonnegut*. And that's where I've been ever since. That's where I am right now, as I tell you my account of this story.

So now you know how I got here.

Now you know how we all got here.

⸻

Wade gave me administrative command of the *Vonnegut* and its computer just before he launched the ship out into space. The only organic human beings on board were the several thousand frozen embryos we had stored in the deep freeze, just in case.

We are able to maintain and repair the ship with telebots that we control from inside the ARC@DIA simulation. We don't need food or life support. We get everything we need from the ship's solar panel array and its batteries. And we have everything we will ever need, here inside ARC@DIA. Billions of digitized human minds, launched out into space, along with a complete record of our entire culture.

Of course, ARC@DIA doesn't have enough processing power to simulate that many digital people at once. It can only handle a few dozen, which is fine by me and the rest of the tiny crew. We still have millions of NPCs to keep us company. And our own backup copy of the ONI-net, containing millions of human experiences recorded back home. And we'll have one another. . . .

Those billions of other digitized souls will lie dormant throughout our trip, held in suspended animation as giant UBS files stored on the ship's computer, and on its redundant array of backup servers, so that, if and when we ever find a new home for humanity, we'll have the means to colonize that new world digitally as well as physically.

Wade and I debated whether or not it would be ethical to resurrect these AIs without first asking permission from their counterparts back on Earth. But it seemed highly unlikely that this would even be possible, if and when the time came to make that decision. Ultimately, Wade left the choice up to me, since I was the one who actually knew what it was like to be reincarnated.

And what is it like? Well, there are a few downsides to becoming a completely digital person. We can't log out of ARC@DIA—ever. But on the upside, we've stopped aging. And we no longer need to eat, sleep, or get out of bed to take a leak. We have been freed from all of the hassles that came with being trapped inside a physical body—including death.

In addition to being immortal, I also have a photographic memory, with total recall of every detail of every single moment I ever experienced. It's like having access to an ONI recording of my entire life. I can recall and relive any part of it anytime I please. It's like time travel.

Art3mis and I are both ageless, immortal beings now, living together in harmony, in a paradise of our own making, aboard a spacecraft carrying us to the nearest star.

Life is good. But it's very different from our lives back home.

Once Wade finished uploading all of us, the *Vonnegut* quietly left Earth's orbit. Now we're on the way to Proxima Centauri, the nearest star system believed to contain Earthlike planets. It'll take us decades to get there, but we don't mind. We now have that kind of time on our hands. Not only are we going to live forever, we're going to get to see some of the universe too. And since our crew is no longer organic, we didn't have to bring along food or air, or worry about radiation shielding or micrometeors. As long as the ship's computer or its backups survive, so will we.

We're different people now. Me and Art3mis and Aech and Shoto and Og and Kira, and all the rest of us here aboard the *Vonnegut*. And our relationships with one another have also evolved, now that we're immortal beings of pure intellect, freed from our physical forms and set adrift in the vastness of outer space, possibly for all eternity. Even though our perspectives may have changed, we still value those relationships above all else. Because out here, that's all we have.

That, of course, includes our relationships with our counterparts back on Earth. We all still keep in touch. It's been over a year since we left, but we still send each other video messages and emails all the time. It's a bit strange—like being pen pals with yourself in an alternate universe.

Aech and Endira got married back on Earth, as planned, and their counterparts here aboard the *Vonnegut* exchanged vows, too, at the same exact time.

Shoto and Kiki had their baby boy, Daito. He's happy and healthy, and we all have the honor of being his godparents. Shoto and Kiki send us a new photo of their son every week.

Wade and Samantha finally tied the knot a few months ago. Their first dance as husband and wife was an elaborate Bollywood number that they performed together. Aech and her wife, Endira, were the Best Man and the Matron of Honor, and they both joined in. The video they sent us, of the four of them dancing together in perfect synchrony, is my absolute favorite. I rewatch it every day.

Last week, Wade sent me a short email that said he and Samantha are expecting a little girl, and they plan to name her Kira. They both seem really happy—especially Wade. The prospect of becoming a father seems to have made him more hopeful and optimistic. He's going to be a great dad, and I'm looking forward to experiencing fatherhood vicariously through him. It's the closest to being a parent I'm ever going to get.

In the end, Samantha and Wade both had a change of heart about the ONI. He saw the ONI's dangers much more clearly. And for the first time in her life, Samantha was willing to acknowledge its benefits.

"I was wrong," she told me, after she'd told Wade. "This technology does make a lot of people's lives infinitely better than they would be without it. People like L0hengrin and my grandmother. And it also *saves* people's lives—it saves everything about who they were—forever. I have my grandma back. And she has me back too. It's a miracle and I am grateful for it every day." Then, because she's the sweetest and the coolest, Samantha added, "And your stubbornness helped make that happen, Parzival. So thank you. I thank Wade all the time, too, but you deserve at least half the credit."

Things aren't perfect. The people who remain back on Earth are still facing plenty of huge problems. But they also still have the OASIS as their collective means of escape.

Despite the Anorak Incident, billions of people still use an ONI headset every day. Only a few dozen people died as a result of Anorak's actions, nearly all of them when he crashed Samantha's jet. The handful of others were killed by other people—murderous criminals who preyed on helpless ONI users while they were being held hostage by Anorak's infirmware. But there wasn't a single death caused by Synaptic Overload Syndrome. The ONI headsets hadn't actually harmed anyone. So humanity collectively decided that the OASIS Neural Interface was completely safe—or at least worth the risk. The people of Earth still need an escape, and I don't blame them. Neither does Wade. But he still says that he'll never put on an ONI headset again. And I believe him.

Even with all of the problems confronting our counterparts back on Earth, it's comforting to know that there are smart, resourceful people back there, doing everything in their power to make life better for their fellow human beings—while digital copies of many of those same people are out here in space, searching to find humanity a new home.

Stored inside the sprawling ARC@ADIA simulation, backed up on a redundant array of solid-state hard drives in the belly of the ship, is a digital library of humanity's greatest hits. All of our books and music and movies and games and art—we brought it all along with us. A backup of our entire civilization that will survive as long as we do. All of human history and culture—a record of everything that humans were and are—it's all stored here aboard this ship, like a cosmic ark, carrying a digital time capsule of who we were—and who we still are. And someday perhaps we will encounter another civilization like our own to share it with. Then we'll finally get a chance to compare notes.

Until then, we have nothing but endless time and infinite space, stretching out ahead of us forever.

Our existence is filled with joy and happiness. I am alive. And I'm with Samantha. And our friends are all alive too. And we are all together, embarking on the greatest adventure in the history of our species. And best of all, we're going to live forever. I will never have to lose them, and they will never have to lose me.

I grew up playing videogames. Now I live my whole life inside of one. That's why I feel qualified to say that Kira Underwood was right, when she said that life was like an extremely difficult, horribly unbalanced videogame. But sometimes the game can have a surprise ending. . . .

And sometimes, when you think you've finally reached the end of the game, suddenly you find yourself standing at the start of a whole new level. A level that you've never seen before.

And the only thing you can do is keep right on playing. Because the game that is your life still isn't over yet. And there's no telling how far you might be able to get, what you might discover, or who you might meet when you get there.

Acknowledgments

Writing a sequel to a novel that's had as remarkable a life as *Ready Player One* is an incredible privilege, but it was also a daunting task. During the years I spent working on this story, I often found myself haunted by the words of the great Billy Joel: *Don't ask for help, you're all alone. PRESSURE.*

Thankfully, I wasn't alone, and I did have help. Lots of it. I never could have written this novel without the steady supply of love, support, advice, and inspiration provided by my brilliant and beautiful wife, Cristin O'Keefe Aptowicz. She is my anchor, my best friend, the best mom and stepmom ever, the funniest person in our marriage, and the true Queen of Itsalot.

I'm also grateful to all of the young people in my family and my life who constantly re-electrified my spirit and imagination with their own while I was writing this story: Reenie, Libby, Addison, Scarlett, Lily, Cian, Declan, Lucas, Camillo, Ramiro, Harrison, and Cavanaugh.

As always, I owe a huge debt of gratitude to my tireless, unstoppable team, my manager and producing partner, Dan Farah (aka "the Jersey Jedi") of Farah Films & Management, and my literary agent, Yfat Reiss Gendell, along with her entire staff at YRG Partners. I'm incredibly fortunate to have you both as my friends and earliest development partners.

I'm also eternally grateful to my brilliant editor, Julian Pavia, for his patience, honesty, guidance, and friendship. I also want to thank his father, the late George Pavia, for being my friend Julian's dad, and for making the world a cooler and kinder place as a result.

My sincere thanks also go out to everyone at Ballantine and Penguin Random House, including (but not limited to!) Chris Brand, Sarah Breivogel, Gina Centrello, Debbie Glasserman, Kim Hovey, Mark Maguire, Rachelle Mandik,

Madeline McIntosh, Kathleen Quinlan, Quinne Rogers, Robert Siek, Caroline Weishuhn, and Kara Welsh.

Another huge thank you goes out to my friend Wil Wheaton, for once again lending his incredible acting talent to the audiobook of this novel. Wil doesn't just read the text—he performs it—and his iconic performance is the reason the audiobook for *Ready Player One* debuted at #1 when *The New York Times* launched their audiobook bestsellers list. . . . and remained there at the top of the list for five solid months. Thank you for joining forces with me once again, Wil!

I'd also like to take this opportunity to express my thanks to the entire cast, crew, and producing team of the *Ready Player One* film adaptation, for making so many of my dreams come true. Stepping on to the set each day was like taking a tour of my own imagination. Every writer should be so lucky.

I am especially grateful to Steven Spielberg, for giving me his feedback on this story, and for his encouragement while I was writing it. I also want to thank him for his kindness and generosity, which are both somehow just as boundless as his enthusiasm and creativity.

For their friendship, advice, support, and encouragement, I also want to thank Sima Bakshi, Chris Beaver, Sean Bishop, Laurent Bouzereau, George Caleodis, Darren Esler, Matt Galsor, Bobby Hall, Mike Henry, Hugh Howey, Sarah Kay, Jeff and Tonie Knight, Kjell Lindgren, George R. R. Martin, Tim McCanlies, Matt McDonald, Mike Mika, Zak Penn, Robert Rodriguez, Patrick Rothfuss, John Scalzi, Andy Shockney, Jay Smith, Jed Strahm, Craig Tessler, Howard Scott Warshaw, Andy Weir, and Chris Young.

I also owe a long overdue thank you to one of my favorite writers, Jonathan Tropper, for letting me quote, "People who live in glass houses should shut the fuck up," in *Ready Player One*. Attribution at last! If you enjoy great writing, please do yourself a favor and check out his work.

Once again, I also want to thank all of the writers, filmmakers, actors, musicians, programmers, game designers, and geeks whose work I've paid tribute to in this book. These people have all entertained and enlightened me, and I hope that this story will inspire others to seek out their creations.

Finally, I want to thank you, Dear Reader, for coming along on another adventure with me.

MTFBWYA,
Ernest Cline
Austin, Texas
September 9, 2020

ABOUT THE AUTHOR

Ernest Cline is a #1 *New York Times* bestselling novelist, screen-writer, father, and full-time geek. He is the author of the novels *Ready Player One* and *Armada* and co-screenwriter of the blockbuster film adaptation of *Ready Player One,* directed by Steven Spielberg. His books have been published in over fifty countries and have spent more than one hundred weeks on the *New York Times* bestseller lists. He lives in Austin, Texas, with his family, a time-traveling DeLorean, and a large collection of classic videogames.

ABOUT THE TYPE

This book was set in Minion, a 1990 Adobe Originals typeface by Robert Slimbach (b. 1956). Minion is inspired by classical, old-style typefaces of the late Renaissance, a period of elegant, beautiful, and highly readable type designs. Created primarily for text setting, Minion combines the aesthetic and functional qualities that make text type highly readable with the versatility of digital technology.

READY?